"Why don't you let me help you with that stuff?"

H.L. jerked away from the wall he'd been holding up. "That's a pretty heavy blanket for a little girl like you."

If there was one thing Rose resented more than H.L. considering her a weakling, it was him thinking of her as a *little girl*. She glowered at him from under Fairy's neck as she flung the blanket over the mare's glossy white back. "I am *not* a little girl, Mr. May. And I'm quite strong. If I weren't, I wouldn't be able to perform my act, would I?"

Thank goodness he didn't laugh. He grinned, but Rose thought she might be able to stand that—although she wasn't sure. His grin flashed two whole rows of gloriously white teeth that made a remarkable contrast against his tanned face. He looked too healthy to be a reporter. Rose had always been told reporters stayed indoors and drank all the time, and were mostly consumptive and dying. This specimen looked awfully darned robust to her.

"I suppose not," he said through his grin.

She sniffed.

"All right, Miss Gilhooley, I promise I won't offer to help again. And I also promise I won't get in your way." He held his hands up, palms out, as a peace offering.

"No?" She made sure she appeared as skeptical as she sounded, because she didn't want him getting any ideas.

"No."

Fiddle. Rose wished his eyes wouldn't twinkle like that.

Dear Romance Reader,

In July of 1999, we launched the Ballad line with four new series, and each month we present both new and continuing stories set everywhere from medieval England to the American West—the kind of passionate, romantic stories you love best, written by the most gifted authors. At the back of each book, we tell you when you can find subsequent books in the series that have captured your heart.

Getting this month off to a dazzling start is **Outcast,** the debut story in the passionate new series *The Vikings,* from long-time reader favorite Kathryn Hockett. When a woman proud of her Viking heritage meets the Nordic warrior in search of her father's oldest son, she proves a woman's strength—in battle and love. Next, ever-imaginative Alice Duncan takes us to the 1893 World's Fair in Chicago with her new trilogy, *Meet Me at the Fair.* Everything's **Coming Up Roses** for a trick rider in Buffalo Bill's Wild West Show—until she meets the man who threatens to steal her heart.

Linda Devlin returns this month with **Cash,** the long-awaited sixth installment in the *Rock Creek Six* series, in which a legendary ladies' man—and gunslinger—must face up to his past, and the future he glimpses in the smile of a certain woman. Finally, Corinne Everett ends *Daughters of Liberty* with **Sweet Violet,** as a young Virginia woman determined to find adventure in England discovers danger instead—along with a surprising chance at love.

What a fabulous selection to choose from! Why not read them all? Enjoy!

Kate Duffy
Editorial Director

MEET ME AT THE FAIR

COMING UP ROSES

ALICE DUNCAN

ZEBRA BOOKS
Kensington Publishing Corp.
http://www.kensingtonbooks.com

PROJECT FLIGHT

PROLOGUE

Deadwood, Kansas
March 1887

William F. "Buffalo Bill" Cody stared at Rose Ellen Gilhooley as if he'd never seen anything even remotely as wonderful as her in his life. Rose hoped she wasn't misinterpreting his interest because she really needed him to like her.

"Whoo-eee!" the former-scout-become-entertainer hollered when Rose performed one of the more lethal tricks her Sioux pal, Little Elk, had taught her several years earlier. Cody even waved his hat in his excitement. "Little gal, you are really something!"

After she'd successfully maneuvered her body underneath her horse's belly and had emerged safely on the other side—without benefit of a saddle or reins—Rose steadied herself, sucked in a deep breath, said a silent prayer, and leaped, landing with her bare feet on Gingerbread's back. She balanced perfectly without, she hoped, looking as if she'd had to struggle to do so, and threw her arms up in the air in a gesture of triumph. Her brother Freddie had told her she looked like an angel ascending when she did that. Freddie used a lot of high-flown language, since he read a lot. Rose's education wasn't as grand as Freddie's, and all she really hoped for today was that she looked like somebody Buffalo Bill Cody could use in the Wild West.

She knew her mother was nervous. Rose could see her from the corner of her eye: gaunt, thin, weathered, looking much older than her forty-three years, thanks to poverty and grinding hardship. But Rose's mother, for all the discomforts of her life, loved her children beyond anything. Rose's one wish, the reason she was performing her heart out for Cody today, was that she could earn some money by doing so, thereby helping her family and easing the burdens of her mother's life.

Sliding down until she rode astride the big bay gelding, Rose kneed him, giving the signal to end the show with a flourish. Obeying her command, Gingerbread raced twice around the meadow and then stopped abruptly in front of Cody, rearing and pawing the air, as Rose had seen wild stallions do on the plains.

Buffalo Bill applauded extravagantly when Gingerbread took a classy bow, as Rose had also taught him to do. She executed a grand bow from horseback herself, sweeping her battered hat from her head. Of course, if she got the job, she'd no longer have to use battered hats.

"By golly, gal, you are really something! I thought your brother was exaggerating when he begged me to come out here and see you, but he wasn't. By God, he wasn't!"

He probably was, actually. Freddie was always praising her to the skies. This time, his zeal might have paid off. Rose slid from Gingerbread's back and clicked for the horse to follow her up to Cody, who stood at the door of the three-room sod hut in which the Gilhooley family had lived since they moved to the territory. The move had taken place years before Rose's birth.

Because she'd learned early that a poor person had to use the gifts God gave her and not to be bashful in expressing her needs, Rose didn't shy away from asking the famous man the question that was uppermost in her mind. "Do you think you can use me in the Wild West, Mr. Cody?" She'd given him a dazzling exhibition of her shooting skills, too, but she knew he already had a couple of female sharpshooters. The most famous of them, Annie Oakley, was, according to Freddie, better even than Rose at shooting. Therefore, Rose had spent most of today's presentation on riding, at which even she acknowledged her superiority.

Nobody could beat Rose when it came to trick riding. Not even Little Elk, not any longer. Little Elk had told her so himself.

"By golly, I've never thought about hiring us a bareback rider, little gal, but I surely do think it's about time."

Her heart thrilled at his words. She'd all but worshiped this man for years. "Thank you so much, Mr. Cody."

Cody stuck out a big hand for Rose to take. She wasn't used to shaking hands with men, but she didn't shrink from that, either. She took Cody's hand, which was so large it swallowed hers, and shook it heartily.

"Call me Colonel, little gal. Everybody does."

"Colonel Cody." Rose would call him anything he asked, as long as he'd hire her.

"Sergeant Gilhooley told me that you—"

"Who?"

Buffalo Bill laughed. Rose wished she hadn't interrupted him, but she wanted to know who Sergeant Gilhooley was. Nobody in her family had joined the army that she knew about.

"Your brother Frederick, little gal. I like to assign ranks to my friends, don't you know?"

"Oh." No, she hadn't known, but that was all right with her, too. "I see."

"So, Sergeant Gilhooley told me that you're mighty eager to get started in your new career as a bareback rider with the Wild West. Is that so?"

"Yes, sir!"

He winked at her. "In that case, when can you pack? I've got to be in New York City next week, and we have to get the show together. We're on our way to Europe."

Europe! Good Lord. Rose shot a startled glance at her mother, whose face held a poignant combination of elation and sadness. Rose knew her ma would hate to see her go, no matter how much she'd be able to use the money Rose would be sending home. She stammered, "N-next week? New York? *Europe?*"

The world-famous buffalo hunter and scout nodded, still grinning up a storm. "You and I'll have to catch the train from Deadwood tomorrow." Cody gave her a sympathetic smile. "I know it's quick, and it'll be a big change for you." He turned to Mrs. Gilhooley. "And for you, ma'am. I know you'll miss your daughter something awful, but she's the best little rider I've ever seen. And I've seen plenty, believe me. We can use her." He allowed his glance to slide over the pathetic Gilhooley family farm. "And I suspect you can, too."

"Yes," Mrs. Gilhooley said softly. It was the first word she'd spoken since before Rose had started demonstrating her riding skills.

"Tomorrow." Rose swallowed hard. Then she straightened and grinned at the man who looked as if he was going to be the salvation of her family. "Tomorrow it is, Colonel." She snapped a smart salute, and Cody chuckled again.

She left with him on the train from Deadwood at noon the next day. There was no parting fanfare except from her family and the few of their friends and neighbors who'd heard the news in time to witness the departure of her train. Cody had made arrangements for Gingerbread to travel with them. Rose tried hard not to cry as she waved good-bye to her mother, brother, and sisters. Her mother didn't even make an effort not to cry.

Thus it was that Rose Ellen Gilhooley began her career with Buffalo Bill's Wild West. She was sixteen years old.

ONE

Chicago, Illinois
May 1893

H.L.—which stood for Horatio Lambert, although no one who knew him ever called him anything but H.L.—May strolled through the entrance of the Columbian Exposition and on to the White City. He and his friend Sam Trimble ambled along, eyeing it all with pure fascination. As they did so, H.L. mentally started composing the first of several articles he aimed to write about the 1893 Chicago World's Fair.

This place was great! Although he seldom allowed himself to feel enthusiasm for anything because he had an image of the world-weary, jaded journalist to uphold, he was in secret totally, unconditionally, and absolutely fascinated by this Exposition.

"We've got to take in Buffalo Bill's Wild West, too, don't forget," his buddy Sam said. He, too, was a reporter for the *Chicago Globe,* although Sam didn't cherish his journalistic image as much as H.L., probably because he hadn't had as much to overcome as had H.L. Starting with his atrocious name.

Why any loving mother and father could saddle an innocent baby with a name like Horatio Lambert was beyond him. Hell, it wasn't as if they'd had any rich uncles or grandfathers to appease. The Mays had always been as poor as church mice. H.L. had grown up on the banks of the Mississippi River in a small town in Missouri. "Like Tom Sawyer," H.L. often told folks with a wink.

It had been a good boyhood, he often thought. And if H.L. had engaged in fisticuffs a good deal more than Tom Sawyer ever had, it was only because his folks had erred when they'd named him. He'd learned to defend himself early on from bigger boys who teased him for having such a prissy name. By the time H.L. was twelve, he'd grown tall and brawny, and was able to flatten anyone who made the mistake of calling him "Horatio Alger"—the last kid who advised him to "go west, young man," had lost two teeth—or "Horatio at the Bridge," or any one of a number of other titles they considered funny.

H.L. didn't even want to *think* about the joy his middle name had brought him. *Lambert.* Good God. If H.L. ever, heaven forbid, got married and sired a son, he was going to name him something decent. Something manly. Something the poor boy wouldn't have to defend with his fists.

Breathing deeply of the stockyard-scented air, H.L. smiled at his shorter, lighter-weight associate. "Damned right, we'll see the Wild West. You know, I hear some people come to Chicago, take in Buffalo Bill's show, think they've seen the whole Exposition, and go home again."

"People can be asses sometimes," Sam commented with a laugh. "I want to see Annie Oakley. I understand she's some kind of phenomenon."

H.L. nodded. "Me, too. And that other woman, too. The horseback rider. What's her name? Rose Gilhooley? I hear she can ride like an Indian."

"I hear she *is* an Indian," said Sam.

"With a name like Gilhooley?" H.L. guffawed. "I doubt it."

"Might be a half-breed."

H.L. shrugged. "Might be."

"Anyhow, I read somewhere that it was a Sioux Indian who gave her the name she uses in her act: Wind Dancer."

H.L. nodded. "I read the same thing, although it was on one of Cody's publicity dodgers. Who knows if those things tell the truth or not?"

"It might be, H.L. You're too cynical, you know that?"

H.L. only laughed. He cherished his reputation as a cynical big-city reporter. God knows he'd worked hard to get it. He flexed his hand in memory of his bruised knuckles.

The two men, who'd not only received dispensation from their editor to visit the Exposition any time they felt like it during the fair's first month but, thanks to H.L.'s silver tongue, had even talked the newspaper into paying their fifty-cent entry fee as well, felt as free as birds. H.L. was used to feeling free, but he knew Sam wasn't. Sam was married and had two children. H.L. shuddered at the notion of being tied to so enormous a responsibility as a wife and family.

H.L.'s entire life had been spent getting free from things, starting with his lousy name. After he'd wrestled his name into submission, he'd plowed through poverty and ignorance until he'd earned a scholarship to Missouri University, graduated with honors, moved to Chicago, and proceeded to bully and write his way into a job as an ace reporter. He'd worked like a demon, fought like John L. Sullivan, and had made it. All on his own. It would take somebody mighty special to get H.L. May to put on shackles voluntarily. H.L. didn't think there was a woman alive who could do it.

"And we've got to see the Midway Plaisance, too," Sam said, looking too innocent for H.L.'s credulity to swallow. "We've been here three days in a row and haven't set foot there yet."

Lots of folks arrived at the Exposition via its street entrance at the Midway, but H.L. and Sam had decided to take the scenic route from downtown Chicago. They'd come on a steamboat and landed at the pier. H.L. figured he might alter his route one of these days, but the steamer was such a peaceful way to ride.

"You just want to see Little Egypt," he said with a knowing grin.

"I do not! Anyhow, she's part of the Middle Eastern exhibition, so when we go there, we'll have to see her. That dance of hers is a cultural experience, H.L."

It amused H.L. when Sam, in spite of the sober and dignified expression on his face, blushed. "Sure, Sam. I'll buy that one if you'll buy a bridge from me."

"Dash it, H.L., that's not fair."

"Right." H.L. shook his head. Lordy, when a fellow tied the knot, his life truly ended. H.L. would rather shoot himself and get it over with all at once than die a slow death via the tortures of matrimony.

"Crumbs, H.L.," Sam muttered after a pregnant pause, "I'm taking Daisy and the kids to the fair next week. I can't very well see Little Egypt with Daisy and the kids, can I?"

"Guess not." H.L. stuck his hands in his pockets and started to whistle. God, he loved his life!

"Whoo, will you look at that! I don't think I'll ever get tired of seeing it." Sam's voice held awe.

As well it might. The backers of this World's Fair had done a magnificent job of turning a swamp into a fairgrounds. H.L. was impressed as all get-out as he gazed at the Grand Basin, the huge reflecting pool in the center of the Court of Honor. An elaborate fountain and a gilded statue of the Republic, complete with scepter and orb, resided in the Basin. It was truly an extraordinary sight.

"You know, Sam, all of this is so fascinating, I'm not sure I even care about seeing the Wild West," H.L. said as he entered the Machinery Hall and stared at the 435,500-square-foot room. It was crammed to the ceiling with exhibits ranging from book-folding machines to knitting machines, to gigantic hydraulic engines. "I've never seen anything like this."

Sam, also stunned by the immensity and magnificence of the Machinery Hall, whispered reverently, "That's the whole point, H.L. Nobody has."

Mrs. Frank Butler, better known to her many admirers as Annie Oakley—although she'd started out in life as Phoebe Ann Moses—shuffled through a deck of cards, sorting out the various aces, sevens, tens, and other cards with appropriate suit marks in their centers. During her sharpshooting performance, she'd shoot out the center pips. The cards, thus decorated by "Little Sure Shot," Sitting Bull's honorary name for her, would be sold later to Wild West attendees.

Annie's white poodle, George, snored on an embroidered pillow at Annie's feet. Annie used George in her act with the Wild West sometimes. George had a remarkably phlegmatic personality for a poodle and never shied away from the sound of gunfire.

Rose Gilhooley, who considered Mrs. Butler her very best friend in the whole Wild West show, if not the entire world, was helping Annie sort cards. "I don't know why they didn't let Colonel Cody set up inside the Exposition. Doesn't seem fair to me."

The late-spring day was fine, and the two ladies were working in Annie's big tent, which had been set up for her use during the run of Buffalo Bill's Wild West. The Sioux attached to the show had constructed a small village for themselves, and dozens of other tents housed the rest of the 600 members of the cast and crew that traveled with the Wild West. A herd of buffalo and a herd of horses also traveled with the show, and were pastured near the tent villages. Cody's entourage included a stagecoach, a veritable arsenal of firearms, pounds of blank ammunition, dozens of mules, and wagonloads of costumes, set pieces, props, and backdrops, as well. It took acres of land to house the large operation.

Annie chuckled. "You just think the colonel's perfect, is all. According to the Fair Directory, the Wild West is just entertainment. The Exposition is supposed to be an educational experience."

"Colonel Cody says the Wild West is an educational exposition. And it really is, Annie." Rose eyed the other woman, whom she admired immensely. "Don't you think so?"

A tiny stab of disappointment struck her. She hated it that Annie, who liked and admired the colonel, didn't appreciate him in the same worshipful way Rose did. As far as Rose was concerned, William F. Cody had been her family's deliverer and would forever be her personal hero.

Annie sighed. "As to that, we offer reenactments of historical events."

Rose nodded vigorously. "Yes, and that's the whole point. Think about it. The colonel's life is so colorful—and it's all true. Why, he rode the longest Pony Express route ever when he was only sixteen years old! And that was way before he started scouting for the army."

Annie leveled a look at Rose over the ace of spades. "You were feeding your whole family when you were sixteen years old, Rose."

Rose shrugged. "Well, yes, but that's only because I had to, after Papa died. Freddie couldn't ride or shoot for anything, and I was a dead-eye shot. Anything the family didn't eat, we sold at market. You know all about that, because you did the same thing."

"Hmph." Annie's lips pursed, as they always did when Rose spoke of her older brother.

Feeling defensive about Freddie, whom Rose loved with all her heart, and who was a sweetheart even though he couldn't hit the side of a barn with a buffalo rifle, Rose said, "Freddie does his part, all right. He took care of the farm and did all the hard labor around the place before he married Suzanne. Plus he worked in Mr. Lovelady's hardware store in town. Still does, for that matter, and he still helps Ma with our farm, although with the money I send home, Ma's been able to hire a farm hand, too." She frowned. "I'm trying to talk her into moving to town. She doesn't need to work the farm any longer."

Annie gave her a sharp glance. "You're the one who provided the meals. I did the same thing, so I know how hard it was for you. The colonel rode a horse a long way, and probably had a wonderful time doing it. He wasn't feeding his family. There's a lot to be said for being willing and able to keep one's family in food and shelter, Rose Gilhooley. Personally, I think it's a lot more important than riding a horse for a long way. It's called shouldering one's responsibilities."

Rose giggled at Annie's ferocity and the thought of Buffalo Bill Cody as a young lad, riding for the Pony Express. Rose would bet her last dollar that he'd had a good time, indeed. "I suppose so, but it's sure not as romantic."

"Romantic," Annie repeated, as if the word were possibly the most ridiculous one in the English language.

"Yes. Romantic. And don't forget about his army exploits, either. I don't think it's ridiculous to reenact Custer's massacre."

Annie lifted one arm in the air, her hand curled into a fist as though she were holding a sacred object, slapped the other hand over her heart, and intoned dramatically, "The first scalp for Custer!" Letting her arm drop and picking up another deck of cards, she added, "Ugh."

"Oh, Annie, I know you're wrong. I think the colonel is the most wonderful man I've ever met."

"That's because you haven't met very many men, darling Rose."

They both laughed. Rose knew Annie was only trying to spare her the disappointment of one day discovering William F. Cody to be a mere man, but she didn't really need any lessons about that sort of thing. Rose had grown up rough.

She also knew that, in spite of her lack of enthusiasm in this instance, Annie adored the colonel.

Besides, Rose had met plenty of men in her life, no matter what Annie thought. She'd met drunkards and gunfighters and gamblers and cowboys, all by the time she was old enough to talk. Deadwood was a dangerous place, and Rose had learned to duck almost as soon as she could walk, because the lead flew like birds around the town.

By this time in her life, she could tell a good man from a bad one, and a faker from an honest man. Whatever Annie said, Rose Gilhooley knew very well that William F. Cody wasn't a plain, common, garden-variety man. And if Rose chose to find a little romance in life where she could, she didn't think it was Annie's place to knock her fantasies around. The good Lord knew, Rose had seen little enough of romance in her twenty-two years. But since she loved and admired Annie Oakley almost as fiercely as she did Buffalo Bill Cody, she'd never complain.

She did, however, sniff, "Well, *I* think the Wild West is much more than a show. *I* think it's an educational experience, and ought to have been allowed to be set up on the Exposition grounds."

"Hmmm. Maybe, but it's still mostly for the amusement of the people who come to see it, what with the Indians attacking the Deadwood Stage, and the buffalo hunt and all. I think those things can truthfully be considered as mere entertainment. You have to admit that the colonel *does* alter historical facts from time to time."

"Maybe, but I don't think there's anything *mere* about it," Rose said huffily. "If anyone thinks you woke up one morning being able to shoot the way you shoot, or that I woke up one morning being able to ride the way I ride, or that they're ever going to see how the Sioux lived before they went to the reservations anywhere else, they're just plain nutty."

"People don't think about things like that unless they have to," Annie told her dryly. "You and I might have had to shoot our families' meals before we were old enough to think, but not too many other folks in today's world have that problem."

"I guess not."

"Did you do those reading and writing exercises I gave you yesterday?"

Rose heaved a sigh. She hated not being better at reading, writing, and ciphering, but that was one of the many prices she'd paid to help her family survive. First she'd brought home their food when she still lived on the farm outside Deadwood. Now she was "Wind Dancer, Bareback Rider Extraordinaire" for Buffalo Bill's Wild West. She didn't regret one single aspect of her life—unless it was the poverty that had driven her to work so hard to begin with—but she still wished she'd been able to go to school.

"I did. It's getting easier."

Annie, with a sympathetic smile that embarrassed Rose, reached over and patted her on the knee. "Of course it's getting easier, dear. You're doing very well. It's quite difficult to learn your letters and numbers when you're an adult and have to hold an exacting job at the same time."

"You did it."

"Yes, but I had a little more background to begin with." She shook an admonishing finger at Rose. "It wasn't easy for me, either, and I know it's not easy for you. And that's not your fault."

"I guess." Rose still felt like a stupid lump every time she had to ask Annie to help her decipher words in the letters she received from fans who'd seen her perform in the Wild West. She figured any self-respecting adult human American, especially one whom others admired, ought to be able to read the letters she got. No matter how many times Annie assured her that ignorance and stupidity were too different things, Rose still felt stupid.

TWO

"I believe they're in here, Mr. May."

The two women looked at each other as Frank Butler's slightly accented voice reached them. Annie sighed. "Who's he got in tow now?" she asked, although she smiled as she did so. Frank Butler, her Irish husband and a champion sharpshooter in his own right, was also her business manager. As such, he tried to garner as much publicity for her as he could.

Grinning, Rose said, "Whoever it is, I'm sure he'll love you, Annie. You're so . . . perfect." Rose was honestly only a little bit jealous of Annie's fame, mainly because Rose knew Annie had earned it. Annie was also small and pretty and elegant, and every inch a lady.

Rose herself was small and guessed she was sort of pretty, but she felt thoroughly deficient in the ladyship and elegance departments. Annie was trying to help her there, too. So far, she'd managed to correct Rose's grammar for the most part—Rose slipped up occasionally when she was nervous—had taught her how to eat with a knife, fork, and spoon and not to drink her tea out of her saucer, and had gone with her on a shopping expedition when they'd first arrived in Chicago. But Rose knew she needed lots more work in order to become a real lady, if she ever could.

Annie sniffed. "Rose Gilhooley, you're being silly. You're ever so much younger and prettier than I am. Who's to say whoever this person Frank's bringing hasn't come here to see *you?*"

Rose felt her eyes pop open. "Oh, no, Annie! That never happens!"

Annie only sighed, patted a stack of cards together, and stood, looking as if she didn't relish whatever this interruption was going to mean. Rose stood, too, feeling nervous. She never felt nervous when she was performing, because she'd practically grown up on a horse and was confident there. Horseback, however, was the only place she felt confident.

The tent flap opened, and Frank Butler came in first. "Howdy-do, ladies. I see you're hard at work, as usual." Frank, a real sweetheart in Rose's opinion—he even wrote beautiful poems that Annie read to her sometimes—winked at them.

"Hello, Frank, what are you surprising me with today?" Annie went over to give her husband a buss on the cheek.

Rose had never seen Annie or Frank show any but the mildest displays of affection for each other in public, even though she knew their love ran deep. Annie had told her so. So had Frank, for that matter. And there were the poems he wrote, which were so beautiful they made Rose cry.

"I have here a photographer, Mr. Winslow Asher, and a newspaperman, Mr. H.L. May. Mr. Asher has been hired by the Fair Directory as the official photographer for the Exposition, and Mr. May is writing a series of articles for the *Chicago Globe*. They want to interview you, darlin', and take some pictures."

Rose turned impulsively, and gave Annie a hug. "Oh, Annie, that's wonderful!"

"Aye, 'tis," said Frank complacently.

"Frank." Annie shook her head. "You are amazing." She didn't sound as if she considered his being amazing a particularly endearing quality at the moment.

Frank only chuckled. "Say your howdies to the gentlemen, ladies. Annie Oakley and Rose Gilhooley, please meet Mr. Win Asher and Mr. H.L. May."

Always slightly abashed in fancy company—and any company she met outside the Wild West or Deadwood, Kansas, qualified—Rose still managed a dainty curtsy. Annie had taught her *that,* too.

Mr. Asher bowed and shook Annie's hand, then Rose's. "So good of you to allow us to disturb you, Mrs. Butler. Miss Gilhooley."

"Certainly," said Annie.

She sounded as much like a queen as Victoria had, Rose thought. She mumbled, "Sure."

"Ah. Good to meet you, Miss Annie Oakley," said H.L. May. Then he surprised Rose by turning abruptly in her direction. "Say, I've heard you're the best rider anybody's ever seen, Miss Gilhooley. I'm looking forward to watching your act tonight."

H.L. May's smile was a wonder to behold. Rose wished he hadn't shot it at her so suddenly, because it made her heart flop around like a hooked trout and then begin racing. She muttered, "Thank you," and forced herself to maintain eye contact with him. She wanted to bow her head and stare at her own toes.

"I hear you ride bareback and with no shoes on," H.L. went on, to Rose's chagrin.

He seemed to expect some kind of answer, so she said, "Can't balance standing up on a horse's back with shoes on. Hurts the horse, too."

His grin widened, as if her comment had tickled him. "A barefoot bareback rider. I can see the headlines now."

Was he making fun of her? Rose wasn't sure. She peeked quickly at Annie, but read no hint in her expression. Glancing back at H.L., she noticed his eyes this time. Darn it. His eyes were a dancing green that complemented his dark-brown hair, jaunty checked suit, and dashing straw hat. He was big, too, and had muscles. He looked more as if he dug ditches for a living than wrote articles. Rose had always thought newspaper people were thin, pale drunkards who lived in smoke-filled saloons and only staggered home occasionally to write a few newspaper articles. This fellow looked as if he went out every day, tackled life with his own bare hands, and thrashed it to a standstill. "Um," she said. "Really?"

He laughed. He didn't just laugh; rather, he threw his head back and roared. Rose was pretty sure he was making fun of her this time. She frowned. "I don't see what's so funny."

Shaking his head and wiping his eyes with the back of his hand, he said, "There's not a thing funny, Miss Gilhooley, but I'd sure like to be allowed to interview you. I have a feeling you're a true original."

What did that mean? Rose looked at Annie again. This time, Annie evidently read the beseeching quality in Rose's glance, because she smiled encouragement. "That's wonderful, Rose. I think you ought to take Mr. May up on his offer." As if she imagined Rose needed further impetus to accept the request for an interview—and she was right—Annie added, "Think of the publicity for the Wild West."

There probably wasn't another thing Annie could have said that would have made Rose accept H.L.'s proposition. Rose didn't want to be interviewed by him. He alarmed her. But any time she became aware of an opportunity to benefit Colonel Cody, Rose pounced on it. She felt her shoulders sag.

"Say, Miss Gilhooley, I don't bite. Honest."

When she peered up into the face of H.L. May, who looked as handsome, devil-may-care, and dangerous as made no matter, Rose wasn't sure about that. Nevertheless, she knew where her duty lay. She'd been doing her duty all her life.

"Very well. When would you like to conduct this inter-

view?" Her voice sounded stifled. Rose felt stifled. She heard
Annie release a breath of relief and vaguely resented it.

"How about tomorrow?" H.L. suggested. "That way I
can watch you perform tonight and get a better idea for the
direction my article will take."

Rose nodded. "All right." She didn't feel good about this
interview.

Frank Butler patted her on the shoulder, as if he understood her embarrassment and reluctance. "You'll do fine,
Rosie." Frank and the colonel were the only people Rose
knew who called her Rosie. She chalked it up to Frank's
being Irish. She hadn't come up with an excuse for the colonel yet.

"Right," she said.

H.L. May only laughed again.

An air of almost palpable excitement surrounded this
whole fair experience; H.L. had made note of it, and promised himself that he'd do his best to make his readers feel it.
The Columbian Exposition's purpose, according to its directors, was to celebrate the 400th anniversary of Columbus's
discovery of the New World in 1492. Nobody seemed to care
much that the Exposition had opened a year late, in 1893.

On a more fundamental level, the fair was a celebration
of American ingenuity and invention. Other nations featured
exhibits at the fair, too, but it was the United States and its
accomplishments that most people were here to honor.

From a band of settlers rebelling against a repressive British government, the United States has grown into a great
nation—and all in a matter of a little more than a hundred
years. By God, those bull-headed American pioneers had
wrested independence from a tightfisted British lion with an
organized and well-trained army at its beck and call.

In H.L.'s not-so-humble opinion, the citizens of the
United States of America had a right to celebrate. The entire

nation exuded a cockiness and confidence that rubbed some folks the wrong way, but H.L. reveled in it. He harbored the same cockiness and confidence about himself.

And he was going to make sure the citizens of the United States recognized the treasure they had in little Rose Gilhooley. H.L. May was going to make Wind Dancer a household name. He vowed it as he headed back to the Midway to meet Sam.

He found his colleague waiting for him near the brand-new, never-before-seen wheel invented by Mr. W. G. Ferris. The Ferris wheel was rapidly becoming the most popular exhibit at the fair. H.L. and Sam had already ridden on it twice, and not merely because H.L. approved of any man who used only his initials, but because the experience of the wheel was so exhilarating. H.L. found himself wondering suddenly if little Rose Gilhooley, who looked and sounded about as innocent as the new dawn, had ridden on it yet. He thought it would be fun to introduce her to the sights of the big city.

"Want to ride it one more time before we take in the Wild West?" Sam asked.

Noting his friend's wistful voice and the expression of pleading in his eyes, and understanding Sam's longing, H.L. grinned. "Sure. Why not?"

After the two men took their seats on one of the Ferris wheel's passenger coaches, each one of which accommodated sixty people, H.L. said, "Say, Sam, I met Annie Oakley and Rose Gilhooley this afternoon."

Sam offered H.L. some of his buttered popcorn, a delicacy sold in cone-shaped paper sacks at the Exposition. "Yeah? Is Gilhooley an Indian?"

Considering pretty little Rose Gilhooley, H.L. shook his head. "Nope. I don't think there's a drop of Indian blood in her."

Sam shrugged. "I hear Annie Oakley's the best shot the world's ever seen. And that Gilhooley girl is supposed to be a great rider. I'm looking forward to seeing both of them tonight."

H.L. barely noticed Sam's mention of the famous Annie Oakley. "Haven't seen her ride yet." He popped some puffed corn into his mouth. "She's cute as a button, though."

"Who?" Sam looked at him, obviously puzzled.

"Gilhooley." At once, H.L. knew *cute* wasn't the correct word to describe Rose Gilhooley. He wasn't sure what was, but he aimed to find out.

"Really? Is she small, too? I hear Annie Oakley's really tiny. I can't imagine anyone being big and doing the things Gilhooley's supposed to do on a horse. The horse wouldn't survive." Sam laughed heartily.

"She's small." H.L. chewed another mouthful of popcorn thoughtfully. There was something about Rose Gilhooley that excited him. As a reporter. He had a strange, instinctive feeling about her. He'd never quite had it before, but it reminded him of the times in his life when he'd known, without any evidence other than his gut, that he'd found a story. And not just any story, but a *story*.

"I'm looking forward to seeing her ride tonight," Sam said around a mouthful of popcorn.

"Yeah. Me, too."

H.L. didn't know what these feelings of his meant exactly, but he had a dead-certain instinct that Rose Gilhooley and her story were going to be the making of his career. He couldn't recall ever being this exhilarated about a story in his entire life. He was going to write the best damned article the city of Chicago had seen since the fire. And it was going to be about Rose Gilhooley.

"By God, she's amazing." Sam's eyes were bulging, and he spoke in a hushed voice as they watched Rose Gilhooley perform in the center of the field where the Wild West had been set up. He and H.L. got to view the Wild West from front-row seats, thanks to their newspaper jobs. Cody, a showman to the core, always treated the press like royalty.

H.L. was too engrossed to respond to Sam's awe-inspired comment. He'd never seen anyone do the things on horseback that Rose Gilhooley, the so-called Wind Dancer of the Wild West, was doing right now.

For her act, Rose wore a modified Indian outfit, although H.L.'s cynical side made him wonder what self-respecting tribe would have the gall—or the funds—to wear such a thing. It looked as if it had been fashioned out of buckskin and glitter, with long, dangly fringes and elaborate beadwork. It was not, properly speaking, a dress, or even a robe.

Rather, Rose's costume sported a split skirt with elastic around the two leg openings that reminded H.L. of the bloomers ladies wore these days for bicycling—and when they wanted to prove to the world that women could wear trousers as well as men. H.L. didn't begrudge anyone, even women, a dash of defiance. The good Lord knew he had more than his share of that particular character trait himself.

Whatever the bottom part of Rose's costume was called, it sure looked good on her. H.L. didn't think he'd ever seen bloomers or any other type of trousers set off to better advantage.

Her act was enough to make strong men faint, too. She'd entered the arena at a dead run, on a horse as white as milk. The horse had torn out through a canvas tunnel as if it had been shot from a cannon, it moved so fast. Rose had been bent over, practically hugging the horse's neck, as if she were trying to create as little wind resistance as possible. The audience had barely caught its breath after her spectacular entrance when it lost it again with an audible *whoosh* as she performed her first trick.

H.L.'s heart, a generally reliable, rock-solid organ and one not easily stirred, had shot into his throat when she'd suddenly sat up straight and then dived head-first off the horse's back. A cry of terror and dismay had gone up from the bleachers as the audience feared Rose had taken a probably disastrous tumble.

But it was all part of the act, as they realized an instant later, when Rose's body slid beneath the horse's belly and she emerged on the other side. In one fluid movement, she then climbed up on the horse's back again. It looked as if she had suction cups on her fingers, since she used neither saddle nor bridle. She guided the horse with nudges and pats of her knees, feet, and hands.

Even H.L., who prided himself on his unflappability, as well as on the knowledge that he'd seen and done pretty much everything dangerous there was to do in the world, had gasped in astonishment. The cheer that went up when Rose safely sat once more on her dashing steed rocked the bleachers.

And then, as if she hadn't frightened everyone to near apoplexy already, she scarcely gave them time enough to swallow their hearts when she was off again. She leaped onto the horse's back as if her legs were on springs, and stood straight up as the horse raced around the arena.

The Indian-style costume she wore was very effective. Even though she had darkish hair, Rose Gilhooley couldn't pass for an Indian in a million years. For one reason, her hair was curly, although it was drawn back tightly tonight. But H.L. remembered very well that her eyes were blue. Robin's-egg blue. Sky blue. Sapphire blue. Gorgeous blue. And they were as big as saucers.

He grimaced, wondering what was wrong with him that he'd recalled her big blue eyes in such poetic terms. Then he comforted himself with the reasoning that he was only thinking of descriptive words to use in his articles. That made him feel better, and he went back to contemplating the rest of her.

On to her hair, then. He knew, because he'd seen it unbound, that it was a very shiny, very dark brown. Chestnut brown. In order to more thoroughly convey the Wild West image Cody required, she also wore some type of headband that seemed to drip feathers behind her as the horse rampaged through the arena. The feathers were colorful and reflected the light to perfection.

Cody had made sure there was abundant light flooding the arena, even though his show went on after dark. H.L. thought there must be sparkly things glued or sewn onto Rose's feathers to make them glitter and shine in the floodlights. The same was true of the beadwork on the bodice of her Indian-style costume.

Her bloomers were heavily embroidered and sported no beadwork, probably because she didn't want to scratch the horse during her acrobatic routines. They only reached her knees, too, so the audience was treated to quite a display of her shapely calves. The rest of her wasn't bad in the curve department, either, H.L. noticed with interest when the horse finally slowed to a trot and Rose slid down astride it. She didn't stay there for long, but jumped up onto the horse's back again and stood in her bare feet as she balanced with seeming ease, her arms outstretched.

He squinted narrowly and decided she wasn't wearing a corset. Well, how could she, and survive the rigors of *that* act? The poor creature would faint dead away during her first trick if she had to strap all that whaleboning around her midriff. H.L. approved. He liked the natural female shape. A lot. He explored it whenever he got the chance, in fact. He wouldn't mind exploring Rose's curves by hand, actually.

Shaking himself hard, he wondered where that thought had come from. He might take a certain pride in a local repute among his peers at the *Globe* as something of a ladies' man, but he was certainly no defiler of virgins. H.L. would stake his virile reputation on the certainty that Rose Gilhooley was a virgin.

Innocent. That was a better word for her than *cute,* but it still didn't capture the essence of Rose.

Beside him, Sam squeaked. "Jesus H. Christ, H.L.! Did you see that?"

H.L. had seen it. He was, however, unable to speak since his heart had lodged in his throat again. He wished it would stop doing that.

"How does she *do* those things?" Sam gasped. Then he joined in the roar of cheers.

So did H.L. He and Sam jumped to their feet, applauding wildly and whooping until H.L.'s throat felt raw.

From standing on the horse's back with her arms lifted in a pose that brought to H.L.'s mind an image of perfect freedom, Rose had suddenly done a spring that shocked the audience into a gasp of alarm, and then landed on her hands. On the horse's back. And then she'd done the splits. In midair. On the horse's back. While standing on her hands. That's when the audience had roared and risen, astounded by Rose's phenomenal skill.

"By God," H.L. whispered to himself. "She's rock solid. Rock solid, by God." He'd never seen anyone ride a horse with as much assurance as Rose Gilhooley.

He found it difficult to reconcile the small, insecure-seeming child-woman he'd met that afternoon with this fabulous performer. "By God, I'm going to do it," he vowed, again to himself.

Sam, who'd been caught up in the thrill of the moment, heard H.L. that time. Still standing and clapping, he leaned toward H.L. "What? You're going to do what? I didn't hear you."

"Nothing." H.L. sent an ear-splitting whistle through his teeth, as he'd done when he was a boy trying to demonstrate a level of approval for which words weren't enough. He couldn't recall the last time he'd been moved to express himself thus. But Rose Gilhooley was a goddamned inspiration.

By God, he was going to do more than write one puny article about her. He was going to make her the centerpiece of a whole series of articles. He was going to write about her the way nobody had ever written about anyone before in the history of the world.

He was going to get to the bottom of her talent and tell the world about it. He was going to make her more famous than Buffalo Bill Cody himself.

Rose's gift was more than mere talent. H.L. knew it. Her entire personality, spirit, and essence went into her act. Nobody—*nobody*—could perform the way she did unless she threw her whole heart and soul into it.

H.L. had never understood that kind of dedication. His own love of the English language and of the written word had driven him to become the best writer he could be, but he was damned certain he didn't possess the depth of talent and single-minded dedication being demonstrated right this minute by little Rose Gilhooley. Hell, he was a natural writer, and he earned a living at it. Rose might be a natural rider, but she was more than that, and he wanted to dig around until he found a definition for whatever it was she possessed.

How old was she? Twenty-two? And she'd been with Buffalo Bill's Wild West for six years? She'd been riding like that since she was *sixteen?* Jesus. By the time he got through with Rose Gilhooley, he'd understand the phenomenal female inside and out, upside and down, absolutely, positively, and with no room for doubt.

H.L. didn't know how long her act lasted. It couldn't have been long, because the horse wasn't even sweaty when Rose signaled it somehow—to the audience, her commands were invisible, although the horse obeyed them instantly—to a halt in a shower of dust, made it twirl around like a ballerina—a *horse,* for God's sake!—then took one last prancing dance to the center of the arena, leaned over, patted the horse's neck, and threw her arms in the air as the horse—the *horse,* by God, and H.L. had never seen the like—bowed!

Rose herself swept a dainty bow from the horse's back and threw kisses to the audience. She reminded H.L. of pictures of angels he'd seen in church. Not that he'd seen the inside of a church for years, but it was still what Rose reminded him of.

She sat on her horse in the center of the arena for a minute or two, looking unbelievably serene and delicate considering everything she'd just done, acknowledging the audience's whoops and cheers. She made the horse turn a slow circle as she waved back at her fans. H.L. was sure the whole thing was planned and rehearsed, but it looked natural when Buffalo Bill himself rode out on a comparably white mount and gave Rose a big hug from horseback. The audience went wild.

Then Rose Gilhooley took one last bow, saluted cheerfully at the crowd, and rode out of the arena.

And the show went on. But H.L. didn't care about the rest of the show. With a clap on Sam's back that made his fellow journalist jump, H.L. got up. "I've gotta go, Sam. See you tomorrow. Give my best to Daisy and the kids."

Startled, Sam half-rose. "Wh-what? Where are you going, H.L.? I thought you were going to—"

H.L. was already running up the aisle. He called back over his shoulder, "Gotta go. See you later, Sam. Gotta start researching these articles I'm going to write."

Glancing back once, H.L. saw Sam staring after him, dumbfounded, but he didn't care. He wanted—no, he *needed*—to talk to Rose Gilhooley. Now. Not later. Now. Right this minute. While he was still under her influence.

THREE

To the accompaniment of cheers from the crowd, Rose directed Fairy, the pretty white horse Colonel Cody had given her and which she'd trained because Gingerbread was getting old, out of the arena. Even though she sometimes thought living in a traveling theatrical exhibition was an odd way to live, she was happy. It was fun to entertain people.

She was greeted by smiles and friendly waves from other members of the cast as she rode Fairy through the group of people gathered to head out into the arena for another educational depiction of Old West activities. The show was a self-contained community, and Rose felt secure within its limits. The rest of the world scared her, but the Wild West was home.

Next on Cody's agenda was a reenactment of the Battle of the Little Big Horn, so there were hundreds of cast members, both soldiers and Indians, as well as horses, ready to ride out into the arena. Therefore, Rose got to greet lots of friends as she maneuvered Fairy through the mob.

Little Elk, the same Sioux who'd helped her refine and expand her riding skills, gave her a brief salute with his highly decorated tomahawk. (Reality, to Colonel Cody, sometimes required augmentation.) "Good riding, Wind Dancer." His guttural voice always held a smile when he spoke to Rose.

"Thanks, Little Elk. It's all your fault, you know." She sent him a grin, which he acknowledged with a nod.

"You were wonderful, Rose. I've never seen you ride better or with more grace and assurance." Annie Oakley walked up to pat Fairy's neck and hold out a pair of moccasins to Rose.

Rose always put on the moccasins after her performance, and she did so now, slipping them on before she dismounted. Although she had to do her act barefoot, she knew it was both unsafe and improper to tromp around the fairgrounds without shoes on. The colonel was very careful to maintain a sanitary workplace, but no one wanted to take a chance of contracting lockjaw, which was always a risk when one worked around horses. Rose knew, too, that no real lady would ever walk barefoot, and though she knew she was no real lady, she always pretended to be one, if only for Annie's sake.

"Thanks, Annie." Rose gratefully took the hand Annie held up to her and slid from Fairy's back. "It's a good crowd. They're going to love you."

Rose was in great shape physically and made sure she stayed that way, never eating too much or too little and doing stretching exercises with her wrists, hands, arms, and legs every day. But the act was hard on her body. Her hands and wrists, which had to bear the brunt of her weight during her act, got an especially rigorous workout. She vigorously shook them after she landed.

After giving them a thorough shake, she wiggled her fingers and turned her wrists as she'd seen dancers in the Egyptian exhibition do. Little Egypt herself had shocked Rose slightly, because she wore a rather scandalous costume. She appreciated having witnessed her dance, though, because she'd learned movements that helped limber up her fingers and wrists after a hard show. Anyhow, as far as costumes went, some folks were shocked by Rose's. Rose sniffed with dented dignity.

The feathers on her elaborate headdress were quite effective during her act, but they bothered her once she dismounted. The long ribbon to which they were attached trailed behind her, and the feathers tickled her calves.

She left Annie and the rest of the Wild West cast and led Fairy beyond the arena to the stable area, carefully unpinning the headdress as she walked. Once, during a performance in Italy, she'd almost lost the headdress due to inadequate pinning. These days Rose made extra-specially sure the silly thing was secure. Fortunately, her dense, curly hair helped hold the pins in.

"Miss Gilhooley! Miss Gilhooley!"

Rose jumped and whirled around when she heard her name being called in such excitement. Usually during Cody's reenactment of the Battle of the Little Big Horn, nobody paid attention to anything else, unless a crisis of major proportion had occurred. Whatever could be wrong?

She frowned when she saw that newspaper reporter— what was his name? H.L. Something?—burst through the crowd of performers and stage hands rimming the arena tunnel and hurry toward her. Whatever his name was, she remembered clearly that he'd found her amusing earlier in the day. In point of fact, he'd laughed at her.

Rose, who felt naive and unsophisticated around big-city folks, resented being laughed at. She didn't smile as H.L. Whoever-he-was hurried up to her. Nor did she speak.

Evidently this person, who seemed to have a rather high opinion of himself, didn't need anyone else when it came to carrying on a conversation, because he spoke without waiting for a response from Rose. Rose decided she didn't like him.

"Miss Gilhooley, I just wanted to tell you that yours was the most spectacular performance I've ever seen in my life."

Hmmm. Rose forgave him a trifle for making her feel small and insignificant earlier in the day. "Thank you."

She'd learned long ago not to trust strangers. She'd had men try all sorts of unkind, not to mention occasionally downright improper, maneuvers on her in the six years she'd been with the Wild West. Colonel Cody, bless him, tried in all ways to protect the female members of his cast, and generally sent pushy fellows off with a flea in their ear. Unfortunately, Cody wasn't here now. He was in the arena fighting off Indians and could not, therefore, fight off H.L. Whoever.

Before she could turn and continue to the stable with Fairy, H.L. grabbed her arm. Again she whirled around, this time snapping out, "Stop that!"

Fairy whickered, unnerved by Rose's sharp command.

H.L. released her instantly. "Sorry." Despite the word, he appeared unrepentant. "But I've got to talk to you, Miss Gilhooley."

If Fairy was unnerved, Rose was completely upset. She was routinely accosted by press people, but not when she was alone, right after an act, with her horse; and certainly not by one who appeared all but deranged with agitation. Members of the press usually approached her in the daytime, by appointment, and behaved in a respectful and respectable manner.

Right now she needed to attend to Fairy. She needed to calm down, too. Her concentration during her act was so complete as to involve her entire self, inside and out. It upset her routine to have people approach her before she'd had time to collect herself.

She also felt uncomfortable talking to people unconnected with the show while she was still in costume. Rose might have been born on the frontier and grown up in unusual circumstances, but she knew propriety from impropriety, and this costume was a decidedly improper one in which to conduct a polite conversation.

"I don't have time to talk to you right now, Mr.—" Drat, she could only remember his initials. "Whatever your name is," she concluded grumpily, irked that he, of all people, should have caught her unprepared.

"I'll walk with you," he said blithely. "Maybe I can help you."

"I don't need your help, thank you. Besides, I'm sure you wouldn't know what to do for a tired horse."

She'd meant it as sort of an insult, although Rose was too polite to be rude to strangers unless severely tried, which she was at the moment. H.L. only laughed. "Hell, you can teach me!"

Rose felt her eyes open wide. She might be unsophisticated, and she might have grown up on the American frontier and have little formal education, but she wasn't accustomed to men swearing in front of her. She barked, "I most certainly can*not!* I have work to do. Will you please excuse me, Mr.——" Blast. She'd done it again.

"May," he supplied nonchalantly, as if she hadn't just told him to get lost. "H.L. May. And I'm going to write about you, Miss Gilhooley. Your act was the most amazing thing I've ever seen."

This time, she wasn't so willing to forgive him. He was beginning to worry her, in fact, with his leechlike adherence to his purpose and his feverish intensity of manner. Since his avowed purpose was in direct opposition to her own, which was to enjoy a little quiet time with Fairy after a difficult act so that they could both relax, she didn't appreciate him one bit.

She stopped walking, causing Fairy to whicker again. Fairy didn't like disruptions to her schedule any more than Rose did. She decided to be blunt. "Mr. May, you're annoying me. I have to take care of my horse, and I don't need help."

"Aw, hell, Miss Gilhooley, all you need to do is answer a couple of questions tonight. We can talk more later. I won't be in the way. I promise."

"You're already in the way," Rose said through clenched teeth.

He laughed again. He was, without a doubt, the most impervious, not to mention aggravating, person Rose had ever met. Well, except for the few occasions when she'd been accosted by men who were liquored up. Rose knew liquor did horrid things to men. On those occasions, however, she'd been armed. At the moment, all Rose had with which to defend herself were her fingernails, and she kept them short because of her act. Well, and her feathered headdress, which only tickled. A whole lot of help *that* would be.

"Nonsense," H.L. said jovially. "I promise I won't be a nuisance. I'll just tag along. That way I'll get to write about what you do after your act is over."

He gave his head a small shake, and Rose thought she detected reverence in his expression, although it was difficult to tell since he was so brash and rude. Reverence from this source would also be incredible, so she decided she'd been hallucinating.

"I swear, I've never seen *anything* like your act. You're amazing."

Bother. She guessed she couldn't shake him off her tail. And, although she hated to admit it, it *was* sort of flattering to have a cultured big-city reporter so enamored of her showmanship. However, she still didn't view with joy the prospect of having him ogle her corsetless body while she rubbed Fairy down.

"Well," she said with less than her customary courtesy— he really was a most aggravating fellow—"I guess I can't stop you." She turned and clicked to Fairy, who walked beside her obediently. Rose reflected that it was comforting to have *something* obey her commands, even if H.L. May was too dense to do so.

"Great." H.L. seemed totally undismayed when Rose took off for the stables without waiting for him. He merely trotted along next to her.

Rose cast him a sidelong glance from the corner of her eye and was irked to observe that he didn't show the slightest degree of embarrassment. She'd known for six years now that newspaper people were aggressive sorts and inclined to be pushy and insensitive, but she hadn't understood until this minute that some of them had no feelings at all. It was quite vexatious.

She also felt a little edgy, knowing she was hemmed in on both sides. Generally, she had only Fairy beside her as she walked to the stables. She would have felt much more comfortable without H.L. May walking with them. She kept expecting him to say or ask something awkward or embarrassing.

Nevertheless, Rose knew Colonel Cody courted the press, so she aimed to do her duty by him. She didn't give a rap about H.L. May or his articles, but Rose held up William F. Cody almost as a saint in her life, and she'd not disappoint him if she could help it.

This reporter made her awfully nervous, though. Rose had the disheartening feeling that she'd be less anxious if H.L. May were a plain man. Or old. Or obviously dissolute and dissipated. Or short, soft, and flabby. Unhappily for Rose, he was none of those things.

H.L. May was a large, robust, young, healthy-looking fellow, with a charming grin, a handsome face, lovely eyes—they looked dark in the dim light leaking from the arena, but Rose recalled that they were a dancing hazel-green. He also towered over her, although that wasn't hard to do.

Rose frequently felt insignificant, but the feeling most often occurred when she was contemplating her lack of formal education and her frontier upbringing. She was unused to feeling insignificant just because she was small. Her overall smallness worked to her advantage, however, in the most important area of her life: her work.

At the moment, if she'd been able to grow six inches and gain thirty pounds, she'd have done it instantly, because then H.L. May wouldn't seem so overpowering to her. Or maybe he would. With a sigh, Rose decided that H.L. May was uniformly bad news in her life, and there probably wasn't anything she could do about it, even with help from a miracle growth spurt.

"Here's the stable," she grumbled.

"Aha. Where the *real* work takes place." H.L. sounded smug.

Rose shot him another glance, this one more sour than before. What did he mean, the *real* work? If he thought doing all those tricks in front of thousands and thousands of strangers was easy, he didn't know real work from his own hind end. She chose not to say so, knowing he could use words better than she and fearing she'd lose any verbal battles he cared to wage.

Shoot, she was already thinking of their relationship, if you could call it a relationship, in terms of warfare. This boded ill for any articles he aimed to write about her.

At least Fairy was happy. The small mare pranced gaily into the stable, knowing she was going to be groomed, covered with a snug blanket, led to her comfy stall, and given food and water. Colonel Cody gave his animals only the best, too, so Fairy would get a share of oats this evening, as she always did after a show.

"There you go, girl." Ignoring H.L. and determined to carry on with her job as if he weren't there, Rose clicked to Fairy, who obligingly walked over to stand near the things Rose used to brush her and rub her down. She was a good horse. Given tonight's company, Rose blessed her for it. Fairy represented normality under abnormal circumstances.

"That horse is sure well trained," H.L. observed, watching with interest.

Rose dared to glance at him. She wasn't pleased to find him relaxed, leaning against the stable wall, his arms crossed over his chest, and watching her acutely, as if his eyes functioned as tiny motion-picture cameras. Rose had seen an exhibition of motion pictures at the fair. She got the impression his brain was recording and cataloging everything his sharp green eyes saw.

"Yes, she is." She went to where her tools were laid out, picked up the currycomb, slipped her hand under the leather strap, and began working on Fairy's beautiful white coat. Rose had contemplated naming the lovely mare Buttermilk, but decided she was far too dainty for such a countrified name. The name *Fairy* suited her much better.

If Rose were a horse, she had a feeling nobody would think twice about naming *her* Buttermilk.

Fiddle. She had to stop thinking things like that. H.L. May brought out the insecurities in her, and that was not a good thing if she wanted to impress him. Which she did. For the colonel's sake. For her own sake, of course, Rose didn't care.

Who do you think you're fooling, Rose Gilhooley?

She managed to suppress a snort laced with self-disgust in time to prevent it from hitting the air. Blast H.L. May, anyhow. He rattled her. Rose didn't allow herself to be rattled very often these days. She'd learned in six years of hard work with the Wild West how to keep herself to herself and to appear quiet and dignified under the most trying circumstances. She definitely didn't want to have her humble origins splashed all over the newspapers.

Well . . . She thought about it as she brushed the mare's coat with a soothing rhythm. . . . She guessed she didn't honestly care if people knew about her hard beginnings. What Rose didn't want folks to know was how dumb she was.

Annie would figuratively smack Rose for calling herself dumb, even to herself. Annie, whose upbringing had been almost exactly like Rose's, had lectured her often about how a body couldn't choose the life into which she was born, and that it was what one did with one's life after one was dumped out onto this earth that counted. Annie invariably went on to say that Rose had *made* something of herself, and she ought to be proud of it.

As for her education or lack of it, that wasn't Rose's fault, either, Annie always said. What's more, Rose was constantly striving to improve that aspect of her life. Therefore, according to Annie, Rose ought to hold her head high and take a backseat to no one.

The good Lord knew, Rose thought as she brushed, that Annie herself never took a backseat. She'd made sure she learned how to read and write, even though she hadn't had any schooling, and she was as dignified and self-assured as Queen Victoria herself. Rose sometimes wondered why Annie was so self-confident, and whether she herself would ever learn how to be that way. She doubted it more often than not.

"Who trained him?"

Having become involved in her own glum musings, Rose had almost forgotten about H.L. May's presence in the stable. Her head jerked up, and she stared at him. "Who? I mean what?" She stamped her foot in frustration, causing Fairy a moment of uneasiness, which Rose allayed by cooing softly to her.

H.L. nodded at the horse. "Who trained him? That horse you're brushing?"

Him? Rose stared hard at H.L. May for only a second before transferring her gaze to Fairy. "This," she said, trying not to sound as surprised as she felt, "is a mare." Eyeing H.L. once more, keenly, she added, "A mare is a female horse."

He laughed. He had a loud laugh, and it seemed to bounce off the wooden stable walls. Several of the horses that weren't being used in tonight's show shuffled and huffed. Rose knew exactly how they felt. She'd have liked to heave the currycomb at Mr. H.L. May's head, but she knew that would probably only amuse him, too.

After what seemed like hours, H.L. stopped laughing and said, "Ah. Well, then, who trained *her?* Whoever it was did a darned good job."

Rose eyed him for approximately ten seconds more before she ground out frigidly, "Thank you. For your information, *I* trained her. Who did you *think* trains the horses I'm expected to risk my neck riding?"

He laughed again. Naturally. Rose might have predicted as much.

"Ah, I see," he said after another several hours of his impertinent laughter had disturbed the horses and Rose's sensibilities. "I should have known."

"Indeed." Finished with brushing Fairy's glossy coat, Rose replaced the currycomb without doing anything untoward with it, for which she congratulated herself, and took up the comb with which she maintained Fairy's sleek main and tail.

Sometimes Rose braided her horse's tail, but she didn't do so unless the weather was particularly windy. Tonight she hadn't. The colonel had told her that when an audience witnessed the free-flowing tail of a fast-moving horse, they went crazy with excitement, and Rose always tried to please the colonel. Even for the colonel's sake, however, she wasn't going to risk her neck any more than she had to, and if the wind blew just wrong, Fairy's flying tail interfered with her vision.

Trying her best to ignore her inquisitor, she started combing, making sure she whispered soothing noises to Fairy, in case the horse was as upset as Rose by H.L. May's continued presence.

It wouldn't be so bad if he weren't so . . . so . . . obtrusive. But he was. Rose had a suspicion that even if he were to be polite and keep his mouth shut, she'd still know he was there. He had a commanding presence. Sort of like the colonel's, only nowhere near as restful.

"You did a really good job training her," H.L. observed.

As if *he* knew anything. He couldn't even tell a mare from a gelding! "Thank you."

Although Rose had told herself she wanted H.L. May to shut up and go away, when he *did* remain silent he made her even more nervous than when he talked. She discovered this unnerving fact when a space of quiet ensued after her last frigid thank-you.

Blast the man, what was the matter with him? For that matter, what was the matter with *her?* It wasn't like Rose Gilhooley to be this anxious around newspaper people. Not any longer. During the first year or so of her tenure with the Wild West, she'd been as nervous as a cat on a hot rock every time anyone connected with the press came around. But that was only because she'd been so conscious of her shortcomings regarding language usage and proper grammar. She'd studied hard in the ensuing years, however, and now she could hold her own around most of the press buzzards, as she'd come to think of them.

At least the reporters in Europe had been polite. This H.L. May person was rude and intrusive, and Rose wished he'd either get on with it or leave. Her nerves crackled uncharacteristically. Perhaps she was only tense because she'd not had her quiet time alone with Fairy.

Twaddle. She'd been pursued by newspaper people plenty of times after a show. Everyone who saw her considered her act spectacular, and most folks wondered how such a tiny, delicate-looking girl could do the amazing things she did.

Ha! If they only knew. Rose was about as delicate as bear jerky. She never admitted it to members of the press. When H.L. finally spoke again, Rose was so involved in her own tumultuous thoughts that she jumped in alarm.

"Say, Miss Gilhooley, I get the feeling you don't like me much, but I'm really not such a bad fellow."

Involuntarily Rose slapped a hand over her thumping heart. She turned to stare at H.L. through slitted lids. Blast him, anyway! How dare he lull her into thinking he wasn't going to talk any more, and then say something like that?

Well . . . Rose realized instantly that she'd just been irrational. She chalked up this aberration in her normally clear thought patterns to H.L. May's influence, too.

After she'd caught her breath and her heart stopped thundering, which took approximately five seconds, she said, "Don't be ridiculous, Mr. May. I don't dislike you. I don't even know you."

His grin made her heart stop for a second. She felt the heat creep into her cheeks, and this time she wanted to heave the mane-and-tail comb at him. Instead, she put the comb in its place with the precision that had been drummed into her by Annie Oakley and Colonel Cody, both of whom liked to keep things neat, and walked over to Fairy's own personal stall, where the mare's special blanket hung over the railing. Rose had embroidered Fairy's name on the blanket with her own fingers, under Annie's tutelage. She picked it up and carried it back to the mare.

"Hey, why don't you let me help you with that stuff?" H.L. said, jerking away from the wall he'd been holding up. "That's a pretty heavy blanket for a little girl like you."

If there was one thing Rose resented more than H.L. considering her a weakling, it was him thinking of her as a *little girl*. She glowered at him from under Fairy's neck as she flung the blanket over the mare's glossy white back. "I am *not* a little girl, Mr. May. And I'm quite strong. If I weren't, I wouldn't be able to perform my act, would I?"

Thank goodness he didn't laugh. He grinned, but Rose thought she might be able to stand that—although she wasn't sure. His grin flashed two whole rows of gloriously white teeth that made a remarkable contrast against his tanned face. He looked too healthy to be a reporter. Rose had always been told reporters stayed indoors and drank all the time, and were mostly consumptive and dying. This specimen looked awfully darned robust to her.

"I suppose not," he said through his grin.

She sniffed.

"All right, Miss Gilhooley, I promise I won't offer to help again. And I also promise I won't get in your way." He held his hands up, palms out, as a peace offering.

"No?" She made sure she appeared as skeptical as she sounded, because she didn't want him getting any ideas.

"No."

Fiddle. Rose wished his eyes wouldn't twinkle like that. He was too good-looking for her peace of mind, and that was a very bad thing. Rose knew all about newspaper men. She understood they were men of loose morals and looser tongues. Annie, Rose's model for all things proper, had often told her so.

Annie's opinion of men in general wasn't very high. Her husband, Frank Butler, was a model of masculine perfection, but there wasn't another man in the world who measured up to Frank—not even Rose's personal hero, William F. Cody.

Rose trusted Annie's opinions absolutely. Since Rose had joined the Wild West, except for that one awful year when Annie had absented herself—she'd not condoned the inclusion of another lady sharpshooter in the Wild West—Annie had substituted for Rose's family. Mother, Father, teacher, moral arbiter: Annie had been just about everything to Rose.

"Heck, no," H.L. said. He walked over to stand on the other side of Fairy and helped Rose straighten out the blanket. Rose wished he hadn't done that. "I'm really a great guy. And I'm going to write a series of articles about you that will bring you to the attention of the world."

Rose squinted at him, this time from over Fairy's graceful neck. She had to stand on tiptoes to do it, but that was all right. She wanted to make sure he knew she wasn't any old backwoods hick. "I've performed in front of the crowned heads of Europe, Mr. May, not to mention most of the celebrities in the United States and its territories over here. What can you do for my reputation that Colonel Cody hasn't already done? I'm sure I don't need any publicity from *you*."

She placed special emphasis on the *you* in order to make him understand that she considered him a mere scribbler and worth little in the overall scheme of things. She didn't, of course, but she'd die sooner than let *him* know it.

"Nonsense. All performers can use publicity. And you're really something."

She was? Since she didn't know what to say, Rose remained silent, only leading Fairy to her stall. Fairy was glad to be home. She let Rose know as much by nuzzling her cheek before retiring for the night. Rose's eyes filled with tears. At least Fairy appreciated her. Because she didn't want H.L. May to know how much he was affecting her, she kept her back to him as she retrieved a bucket, got some grain, filled Fairy's feed bin, and checked her water supply.

"There you go, girl." Rose patted the mare's white rump and, unable to delay any longer, left the stall. With a sigh, she closed and locked the stall door, then sucked in a breath redolent of sweet hay and horses, and turned to confront her tormenter.

"What exactly do you expect to accomplish with these articles, Mr. May? And why do you want to write about me? Wouldn't you prefer to concentrate on a more famous performer?"

Annie Oakley was forever being written about. Annie was used to it. Rose wasn't. She feared she might get big-headed if reporters suddenly started paying attention to her. Worse, she feared that once they got to know her, they'd despise her for her many deficiencies of education and refinement. In Rose's opinion, that would be much worse than anonymity.

"Everybody writes about folks who are already famous, Miss Gilhooley. I'm interested in you."

"Hmmm." His statement might be taken in more ways than one if Rose weren't so certain of her position in life, which was quite low. If she hadn't been so superior a natural rider, she'd still be living on a miserable farm outside Deadwood, Kansas, illiterate, ignorant, and shooting game for a living. It was pure dumb luck—and her brother, Freddie— that had brought Rose to Colonel Cody's attention.

H.L. lifted his arms as if he were presenting Rose to the world. "You're a true phenomenon, Miss Gilhooley! I've never seen anyone ride like you do. You've got to be the most sensational performer I've ever seen, and you put on an absolutely amazing bareback riding act. Why, you put every single one of the circus performers I've seen to shame."

"Thank you."

"And I'm sure your story is fascinating. According to the publicity dodger Cody sent to the newspaper, you've been with the Wild West for six years. You must have started when you were a baby!"

"I was sixteen," Rose muttered, peeved. Why did this man persist in thinking of her as a child? She didn't want him to. Or maybe she did.

Fiddlesticks. H.L. May made her brain hurt.

"That means you're only twenty-two years old right now. Do you realize what most twenty-two-year-old women are doing with their lives these days?"

Getting married to nice men and having babies, Rose thought unhappily. She said, "No."

"Well, neither do I, really." H.L. laughed.

This time his self-mocking laughter charmed Rose. She considered her reaction an unhappy indication of her underlying moral depravity. Annie had told her over and over again that poverty did not equate to moral depravity, and Rose tried to believe her, but she had her suspicions.

"I do know, though," H.L. went on, "that most of them aren't riding horses as star performers in the premier Wild West show in the world, as you are."

"I'm sure of it," Rose said dryly. For one thing, they didn't have to, and she did.

Because she wasn't feeling too good about herself at the moment and, moreover, didn't want H.L. May to agree with her self-assessment, she added, "What I do takes a lot of skill and even more practice. Most people, male or female, aren't willing to put so much time and effort into perfecting a skill." That was quite good. Rose tried to think of some of the other things Annie and the colonel had said of and to her in their ongoing efforts to boost her self-esteem. She couldn't think of any.

"That's right," H.L. said energetically. "And I'm going to show the world exactly what you've made of yourself."

Instantly, all of Rose's insecurities leaped to attention. "What do you mean by that?" She slammed the bucket back into place and was sorry at once when Fairy whinnied and fidgeted in her stall.

H.L. blinked at her. "Nothing bad, honest. Why won't you trust me, Miss Gilhooley? I don't intend anything of an improper nature, believe me."

The way he said it made Rose understand that being improper with her was about the last thing in the universe he desired. Oddly enough, knowing that his intentions were honorable didn't make her feel significantly better. Nevertheless, she said, "Of course not," because she felt she should. This was so embarrassing.

She stood as tall as she could—which, at five feet, one inch, wasn't very, although she was a whole inch taller than Annie Oakley—and tried to sound dignified when she next spoke. "I need to go to my tent and change out of my costume, Mr. May. Is there anything else you wish to say to me?"

He looked exasperated. "Of *course* there's more I wish to say to you! Damn it, I want to write about you!"

Rose drew her shoulders up even more rigidly. "Please don't swear at me, Mr. May."

The roar of the crowd and the rat-a-tat of gunfire let Rose know that the Little Big Horn reenactment was about over. Pretty soon, General Custer would be the last man standing and would die a brave and honorable death—although how anyone could know how he died was beyond her, unless Colonel Cody had managed to get one of the Indian participants to yak, and they generally wouldn't—and Rose didn't want anyone to catch her alone in the stables with H.L. May. They might get the wrong idea.

"Sorry, Miss Gilhooley." Again, H.L. May sounded unrepentant about his use of impolite language. "But I need to spend more time with you. A lot of time. Don't you understand? I want to write a whole series of articles about the Columbian Exposition, and I want more than one of them to be about *you!*"

"What you want and what I want are two different things, Mr. May," she said stiffly. "I shall be more than happy to sit for one interview with you so that you can write your article."

She knew good and well that the colonel had been made rich and famous through dime novels, theatrical exhibitions, and newspaper articles documenting his exploits, but the notion of someone writing such things about *her,* little Rose Ellen Gilhooley, dismayed her. For heaven's sake, she didn't want the whole world to know she was an uneducated boob! She'd never say so to this man.

"Nuts. I'll bet you anything that if I approached Buffalo Bill about doing a series of articles about you, he'd give me his blessing."

Rose glared at him—and gave it up. He was right. "There's no need to ask the colonel," she muttered. "How do you want to approach this assignment of yours?"

FOUR

H.L. May's smile almost knocked her over backward. "We're going to have to spend a lot of time together."

All of Rose's suspicious instincts rose up in alarm. "What do you mean?"

He shrugged, as if he couldn't conceive of anyone ascribing less-than-chivalrous motives to his words. "I want to do a series of interviews with you, but I don't want them to be stiff and stuffy. I want to chat with you in a relaxed atmosphere."

Fat chance of that ever happening, Rose thought sourly. She'd relax around H.L. May the day the earth stood still. "How do you propose to accomplish that?" At least she was speaking properly. Rose was rather proud that her rattled innards didn't express themselves in poor grammar.

His speculative gaze made her nerve endings perk up and quiver. She definitely wasn't sure about this man and his motives. Rose knew she was no femme fatale, but Annie had often told her that men didn't care how pretty a girl was. *If you're a woman, you're prey,* Annie had said, and Rose believed her.

"Say, Miss Gilhooley, have you been up in the Ferris wheel yet?"

Rose blinked at him. "The Ferris wheel? Why, no." She'd been wanting to ride on the spectacular invention, but she wasn't about to wander around this enormous Exposition, teeming with all kinds of people, by herself. She and Annie had been intending to ride the wheel one of these days, but so far Annie hadn't had the time.

"How would you like to ride the Ferris wheel this evening?"

"This evening?" Rose was so startled, she spoke more loudly than she'd meant to. "But—but—but . . ."

"I give you my word of honor I only want to show you the wheel, Miss Gilhooley."

The way he said it, as if he were talking to a small child who needed to be humored, didn't do anything to settle Rose's uncertainty. Although it was absolutely true she had no wish to be obliged to fend off improper advances, she also wouldn't mind knowing that H.L. May thought of her as a grown-up adult human female toward whom he might conceivably want to make an improper advance or two. For heaven's sake, she wasn't all *that* young!

She had a feeling she was missing some very important point somewhere, but she had no notion what it could be. "Um, I'm not sure I ought to do so tonight, Mr. May. I have to get plenty of rest, you know, and—"

"Applesauce!"

Rose objected to him interrupting her in that peremptory way. She was, after all, something of a star. A smallish star, granted, and one without a whole lot of twinkle, but she deserved at least as much respect as anyone else in the world.

That being the case, she propped her fists on her hips and frowned at him. "You may think my act is easy for me, given my level of expertise, but it's not. For your information, I need sufficient sleep and so forth in order to make sure I don't kill myself out there. And my concerns are *not* applesauce!"

"Of course they're not."

He was humoring her again, using that mollifying, condescending tone Rose hated. She turned around and snapped, "Some other time."

She'd stomped clean out of the stables before she realized H.L. May hadn't gone anywhere. Nor had he been intimidated into remaining in the stables. She ought to have known better than to think anything she could say or do would sway this nosy, pushy, aggravating reporter. He was right there by her side, grinning like an imp. She sighed heavily.

H.L. May gazed down at Rose Gilhooley and thought that she, while annoying as hell, was absolutely adorable.

"Come on, Miss Gilhooley." He used his most persuasive tone on her. It had always worked on women before. He couldn't imagine artless little Miss Rose Gilhooley being less susceptible to his many charms than any other female in the world.

"I have other things to do." She didn't slow down, but continued to march along as if she were trying to kill roaches as she walked.

Whoa, she sounded ferocious. H.L. hadn't reckoned on her being twice as stubborn as most women, susceptible or not. Although . . . He guessed she'd worked hard to get where she was. That must take a lot of grit and determination. Stubbornness was probably only an outgrowth of those qualities.

But that was the whole point, he reminded himself instantly. He wanted to find out what made her tick. What had motivated this tiny woman to become the best in the world at what she did, especially since what she did required an astonishing level of stamina and skill? Damn it, she wasn't going to get away with this peremptory dismissal.

"Wait a minute, Miss Gilhooley." He put a couple of fingers on her arm, and she jumped. Lord, she was touchy. "Sorry."

She wheeled around and scowled again. "I don't like people I don't know touching me, Mr. May."

So . . . did she like people she *knew* touching her? H.L. would have liked to ask, but didn't dare. She might slap his face, although she'd probably have to stand on her tippy-toes to do it. Jeez, she was cute. "I beg your pardon." He tried to sound humble. "But you *did* tell me I didn't need to ask Buffalo Bill's permission to interview you. And I'm sure he'd approve of what I have in mind as publicity for you and, by extension, the Wild West."

H.L. found the lightning-quick change in her demeanor both intriguing and significant. All he had to do was mention Cody's name, and Miss Rose Gilhooley went tame. It was akin to what that Russian fellow, Pavlov, had demonstrated with his dogs. Only Miss Gilhooley didn't start salivating when the colonel's name was mentioned; she started being agreeable. H.L. decided to remember this for future dealings with her.

"Are you trying to blackmail me, Mr. May? It won't work. I'll do pretty much anything for Colonel Cody, because I think he's one of the great men of our day, and he's—well, he's been wonderful to me. But I won't compromise myself for him or anybody else."

H.L. was honestly shocked, and that surprised him. Before he met Rose Gilhooley, he'd considered himself fairly unflappable. *"Compromise* you! What the hell do you think I'm planning to do to you on that wheel, anyway? Damn it, Miss Gilhooley, all I want to do is write about you!" He was pleased when she blushed brick red.

"I didn't mean that."

"No?" Noticing that his reaction had slightly cowed her, H.L. resolved to take advantage of it. He adopted his best wounded expression. "That's what it sounded like to me."

"Well, you heard wrong, then." Now she sounded exasperated. "But you don't understand! As a performer, I have to be twice as careful with my reputation as anybody else. Annie has told me so often."

"Annie?" All of his reporterly instincts jolted to attention. "You mean Annie Oakley?"

"Yes."

"You were with her this afternoon, too. Do the two of you spend a lot of time together?"

"Yes. She's my very best friend."

Hmmm. The little bareback queen sounded a trifle defensive. This was awfully interesting stuff; H.L. wasn't about to let it slip away. "I see. Well, for your information, even if I had something dastardly in mind for you, I wouldn't be able to accomplish it on the Ferris wheel. The thing's too public, for one thing, and there would be fifty-eight other people in the carriage with us. And for another thing, I'm not that sort of man."

She started walking again, but she gave him a look he'd have resented if he didn't find it so darling. "Is that so?"

"Yes." He didn't have to trot to keep up with her, although she walked mighty fast for such a shorty. "Anyhow, I know you'll enjoy it. You haven't lived until you've seen Chicago and the Exposition at night, all lit up, from the top of the Ferris wheel."

That got her attention, by God. Her eyes were huge when she glanced up at him. "Really? I've been wanting to go, but there's so little time."

"You've got time right now," he pointed out.

Thunderous applause reached them from the arena. Rose paused to watch. When H.L. did likewise, he saw what looked like a million mounted men, some in soldiers' uniforms and some in breechclouts and feathered headbands, galloping out of the arena. Rose waved to several of them.

Colonel Cody and an Indian gentleman spotted Rose and H.L. and trotted over. Rose smiled with unfeigned admiration, and what looked to H.L. like adoration, at Buffalo Bill.

"Sounds like the crowd loved you as usual, Colonel."

Buffalo Bill saluted H.L. and leaned over to give Rose a kiss on the cheek. "That they did, Rosie. I see you're giving an interview. Good work!" He reined his white horse around and trotted back toward the arena. "Got to take another bow and introduce Missie. Have fun, Rosie! Show that reporter fellow a good time. It'll be good for the Wild West!"

Rose frowned.

H.L. grinned.

The Indian did neither. Rather, he stared at H.L. in a noncommittal way for so long that it actually made H.L. uneasy, which was a feat few men had accomplished. Slightly peeved, H.L. said, "Hello, there. My name's H.L. May. I write for the *Globe*." He reached up to shake the Indian's hand, but the gesture was ignored. H.L. chalked it up to cultural differences.

The Indian transferred his unreadable gaze to Rose. "This man bothering you, Wind Dancer?"

The fellow's voice was deep, sort of guttural, and it made H.L. think of prairie grasses blowing in the wind, which was weird, since he'd never seen prairie grasses blowing in the wind. Uneasily, he eyed the rifle gripped in the man's hand and the tomahawk stuck in his waistband. "I'm not bothering her."

Rose opened her mouth, and H.L. held his breath. He didn't think this guy would scalp him, but he wasn't sure. After keeping him in suspense for several seconds, Rose finally said, "No. I guess he's not really bothering me. Little Elk, this man is a reporter who wants to write an article about me."

"More than one article," H.L. hastened to correct her. "She's great, and she deserves lots of publicity." He grinned at the Indian, who didn't grin back, the same way he hadn't shaken his hand. H.L. sighed.

"She's the best rider in the world," Little Elk said matter-of-factly.

Rose gave him a pretty smile. "Little Elk taught me everything I know how to do on horseback. He has to say that."

At long last, the Indian grinned. "Naw. You're great." He made a brief gesture to H.L. "What you going to do with her?"

H.L. cleared his throat. Shoot, this was worse than asking a proper lady's father if he could come a'courting. "I was only going to take her on the Ferris wheel. The lights of the fair and the city are wonderful to see at night from on top of the wheel."

Suddenly, Rose gave a start and brightened visibly. "Say, I have a splendid idea! Why doesn't Little Elk come with us?"

Damn. H.L. squinted first at Rose, and then at the Indian, who looked smug. H.L. didn't know Indians could do that. He thought they were supposed to be stoical and impassive.

What the hell. He shrugged. "Sure. Come on along."

At least his acquiescence in the matter prompted Rose to quit arguing with him. That was a good thing.

Little Elk chomped popcorn contentedly. So did Rose. This really *was* fun. She'd never been to a fair. In England, she'd been introduced to Queen Victoria herself, not to mention the Prince of Wales—he was so portly that she and Annie had privately referred to him as the Prince of Whales—and his wife, and a whole bunch of titled folks. She'd also met the kaiser and several more royal people in Europe, as well as an African chief, a Polynesian something-or-other, and a Chinese mandarin. But she'd been working then. Her life hadn't afforded her many opportunities to relax and behave like other young women, who, she presumed, visited entertainments whenever they were moved to do so.

But at this moment, she was visiting the most spectacular exhibition the world had ever seen, in the company of one of her best friends and an alarmingly exciting man. She glanced up at H.L. May and was thrilled all over again.

Her reaction to him both troubled and puzzled her. She didn't really like him. He was too cheeky and aggressive for her taste. He also made her feel like a backwoods yokel. Granted, that wasn't a difficult feat to accomplish, but all

Rose had to do was *look* at H.L. May, as she was doing now, to feel insignificant, unlettered, and worthless.

At the moment, he was surveying the milling throng and the astonishing display of electrical lighting all around them as if he were a monarch eyeing his kingdom. *He* didn't find all this tumult and inventiveness intimidating. *He* acted as if he'd created it himself, like God.

Oh, dear. She was becoming blasphemous, and she'd only been in H.L. May's company for a little more than thirty minutes. This didn't seem like a good omen to Rose.

To distract herself, she said, "It is very kind of you, Mr. May, to entertain Little Elk and me this way." There. Rose didn't truly think the man was kind at all. She figured he'd only taken Little Elk along with them because she wouldn't have gone otherwise.

Or would she? Shoot, she didn't know. She hoped she'd have had enough moral courage, or been enough of a proper lady, to resist the lure of an exciting time at the fair.

"Aw, it's nothing," H.L. said, waving his hand in a dismissive gesture. "It's more fun to see the fair with a friend or two along."

"You have *friends?*" Rose could have bitten her tongue as soon as the question popped out of her mouth.

H.L. gave her a sharp glance. "Yes, Miss Gilhooley. I have lots of friends. What kind of man do you think I am, anyway?"

She'd probably better not say. Instead, she mumbled, "I'm sorry. I didn't mean it like that." Lordy, now she'd added lying to her list of defects.

"I'll just bet."

A low rumbling sound came from Little Elk. Rose, who had heard that noise before, but only rarely, glanced at her friend, vaguely peeved. "What are you laughing at?"

"You and your man, Wind Dancer."

"My *man?*" Just as Rose hadn't meant to ask H.L. May

if he had any friends, she also hadn't meant to shriek at Little Elk.

Little Elk winked and offered her more popcorn. She took some because she had to do something or die of embarrassment.

H.L. May, as might have been expected, laughed. He probably thought it was the funniest thing anybody had said in a month of Sundays, since he obviously had no interest in Rose except as a subject for examination and dissertation.

She found that notion so depressing, she decided not to think about it, too, along with all the other things she didn't want to think about. Instead, she turned her attention back to the fair and hoped H.L. would forget Little Elk's comment and her own shriek. "I've never seen so many people in my life outside of an arena."

The manner of H.L.'s smile changed. To Rose, he suddenly looked as if the topic of conversation had turned down a path for which he harbored a degree of fascination most often associated with religious zealotry or romantic love. "You know, Miss Gilhooley, the Columbian Exposition is the most spectacular world's fair ever put on. I've heard it even tops the one they had in Paris a few years back. And I'm going to make sure you see every inch of it."

Surprised, Rose shot him another look. "You are?"

"I am." He nodded once, as if that settled the matter.

"Um . . . Why?"

He looked disgustingly self-satisfied, sort of the way Rose imagined a man who'd just discovered a new continent might look. "Because I've decided exactly how I want these articles to run. The first one is going to be an introduction. The series of articles is going to be a metaphor, you see. At the moment, you're becoming acquainted with the Columbian Exposition, even as the Columbian Exposition is being introduced to humanity. The first article will be an introduction to you." His glance was eager, as if H.L. really wanted

Rose to understand his intentions so she'd cooperate with him in achieving them.

She'd have liked to, maybe, if she knew what he was talking about. She thought it over for a moment. Nope. In order to understand, she'd have to know what a metaphor was, and she didn't. She'd sooner shoot herself than ask H.L. May, so she wouldn't get an answer until she talked to Annie, and that would be far too late to do her any good right now. "Um . . . Is that so?" Her often-present feeling of inferiority reared its ugly head and sneered at her.

"That's so," H.L. said complacently. "As the fair is presented to you, so *you* will be presented to the reading public. Do you see now?"

No. She didn't see at all. Deciding it would be better for her own self-esteem to shuffle a little, she said, "I guess I understand that part. Sort of."

H.L. heaved a sigh, but when Rose inspected his face minutely to see if the sigh might have held disdain or exasperation, she discerned not a trace of either. Actually, the newspaperman appeared quite happy and pleased with himself. "It's simple, really. You're a young woman who was thrown into a life of glamor and showmanship at an age when most young women are only getting ready to leave the schoolroom."

Glamor? For that matter, *schoolroom?* Rose couldn't recall having had anything to do with either of those things thus far in her life. There had been an Indian school not far from Deadwood, but Rose wouldn't have been eligible to attend it even if she'd been able to take time away from feeding her family to do so. "Um, the Wild West isn't actually very glamorous, Mr. May."

She pondered the Wild West as she chewed and swallowed another handful of popcorn. "Maybe it is to the audience," she conceded.

"Right. But that's just it. People see only the finished product. I want them to see it all from the inside."

Rose was so horrified, she stopped walking. H.L. May and Little Elk, who were digging in their paper sacks for the remains of their popcorn, didn't notice she no longer accompanied them until they'd walked about five paces. Then H.L. turned around, a question in his gorgeous eyes. "What? What's wrong?"

"I don't want anybody to see me from the inside, Mr. May." Blast, her voice was shaking. "I—I value my privacy." That was not exactly a lie. The truth of the matter was that Rose's life was so mind-numbingly boring and dull that she'd suffer agonies of mortification if the public, who overtly adored her during her act in the Wild West, learned about it.

Rose was sure his smile was meant to reassure her. "Of course you do. I'm not planning to invade your privacy, Miss Gilhooley. But the public really craves to know more about its icons. And you're rapidly becoming an icon of American womanhood and accomplishment."

"I am?" This was news to her. It might even be flattering if Rose weren't so appalled by the notion of a whole bunch of perfect strangers learning her deepest, darkest secrets.

H.L.'s eyes opened wide in amazement. "What do you mean, 'I am?'? You're one of the biggest female stars of our day! Figuratively speaking, that is to say." He grinned one of his stunning grins. "You're actually about as big as a minute. But you and Annie Oakley are news everywhere."

"Oh." That made it even worse. Rose had come to have a faint understanding of the level of popularity enjoyed by the Wild West and Annie Oakley and, by inclusion, herself, but she sure hadn't known *Rose Gilhooley* was a household name.

Suddenly, she exhaled a whoosh of relief. By gum, it *wasn't* Rose Gilhooley whose name was splashed all over the newspapers all the time. It was *Wind Dancer.* Nobody knew Rose Gilhooley from a hole in the ground.

Feeling much better about life, the fair, the Wild West,

and somewhat better about H.L. May, Rose began walking again and caught up with her comrades in a moment. Little Elk offered her the last of his popcorn, but Rose declined with thanks. A few treats were fine, but she couldn't afford to eat much between meals.

Which reminded her that she hadn't taken any supper yet. She never ate before a performance, because to do so would have been most unwise if she valued her digestion. But the few grains of popcorn she'd consumed had whetted her appetite. As if she'd just reminded it, her stomach growled. Rose was completely embarrassed.

"Say, I didn't think to ask," H.L. said. "But are you hungry, Miss Gilhooley? You probably can't eat before performances." His tone was so natural that Rose was almost not embarrassed any longer.

His perceptiveness made her soften toward him for a second. She didn't dare let the softness linger, because she trusted him about as much as she'd trust a rattlesnake in her bed. "I am a little hungry," she equivocated. "I guess I could use . . . something."

"I have an idea!" H.L.'s expressive eyes suddenly expressed eagerness. "How about we get you a carbonated drink and a hamburger! I'll bet you've never tasted either one of those items."

She blinked at him. "Er, no, I haven't."

"Ha!" H.L. flung his arms wide. "I love this fair!"

He was certainly an enthusiastic young man. Rose found herself reluctantly fascinated by him. He was so free with his emotions and gestures. Rose had tried to hide herself behind her Wind Dancer persona for so many years, she couldn't even imagine being so open and spontaneous.

"Before the Columbian Exposition opened, *nobody'd* ever tasted a hamburger or a carbonated drink, Miss Gilhooley! They're being introduced here, at this fair!" He stamped the ground beneath his feet as if confirming the solidity of his statement.

"Oh." She glanced at Little Elk, who seemed as interested as she in food. "Um, what's a hamburger?" Rose knew that Little Elk, like most of his Sioux kin, liked to eat meat and resisted the so-called "vegetarian" foods that were being touted as healthy these days. His preference made a lot of sense to Rose, who knew how difficult it was to find meat on the plains, but she didn't even want to try to explain it to H.L. May.

"It's ground-up beef formed into a flat patty, then fried, and served on a round roll they call a bun, with condiments."

What were condiments? As Rose contemplated how stupid it would sound if she asked, H.L. made a question from her unnecessary.

"You can have pickles, prepared mustard sauce, some sort of tomato sauce they call ketchup—I think it was developed by a fellow named Heinz from a Chinese sauce—and onions on the hamburger roll. They're delicious."

Again, Rose and Little Elk exchanged a glance. Little Elk lifted one shoulder in his version of a shrug. Interpreting this as compliance, Rose said, "That sounds nice, Mr. May. We'd both like to try a—what did you call it?"

"A hamburger. I think there's a vendor here selling sausages on a bun, too. They're pretty good, especially when he dumps on a spoonful of sauerkraut. The fellow's German and calls them frankfurters."

"My goodness." It hadn't occurred to Rose until this conversation that people invented different kinds of foods. Or different ways to prepare, serve, and name foods, she guessed was a more appropriate way of thinking about it. And what was sauerkraut? Rose decided she'd probably never have to know and decided not to remember the word, which made her feel slightly better, since her memory for words wasn't infinite and there were several rattling around in there already.

So H.L. led the way to a food vendor, where he bought

hamburgers and carbonated drinks for the three of them. They sat at one of the outdoor tables placed along the main thoroughfare so that diners could watch fair visitors as they munched.

"This is quite tasty," Rose said. In truth, she was finding it difficult not to gobble her hamburger, it tasted so good and she was so hungry.

"Good," agreed Little Elk, who looked as if he wouldn't mind eating another three or four of the delectable meat sandwiches.

"I like 'em." H.L. was clearly pleased with himself as he, too, indulged in a hamburger. "How do you like your soda?"

"Soda? Is that what they call this?" Rose held up her drinking glass, which fizzed amusingly. She took a tentative sip and giggled. "It's very good, but the bubbles tickle." When she glanced at H.L., she discovered him gazing at her speculatively, his sea green eyes gleaming. She wasn't sure what to make of his expression, but it worried her.

"I don't suppose you've ever tasted champagne?" he asked in a quiet voice.

"No." Because the question and his expression disconcerted her, Rose turned to Little Elk. "Do you like your soda, Little Elk?"

The Indian nodded. "Good."

"Would you care for another hamburger? I know how much you like to eat."

Although she smiled at her friend to show she didn't mean anything unkind by her remark, it occurred to Rose that it hadn't been her money that had provided the first round of hamburgers. She supposed it might be considered impolite for her to offer H.L.'s guest more food.

But that didn't really matter, she decided instantly. Rose might send most of her money home to her family, but she made a large enough salary that she was able to keep a supply of pin money on hand. And if buying Little Elk another hamburger would make her feel less uneasy in H.L. May's company, the money would be well spent.

Little Elk nodded. "I like it."

"Wait right here," H.L. said as he got up from the elaborately molded ceramic bench. "I'll get you another one." As he loped off toward the hamburger concessionaire, he shot back over his shoulder, "Be right back."

Rose watched him in dismay. She oughtn't have done that; she knew better. Although she possessed no understanding at all of the polite nuances of behavior required in sophisticated society, her mother had drummed proper manners into her when she was a child. She'd just made a big gaffe, and she was mortified.

"Wait here," she told Little Elk, leaping up from the bench and hurrying after H.L. "I'll be right back."

She had to run to catch up with the long-legged reporter. "Mr. May! Mr. May, wait a minute."

He turned, surprised. "What's the matter, Miss Gilhooley?" With a wicked grin, he asked, "You want another hamburger, too?"

"No!" Exasperated, Rose started digging around in her skirt pocket, where she carried some change. "I'm quite full, thank you, but it was I who offered Little Elk another one of those sandwiches, so I ought to pay for it."

"Tut, tut. I invited you to come with me tonight," he reminded her. "This evening is my treat."

"You didn't invite Little Elk," Rose muttered, conscious that her friend's company tonight was a direct result of her own cowardice. "I should pay for him."

"Pshaw. Don't be silly."

"I'm not being silly!" Heat crept up the back of her neck. Rose wondered if she was making too much of this. Probably. H.L. May rattled her composure more than any other human being she'd ever met. "Here." She thrust a silver dollar at him.

He looked down at it and didn't make a move to take it. "Pooh."

"Blast you, H.L. May! You drive me crazy!"

His slow grin stampeded the heat at the back of her neck into her cheeks. Rose imagined she now glowed like one of those electrical lights hanging all over the place at the exposition.

"I'm not sure driving you crazy is a bad thing, Miss Gilhooley." He took her demurely gloved hand and folded her fingers over the silver piece. When he was through, her hand was firmly secured in his own. "Keep your money. This night's on me."

He leaned close to her when he said it, and his warm breath fanned her already burning cheek. Two strong and contradictory impulses warred in her. On the one hand, Rose wanted to turn around and scuttle away as fast as she could. On the other hand, she wanted to throw her arms around H.L. May's broad shoulders and cling for dear life. The strain of dealing with the wildly disparate hankerings held her rooted to the spot, staring into H.L.'s magnificent, hypnotic eyes.

"You have beautiful eyes, Miss Gilhooley," he whispered after what seemed like three or four hours.

Rose swallowed, opened her mouth, discovered her brain was barren of words, and shut it again.

"In fact, taken as a package—a very small package— you're a most appealing female."

Rose felt her knees go weak. Good heavens, what was he saying? Her ears buzzed. Her mouth went so dry, she wouldn't have been able to talk even if she could have found a word or two in her brain somewhere.

H.L. slowly released her hand and patted her on the shoulder. "You just go back to your friend, Miss Gilhooley. I'll bring him another hamburger."

She managed to nod, although she could have sworn she had no control over her muscles. He chucked her under the chin, grinned more broadly, and walked away from her. Sauntered away from her. Swaggered away from her. As if he'd just scored a home run and won the game for the home team.

Rose swallowed hard as the bones in her legs stopped melting and her knees straightened. She realized her mouth was hanging open and shut it. She blinked.

Damn him! Rose, who would never, ever speak a profanity aloud, and who virtually never even thought profanities, wanted to fling hundreds and hundreds of *damn*s, *hell*s, and *bastard*s at H.L. May's wide back.

Instead, she whirled around and stomped back to Little Elk.

Offhand, she couldn't recall another time in her life when she'd been so completely and utterly humiliated. And all because a handsome man had sweet-talked her.

"Ooooooh! That man drives me *crazy.*"

She resented it when Little Elk's chuckle rumbled out.

FIVE

H.L. didn't know why he'd flirted with Rose Gilhooley. Hell, she was just a kid, really. He kicked at a wad of paper in his path as he, Rose, and Little Elk stood in line for the Ferris wheel.

Worse, she was now mad at him. She'd been almost relaxed before he'd succumbed to his urge to flirt. Now she'd gone back to being stiff as a poker, frigid as winter, and as uncommunicative as one of those sightless, earless fish somebody'd discovered in an underground river somewhere in a cave. When she did speak, she used words of one syllable. Hell, she used *sentences* of one syllable. Damn it, what had possessed him to spoil it all? He needed her cooperation, not her enmity.

He inspected her closely when they reached the head of the line, and offered a hand to help her into the carriage. She didn't want to take his hand; she resisted taking it, even; but he didn't give her a chance to scramble inside unaided. He simply grabbed her hand and held on. He also revised his opinion of Rose Gilhooley.

All right, so she wasn't just a kid. She was curvy as hell, and fully grown, even if she wasn't very big.

Well, how could she be big and perform her act so effectively? Annie Oakley was even smaller than Rose Gilhooley, although with her, slightness didn't seem so odd. After all, Annie Oakley was a sharpshooter. That required skill, but no outrageous degree of athletic ability. What Rose Gilhooley did on a horse was masterful, and it *had* to require the strength of a Hercules.

Yet she was a tiny, delicate-looking, remarkably pretty young woman who, if you didn't know better and you saw her walking on a street, you'd think was a normal, everyday wife and mother. Or at least . . . maybe not a wife and mother, but a clerk in a department store. Or a typewriter for some attorney's firm. A secretary at a bank somewhere, perhaps. Or somebody's kid sister.

You sure wouldn't look at her and think: *Wind Dancer, Bareback Rider Extraordinaire.* He grinned to himself. She was a goddamned Herculette, in actual fact. He'd have to remember that description when he wrote his first article.

Funny thing was that you didn't notice how tiny she was when she was performing. You only noticed how incredible she was.

It was later, after you'd met her, that you realized she was an adorable, not to mention eminently ravishable young woman. Damn. He almost wished he hadn't noticed.

But that was stupid. H.L. May could withstand lust. And anyway, he wasn't sure *lust* was the right word. He certainly felt a powerful attraction to her, but *lust* didn't exactly express it. He consoled himself with the thought that he was excited about this writing assignment, and that his enthusiasm was undoubtedly the only reason he felt this . . . interest. Yes, indeedy. Interest. That was it. Fascination, even.

How nonsensical of him to think of it as lust.

H.L. caught a flash of one of Rose's well-turned ankles, recalled how shapely her legs were, and had to fight down a surge of sexual awareness.

Damnation. That wasn't mere interest.

Unless . . . Ah, of course. That was it. H.L. had read a monograph written by one of that German doctor Breuer's colleagues, Sigmund Freud. Freud claimed that nearly every human emotion had something to do with one's sexual drive. Therefore, H.L. understood that sometimes, when one was particularly intrigued by a subject, one's carnal nature, being the notoriously ungovernable monster it was, turned one's intrigue onto sexual channels. That's the way the human brain worked. It had nothing to do with Rose herself in relation to him, H.L. May, skeptical and jaded newspaper reporter.

H.L. smacked himself upside the head with the heel of his palm. Who was he trying to kid?

"Mr. May! Whatever is the matter?"

Damn. Rose clearly hadn't missed his self-inflicted attention-getting gesture. He grinned at her to show her that all was well in his universe. "Mosquito," he lied glibly. Hell, this whole Exposition was built on what used to be a swamp. Mosquitoes were possible. Besides, her alarm at his unexpected self-punishment had at least jolted more than one word out of her.

She gave him a small frown that made her appear like a very prudish, very delicate schoolmarm. "It looked as if you might have hurt yourself. Perhaps you ought not to be so violent with the mosquitoes."

Then she smiled puritanically, and desire swept through H.L. like a tidal wave. This was really stupid, especially when he knew she'd been trying to be sarcastic. As if she could ever out-sarcastic *him,* of all word-loving people.

He was distracted—thank God—when the wheel moved and Rose expelled a tiny squeal. Then she looked embarrassed. He wanted to hug her.

"Wheel's moving," mumbled Little Elk. His dark eyes glittered like onyx. He'd eaten three hamburgers altogether, as H.L. and Rose had sat in silence, Rose staring off into the distance and H.L. wondering what to say. Neither the Indian nor Rose seemed to be troubled by silence. H.L. was used to being in conversation when he was with people, so he didn't enjoy the lack of chatter, but he endured.

He didn't begrudge Little Elk a single one of those hamburgers. Or even the silence, if it came to that, because it was a new experience for him. It was interesting to get to know people from other walks of life and to observe both how they lived and how they tackled new experiences. H.L. loved people of all shapes, sizes, ethnicities, colors, and creeds. That's why he'd gone into the newspaper business in the first place.

On that happy understanding, he told himself *this* was why Rose excited him so much: because she was so different from the other women in his life. And the other men, too, for that matter.

Here she was, a perfectly ordinary-looking female—well, perhaps prettier than most, especially when those gigantic blue eyes of hers sparkled like gemstones as they did now— but she'd lived such an incredible life. They hadn't started the interviewing process yet, but if Cody's advertising circular was to be believed, she'd been born and grown up on the wild, western frontier near Deadwood, Kansas, one of the most notoriously dangerous towns in the United States and its territories. Hell, she'd already told him she'd been taught to ride by this Sioux Indian. A Sioux Indian, for the love of God! For all H.L. knew, Little Elk was one of the band of Sioux who'd wiped out Custer and the Seventh Cavalry at the Little Big Horn.

Squinting at Little Elk once more, H.L. decided he was allowing his romantic side to get the better of him. Little Elk would have been a small child in 1876. He most likely hadn't done any killing or butchering of soldiers—although everyone in the United States had read stories about what women and children did to the soldiers after the massacre. H.L. shuddered briefly, unable to reconcile Little Elk, who seemed like a very nice fellow, with such savagery.

"Oh, look at that!"

H.L. frowned when he saw Rose grip Little Elk's arm and point at the scenery. Why was she hanging onto Little Elk? It was H.L. who'd given her this exciting opportunity to see the world's fair from on high. If she was going to hang onto anybody, it ought to be *him,* H.L. May, damn it.

"Lights," Little Elk said, with what H.L. considered remarkable brevity under the circumstances.

In reality, the Ferris wheel had begun its ascent, and the three of them were now hanging, along with dozens of other fair-goers, in a carriage swinging from a steel frame, and observing a panoramic vista of the entire Columbian Exposition.

H.L. knew that in another couple of minutes, when their carriage rose even higher, they'd be able to see the city of Chicago spread out before them. And then they'd see Lake Michigan and all the boats floating out there, many of which were decorated for the fair.

A person got a dramatic and fascinating view of the world from up here. H.L. liked it. He wanted to put an arm around Rose's shoulder and hug her small body close to his big one and point out all the sites of interest in Chicago that he could make out from up here in the air.

Of course, you could see more of those sites in the daytime, but there was something about the night that made cuddling up with a pretty girl an alluring prospect.

And if he so much as tried to do such a thing, she'd scratch his eyes out. Probably shove him out of the gondola. H.L. entertained a mental vision of himself flying through the air to land with a *splat* on one of the concession stands below. He sighed. There was something the matter with him tonight, and he didn't know what it was.

"I should say there are lights." Rose's voice was nearly all breath, she was so excited. "Oh, my goodness, I've never seen anything like it."

"Spectacular, isn't it?" H.L. didn't mean to sound smug. Nevertheless, he was responsible for Rose's seeing these astonishing sights, and he wanted her to remove her hand from Little Elk's wrist and pay attention to him.

"Oh, my, yes! It's truly incredible, Mr. May."

She finally let go of her friend and, folding her hands in her lap, gazed out at the lights. She only glanced briefly at

H.L., and he decided something had to be done. After clearing his throat, he said, "I'll bring you here during the daylight hours one of these days, Miss Gilhooley. We can conduct an interview on the Ferris wheel as well as anywhere else, I suppose."

"It must be wonderful during the daytime, too."

"It is." He was delighted to note that she seemed to have forgotten she was angry at him. He was also pleased to note that her blue eyes were as bright as stars.

Rose insisted H.L. walk them back to the Wild West encampment after they alit from the Ferris wheel, maintaining that it was late and she and her companion needed their rest. She was polite about it, but H.L. sensed he'd better not press his luck with her tonight if he wanted to continue interviewing her for his articles. He was so exhilarated about writing those articles, he fairly tingled with it, and he hated the notion of parting with Rose so soon.

He had his hands stuffed into the pockets of his seersucker suit when he delivered Little Elk to the Indian compound.

"Good night," Little Elk said in a way that conveyed to H.L. that he was expressing gratitude for the evening's entertainment.

"Thanks for coming," H.L. said back, and the two men parted company. H.L. got the feeling he'd passed whatever test Little Elk required of a white man before he deigned to approve of him. "See you later," he added to the Indian's back as Little Elk strolled off.

Little Elk didn't turn around, but only lifted a hand in a gesture of dismissal. H.L. would have liked to interview him, too, but decided he'd best not press his luck right now. If all went well, he could conduct interviews later with Little Elk and perhaps some of the other Sioux traveling with the Wild West. He and Rose walked on to the tent village occupied by the white members of the Wild West's cast and crew.

Rose led the way to her tent, where she turned and stuck out her hand.

"Thank you very much, Mr. May. The fair is a wondrous place, and I loved riding on the Ferris wheel."

H.L. looked for a couple of seconds at her hand before he sighed and took it in his much larger one. It had, of course, not escaped his attention that Rose had donned a little hat and prim gloves before she'd set out with him to see the fair. From this he deduced that, while she might earn a living as an entertainer, at heart she was pure middle-class American morality. He guessed that was interesting, although it pretty much put the kibosh on any sexual fantasies he might think about harboring in her direction.

As if thought had anything to do with it. He sighed again.

"Say, Miss Gilhooley, I know you have to practice a lot and need to get plenty of rest and all that, but I'd really love to show you Chicago from the Ferris wheel in the daylight. It will be a good use of time, too, because, as I already said, I'll be able to interview you as you see the city." He gave her one of his most winning smiles, the smile he most often reserved for ministers and politicians from whom he was trying to pry information without their awareness.

Rose gave him an uncertain look. "Yes, you said that before, Mr. May. And I have already agreed to be interviewed. Did you forget?"

She was so damned cute, H.L. couldn't contain his grin. "Nope." He tapped his forehead. "I've got a great memory. Just wanted to make sure you did, too."

"I see," Rose said repressively.

Undaunted, H.L. only grinned more widely and said, "So, how about tomorrow?"

Her mouth pursed into a moue of uncertainty that made H.L. want to kiss it soft again. Good God.

"Well . . ."

"It's publicity, Miss Gilhooley. *Free* publicity," he reminded her, aiming for a funning, friendly tone of voice.

Deciding it wouldn't hurt to drag Buffalo Bill into the conversation, he added, "Colonel Cody will be pleased."

This time it was she who sighed. "I suppose you're right." She hesitated another moment, fiddling with those prim white gloves of hers. Then, as if she didn't want to say it but couldn't help herself, she added, "And I really would like to go up on the Ferris wheel again."

"You bet!" H.L. never let an interesting opportunity pass by without leaping at it. "And then we can visit some of the other exhibits. I want to get your impressions of all the modern inventions being shown here at the fair. In the Machinery Hall, there's a printing press that's a hundred and fifty years old, and there are all sorts of brand-new inventions being shown here, too. You can see everything from moving pictures to horseless carriages to new foods—well, you had some of the new food tonight. It's great stuff, all of it."

"I did enjoy the hamburger," she admitted.

She gave him a shy smile, and he had to fight the urge to pounce on her like a wolf on its prey. Hell's bells, he wasn't normally a predatory sort of fellow; he guessed her innocence brought out the worst in him or something. To guard against further sudden impulses, he jammed his hands into his pockets once more. "So, what time would you like to do these things tomorrow, Miss Gilhooley?"

"Tomorrow?"

She sounded doubtful, which irked H.L. a bit. "Sure. Tomorrow. Newspapers in Chicago are printed every day, Miss Gilhooley. I've got to write a whole series of articles, don't forget."

"Oh." She appeared slightly perplexed. "I guess I didn't think about that part."

H.L. didn't roll his eyes, because he was certain she'd not appreciate it. "Yes, well, that's the way newspapers around here work. Now, for example, while you get your rest, I've got to go back to the office and write up my first impressions of the Exposition. I'd like to get started on the articles about you and the Wild West tomorrow."

"I see." She licked her lips. It was a simple gesture, borne most likely from rattled nerves, but it made H.L.'s insides clench and a wave of lust spike through him. "All right, then. I have to take care of my horses in the morning. I'm usually finished by noon or one o'clock. Will that be all right?"

He smiled at her, having managed to subdue all improper impulses, although he had a feeling they might pop up again later. "That would be super. I'll come by here at noon and take you to lunch. Say, I'll bet you haven't sampled half the food they're selling here. You've got to try a baklava at the Middle Eastern place. It's great stuff."

"A what?"

He gently flicked a finger against her cheek. "I'll teach you the word tomorrow, sweetie." He knew instantly that he'd made a grave mistake and hurried to correct it. "I mean, Miss Gilhooley. Sorry. Didn't mean to take liberties."

She'd stiffened up like a frozen fish, lifted her chin, and glared at him with eyes as icy as Lake Michigan in January. "I should say not!"

"Right." H.L. removed his hat, thinking a bit of formal politeness would be in order at the moment. "See you at noon tomorrow, then, Miss Gilhooley."

She remained mute for a couple of moments, then said frostily, "Good night, Mr. May."

H.L. strolled away thinking, *Miss Gilhooley. Mr. May. I haven't been this formal since I took first communion.*

That was all right, though. He'd break down her defenses one of these days. And then it would be every man for himself. Or, in this case, woman.

H.L. took a street car back to the *Globe*'s office and wrote his first article about the Columbian Exposition, feeling better about things in general than he had for months.

* * *

The next day dawned clear as a bell, warm as toast, and only slightly breezy, and Rose got up feeling fine, which surprised her a bit. When she'd turned in the night before, she sort of expected she'd arise feeling as if she'd made a fool of herself. Evidently, either the gods were smiling down on her, or she hadn't come across as stupid as she felt while enjoying the evening with Little Elk and H.L. May.

H.L. May. Fiddlesticks. Rose wished she could stop thinking about him. She knew he was exactly the wrong sort of fellow to take up with, even if he'd ever want to take up with *her,* which was so unlikely as to be off the scale of improbabilities.

Nevertheless, she felt good as she ate her breakfast with Annie and Frank, greeted those of her fellow Wild West companions who were up and about before noon, and walked to the stables. She liked the smell of the fair; it was dusty and rather windy, and a slight taint of swamp and stockyard lingered in the air, but the overall aroma of the Wild West was one Rose imagined she'd remember until the day she died. Horses, buffalo, leather, dust, the unique smell of the food cooked by the Sioux in the neighboring tent city; it was meat and drink to her, and she loved it.

She didn't expect H.L. May to arrive at her tent at twelve noon. She expected him to keep her waiting. After all, he was a sophisticated big-city newspaper reporter, and she was a hick.

Instantly, Annie rose up in her mind and started to chide her.

Exactly what do you mean by that, Rose Gilhooley? You're no hick! You're a star with Buffalo Bill's Wild West.

Rose decided that, although Annie might be right about her technically, she didn't feel like a star. She felt like a hick.

H.L. May doesn't have to know what you think of yourself, for heaven's sake!

Rose, who had been practicing bows with Fairy's stable-mate, Betsy, another small white mare, gasped when understanding smote her, hard, in the brain. By heavens, Annie was right! Rather, Rose's mental image of Annie was right, which amounted to the same thing.

H.L. May *didn't* have to know that Rose considered herself a hick if Rose didn't choose to let him in on her inner insecurities. Even though she didn't feel confident and secure on the inside, she could act as if she did outwardly while in his company, and he wouldn't ever know the difference. Why would he?

She felt pretty good after she'd come to this conclusion. The prospect of seeing H.L. again dimmed her pleasure slightly, but not enough to interfere with her lesson. Anyhow, another part of her could hardly wait to be in his company today. Rose considered that part of her slightly traitorous.

"You look beautiful, Miss Gilhooley!" a cheery voice called from the grandstand.

Surprised, Rose glanced up from the bare back of the horse she was training, and saw none other than H.L. May. Jehosephat! She'd been correct about him, all right: he wasn't on time. Only instead of being late as she'd expected him to be, he was early.

Totally discomposed at this further illustration of the many ways in which H.L. May was not what she needed in her life, Rose glowered at him. "I thought you were coming at noon!" She didn't dare speak loudly or unpleasantly, because that would have upset Betsy. Rose knew horses. She knew horses a whole lot better than she knew men, for sure.

H.L. hauled his watch out of the pocket in his vest and held it up so that its gold chain glinted in the sunlight. "It's almost noon. I'm glad I came early so I can watch you work!"

Rose wasn't glad about it. She'd like to conk him on the head, actually. And now that she knew he was watching her, she was too flustered to work because she'd transmit her anxiety to Betsy, sure as anything. Upsetting a horse was a certain way to undo any bowing lessons she'd been able to impart. She called out in a sweet voice, "Wait there for a minute. I'll just stable Betsy and tidy up."

"Sure thing!"

If it was such a sure thing, why didn't he sit down again, blast him? Rose watched in mounting trepidation as H.L. bounded down from his seat in the grandstand and came to tarry in the ring, waiting, she was sure, to see which way she went so he could tag along.

Piffle. Rose was beginning to feel haunted, harassed, and beleaguered by this nosy parker of a reporter. If she didn't find him so impossibly attractive, she might just up and tell him to take a hike.

Good Lord! She hadn't meant that—the attractive part, not the taking-a-hike part. Surely she hadn't.

She feared she had. Bother.

Fortunately for her, she saw Little Elk walking around the perimeter of the arena, scanning the ground. He sometimes went hunting for coins lost by careless audience members. Rose thought that seizing such an unusual business opportunity was quite enterprising of him. She called out, "Little Elk."

He glanced up and raised his hand in greeting. Rose squinted at him hard. What was he holding? It was small. It was wrapped in what looked like brown butcher paper. As he began to walk in Rose's direction, he lifted it to his mouth and took a bite, and Rose understood. He'd gone out and bought himself a hamburger.

With a deep sigh, wishing her good friend hadn't demonstrated quite so palpably in front of H.L. May his approval of something Mr. May himself had done, Rose asked, "Can you please take care of Betsy for me? I have an appointment with Mr. May."

Little Elk nodded, glanced at H.L., and grinned. He held up his hamburger for H.L. to see. The reporter waved and grinned back. Now Rose wished she could conk both of them.

Nevertheless, recalling her new-found realization regarding her feelings of inferiority and hick-hood, she opted not to throw a tantrum. It was just as well, since she didn't think she could throw one if she tried, having had no practice. In an effort to appear unperturbed by H.L. May's early arrival, she smiled at him with what she hoped looked like serenity when he walked up to her as she was handing Betsy over to Little Elk.

"How do you do, Mr. May?"

He looked slightly taken aback by her formal manner. "I'm all right, thanks, Miss Gilhooley. You?"

She fought a grimace. How could she appear prim and proper if he wasn't going to help her out? This wasn't fair. With a sigh, she said, "That's nice. I'm fine, too, thank you. Um, will you excuse me for a moment? I didn't expect you quite so early, and I still have to tidy up."

"You already look mighty tidy to me," he told her with a wider grin, and he winked at her.

She couldn't help herself; she frowned. Was he trying to flirt with her again? Did he think she was *that* sort of woman merely because she worked as an entertainer? If he did, he had another think coming.

"Thank you." She spoke in freezing, measured accents. "However, I prefer that you either go with Little Elk or remain here while I prepare for our scheduled appointment."

"Yes, *ma'am*," H.L. barked.

And then—Rose could hardly believe her eyes—he had the effrontery to salute her! Rose gaped for a second before she caught herself and stopped. She snapped, "Fine," turned on her bare heel—she was at *such* a disadvantage here—and stamped off to her tent, forgetting to put on her moccasins.

Once in her tent, she fairly ripped the clothes from her body. She always dressed in an old, worn-out costume when she was working with her horses, which made her recent encounter with H.L. May that much worse. More than anyone else in the world, she didn't want him to see her looking dowdy, or think she was too poor to buy nice clothes. Or worse, think she had no taste and dressed like that all the time because she was too stupid or too rustic to know how to dress herself in a big city. Granted, she didn't keep much of her sizable salary for herself, but she could still afford decent clothes.

No matter what she did, he undermined her—and she'd only met him yesterday! Grumbling to herself, she plowed through her traveling trunk to find the nicest, prettiest, newest, and most comfortable outfit she owned. Even to teach H.L. May a lesson, Rose didn't fancy strolling for miles at the Columbian Exposition in uncomfortable clothes.

Because the late spring day was warm, Rose selected a pretty walking skirt in lightweight yellow-checked gingham. The skirt looked lovely on her, especially when she wore it with a pretty lawn shirtwaist and the yellow jacket she'd bought especially to go with the skirt. She topped everything off with a charming confection of a tiny straw hat with a yellow satin ribbon circling its crown. One yellow rose attached to the ribbon brought everything together.

This was the prettiest outfit she'd ever owned, and she'd felt wonderful when she'd worn it for the first time. She and Annie had bought it their first week in Chicago when they'd gone shopping expressly for summer clothing. They'd both heard how hot and humid Chicago could be during the summer months, and the Exposition was scheduled to run through the summer months until some time in October.

In spite of how good she knew she looked, Rose was in a foul mood when she left her tent to meet H.L. May. Then she realized she didn't know where he was. She'd been so miffed by his comment and wink, she hadn't stuck around long enough for him to tell her where she could find him.

Bother. On the off chance that he'd done something cooperative for once and gone with Little Elk to the stables, Rose headed there first. Wonder of wonders, there he was! She was surprised, as she'd been certain he'd lead her on some kind of chase.

On the other hand, if he'd tried to do that, Rose wouldn't have played his game. She'd have just gone back to her tent and . . . and what? Eaten lunch alone, she guessed. Aw, mud puddles. She might as well give it up and admit she couldn't win with H.L. May.

On that depressing thought, she took a deep breath, steeled her nerves, and was about to enter the stable when a commotion behind her stopped her in her tracks.

"It's her!" came a child's shrill, excited voice.

Thinking something unusual had happened, Rose turned to see what it was. All she saw was a man standing about fifteen feet away, peering her way. He had two little boys in tow, both clad in darling sailor suits. One of the boys was pointing at the stable. When Rose turned to determine what could be the matter with the stable, she saw nothing amiss.

"It *is* her," the other little boy exclaimed. He was every bit as excited as the first one.

"Now, boys," said the man—Rose presumed he was their father. "Let's calm down."

"But it's *her!*" the first little boy shouted joyfully, and he broke away from the man and charged straight at Rose.

Merciful heavens! These little children must be fans! Rose had never been attacked by fans before, although she'd seen them swarm all over Annie more than once. She guessed it was a good thing these were relatively small representatives of the species.

Before she'd had time to brace herself, a large figure loomed at her side, stooped, and scooped the little boy up in his strong arms. "Whoa, there, Buster. Watch it. This is a lady, not a circus clown."

"Mr. May!" Rose, whose first reaction to rescue had been relief, became angry when she realized who her rescuer was.

"Say, mister, put down my boy!" the child's father hollered. He hurried toward Rose and H.L., his other son running to keep up with him.

Rose didn't like *that* much, either.

"Does this little hooligan belong to you?" H.L. sounded as if he aimed to pitch the child over his father's head, the way he might throw a baseball or heave a lance.

"Don't you call my boy a hooligan!"

Bother. Why couldn't her association with H.L. May be normal? Whatever *normal* was.

SIX

H.L. was flabbergasted. How dare this man yell at him for protecting Rose from his marauding monster of a child? Thrusting the wriggling boy at his father, who caught him even though the gesture surprised him, H.L. barked, "Take your kid, then, and teach him some manners. Miss Gilhooley isn't accustomed to being mauled by uncouth brats."

"Oh, now, Mr. May, please . . ."

Disregarding Rose's protest, H.L. scowled at the now furious father.

"What do you mean, manhandling my boy like that?"

H.L. leaned toward the man. "What do *you* mean, allowing the kid to attack Miss Gilhooley?"

Rose tried again. "But . . ."

Disregarding Rose in his turn, the father hollered, "He didn't attack her!"

The two boys drew back. The one who'd made the dash for Rose looked as if he was feeling guilty about his misdeed and ashamed he'd made his father angry. Rose judged him to be around seven years old, but he was upset enough that he stuck a thumb in his mouth. From the expression in his big, scared eyes, Rose guessed this was a behavior he only resorted to when he was under extreme duress. Her heart softened. Poor little tyke.

Since the idiotic men were busy shouting insults at each other, Rose decided to deal with the children herself. Stepping away from the combatants, she smiled sweetly at the boys and knelt, giving scant thought to her new yellow-checked gingham skirt. Holding out a hand, she said, "Hello, there. My name is Miss Gilhooley. I think you might have seen me ride in the Wild West. Is that so?"

The dasher, his brown eyes huge, nodded. The other boy, younger by perhaps a year, whispered, "Yes'm."

"Would you like to have a souvenir of the Wild West?"

Both children nodded.

"You interfering scoundrel, you had no right to touch my child!"

"Your child had no right to attack a woman on the street!"

"He didn't attack her, and this isn't a street!"

Rose shook her head, marveling at the relative insanity of adult human males, and dipped into the small handbag she had decided to carry with her on her outing with H.L. She withdrew two small rosettes with blue ribbons dangling from them. They were advertising pieces with her Wild West name, *Wind Dancer,* printed in gold lettering on the ribbons. Buffalo Bill had created them for this exact purpose. He claimed that you never could predict when you'd have an opportunity to advertise the Wild West, and children loved to wear blue ribbons. He maintained they made them feel important, and Rose had never found a reason to disbelieve him. She supposed the idea had originated with Annie Oakley and the championship shooting medals she always wore during her performances.

Although Rose normally handed out the ribbons after a show, she always carried some with her, just in case. She was glad for her decision to do so as she held two of them out to these children now. She'd never used them to calm little boys whose fathers had become embroiled in shouting matches with newspaper reporters before. Rather sourly she told herself she might have expected H.L. May to get her involved in a dispute. It was just like him.

The ribbons worked wonders on the boys, however. The

colonel would have been proud. The children, their eyes growing bright and losing their fearful cast, walked up to Rose. The dasher's thumb popped out of his mouth, and he reached for a ribbon with a damp hand. The other boy grinned broadly as he took his.

"Let me help you pin them on," she offered.

When the larger of the boys moved up a step, she asked, "What's your name?"

"Jesse Lee Wojinski, ma'am." He fairly glowed as Rose pinned the rosette on the lapel of his sailor suit.

"There you go, Jesse Lee." Rose turned to the smaller boy. "And what's your name, sweetheart?"

The little boy blushed scarlet. "Ernie James Wojinski."

She thought they were both adorable. "Here's your blue ribbon, Ernie James." Rose pinned a rosette on his lapel, too.

The two children had stood to attention as Rose attached their ribbons. When she was finished, she stood back and beamed down at them. "There, now. You look just like—like Colonel Cody himself!" She'd been going to say they looked like Annie Oakley, but decided it would be more diplomatic to use the colonel's name with boys.

The children were ecstatic.

"Thank you, Miss Gilhooley," said the dasher.

"Thanks, Miss 'Hooley," said his brother.

"I don't care what you say, you blasted interloper! Don't you dare call my children brats! It's not their fault they loved watching Wind Dancer ride!"

"It's not their fault they didn't knock her over backwards, you mean!"

Rose cleared her throat, hoping either the boys' father or H.L. May would hear her and cease his yelling. She should have known better. Neither man paid her the least heed. In fact, the fight seemed to be heading perilously close to becoming a physical confrontation.

Not wanting to be associated with an embarrassing brawl, Rose came to the conclusion that, whereas being ladylike and polite was a good way to behave most of the time, at other times, harsher measures were required. Therefore, although she'd never have done this under normal circumstances, she put two fingers in her mouth as her brother Freddie had taught her to do in Deadwood many years before, and whistled.

The sound pierced the air like a volley of Sioux arrows. H.L. May and his adversary both clapped hands over their ears and spun around. They looked to Rose as if they were trying to determine from whence the attack was being launched.

The two little boys laughed and clapped as if Rose had done something marvelous.

Rose said, "Thank you." She glared at H.L. "Are you quite ready to resume our interview, Mr. May?"

H.L.'s mouth had opened in what looked like fury before he caught sight of Rose. Then his eyes widened, his rage seemed to evaporate, and he stared at her. Rose had no idea what his problem was now, but she appreciated his silence.

Turning to Jesse Lee and Ernie James's father, Rose said sweetly, "Your sons are delightful, Mr. Wojinski. I'm glad they enjoyed the Wild West. Now, if you'll excuse us, we need to be going."

Mr. Wojinski, too, seemed stunned. Deciding to take advantage of the two men's silence, Rose grabbed H.L.'s arm and yanked. Hard. He stumbled forward before he caught himself and straightened. Then he cast one last glare at Mr. Wojinski before he took in the sight of the two little boys, who stared at Rose as if she were a goddess and they were worshiping her.

The boys' father gave H.L. a final vicious scowl and took his sons by the hand. "Let's go, boys. I'm glad to see Wind Dancer is nice, even if she runs with some rough company." He turned them around and stamped away.

The two small voices rose in a duet. "Oh, she's *real* nice, Pa!"

After a few more tense moments, H.L. said, "Hunh."
With a curt nod, he turned away from the Wojinskis and went
with Rose.

She waved daintily at the little boys, who were staring at
her from over their shoulders, and minced off. H.L. wondered if her feet hurt, confined in shoes as they were now.
Did she wear shoes all the time except when she was performing? He was about to ask, when she spoke first.

"What do you mean, getting into a fight with that nice
man?"

Astonished, H.L. blinked as he peered down at her.

She looked absolutely gorgeous in that yellow thing. Yellow did wonders for her dark chestnut hair and blue eyes,
especially when they were glinting as they were now. And
her cheeks were rosy. With anger. Good God, she was furious.

"I can't take a step in your company without you doing
something outrageous or saying something horrid. I don't
know why I consented to this interview with you, anyway!"

H.L. gulped twice before he could speak. Two things interfered with his thought processes, which were normally
quicker than lightning. The first thing was how good she
looked. The second was anger. She was mad at him! *She* was
mad at *him,* the man who'd just saved her from being mauled
by a couple of dirty little brats!

"What do you mean, saying something horrid?" His
voice was very loud. He gentled it with difficulty. "Damn it,
Miss Gilhooley, that monster was going to get his sticky
fingers all over you!"

"Pooh. He's a charming little boy. And sticky fingers
can't do permanent damage."

"Charming! No permanent damage? Why . . . why . . ."
But H.L. didn't know what to say. He gazed at Rose and
realized his very essence would have been wounded if she'd
been damaged in any way whatsoever, even with imperma-
nent sticky fingerprints, by that child's attack. Or so it would

have been if he'd had any sensibilities to crush, which, of course, he hadn't.

It couldn't be denied, however, that at the moment she was a vision. She was a perfect, tiny, tidy wonder of a woman. Since he couldn't say those things or he'd ruin his image, not to mention his sense of personal dignity, he summed up his tumultuous feelings with a savage, "Nuts!" He yanked his straw hat down low on his forehead, stuffed his hands into his pockets, glowered, and kicked at impediments in his way.

Rose lifted her chin. "There's no need to pout, Mr. May. I shan't break our agreement."

"I'm not pouting. Anyhow, what agreement?" he muttered gruffly. "We didn't have an agreement."

Damn it, why'd she quit walking? He stopped, too, and wheeled around to glare at her. "Well? We didn't have an agreement. Exactly. I mean, we didn't sign a contract or anything."

She stared up at him for one full, fulminating moment before she spat out, "Fine." She turned and started to walk away from him.

H.L.'s heart did something it had never done before in its life: It screamed in anguish. Clutching a hand to his chest in reaction, H.L. wondered what the hell was going on.

He hadn't reached a conclusion before he'd begun running after Rose. He guessed he'd have to figure out this inexplicable chest pain later, although he knew it had something to do with Rose Gilhooley and the fact that she was leaving him. He couldn't let her do it. That was the only thing he knew for a rock-solid certainty.

"Hey!" he hollered. "Wait up, there! You can't walk away from me like that!"

She turned abruptly. The color in her cheeks had deepened. She looked every bit as furious as Mr. Wojinski had when H.L. had called his son a brat.

"Oh?" She looked as if she were boiling on the inside,

but her voice was as cold and sharp as icicles. "You just said we have no agreement, Mr. May."

"Damn it, you know I was lying!"

"Ohhh," she voiced, sarcastic as all hell. "So you admit it, do you?"

"I didn't mean it like that!" He stomped up to her. He was surprised when she held her ground. He'd sort of expected her to be intimidated, although why he'd expected that, he had no idea. Anybody who could face a horse that weighed a hundred times what she weighed and could squash her without half trying, and then ride that same horse in a death-defying manner that shocked and astounded the masses on a daily basis, couldn't very well be a shrinking violet, could she?

"No?"

The word hit him like a hailstone rapping on glass. "No." He sucked in several pecks of air sweetened by the scent of May flowers and buttered popcorn.

He knew what he had to do, but he didn't want to do it. He did it anyway. "I beg your pardon, Miss Gilhooley. I was wrong. You were right. We did have an agreement." The next part was the hardest, but he pushed the words past his reluctance. They fell into the atmosphere like small, dried-up pellets of cheese. "I'm sorry I got mad at that guy. I guess I was afraid for you when I saw that lousy kid shooting at you like a bullet."

"Lousy kid?" If she wasn't incredulous, she was doing a good imitation. "He's a little *boy,* Mr. May! He's too young to have become lousy yet. He was excited. What's more, he was a fan of mine! He's not yet had enough time in this life to turn rotten—not like *some* people."

That meant him, of course. H.L. gritted his teeth and didn't mount a defense. Obviously, Miss Rose Gilhooley hadn't run up against some of the juvenile delinquents H.L. had encountered during his newspaper career. Now *they* were rotten, no matter how young they were. "Right." He really hated apologizing for hollering at that brat's father. "I beg your pardon."

She sniffed. "It's not my pardon you should be begging. It's that poor man's. Mr. Wojinski."

"Wojinski. Figures."

She rounded on him again. "And exactly what is *that* supposed to mean?"

"Nothing, nothing." He wasn't about to go into the cultural divisions abounding in the city of Chicago. It did occur to him, though, that it might be fun to take Rose to the different neighborhoods and gauge her reactions to them. Not that H.L. had anything against Poles. Even though many of them leaned toward political anarchy and were inclined to be socialists and live in tenements that smelled like boiled cabbage, they were easier to tolerate than, say, the Irish, who tended to drink a lot, become belligerent and very loud, and get into scraps. Or the Italians, who formed tight brotherhoods, extorted protection money from shopkeepers, and stabbed each other all the time. "I'm sorry, Miss Gilhooley." Sucking in another deep breath, H.L. then said something that nearly choked him. "Please forgive me."

She squinted at him for a good thirty seconds. H.L. wanted to grind his toe in the dirt, as he used to do when being given a dressing-down by various teachers following his many altercations over his name. He'd nearly started squirming before she finally let up on him.

"Very well. But I trust you won't create another disturbance of a like nature."

H.L. bellowed, "You trust I won't—" He broke off abruptly. If he yelled at her, she'd go away, and he'd die. Perhaps not die. But he knew he'd best keep quiet for a while. Therefore, he produced a small, tight smile and said, "Fine, then, shall we be off?"

She nodded imperiously. He wondered if she'd learned that from the queen. The notion tickled him, and his mood climbed uphill as they took off.

It was Rose who broke the silence that had fallen between them. "Where are we going first?"

"I'm going to feed you first off," he said, feeling almost chipper again. "We're going to have our lunch at the Street in Cairo."

"Oh, I've heard about the Street in Cairo."

H.L. smirked inside. Everyone had heard about the Street in Cairo. Before the fair was a week old, the Street in Cairo had become famous throughout the land, probably because it was more exotic than anyone in the United States had conceived of before viewing it. A reproduction of a seventeenth-century Cairo street, it gave visitors an intriguing view of what life in Egypt might have been like—and perhaps still was. "Good. I'm sure you'll find it fascinating, and I think the food's quite tasty there. Hope you'll like it."

"Um, I'm sure I shall."

When he glanced down at her, he was disturbed to see the expression of bemusement on her face. Shoot, maybe she didn't like Middle Eastern stuff. She'd probably never tasted any of those spiced and roasted meats that H.L. loved that they served up with some kind of grain they called couscous, or anything even remotely resembling them. Hell, hardly anybody had, until this fair.

Because he didn't want to irk her again, and even though he wanted to take her to the Egyptian place, he decided it would behoove him to do some prior probing. Better that than earn more of her enmity. "Er, do you have any digestive difficulties, Miss Gilhooley?"

The glance of shock she shot him couldn't possibly be feigned. "Digestive difficulties? What do you mean? What do they serve you there?" She sounded almost frightened.

"Calm down," he said soothingly. "The food's good. It's only that they use spices most Americans aren't used to."

"Oh."

"Is there any particular food you don't like?"

"Um, no."

Her gaze held abundant suspicion. H.L. didn't appreciate it, since he'd never done anything to deserve it. That is to say, he hadn't done *much* to deserve it. How was he supposed to know she enjoyed being attacked by miniature monsters? He'd been trying to protect her person. At the moment, he was only attempting to protect her digestive system.

"Trust me," he pleaded. "If you don't like it, we can eat something else. You only have to taste it. I promise."

"But I don't want to waste money, either."

"It's not going to be your money," H.L. exclaimed, miffed that she'd even think such a thing. "I'm paying. Or the *Globe* is. This is a business expense, for crying out loud!"

"That's not the point. I don't want to waste the *Globe*'s money, either." She shot him a baleful glance. "I'm not accustomed to flinging money around indiscriminately, Mr. May."

Damn, she was a pain in the neck sometimes. H.L. discovered in that moment that, when he wasn't wanting to kiss her silly, he was wanting to turn her over his knee and spank her. "Let me worry about the *Globe*'s money, please. The *Globe* is accustomed to paying for what it gets in news. Your mission today is to grant me an interview and enjoy yourself. That's going to be part of the article; don't you understand yet?"

She lifted her chin some more. "You needn't speak to me as if I were a nitwit, Mr. May. Merely because I don't like to waste money doesn't mean I'm stupid."

He was honestly surprised. "Of course not! I don't think you're stupid. Why'd you say that?"

The glance she cast him held at least a ton of doubt. H.L. narrowed his gaze and wondered why. He'd not said anything that might make her think he thought she was stupid, had he? Granted, they'd disagreed a few times—all right, they'd disagreed a lot of times. Most of the time, in actual fact. But disagreements didn't equate to stupidity. On the contrary, H.L. loved to discuss things with people who dis-

agreed with him. Such conversations whetted his appetite
and sharpened his wits.

"It doesn't matter," she said at last.

The Street in Cairo was on the Midway Plaisance, where
the Ferris wheel was also located. The Fair directors had
envisioned their enterprise as a complete educational experience. Although they'd relegated amusements to the Midway, they'd also had many foreign nations set up their
exhibitions there. Since the Midway was close to where the
Wild West had set up shop, that was ginger-peachy with
H.L., who was hungry.

He watched Rose as her eager gaze took in all the sights
and sounds of the Midway, and words swirled in his brain,
occasionally plopping into place in perfect, brilliantly constructed sentences. He could hardly wait to write about
Rose's discovery of the fair and all the new and exciting
things it held. "After we eat," he told her, "let's see some of
the other foreign exhibits. Have you seen Little Egypt
dance?"

After shooting him a startled glance, she blushed. "Yes, I
have. Annie and I saw her dance when Colonel Cody took
us there. We didn't get to see any of the other exhibits." Her
brow furrowed into a tiny frown, as if she weren't sure the
colonel should have done that.

She was about the most charming young woman he'd ever
encountered, even if she was stubborn as a mule and argued
with him about everything. "Interesting, huh?"

"Very."

H.L. would have laughed at her repressed tone if he could
have trusted her not to run away if he did. "There are lots
of other things to see here on the Midway besides Little
Egypt and the Ferris wheel. There's an entire African tribe,
a Moorish palace, a German village, and a whole hall de-
voted to beauties of the world. They've got a snake charmer
and fortune tellers, and just about everything anybody could
ever have an itch to see."

Her eyes were so big, H.L. wished he could remember more of the delights to be experienced on the Midway. It would be interesting to see how much larger those beautiful blues of hers could get. Alas, he ran out of inspiration and had to settle for Rose's breathy, "My goodness!" It would suffice.

There were so many sights and scenes to be gawked at and exclaimed over, from bejeweled daggers, silks, and wood carvings to donkey boys, a mosque, and camels, that it was almost two o'clock by the time they finally made their ways to the Egyptian restaurant. H.L. ordered a dish made of chunks of skewered meat, spiced and roasted over an open fire, for both of them. To accompany the meat dish, he ordered a kind of sweet tea that he liked a lot and that he assumed was some kind of Egyptian delicacy. Or Moorish. Or Moroccan. Hell, all he knew was that it tasted good. Some sort of stuff that wasn't rice but looked vaguely like it, called couscous, and a dark-green salad composed of wheat kernels, parsley, onions, and chopped-up tomatoes accompanied the skewered meat. It was all nectar to H.L.

He watched Rose as she surveyed her plate. "So, what do you think?" He was anxious that she like her meal. She must be hungry. The sides of his own stomach were rubbing against each other, he was so empty.

She didn't lift her gaze from the foreign concoction residing before her. Looking vaguely dubious, she leaned forward and sniffed delicately. "It smells good." She seemed more cheerful after this pronouncement.

"Sam and I ate this same thing yesterday. It's delicious." H.L. spoke with decision as he slid a piece of meat off its skewer and speared it.

"Who's Sam?"

"Another reporter with the *Globe*."

"Ah." Rose continued to gaze at her food for another moment. Then she pulled off her gloves, picked up the end of a skewer, maneuvered a piece of meat from it, and stabbed it with her fork. She cut it in half before she popped one of the halves into her mouth.

It pleased H.L. more than he could express when her eyes opened wide again. He recognized the delight dawning in them, and felt as if he'd done something wonderful. That was probably ridiculous, but he couldn't help himself.

After she swallowed, Rose said, "Oh, my, this is delicious!"

"Told you so." H.L. couldn't recall when he'd felt so self-satisfied.

She then forked up a small bite of the parsley salad, chewed it, and swallowed. "Oh, I *really* like this! Do you know what it's called?"

"Uh-uh, but we can find out." H.L. hadn't thought much about the oddly concocted salad, not being the vegetable-loving sort, but he waved at a handsome, dark-visaged, white-clad, turbaned waiter, who came over to stand before them. He looked more dignified than any other waiter H.L. had ever seen, but he still asked, "Does this salad have a name?"

"Taboule, sir," the waiter replied.

"Taboule?" Rose blinked up at the man, whose mien softened slightly as he gazed at her.

Well, and why wouldn't it? H.L. thought smugly. Rose Gilhooley would be an ornament to any setting.

The waiter bowed at her. "Yes, ma'am."

"It's delicious," Rose said, her cheeks pinkening slightly. She looked as if she wasn't sure it was permissible to compliment waiters on meals.

H.L. was proud of her. He knew he hadn't any right to be; after all, she was nothing to him but a news story. But she was so precious. So polite and charming. So . . . He'd have to think about it. He seldom had trouble coming up with the best words to use in describing anything, but Rose had him buffaloed. Every time he contemplated her, he fell short of achieving the perfect word to assign to her.

The waiter said, "Thank you, madam." He even smiled. Rose's blush deepened.

Yanking his brain away from words, H.L. decided this encounter had lasted long enough. He didn't want any Middle Eastern swami—whatever a swami was—to get any ideas about ravishing the delectable Rose. If there was any ravishing to be done in that quarter, H.L. May would be the ravisher.

He didn't mean that.

Or did he?

Damn. As he wondered if he were losing his mind entirely, H.L. spoke rather sharply to the waiter. "Thanks a lot. That answers our question. We'll call if we need anything else."

The waiter's expression turned blank once more, and he bowed formally and moved away from their table. H.L. felt a little silly.

"There was no need to be rude to the poor man, Mr. May."

Damn it all, there she went again. H.L. glanced from the waiter's back to Rose's face, ready to do battle, when her expression stopped him. She was clearly embarrassed about something. What the hell was going on?

Rose went on, "If it was improper of me to speak to the waiter, I'm sorry, but it's certainly not his fault."

Since H.L. didn't understand her point here, he didn't have a clue what to say.

She took a deep breath and blurted out, "If you *must* know, I'm not used to dining in restaurants." She bowed her head and frowned at her plate. "I grew up on the frontier, for heaven's sake. It may seem countrified to you, but in Kansas we're generally polite to people, whatever their station in life—even those who serve us meals."

Still confused, H.L. said, "I beg your pardon? I'm not sure what you're talking about, Miss Gilhooley."

She lifted her head and glared at him, unquestionably

exasperated, and H.L.'s confusion grew. He began to feel as though he and Rose were performing parts in two different plays that had somehow ended up on the same stage at the same time by accident. The sensation was uncomfortable.

Rose snapped, "Fiddlesticks! Just answer me this, please: Was it wrong of me to have told the waiter I found my meal tasty?"

"Good God, no!" H.L. couldn't account for the expression of relief on her face.

"Good. I'm glad of that, anyhow." She seemed to relax as she speared the other half of the meat cube she'd cut up earlier. "That settles that, then."

"I guess so." Befuddled and without the least understanding of what mental machinations had just occurred in his lovely dining companion's head, H.L. decided to solve that riddle later, along with all the other Rose riddles he was storing up. The food was too good and he was too hungry to worry about it now.

He was stuffed to the gills by the time they'd polished off their lunch and crowned it with one of the melt-in-your mouth baklavas he loved so well for dessert. Rose had told him she was too full for dessert, but he'd insisted. When, with her first bite, she looked as if she were experiencing heavenly ecstasy, he was satisfied.

Patting his stomach as they left the restaurant, he said, "I feel better now. I seem to have lost my appetite, in fact."

Rose smiled up at him. H.L. nearly fell over backward. He couldn't recall her smiling at him in unalloyed pleasure before. A mad urge to keep the expression on her face assailed him.

"That was one of the very best meals I've ever eaten, Mr. May. Thank you for giving me the experience."

"You're welcome." His tongue felt bulky and didn't seem to want to work with its normal glib suavity. Rose Gilhooley did something to him; he wasn't sure what it was, but it had never happened before. He didn't altogether trust it.

After he cleared his throat in a vain attempt to get his tongue and brain coordinated, he gave it up and decided he might as well start with the basics. "Say, Miss Gilhooley, I don't know about you, but I need to visit the comfort station. I expect you might need to powder your nose, too."

"Powder my nose?" She gazed up at him blankly.

He grinned down at her. "Yeah. Euphemisms. You know. Powder your nose?"

Her blank look remained as she answered him. "Er, yes. Yes, of course."

So H.L. led them to the end of the Midway, where the comfort stations, fabulous in their own right, had been built. "I'll meet you here in a few minutes," he said as he sauntered off to the men's side of the building.

"Right. In a few minutes."

Glancing back over his shoulder, he saw Rose gazing after him, looking puzzled. As soon as she saw him, she blushed, turned, and hurried to the women's side of the building.

SEVEN

Rose couldn't decide whether she'd made a total fool of herself or only a partial one, but she had her fears. But how was she supposed to know that a "comfort station" was where one could relieve oneself? Fancy words that folks used for things like privies had never been a part of her experience. And what was a *euphemism?*

She felt really stupid. It was true that she'd been to Europe. She'd even met queens and emperors and kaisers— and why the Germans didn't just call him a king like the rest of the countries did was a mystery to her—but she'd never encountered a "comfort station" before this Exposition.

Now that she knew what it was, she wondered what H.L. had meant with his comment about powdering her nose. Did he think her nose needed powder? Did he think it was too shiny? After she relieved herself, which was the first and most vital order of business, she peered into the elaborate mirror set up for female fair-goers to view themselves, presumably with an eye toward improvement.

Her nose did appear to be a trifle pink. She probably ought to have powdered it before walking so far in the sun, actually, but Rose didn't use powder. The truth was that she didn't use any paint at all, even during her performances, because she'd never thought about it. She did now. She held no moral qualms about using face powder if it would make her look better as she performed. Lord. Here was one more thing to discuss with Annie, she supposed.

Because the weather was warm, and the world-famous Chicago winds had blown up a lot of dust, Rose splashed cool water on her face and wiped it dry with a towel handed to her by an attendant. An attendant! She'd never heard of such a thing. She smiled politely and said, "Thank you," and her mind slid back to the waiter.

Dagnabit, she wished Annie had taught her how polite ladies acted when they went out to restaurants and dined with gentlemen. Annie knew, because she'd had more experience than Rose at these things. Rose had never thought about asking her how one was supposed to behave in a restaurant. Until H.L. May barged into her life, Rose hadn't even considered that she might be made to feel foolish because she didn't know whether it was proper to talk to a waiter or not. When she'd eaten in restaurants before, she'd done so as part of her Wild West duties, and the colonel had done all the talking.

"Bother." It would do her no good to stand here staring at herself and brooding. Since she'd learned a little bit about tipping in Europe, she handed the attendant a one-cent piece, thanked her again, and bracing herself for further humiliation, walked outside to find H.L. May.

He was waiting for her. When he spotted her, he gave her one of his unfairly spectacular smiles and strode over to greet her. He had a long stride. And a confident one. Rose allowed herself a single moment to feel small, insignificant, and stupid before she braced herself and smiled back at him.

"You look beautiful today, Miss Gilhooley. Did I already say that?"

Rose felt herself flush. "I can't remember."

"Well, if I forgot to tell you so before, please allow me to do so now. You do look beautiful."

"Thank you." Was it proper to say more than *thank you* when a man told a woman he thought she was beautiful? Rose had no idea, so she kept quiet.

H.L., evidently not expecting an elaboration from her,

inhaled deeply and glanced around as if he were glorying in the day. "All right, how about we go to the Japanese pavilion next? Have you been there yet?"

Thank God she'd managed to squeak past the beauty comment. "No. I haven't really seen much of the fair yet. We've been quite busy at the Wild West." Excuses, excuses. Rose, inferior being that she was, hadn't wanted to explore the Exposition with anyone but Annie, since Annie understood her and never made her feel backward or dim-witted. Now she felt sort of silly about her lack of adventurousness.

"Great."

She shot him a glance, wondering what was so great about being a coward, but she didn't perceive anything on H.L.'s face that might signify he knew why she hadn't seen the fair. Thank goodness. Maybe pretending not to be a hick was working. Of course, pretense wouldn't save her indefinitely, since she didn't honestly know what could be considered hicklike and what couldn't. Talking to waiters sprang to mind.

Taking her courage in both hands, she decided to ask. Why not? She'd already admitted to having had no experience in dining out. "Um, is it considered ill-mannered to talk to waiters, Mr. May?" Because she thought that sounded too stupid to stand alone, she hurried to add, "I mean, in Kansas, we just talk to everybody."

He shot her a glance filled with surprise. "Ill-mannered? Of course, not. Why'd you think that?"

Because she was a bumpkin? No. She couldn't say that. Rose licked her lips as she scrambled through the sludge in her brain for a less damaging response. "Um, I only wondered. I mean, I wasn't sure if I should have told that man that I enjoyed my meal back there in the Egyptian restaurant."

She wished she hadn't said anything at all when H.L.'s expression of disbelief intensified.

"Why not? I mean, why should you think it was wrong to

tell the man you liked his cuisine? After all, he's probably happy to know it."

"Oh. Good." What was *cuisine?* For only an instant, Rose wanted to cry. Firming her resolve to behave like a lady, she suppressed the urge at once. She'd ask Annie tonight. Let's see. That was *euphemism, cuisine,* and what else? Oh, Lord, she'd forgotten already. She wished she dared write these words down. Oh, yes, she remembered now. *Metaphor.* She'd forgotten to ask Annie that one. Bother.

"Anyhow, I think you'll enjoy the Japanese Pavilion. Did you know they eat raw fish in Japan?"

"Raw fish? Good heavens." Rose really didn't want to hear about eating raw fish on a full stomach, although she didn't say so.

"They call it sashimi. I'm not sure it's altogether raw. I guess they treat it somehow. They eat a lot of rice in Japan, too."

"Oh, sort of like they do in China?" At least she knew *that* much.

"Right. Rice is a staple for a lot of countries."

What was a *staple?* Mud puddles. Here was another word for Annie, Rose guessed. In spite of her resolve not to, she felt stupid. She only nodded as they walked up to a lovely building.

"I suppose we should have gone to the Moorish palace after that lunch, but I thought you'd be interested in Japan. They have lots of earthquakes there, and volcanoes. There's a photograph of a volcano erupting."

"My goodness. It sounds interesting." If all she had to do was look at photographs and so forth, maybe she wouldn't be expected to know too many words. As long as she didn't have to read anything aloud, she'd probably survive. She could read to herself pretty well now if she was given time to decipher the hard words, but she still wasn't comfortable reading aloud, although she practiced every evening. Annie would assign Rose some pages, and she'd listen and embroider while Rose read them to her. She was getting better. Annie told her so every day. She'd die of embarrassment if she had to read aloud in front of H.L. May, however.

"The Japanese have a very stylized artistic form, too. I think you'll enjoy it. It's really different from ours."

"I'm sure." She didn't know what that meant, either. Stylized? Was that an art term? Rose wanted to be in the stable with Fairy and Betsy, who never expected her to know unusual words.

She was beginning to get itchy. She'd agreed, after all, to accompany H.L. May today because he said he was going to interview her. There had been neither hide nor hair of an interview that she could see thus far, although the day had been enjoyable except for the word issue.

That was what worried her the most. Not the big words; the enjoyment. She had a gnawing, itching, *irritating* feeling in her innermost being that, in the long run, it would be better for her if she found nothing whatever about H.L. May or his company enjoyable. He was, after all, a well-educated big-city newspaper reporter who wrote entire sentences for a living, for heaven's sake, and she was an undereducated booby. He'd find her out pretty soon; there was probably no way to avoid it. And then he'd look down on her. Laugh at her. He might even tell the world, through his position at the *Globe,* that in reality Wind Dancer was only a dumb cluck from Kansas.

Rose didn't think she could abide being ridiculed in print. It was difficult enough for her to know inside herself that she was uneducated. Reading banner headlines proclaiming her stupidity would be completely mortifying.

Not, of course, that any article about her would be headline news, but it would feel like it to her. Although the serenity of the Japanese pavilion appealed to her jumbled emotions, Rose decided it was time to tackle some pertinent questions and get some solid answers. She cleared her throat.

"What's up?" H.L., who appeared relaxed and happy and absolutely at home, smiled at her.

His smile gave her a palpitation in the chest region, and her skin heated up. This was getting ridiculous, and she despised herself. That being the case, she spoke in a more severe tone than was perhaps necessary. "I had believed you wished to interview me, Mr. May. Don't you think it's time to get started?"

He lifted one of his eyebrows, the result of which was to give him an ironical expression that did nothing for Rose's peace of mind. "You in a hurry or something? I thought you didn't have to perform again until tonight."

"I don't. However, I like to have some time to compose my thoughts before a show, and I have to prepare Fairy."

"Fairy's your horse? That's the one you rode last night, isn't it?"

"Yes. She's the one." What was this *it* nonsense? Rose didn't like thinking of her horses as *its,* and she would have scowled at him, but she was afraid of seeing his handsome face sneering at her again.

Not that he'd actually sneered, but he'd looked mighty teasing, and she didn't think she could tolerate another one of those looks without blushing and stammering, and that would be horrid. She gazed stonily at a magnificent landscape, framed and hung on the wall in front of her. The artist's rendering of the cherry trees, springlike weather, and peaceful river appealed to Rose. She'd never seen a painting like it.

Hmmm. Maybe the way the artist had used his brush was what Mr. May had meant when he'd said the art was *stylized.* Rose would have to ask Annie. She'd like to ask H.L. May, but didn't want to appear any more dim-witted in front of him than absolutely necessary.

"I'm sorry you're in such an all-fired hurry, Miss Gilhooley." He didn't sound sorry. He never sounded sorry, blast him. "But I do believe I mentioned yesterday that my articles were going to be akin to sketches of you discovering the fair."

She frowned at the glorious painting. "I suppose so. Is that what you're doing now? Taking mental notes of my reactions to things?"

"Exactly. I'll also be asking you some questions."

"I see. Well, I think you'd better start asking, because I'm going to have to go back to the Wild West pretty soon."

"Right." H.L. pulled out the gold pocket watch Rose had seen earlier, flipped open the case, and gazed at the dial.

He sounded peeved, which Rose resented. She lifted her chin defiantly and told herself that she was well within her rights to demand that this disturbing man get down to business. After all, she was no wealthy society dame who could loll around all day taking in fairs and Japanese exhibits and stylized paintings. She had a job of work to do, no matter how out of the ordinary it was, and she aimed to continue doing it to the best of her ability. That's what Colonel Cody was paying her for, and that's what she planned to deliver.

"Okay." He snapped his watch shut and slipped it into his watch pocket. He sounded cheerful again.

His relatively good mood surprised Rose, who'd been preparing for another battle. In truth, his attitude took the wind out of her sails, and she didn't know what to do with the fire she'd been storing up to fling at him. He was a most perverse individual, and she thought it was unfair of him to spring moods on her.

"So, let's start our interview, then," he went on, oblivious to her unsettled nerves. "What do you think of this painting? Have you ever seen anything like it before?"

Rose squinted up at him for almost thirty seconds as she mulled over his question and tried to determine if he meant it as it stood, or if it might somehow contain a subtle meaning that he'd ferret out and attack her with later. Although she thought hard, she couldn't come up with any way in which an honest answer on her part might be used against her, so she gave him one.

"I think it's beautiful. And no, I've never seen anything like it. Is all Japanese art like this?" She gestured at the painting, moving her fingers to indicate the intricate brush strokes and the way in which the artist had depicted the movement of water and the glory of the cherry blossoms, not to mention the bushes, which were all quite trim and neat-looking. None of the bushes Rose had seen growing in American meadows had ever looked so tidy.

"Yup. It's very stylized."

Aha! So that *was* what stylized meant! Rose felt a leap of triumph, although she figured it was silly of her to do so.

"However, I once interviewed a sailor who went to Japan with Commodore Perry, and he told me that some of the Japanese countryside actually looks pretty much like this. Evidently, the gardeners there don't believe in letting stuff grow naturally, but clip the shrubs and plants around temples and other buildings into strictly controlled shapes."

"My goodness. It's hard to imagine plants and shrubs really looking like those," Rose ventured, hoping her hesitant comment wouldn't be thought idiotic.

"I agree. It would be interesting to see in person, wouldn't it?"

Thank God. Relief washed through Rose. Because she feared if she spoke now, she'd spoil the effect of her last comment, she didn't, but only nodded.

After another moment spent contemplating what appeared to Rose to be a Japanese mania for tidiness—although it made for lovely pictures—H.L. said, "Say, as long as you have to get back to work, why don't we take in the Ferris wheel again. That way you can see the Exposition and Chicago in the daylight. I promised you a daylight view."

"Oh, I'd like that!" Rose exclaimed.

H.L. laughed.

"What? What are you laughing at?" Rose worried that

she'd done something idiotic by inadvertently demonstrating her eagerness to experience the Ferris wheel again. Was one supposed to conceal one's enjoyment and eagerness? Was that what sophisticated people did?

"Don't worry, Miss Gilhooley. I'm not laughing at you."

That was a mercy Rose hadn't expected.

"It's only that the Ferris wheel is already the most popular attraction in the entire Exposition. You've just proved to me that even ladies who are star attractions in their own right are, in this respect, like all the other ladies who visit the fair."

For some reason, that didn't make Rose feel appreciably better about herself.

EIGHT

And thus it has been proved beyond a doubt to this reporter that even the most well-traveled and famous of performers are, at heart, only human. Wind Dancer, Bareback Rider Extraordinaire, is as fond of Mr. Ferris's new innovation as a seamstress from the South Side.

H.L. sat back in his chair and stared at the words he'd just typed on his brand-new Underwood Invisible Writing Machine. He liked it—the article, that is. The citizens of Chicago would like it, too; he was sure of it.

Would Rose like it? He wasn't sure. He hadn't written anything she *should* object to, but she was a prickly little thing. An adorable, prickly little thing. He grinned at the page before him, remembering their ride in the Ferris wheel.

He'd just heaved a huge sigh when Grover Haley, his editor, walked by, smelling of spirits as he always did, and with a fat cigar stuck in his mouth. Good old Haley. He was one of the old-timers—gruff, cynical, literate, and jaded—and H.L. honored him for it. He was the sort of guy H.L. wanted to be in another twenty or thirty years. Maybe forty. H.L. didn't want to rush anything.

"Your story ready yet, May?" Haley stopped behind H.L.'s chair and peered over his shoulder. Taking the cigar from his mouth, he exhaled a cloud of smoke that blended with the whiskey fumes, creating an incense H.L. would forever associate with newspapers.

"Yup. Right here." He ripped the sheet out of the typewriter. *Real* reporters never turned the platen to remove their stories. Doing so would defy tradition. He picked up the rest of the pages of his story, patted them together, and handed them over. "There you go."

"Good. We've got to get this baby to bed. Took you long enough."

H.L. shrugged. He knew Haley only said things like that because it was an editor's job. Sam, who had looked up from his own typewriter, grinned at him, and H.L. tipped him a wink.

"You're going to do more of these, aren't you?" Haley barked. "Folks are eating them up."

"Absolutely." H.L. felt the deep sense of satisfaction that came from knowing he was going to get to do what he wanted to do and get paid for it for the next ten or twenty days—or more.

Hell, the fair was going to last until October; maybe he could do a story a week until it closed. God bless the Columbian Exposition. And God bless little Rose Ellen Gilhooley. H.L. could hardly wait to take her to the Fine Arts and Liberal Arts buildings. She'd probably been to museums in Europe, but H.L. imagined her art education was scanty at best.

How old had she been when she'd joined the Wild West? Sixteen? Hell, she couldn't have acquired much education in sixteen years. Though Buffalo Bill was a great fellow by all reports, H.L. would bet he didn't provide any schooling for his cast and crew. H.L. had discovered within himself a deep longing to show Rose Gilhooley things, to feed her thirst for knowledge, if she had one. He might be imagining he'd detected one in her, although he doubted it. He wanted to present the world to her even as he presented her to the world.

Sitting back in his swivel chair, H.L. clasped his hands

behind his head, clumped his feet on his desk, and thought about what marvels he aimed to pursue with Rose next. He wanted to learn the story of her childhood and youth. Rather, he wanted to learn the story of her youth before the Wild West. He supposed he could look up Buffalo Bill's performance schedule for six years and find out the story of her years after he'd hired her.

Was she ready to open up to him yet? Frowning into the almost-empty press room, and feeling vaguely comforted by the muffled clunk-clunk of the printing presses that seeped through from the basement print room, he considered the matter.

She was as prickly as a poison ivy rash, and he didn't dare leap into anything with her. It had been hard enough getting her to visit the fair with him in the first place.

Then again . . . H.L.'s frown tipped up into a self-satisfied smirk. He'd really done a pretty good job in softening her up, he told himself. She was so interested in the Exposition now, she probably wouldn't balk at talking to him about other things as well.

God, he was good at his job. He was right up there at the top, in fact. And this series of articles about Rose Ellen Gilhooley was going to make him a household name across the entire nation. H.L. envisioned his Columbian Exposition articles being picked up by newspapers from Maine to California. The *New York Times,* even!

With visions of fame and fortune dancing in his head, and mental images of himself covering earth-shaking events— wars, famines, floods, and fires sprang to mind—H.L. lifted his feet from his desk, stood up, stretched, bade his few remaining colleagues a cheery good night, and sauntered out of the *Globe*'s offices.

"I'm not sure," Annie told Rose.

The Wild West was over for the night. Both women had

been cheered and applauded lustily by a standing-room-only crowd. Rose didn't know about Annie, but she was bushed. It had been a busy day, and an exciting one. As soon as H.L. May had walked her back to the Wild West encampment after their daylight Ferris wheel ride, Rose had written down the words for which she wanted definitions, wishing as she did so that she knew how to spell them.

"I have a dictionary packed in one of my trunks." Annie, still garbed in her costume, the bosom of which bristled with award medals, ribbons, rosettes, and all manner of prizes won in sharpshooting competitions, stood in the middle of the tent she shared with Frank, and tapped her chin with a finger.

"I'll be happy to get it, if you know which one it's in," Rose offered. George snoozed peacefully on the blanket Annie had embroidered for him. Sometimes Rose wished she were a pampered poodle. Life was much easier for pets than for their owners. She didn't want to face H.L. May again until she knew for sure what he'd said to her today. She had a fairly good memory, and had stored sentences in her head rather the way she'd seen books stored on library shelves in some of the big cities she'd visited.

The one she was most curious about was *euphemism,* and why "Would you like to powder your nose?" could be considered one. It seemed like a straightforward enough question to her, yet H.L. May claimed it hadn't been. Rose, who loved stories and would dearly like to be able to read them better by herself, didn't like not understanding things.

"Oh, no, you needn't do that," Annie said. "I'm only trying to recollect which trunk it might be in." She snapped her fingers. "Oh, yes! I remember now."

Rose watched her dart over to a corner of the roomy tent, where two trunks were stacked in order to provide the Butlers with a writing surface. Annie flung the top trunk down with a clunk and opened the bottom one. Glancing over her shoulder at Rose, she said, "We put the empty one on top for this very purpose."

For the purpose of flinging it aside? Rose, tired after a full day, didn't ask. "Is it in there?"

"Yes!" Annie lifted a heavy leather-bound volume. "As you know, I've tried hard to better my reading skills, too, just as you're doing now."

Rose nodded. Yes, indeed, she did know that. It was one of the many things about Annie that made them such good friends. "I'm not sure how to spell the first word," she admitted. "It's *euphemism*. Maybe it starts with a *U?*"

"Let me see." Sitting on the trunk she'd tossed on the floor, Annie thumbed through the well-used book. "Would it be a *U* and an *F?* Or a *U* and a *P-H?*"

"You're asking me?" Rose walked over and sat beside Annie. She was beginning to feel stupid again. Or . . . Maybe stupid wasn't it. Maybe she was only feeling as though she were at a disadvantage. Both conditions were uncomfortable, but being at a disadvantage didn't sound so permanent as did being stupid. It also felt a tiny bit better to think of herself as disadvantaged rather than stupid. Besides that, it was the truth.

"I don't see anything that begins *U-F,*" Annie muttered, following the words in the book with her forefinger. "Here's *Ugrian.*"

"What?"

"*Ugrian.* It's some kind of Hungarian, it says here. Or a Hungarian is some kind of Ugrian."

"Well, that doesn't help us with *euphemism.*"

"No. Let me look up *U-P-H* and see what happens." She flipped some more pages. "Hmmm. *Upheaval, uphill, uphold, upholster.* No *euphemism.*"

Rose sighed, feeling discouraged. "Why does he use words like that, I wonder?"

With a shrug, Annie shuffled back through a big hunk of

the dictionary. "Probably because he can, I reckon. People who like words use them a lot. Look at the colonel."

"That's true. But I usually understand the words he uses."

"But that's only because you and he live and work in the same environment. Don't forget that words are Mr. May's livelihood. He probably knows a whole lot of them."

"True." Rose dropped her chin into her cupped hands, resting her elbows on her thighs. "Are there any more choices? If it doesn't start with a *U-F* or a *U-P-H,* what's left?"

"Let me think."

Annie thought as Rose ruminated on how uncomfortable it could be to spend time with someone who had a grand education when she had no education at all. She suspected she wouldn't mind so much if she didn't *care* so much, but she did care. And she didn't even know why. After all, H.L. May was so far out of her orbit as to belong to another solar system. She sniffed, thinking at least she knew what the solar system was. Thanks to Annie and a book she'd had her read aloud to her a couple of years ago.

It was depressing to know that if Rose hadn't met Annie, she'd be even more of an uneducated blockhead than she was. She wondered if H.L. May would have wanted to interview her six years ago, when she first joined the Wild West. The mere thought of having him see her as she was then made her shudder.

"I have it!"

Startled, Rose cried out, "What? What do you have?"

Annie began flipping quickly through the dictionary. "I remember when I first met Frank. He's Irish, you know, and a Catholic, and it's the first time I'd ever heard of the Holy Eucharist."

"The what?" Rose had never heard of it until this minute.

"Never mind. But the point is that it begins *E-U.* Maybe *euphemism* begins with an *E-U,* too, and doesn't have an *F* in it at all."

Rose blinked at her friend. "Why would a word that sounds like it begins with a *U* begin with an *E,* though?"

"I don't know. It's just the way these things work sometimes. Language is strange. Ours comes from all sorts of other, older, antique languages."

"It does?" It didn't seem sportsmanlike to Rose that the more she learned, the less she knew, but that was the way her education seemed to be going at the moment. She clung to the hope that any education at all was better than none, however, and didn't run screaming from the tent.

"Ah, yes, here we are." Annie stabbed a finger at the page. "Oh, here's *euchre.* I think the colonel and Frank play euchre sometimes."

"I've heard of euchre." This faintly surprised Rose, who hadn't believed she had anything at all in common with those strange words in the English language that began with *E-U.* "It's a card game, isn't it?"

"Yes. Oh, look. And here's a euphonium. I knew a gentleman who played the euphonium once."

From which statement, Rose presumed a euphonium was either a musical instrument or another card game. She didn't say anything, although she was slightly curious. Most of her energy was being expended on wondering about *euphemism* at the moment. Euphoniums could just take care of themselves.

Preoccupied, Annie didn't expound on the definition of *euphonium.* After another few seconds, she lifted her head and beamed at Rose. "It's here!"

"It is?" Rose beamed back, her heart swelling as if it had been she who'd discovered Dr. Livingstone in deepest Africa rather than Mr. Stanley. She hoped the rest of the words she wanted to look up wouldn't be as difficult to find as *euphemism.*

"Ah," said Annie, satisfaction lacing her voice. "I understand now." She looked at Rose. "You told me he asked if you wanted to powder your nose when he really wanted to know if you needed to use the privy?"

"Yes, only he called it the comfort station."

Annie's smile was wide. *"That's* a euphemism, too, my dear."

"It is?"

"Yes. Look. It says right here that a euphemism is the substitution of an agreeable or inoffensive word for another one. So, when a gentleman wants to know if a lady needs to use the privy, he's being polite when he asks if she wants to powder her nose."

"For heaven's sake." Rose's mouth dropped open at the notion of H.L. May trying to be polite. "Goodness gracious. I'll be hanged."

Annie nodded. "All of those things." Her smile faded. "When I met Mr. May, he didn't appear to be the type to mince words—so to speak. Do you suppose he has ulterior motives, Rose?" Reading the shock on Rose's face, she took her arm. "I don't want to alarm you, Rose, but he *is* a man, after all, and you know what men are."

"Well . . . Actually, I'm not sure I do." Rose shrugged self-deprecatingly. "I don't have much experience, you know."

"I know, dear." Annie patted her knee. "Just be careful. He's a handsome devil, and there aren't too many honorable men in the world anymore, particularly not handsome ones."

Rose lifted her chin. "The colonel is an honorable man, Annie, and he's good-looking."

"Yes," her friend said dryly. "But it isn't the colonel who's taking you out gallivanting all over the fair every day, is it?"

"No. I guess not."

"You guess not, indeed. Just watch yourself, Rose. I'd hate to see you get hurt by a sophisticated big-city reporter who's only out for a bit of sport."

Rose felt herself flush. "Annie!" she exclaimed in a mortified voice. "Please, I know how to take care of myself."

Annie heaved a huge sigh. "Yes, yes. I know. You've been taking care of yourself for far too many years already. But you haven't been wined and dined by a cultivated scoundrel, either."

With a gasp, Rose goggled at Annie. "Oh, Annie! Is that what he is? Do you really think so?"

Apparently recognizing that she'd gone too far, Annie again patted Rose's knee. "I'm sorry, dear. I don't know that's what he is. How can I? All I'm saying is that you must guard yourself. Your feelings, most of all. I know you can keep any man from taking advantage of you physically, but no matter how well known you are in show business, you're still a very young woman with little experience of men."

Seeing the logic in Annie's worries, Rose expelled a gust of breath, wishing her best friend weren't so right about her. "I understand, Annie. Truly, I do."

"I'm sure of it, Rose."

Annie gave Rose a sweet smile, and Rose almost succumbed to the urge to hug her. She missed her mother so much sometimes. And her brother, Freddie. She'd been able to talk to her mother about almost anything, and the things she didn't dare talk to her about, she could always talk to Freddie about. Freddie had protected her, although Rose had always pretended she didn't need his help. Still, she knew she could have been in big trouble a few times if Freddie hadn't warded off drunken cowboys, outlaws, gamblers, and other forms of lowlife often found in and around Deadwood.

Sometimes, even with Annie and Frank Butler standing in for her family, she missed her real kin dreadfully. Often, in fact, if she'd been able to wish herself back home to Kansas, she'd have done it.

But that wouldn't be fair to her family. They needed Rose to be doing exactly what she was doing. One day Rose hoped to live with her mother again, whether in Kansas or somewhere else. Every time she thought about her poor, tired mother, Rose's heart ached. She'd given up so many years of her life on the frontier. According to Freddie and her mother herself, Mrs. Gilhooley was healthier and stronger these days, thanks to Rose.

No. Rose knew she had to keep on with the Wild West. For her own sake and her family's. No matter how uncomfortable living away from family could be. At least she had Annie.

"What are the other words you wanted to know about?" Annie asked.

Dragging her brain back from the dismal swamp into which it had been sinking, Rose sighed and said, "Let me see. *Staple.* Mr. May said rice is a staple for the Japanese. And *metaphor.* I don't have any idea what a metaphor is."

So the two ladies looked up words in Annie's dictionary, and Rose repeated the words individually and in sentences until she was pretty sure she wouldn't again forget what any of them meant. God alone knew what the morrow might bring. For all she knew, H.L. May would keep piling words on her until she smothered under a heap of them.

She was so exhausted when she finally got to bed that night, she didn't even turn over for eight hours.

H.L. had decided Rose probably needed one more day of softening up before he began to probe deeply into her background. Or maybe not. He'd play it by ear.

He arrived even earlier at the Wild West encampment today than he had the day before, his eagerness to see Rose propelling him. Not, of course, that he wanted to see Rose because she was *Rose,* but because she was the best story ever to land in his lap. So to speak.

The notion of having Rose Gilhooley on his lap was such an appealing one, H.L. had trouble banishing it from his mind. The problem was solved a moment later when he moseyed into the arena and saw Rose in the distance, practicing with one of her white horses. H.L. couldn't tell the two beasts apart.

Deciding he didn't want to interrupt her, and also that it might be fun to observe her for a while without her being aware of his presence, he found a seat in the grandstand that was partially obscured from Rose's line of sight by a pillar. He drew out a notebook and a pencil and started writing even before he'd sat down.

Rose Gilhooley was an inspiring subject. Seldom at a loss for words, H.L. found they flowed like water from his brain to his pencil to the page when Rose was the subject *du jour.*

As graceful on horseback as a firefly at night, streamed out in lead onto the paper.

> *Miss Gilhooley rides like the wind. This reporter finds it no wonder that her Indian chums gifted her with the name "Wind Dancer." She belongs to the wind, as naturally as if she were herself a force of nature.*

H.L. watched Rose and pondered the words he'd just jotted down. He didn't want to get *too* flowery in his praise of Rose, because folks might get the wrong impression. They might think he was enamored of Rose herself instead of her remarkable skill as a horsewoman.

Not that H.L. didn't think she was cute as a bug, because he did. But, being the cosmopolitan man of the world that he was, he didn't find innocence all that exciting. He liked women with a few years on them. Experienced women. Women who knew what was what. Women who weren't breakable.

Breakable? Where the hell had that come from? H.L. squinted down at the page and realized he'd written, *Miss Gilhooley, for all her poise and gumption, wears an air of fragility that would do a fairy princess proud.* Good God.

H.L. drew a heavy line through that sentence, knowing it was preposterous.

Or was it? He gasped as Rose, using some gesture invisible to her audience, made her pretty white horse rear up onto its hind legs and seem to dance across the field. How did she *do* that. Hell, H.L., who didn't have much truck with horses on a regular basis, would have fallen off and bashed his head long before the horse quit prancing, as it did now. Without waiting for Rose to catch her breath, the horse then took off at a dead run and made two entire circuits of the arena before veering into what would have been center stage, if it had been on one, and stopping with another lift of its front legs. The sequence of events was tremendously dramatic, which he guessed was the point, but they scared the tar out of him for Rose's sake.

Although his intention had been to write most of today's story without Rose's even knowing he was there, H.L. couldn't stop himself from leaping to his feet, cheering loudly, and applauding.

Rose gave a visible start, began to slide sideways, and made a grab for her horse's mane. H.L. watched, horrified. Never in a million years would he have guessed that being startled might cause her trouble on horseback. She was so competent. So secure. So damnably cool when she rode.

His heart, which had flown to his throat—again—when he saw her slip, settled down again when she regained her balance. "I'm sorry, Miss Gilhooley!" he called, meaning it sincerely. "I didn't mean to alarm you."

"For heaven's sake, Mr. May, please don't burst out clapping like that when I'm practicing. I didn't know you were there, and poor Betsy almost had an attack of apoplexy." She guided the horse toward H.L., looking cranky. "And so did I."

H.L. got the impression she'd like to scold him for an hour or two. In truth, he felt bad for having scared her and her horse. Although he wasn't accustomed to offering apologies, he did this time. "I'm really sorry. I didn't realize how fully you concentrate when you're working." He shook his head. "I should have, I guess. You wouldn't be able to do what you do if you didn't have an amazing capacity for concentration."

Her scowl evaporated and was replaced by an expression of bemusement. "Oh. Yes, I suppose you're right."

He eyed her uncertainly. Hadn't she already figured that one out on her own? "Yeah." He cleared his throat. "Um, well, if you're through practicing, how about we visit some more of the Exposition?" He gave her one of his patented charming grins, the ones virtually guaranteed to level rooms full of women, not to mention actors and politicians.

It didn't work on Rose, who continued to frown down at him from her perch on the horse. "I don't know. I mean, I know I agreed to be interviewed by you for your articles, but I didn't realize the interviewing process would take up so much of my time." She appeared more than a little skeptical. "And yours. Besides, you haven't really even interviewed me. All you've done is take me to lunch and on the Ferris wheel."

"Are you complaining, Miss Gilhooley?" H.L. tried for a twinkle, although inside he was peeved. Damn it! It wasn't often he spent this much time and energy on a project. The least this project could do was appreciate him for it.

She heaved an exasperated sigh. "No, I'm not complaining. In fact, I suppose I should thank you."

"Don't strain yourself," he advised grouchily.

Another sigh, this one larger and sounding more exasperated, heaved from Rose's budlike mouth. "I beg your pardon. I didn't mean to sound so ill-natured, Mr. May."

He bowed, aiming for irony. From the sour look on her face, he achieved it.

"There's no cause for you to be upset with me," she said tightly. "I need to take care of Betsy and change my clothes, and I'll be with you shortly."

"Do you mind if I mosey along with you? I'd like to document the care you give your horses."

She slid from Betsy's back. H.L. caught his breath, not having anticipated this action, and fearing for the health of her limbs. But she alighted on the ground rather like a feather coming to rest after coming loose from a bird's tail. Great God Almighty, but she was good on a horse! Without any conscious effort, his brain composed a sentence describing Rose's descent from her horse's back.

"What's the matter?" she asked, squinting up at him as if she suspected him of dire motives. Apparently, she'd heard his gasp of alarm.

This time his grin was spontaneous and wasn't meant to convey anything but pleasure in her company. "Nothing. It just startled me when you dismounted. You sure are an abrupt young lady, Miss Gilhooley. Has anyone ever told you that before?"

She still looked skeptical. "No, they haven't."

"Well, you are. So, may I accompany you to the stables?" Believing he might look less menacing to this innocent girl-woman if he hunched over a little, he did so, and stuck his hands in his trouser pockets. There. If he didn't look innocent now, he didn't know what else he could do.

Rose didn't appear significantly less wary. Nor did she sound it when she said sharply, "You've seen me take care of a horse. It was a different horse, but the principle's the same."

"But I wasn't taking notes then," he said meekly.

She huffed, "Oh, all right. Follow me."

Before she left the arena, she grabbed a pair of moccasins from a nearby bench. H.L. hadn't noticed them there, probably because they were so tiny. Rose slipped them on before she clicked to her horse and moved off in the direction of the stable.

H.L.'s gaze went to her feet. The moccasins, small or not, seemed to fit her perfectly. And, as her bloomerlike skirt ended shortly below her knees, he also got a good gander at her calves and ankles. He couldn't recall ever seeing better-looking legs. With an effort, he dragged his gaze from her lower-body assets and concentrated on her face, which was pleasant to look at, too.

Because he was supposedly here in order to do his job, he decided to ask a question or two as they walked along. "So, Miss Gilhooley, where'd you get these horses? Are they Kansas natives, too?"

She shot him a suspicious glance. H.L. resented it. What the devil was she suspicious of? Surely she didn't suspect him of improper motives, did she? Before he could dwell on it, she answered his question.

"No. The first horse I trained, Gingerbread, is a bay gelding I bought from Little Elk's brother in Kansas. I used him for the first year or so I was with the Wild West, but the colonel thought it would look better if I were to ride a white horse during performances, so he gave me Fairy and I taught her what to do."

"Interesting. So, while you rode your own horse, you were training this one on the side?"

"Not this one. This is Betsy. She's a standby the colonel bought in case Fairy's ever laid up. These two are mares. Gingerbread was much bigger than either Fairy or Betsy."

"I see." H.L. tried to envision the diminutive Rose on a much larger horse, but his mind boggled at the image. "Do you still ride Gingerbread?" He didn't understand why his heart had suddenly started pounding, as if with dread.

"Sometimes, but poor Ginger's kind of old now, and I only ride him for exercise."

"Exercise? Good God, Miss Gilhooley, what do you need to exercise for?"

She looked exasperated again. "Not me, Mr. May; Gingerbread. If a horse just stands around eating all the time, it'll get fat and out of shape. That's not fair to the horse."

"Ah. I see."

There was a lot to this horse business. H.L. decided he was glad he lived in the great city of Chicago and didn't have to worry about taking care of cattle.

NINE

Annie's words swirled in Rose's head as she changed clothes in her tent after tending to Betsy. She'd left H.L. cooling his heels in the stables. *"I'd hate to see you get hurt by a sophisticated big-city reporter,"* Annie had told her.

Was H.L. May only after a bit of sport, as Annie suspected? The notion made Rose's chest ache. Thus far in their short association, H.L. May had been rude, brash, arrogant, and inquisitive, and he'd flirted with her once. But was he dishonorable? She couldn't tell.

Her brain told her to watch her step; that H.L. May had the ability to hurt her more deeply than anything had ever hurt her before, barring the death of her father. Her heart told her to open up, enjoy herself in his company, and let fate take care of itself. The two organs were, in other words, in direct opposition to each other.

Rose told herself she'd be better off ignoring her heart and listening to her brain. If H.L. May's motives were pure, she'd surely suffer less if she followed her brain and told her heart to take a hike. And if his motives were impure, she'd only get herself into trouble if she paid attention to her heart. Plus, if his intentions were wicked, she'd feel like a blithering idiot if she fell for his wiles.

If, that is, he was in fact using wiles on her to achieve untoward goals—which she couldn't tell since she'd had no experience with wiles per se. The men she'd met so far in her life whose intentions had been bad, had been obvious about them. H.L. May, if he were a villain, was keeping his evil intentions a very dark secret.

Her heart said, "Relax."

Her brain said, "Be on guard."

"You're being a fool, Rose Gilhooley," she finally barked at both of them. "He only wants a story."

So much for that. Rose felt calmer once she'd settled the issue, at least for the moment.

She'd worn her pretty yellow outfit yesterday. Today, since the weather promised to be warm and springlike again, she opted for another new ensemble she'd bought during her shopping spree with Annie. The color was a dark navy blue, but the material was a lightweight cotton calico, and the entire ensemble was trimmed in white, like a sailor suit. Annie claimed Rose looked absolutely adorable in it. Rose hoped her best friend was right and not merely being polite. She trusted Annie, who wasn't accustomed to fibbing.

Therefore, as she pinned the accompanying tiny confection of a sailor's hat to her chestnut curls, she felt as confident as a girl in her circumstances could. She was only slightly nervous when she left her tent and walked to the stables to meet with H.L.

A glow of satisfaction suffused her when H.L., who had been speaking gently to Betsy and Fairy, much to the appreciation of the two mares, who were affectionate creatures, turned and saw her. She heard his sudden intake of breath from the door of the stable, and hoped the shadows in the stable were deep enough that he wouldn't detect the sudden rush of color to her cheeks. She felt them get hot and was disgusted with herself.

"My God, you look glorious, Miss Gilhooley!"

Her heart hammered against her ribs like the gunfire in the Wild West during Custer's Last Stand, but Rose managed a credible, "Thank you" and a slight nod of her chin, which she'd lifted for strength.

H.L. strode toward her like a king taking a castle. Oh,

dear, there went her imagination again, spurred on by her insubordinate heart. Rose told her heart to shut up and sit still. She didn't need it to get fanciful on her now. She needed to maintain her poise.

He stopped right in front of her, which meant she had to tilt her head back to see his face. His eyes held the most alarming expression. They reminded Rose of burning coals.

Stop it, she shrieked at her heart and her imagination. Then she scolded her wits for running away and hiding just when she needed them the most. *Pretend,* she commanded herself. *Pretend you're not a bumpkin.*

"I must say, Miss Gilhooley, that it's a pleasure to be in your company. You make me the envy of other men."

"Pshaw," Rose muttered. It was the best she could come up with at the moment, having once more mislaid her wits somewhere in the mush of her emotions.

H.L. crooked his arm, and Rose laid her gloved hand on it. She heard him suck in a gallon or two of fair-scented air and dared a peek up at his face. He was a truly striking man. She wasn't sure if his features could be called classically handsome, but he certainly caught one's eye and held it. If she was an ornament to him, he was an ornament to her, too, and she was glad of it. Rose rather liked the notion of other women envying her because of her escort, although she knew the sentiment did her no credit.

Nevertheless, she felt awfully good as they set out to conquer another day at the fair.

"Fine Arts and Liberal Arts today, Miss Gilhooley," H.L. told her after they'd strolled a few yards, taking in the sights and sounds abounding everywhere around them. "And we're going to visit the Grand Basin, too. Have you seen the statue of the Republic yet?"

"Yes. Annie and I walked through the White City. It's quite a sight, especially at night when it's all lit up."

"It is, indeed. We'll have to visit it together one of these days. I'd like to hear your reaction to it." He frowned down at her. "Say, do you ever have any time off? I mean, at night? I know you can come out after you finish your act in the Wild West, but you don't have much time then."

"We don't perform on Sundays," Rose said, wondering what it would be like to walk out of an evening with H.L. May all by herself, with no Little Elk along as chaperone. The notion made her insides tingle. Her mind, which finally surfaced with a pop, admonished her for being forward, and she hastened to add, "Although Annie and I usually attend an evening church service."

H.L. sighed. "Why doesn't that surprise me?"

A quick glance at him didn't serve Rose in figuring out what *that* was supposed to have meant, so she didn't respond. She did, however, sniff as her head, again in charge, asked her why this man should sound sarcastic about two ladies attending church together. Rose feared this attitude regarding church on H.L. May's part boded ill for her hopes about his intentions.

"I'd like to show you Chicago, too."

Evidently, he'd opted to drop the church and evening issues for the moment. Rose figured it was just as well. "Annie and I went to some of the museums when we first arrived," she muttered.

"Oh, there's a lot more to Chicago than museums," he laughed.

Eyeing him critically, Rose decided his laughter wasn't meant to be snide. "Oh?"

"Absolutely. Chicago's a great place. We have a terrific baseball team, we're famous for our stockyards, and we have some grand buildings."

He smiled down at her, and Rose's heart trampled her head into the mud again. Blast! It was so difficult, constraining her stupid heart.

"I'll bet you'd find the courthouse fascinating. And the train station. They're built upon truly magnificent lines. Not what you're used to in Kansas, I imagine."

Because she *really* wanted to lay to rest this image she had of herself—and that he might have of her—as a hick, Rose said majestically, "I haven't spent my entire life in Kansas, if you'll recall, Mr. May. I saw innumerable grand buildings in London, Rome, and Paris." She added a sniff for good measure.

He laughed. Disgruntled, Rose decided it was what she should have expected of him. How could she flaunt her status as a world traveler if he refused to be impressed?

"That's right. I forgot. You can probably give me lessons on grand buildings, huh?"

"I don't know about the lessons part," she muttered, feeling small and ill informed. Why was it she could feel dumb and insignificant without half trying, but it took an act of God to make her feel good about herself? It didn't seem at all equitable.

He laughed again. Rose sighed and guessed she was doomed to feel like an imbecile in his company.

They'd entered the Exposition through the main gate, which led directly to the Court of Honor and on to the White City. H.L. flung his arms wide in one of the exuberant gestures Rose so envied. "I love this place!" he declared. "Burnham and Root conceived the initial plans, and they hauled in architects from all over. Most of them followed the Beaux Arts style Burnham and Root favored."

Rose heaved a large internal sigh. Here they were again, back to normal: H.L. talking about things that were incomprehensible to her, and Rose wishing she weren't such a booby. Annoyed with him and with herself, she asked, "Who are Burnham and Root?"

"Architects," he replied promptly.

Well . . . That had been pretty easy. Rose ventured another tentative question. "And what's the Beaux Arts style?" She flinched inside, waiting for his sneer of condescension.

She was amazed when he didn't give her one. "It's a style of architecture developed in France. You know how everybody likes to think the French are better at everything than anybody else is." He gave another jolly laugh. "At least, the *French* like to think so."

Rose, who breathed more easily when she realized he wasn't looking down on her for not knowing more about architecture, had actually heard that before, when the Wild West had visited England. The British and the French seemed to have very few good feelings for, and almost nothing good to say about, each other. Rose, feeling more akin to English people than French ones, probably because she understood their language better, figured the English were on the right side of the argument. "I see."

"Poor Root died before the Exposition opened."

That shocked her. "Oh! How awful. I'm so sorry he didn't get to see the fair!"

"Yeah, it was tough. He caught pneumonia."

She shook her head, genuinely sorry for poor Root, whoever he'd been.

"But Burnham and the rest of the architects did a great job, didn't they?"

He'd stopped walking beside the Grand Basin. With another large gesture, he invited Rose to take in the glory of the Court of Honor, the first feature one observed when one entered through the main entrance.

Taking him up on his offer, Rose feasted her eyes on the spectacular array of buildings, electrical lighting, fountains, bandstands, and people before her. It was a sight, all right, and one that inspired awe in her bosom. "It's beautiful," she said simply.

"It sure is."

He shook his head, and Rose was happy to detect a bit of awe in his expression. It was comforting to know that even a sophisticated man of the world could feel genuine emotion every now and then.

"The only building not constructed in the Beaux Arts style is the Transportation building. See it over there? You'll enjoy that one, too. Have you ever seen a horseless carriage?"

Rose gaped at him. Was he teasing her?

As if reading her mind, H.L. grinned again. "Honest Injun, Miss Gilhooley, they're developing motorized vehicles that don't require horses to pull them. Pretty soon the horse will be obsolete."

If she knew what *obsolete* meant, she might be worried. Since she didn't, and there were so many other things with which to occupy her mind, Rose decided to panic later. Because she felt she ought to say something, she murmured, "Oh, my," and hoped it would suffice.

It seemed to. H.L. went on enthusiastically, "After we see the arts buildings, we can visit the Transportation building. It sticks out like a sore thumb, doesn't it?"

Rose didn't think so. She thought it was gorgeous, even if it didn't fit precisely in with the other buildings. Although she realized her opinion didn't matter in the overall scheme of things, she voiced it anyhow. "I think it's lovely."

H.L. grinned down at her as if she'd just done something wonderful. "Yeah. So do I."

This was a commendation she hadn't expected. Her unruly heart leaped happily. Sternly admonishing it to be still, she said, "And it doesn't look at all out of place, either. Rather, I think it adds something." Was that stupid? Probably. Rose sighed.

"I think so, too."

She cheered up.

H.L. pointed to the Grand Basin. "There's a wooded island in the middle of one of the lakes that you've got to see. This is only one of the many lakes, fountains, and waterways around the Exposition."

"Oh."

"I'll take you to see the Wooded Island one of these days, too."

"Um, what is it? The Wooded Island, I mean."

"It's an island with woods on it." H.L. guffawed.

Rose frowned. "Yes, I understand that, thank you very much."

"Sorry. Didn't mean to tease you."

Rose would believe that one when hell froze over.

"The fair directors named it the Wooded Island. It's supposed to be representational of how frontier folks lived when America was first colonized."

"Oh. I see." Shoot, she could demonstrate how frontier folks lived right this minute, if anybody really wanted to know. Rose didn't think it was such a glorious thing to live on the frontier and have to scramble to put food in your children's mouths, but she guessed she'd better not bring it up right now. "That sounds interesting."

Concluding that she hadn't really fibbed, and that it might be entertaining to contrast how the first American pioneers lived with how modern-day American pioneers lived, Rose didn't scold herself. She did expect that most of the first American pioneers might have had a more noble purpose in their hearts than lots of the folks she'd met in Kansas, many of whom had fled west to escape the law. Kansas was mighty rough in spots. "I'd like to see it."

"Good. We can do that another day." He sounded pleased with himself. "Right now, we're taking in Fine Arts. You said you like to go to museums, right?"

Actually, she didn't recall saying that at all, but she didn't argue. "Right." She was particularly fond of the Natural History Museum she and Annie had visited in New York City, but she had a vague notion that not all museums housed stuffed elephants and displays of African artifacts and the like. *Fine Arts,* for instance, didn't immediately bring to Rose's mind images of tanned buffalo hides or Zulu war drums. She didn't mention her musings to H.L., suspecting he'd mock her.

"This place is great," he said warmly. "There are some magnificent paintings in here."

"Ah." So. It was one of those kinds of museums. Rose supposed she should have guessed, since it was called the Fine Arts building. But if this structure housed *fine* arts, what did the *Liberal* Arts building hold? Art that wasn't so fine? These nuances were confusing to a country girl. In the interest of self-preservation, she didn't say that, either.

"Here we go," H.L. said, leading Rose up to the magnificent Fine Arts building. "The building itself is a work of art, as you can see for yourself."

Rose didn't doubt it, although she wasn't all that eager to enter it. Not that she didn't want to learn what fine arts were. But a fellow vigorously waving a baton was conducting a brass band on a covered bandstand in a spirited musical offering. Rose liked it a lot and didn't want to miss the finale of the piece.

Because the high-pitched, tuneful piccolo part appealed to her so strongly, she placed her other hand on H.L.'s arm as he reached out to open the door. "Do you mind waiting to hear the end of this piece, Mr. May? It's so . . . lively." She hoped that didn't sound idiotic.

"It's lively, all right." H.L. chuckled. "Sure. Why not? We have all day. Almost."

H.L. May's chuckle did something to Rose's insides that she didn't trust. He did, however, stop in his headlong pursuit of fine arts. Actually, he didn't even seem put out with her, so Rose guessed she hadn't done anything too appalling or low-class.

"That's a great band, isn't it?"

Surprised by his seemingly easy acceptance of this alteration in his plans for their day, Rose glanced up to study his face. He appeared perfectly cheerful. "I think they're wonderful."

There. She'd offered a firm opinion on something. She felt rather as if this was a test of her ability to perform in the world outside the Wild West. If he didn't make fun of her, perhaps she'd dare to be a trifle more forthcoming in stating her opinions in the future.

"The conductor—see him there? The fellow who's bouncing up and down and waving that baton?"

"Yes. Of course." Rose had even known the leader of the band was called the conductor, although she was certain H.L. wouldn't understand her pleasure in the knowledge. But Deadwood boasted a brass band and, while the conductor thereof didn't direct his musicians with a revolver, as the conductor of the Dodge City Brass Band was reputed to do, Rose had enjoyed their music on many occasions. In truth, she was glad the Deadwood conductor didn't find it necessary to conduct with a revolver. Life in Kansas was already too perilous, and surely listening to pretty music didn't need to be a dangerous affair.

H.L. nodded at the conductor. "His name's John P. Sousa, and he writes a lot of the music his band plays, primarily the marches. I think he wrote that piece. If it's the one I'm thinking of, it's called *Stars and Stripes Forever,* and it's being introduced here, at the Exposition. Nobody'd ever heard it before this fair opened."

"My goodness." Here was another discovery for her to ponder. First it had been the invention of foods, and now it was the invention of musical compositions. She guessed there was a lot to life, if a body had time to appreciate it.

All at once, she experienced an aching longing to bring her mother to Chicago and show her the fair. Her poor mother hadn't been allowed to experience very much of life aside from the difficulties it afforded a woman on the frontier. Rose would love to be able to present the world to her, just as H.L. was presenting it to Rose.

Now there, she thought, was an interesting concept. Sneaking another peek at H.L.'s face, she decided maybe he wasn't so frightening a fellow after all. As long as she could guard herself against making more out of his attentions than was there, she could undoubtedly benefit greatly from his willingness to introduce her to new things. Then she could relate her experiences to her mother via letters.

Rose wasn't great with words, but she knew herself to be adept at creating pictures with them. She tried hard to develop this skill, since it was through her that Mrs. Gilhooley was seeing the world. She hoped that with enough urging, Mrs. Gilhooley and Rose's two younger sisters would agree to visit Rose and the Columbian Exposition before it closed.

The band, with the piccolo's part soaring along above every other instrument—Rose got the impression of a small bird flying over a herd of cattle—came to the thrilling conclusion of their musical offering. Rose was pleased when several people who'd stopped to listen applauded. Believing the musicians and their director deserved the applause, Rose added her accolades to theirs. She found it a joy to be on the giving end of applause for a change.

When she turned to continue on her way to the Fine Arts building, she was embarrassed to find H.L. smiling at her, his overall expression that of a man whose pet had performed some kind of trick to his satisfaction. She said tartly, "What?"

"What what?"

"What are you looking at me like that for?"

"Like what?"

He appeared far too innocent, and Rose frowned, not believing the pose for an instant. "Like I'm a performing bear in a circus and you just taught me a new trick." He threw his head back and laughed as he held the door open for her. Rose frowned as she passed by him and entered the building. She didn't think it was funny.

"Miss Gilhooley, you're priceless."

She was, was she? Rose didn't know what to think about that, so she only murmured, "Hmmm."

H.L. was still grinning when he led the way into the main chamber of the building. Rose blinked, amazed by the size of the room, the number of paintings hanging on the walls, and the many sculptures set here and there on the floor.

"This is a great exhibit," H.L. said as he, too, paused to take everything in. "You can probably tell that the fair directors got artists from all over the world to contribute their work."

"My goodness." Actually, Rose couldn't tell that, but she believed H.L. when he told her so. If she were an artist, she'd like to have her work exhibited here.

"Look. Over here we have a painting by Michel. He's French. The French are big in the fine arts department."

"Ah." So. Fine arts were paintings, were they? And statues, too, from the looks of this room. "Good Lord!"

"What's the matter?"

"Nothing. Nothing. Really." Rose felt herself blush from the tips of her toes to the part in her hair. Why, she wondered but would never ask aloud, did artists seem to enjoy painting and sculpting ladies with no clothes on? A surreptitious peek around at the other fair attendees who were ogling the art works gave her to understand that most of them weren't shocked or offended by these naked renderings. She wanted to fan herself but didn't dare, for fear H.L. would snicker at her small-town ways. Unwilling to further expose her lack of sophistication, and annoyed with herself for her unintentional gasp of surprise, Rose opted to keep her lips pressed tightly together.

H.L. didn't seem to take much note of her outburst, thank goodness. He said, "And there's a lot of Spanish stuff in here, too, although most of the artwork was done by Americans. This is an American fair, after all."

"Yes." She squinted up at him, perceiving an opportunity to direct the conversation away from her faux pas. "You must have haunted this fair, Mr. May, to be so knowledgeable about everything in it."

He chuckled again, and Rose wished he hadn't. She scolded herself for giving him the opportunity to chuckle, in fact, because every time he did it, hot shivers chased themselves up and down her skin, and her heart did funny things in her chest. This was undoubtedly a terribly improper reaction to H.L. May on her part, and one Annie would be horrified to be told about.

Reminding herself to keep Annie's advice about men in mind at all times, no matter what her bullheaded heart did behind her back, Rose snapped, "Well? Did you get to see the exhibits before the fair opened? I mean, was that part of your newspaper job or something?"

"Actually, no. However, I do have a pamphlet the fair directors published before the Exposition opened. It tells about everything that's being exhibited here. This is the largest World's Fair ever put on. It's colossal."

Rose presumed that meant big. She didn't ask, but mentally jotted *colossal* down in her internal notebook, along with *obsolete*. If she and H.L. visited a comfort station today, she'd write them both down in the real notebook she'd thought to stick in her handbag before she set out on today's excursion.

"Look over here, Miss Gilhooley. You'll probably find this interesting. This artist, H. Buck-Brown, is famous worldwide these days. Do any of these scenes look familiar to you?" He gestured at a large plaster statue of an Indian and a buffalo and then at a painting of soldiers on the Western plains.

They sure did look familiar, although Rose was impressed by the overall neatness of Mr. Buck-Brown's renditions of Western life as she'd known it in Kansas. Not to mention the beauty of the scenes he depicted. Rose didn't remember anything beautiful about her Kansas home. If one were to judge by Mr. Buck-Brown's notions of life on the frontier, one could be forgiven for concluding that the West was a virtual paradise. "Um, I don't recall the prairie being that pretty."

He gave her another one of his velvety chuckles. Rose held her breath. "That's because it's old hat to you."

"Old hat?" Instantly, her attention was jerked from the thrill of his voice to a new, and hitherto unknown to her, figure of speech.

"That means it's because you lived there and were used to it. It was all new and fascinating to Buck-Brown when he traveled out west. And he probably went with the express purpose of creating works of art, too. I think artists tend to infuse romance into reality and make things look better than they really are sometimes."

Even though there were some words in H.L.'s explanation with which Rose wasn't familiar, she understood what he was saying. She felt slightly encouraged. "Yes. I see what you mean."

By the time Rose and H.L. toured the Fine Arts building and the Liberal Arts building, Rose was beginning to sort out the different definitions of the arts in her head. Fine Arts were paintings, drawings, sculptures, and so forth. Liberal Arts included the writing of books and poetry and the study of history and language.

Did music fit in there somewhere? She didn't believe she could correctly assume, simply because Mr. Sousa and his band were playing on the bandstand outside the arts buildings, that music was a liberal art. And where did mathematics enter into all this? Or was math a science? Fiddlesticks.

The educational process could be a mighty discouraging one sometimes, she mused sourly as H.L. and she walked back to the Wild West encampment. There was still plenty of daylight left, and Rose didn't really need to rest up for her show tonight, but she'd started to feel as if she were drowning in information. She needed to relax a bit before her head, which had been crammed as full as it could be with new experiences and understandings, either exploded or sprang a leak.

They'd almost come to the Indian encampment when Rose realized from the unusual activity therein that something was amiss. She stopped in her tracks. "Oh, my."

"What's the matter?" H.L. went on the alert instantly. He'd become accustomed to Rose's moods, he guessed, because he understood at once that something was wrong.

"I don't know."

He was annoyed when she took off at a trot, leaving him to run after her or not as he chose. Damn it, the way he saw it, she was his responsibility until he got her safely back to her tent. Obviously, she had other ideas on the matter. He caught up with her in a couple of seconds.

"Hey! Wait up, there. Where are you going?"

"Something's wrong!" She didn't slow down.

"That's no answer," he growled. *"What's* wrong?"

"How should I know?"

She sounded irked, and her annoyance sparked his own. "If something's wrong, shouldn't you figure out what it is before you dash straight into it?"

Slinging him a black look, she snapped back, "Oh, for heaven's sake. If you're frightened, you don't have to come along."

This, naturally, only riled him more. "Damn it, Miss Gilhooley, slow down!"

"No!"

H.L. spotted Little Elk at approximately the same instant Rose did. The two of them cried out in a duet, "Little Elk!"

The Sioux, looking very worried and thereby negating H.L.'s lifelong assumption that Indians didn't visually express emotions, hurried up to them. "Wind Dancer. Mr. May. I'm glad you're here. You know Chicago."

H.L. couldn't deny it. "True. Why do you need someone who knows Chicago?"

"Bear in Winter is gone."

Rose stopped running, gasped, slammed a hand over her heart, and stared at the Sioux, aghast. "Gone? What do you mean, Bear in Winter is gone?"

Little Elk gave his version of a shrug. Holding his open hands out, palms up, he repeated, "Bear in Winter is gone."

"Where'd he go?" H.L. was only assuming this Bear person was a *he*. For all he knew, these two might be talking about a woman, or even a real bear.

"Nobody knows."

Obviously puzzled, Rose said, "You mean, he left the encampment? On purpose? Why'd he do that?"

"No." Little Elk shook his head. "He didn't walk away. Somebody take him."

"Somebody *take*—er, *took*—him?" Rose's voice went shrill with her horror. "Good God, Little Elk! Who took him?"

"Nobody know. It was a man with black hair on his lip and a leg made of wood."

"But why?" Rose asked. "Did Bear *want* to go with him?"

"No. Bear, he cried out, but no one understand that he's in trouble until he's already gone."

"But someone saw him go?"

"Two white men. They didn't speak about it until we asked them if they seen Bear in Winter."

Little Elk spat on the ground, giving H.L. a pretty good idea of the Sioux's opinion of white men. Given the opinion most white men harbored about the Sioux, H.L. didn't begrudge the Elk this turnabout.

"Oh, dear." Rose reeled abruptly to face H.L., her cheeks gone ashen with worry. "Mr. May, you have to do something."

"I have to do something? What can *I* do?"

"For heaven's sake, Bear in Winter has been kidnapped!"

"Yeah. By a wooden-legged man with a black moustache, it would seem. But I'm still not sure what you expect me to do about it."

Rose was getting mad. H.L. recognized the symptoms. Her cheeks went from ashy pale to bright red and she snarled, "You can lead us to the police, for one thing! Does this Exposition have a police station? As Little Elk said already, you know Chicago and we don't."

He guessed she had a point. "There's the Columbian Guard," he said uncertainly. He didn't add that he doubted the gentlemen of the Guard would be awfully interested in the kidnapping of an Indian boy. It wasn't sportsmanlike, and it wasn't nice, but it was the truth.

"Well, then, take us to the Columbian Guard!" Rose demanded. "Somebody has to *do* something!"

Why not? Since he couldn't think of a decent answer to that one, H.L. said, "Come with me. We'll find one of these famous guards. Who knows? He might even want to help us." Still, H.L. had his doubts.

"If he doesn't *want* to help us, he'd better do it anyway," Rose announced with remarkable ferocity, given her size and relative delicacy of appearance.

Little Elk remained silent while they searched for one of the uniform-clad guards hired specifically to keep order at the Columbian Exposition. They did a good job of it, too, for the most part, although H.L. would be much surprised if their expertise extended as far as finding lost or kidnapped children. Especially Indian children. He really didn't want to cast aspersions on his fellow Chicagoans, but he had a notion nobody was going to care a whole lot about this little lost boy. Except, of course, his tribe. And Rose, God bless her.

Speaking of which . . . "Say, how old is this kid, anyhow?"

"Ten, I think." Rose turned to Little Elk, who nodded. "Yes, he's ten."

"That's not very old." Lordy, H.L. hoped whoever'd captured the little boy wasn't a complete lunatic.

Although the *Globe* never published the most sordid of the crimes committed in the wonderful city of Chicago, H.L. knew more than he wanted to about most of them. Child prostitution was far from unheard of, and white slavers took boys as well as girls. Human perversions ran to all types.

The thought made H.L. feel sick at his stomach. He discovered within himself a fervent hope that they could find the little boy before something awful happened to him. He found himself walking faster and faster, until he realized Rose was panting at his side. He slowed down. "Sorry. Didn't mean to race."

"No, that's perfectly all right," she gasped. "Finding Bear is more important than my breath."

"It won't do him any good if you faint," H.L. pointed out, somewhat irked by her sharp tone.

"I won't faint! For heaven's sake, Mr. May, I'm accustomed to much heavier exercise than this on a nightly basis."

"Yeah, but when you ride your horse, you aren't wearing a corset."

She turned brick red and shut up, although she did cast him a look that might have withered him had he been a less hardy specimen of manhood. He was totally charmed, although he knew better than to say so. She'd probably sock him. After sliding a quick glance at Little Elk, H.L. decided he'd probably help her do it.

"Is that one of the guards?" Rose said suddenly.

Glancing in the direction she pointed, H.L. released a breath of relief. "Yes. Better let me do the talking." He was surprised, but gratified, when neither of his companions voiced an argument.

The member of the Columbian Guard they approached appeared very dignified. H.L. hoped his sobriety of demeanor didn't mask an empty head, but he didn't allow himself to hope very hard.

...

TEN

"I expect the boy's just run off to see the fair, don't you?"

Rose stared wide-eyed at the Columbian Guard, whose broad, placid face reflected the same complacency she'd heard in his voice.

Before H.L., who had tendered the initial explanation of Bear in Winter's disappearance, could respond, Rose blew up. "No, we do *not* expect the boy's just run off to see the fair! He's been kidnapped, and *I* expect *you* to do something about it!"

The guard, who was at least a foot taller and a yard wider than Rose, allowed annoyance to dilute some of his complacency. "Now, little lady, there's no need to carry on."

"There's no—" Rose could scarcely believe her ears. She was so irate, her words clotted up and froze in her throat.

"Take it easy, Miss Gilhooley," H.L. May advised.

Feeling betrayed, Rose turned on him. "How *dare* you tell me to take it easy! Bear has been *kidnapped!*" H.L. tried to pat her shoulder, but she swatted his hand away.

"Listen, Miss Gilhooley, I'm on your side, remember?" H.L. hooked a thumb at the guard. "This guy's the one who doesn't give a rap what happened to the kid."

The round-faced guard, who had by this time lost the last vestige of his complacency, frowned at H.L. "Now see here, young man, that's not true."

"It is so!" Rose whirled around and wagged a finger in his face. She had to reach to do it, but she wasn't about to let this matter drop. "A child's life is at stake here, mister, and you're treating it as if it were a mere nothing!"

"Miss Gilhooley."

Rose could tell H.L. was speaking to her through gritted teeth, and she resented it like fire. "Don't you 'Miss Gilhooley' me, Mr. May! This matter is too important to be treated lightly, and this man"—she poked the guard in his chubby chest—"obviously doesn't want to treat it at all!"

The guard took a startled step backward. "My good woman—"

Again Rose verbally cut him off at the knees. "Don't you *dare* speak to me in that scornful voice!"

"Scornful? But—" The guard stopped speaking when Rose didn't.

"You'd better do something about this right this minute, or you'll face dire consequences. I'll see to it!" She had no idea what those dire consequences would be, or how she'd ever be able to deliver them, but she was too angry to consider such trivia at the moment.

"Miss Gilhooley," H.L. tried again, "give the man a minute to think, all right?"

"He doesn't need to think!" Rose bellowed. "He needs to *act!* Immediately! Instantly! That boy's life is at risk!"

Rose had forgotten all about Little Elk, although he was still there. She jumped when he lightly tapped her shoulder.

"What?" When she jerked around to look at him, she was flabbergasted to see a small half-smile on his leathery, oak-colored face. She had to suck in air before she could speak without shouting. "Yes, Little Elk?"

"Let the man talk," Little Elk advised in his grumbly voice.

"Good idea, Little Elk."

Rose would have liked to slap the grin from H.L. May's face. Instead, she turned back to the guard. "All right, then, talk."

"Ahem." The guard appeared flustered.

Rose sneered, imagining this throat-clearing nonsense was merely a prelude for the spouting of more inanities. She managed to keep quiet, but it was a struggle.

"My duties are to provide protection to fair-goers, ma'am," the guard said stiffly, as if he'd rather not be speaking to her at all but perceived no alternative.

"You didn't do a very good job of protecting Bear in Winter, did you?" she snapped viciously.

H.L. muttered, "Aw, cripes."

Little Elk touched her shoulder again. Rose, feeling stifled and miserable, shut her mouth.

"The Columbian Guardsmen can't be everywhere at once, miss," the guard went on defensively. "I'm right sorry about the lad, but I can't leave my post to go gallivanting all over Chicago to find him if he's run off to see the sights."

"He hasn't run off to see the sights!" Rose screeched, unable to contain her rage. "He was kidnapped!"

"Rose," H.L. said, speaking more sharply than she'd ever heard him.

He'd also used her first name, which shocked her so much that her mind went blank and all of her words flew away. She wondered if that had been his intention, the rat.

"Let me talk to this poor man, please," H.L. went on, speaking into the silence occasioned by Rose's state of shock. "We might get farther if we don't accuse him of shirking his duty."

The tightness around H.L.'s eyes belied the silkiness of his voice. Rose, still flustered, noted his dour expression and took heart. Maybe he really was concerned enough to help find Bear.

"True, true." The guard tugged at his fancy uniform jacket and patted his badge. Obviously, he was proud as punch of his status at the Exposition. Rose would like to shove the badge down his throat.

"So, I understand you can't leave the Exposition to search for a lost boy," H.L. said before anyone else could speak.

"But we need to know where the nearest police station is. Is it the one on Fiftieth Street, or is there one on the Navy Pier?"

The guard cleared his throat and concentrated on H.L. Rose got the impression he was happy to be dealing with a sane man instead of a crazy woman, and she'd have kicked him if she thought it would do any good.

"The Fiftieth Street Station is the closest. I advise you to go there, as long as you're certain the lad's nowhere on the Exposition grounds. It's a vast place, you know. Have you looked around the fairgrounds?"

"Oh, for heaven's sake." Rose couldn't even remember the last time she'd been this disgusted. "You've got a band of Sioux Indians here, you idiot! Don't you think they've scoured the Exposition grounds long before this? They're the best trackers in the world!"

The guard, unable to avoid further communication with her, gave her a good, hot scowl before speaking. "Madam, I have no doubt your Indian friends know how to find rabbits and so forth in their native forest. This is a big city they're in now, and life's not so simple."

"Native forest?" Rose goggled at him, astounded that anyone could be so stupid. *"Rabbits!"* Turning precipitately, she grabbed H.L.'s coat sleeve. "Come on, Mr. May. This man is worse than useless. He's a fuddle-headed moron! We must get to a real police station before whoever kidnapped Bear does something awful to him."

She'd have liked to shove H.L.'s sigh down his throat, along with another Columbian Guardsman's badge. However, since he turned to accompany her, only flipping the Guardsman a farewell salute as he did so, she decided to wait until later to scream at him.

"I've never seen such a stupid man," she muttered as the three of them hurried back to the Wild West.

"He's only doing his job," H.L. told her mildly.

"Fiddlesticks!"

"Will police find Bear?"

Rose and H.L. both glanced at Little Elk. His voice was impassive, but Rose knew how worried he was. She shot H.L. a quick look before she said, "I hope so, Little Elk. If the police won't help us, you and I can find him, I'm sure."

"What?"

H.L. didn't stop and stare at her because they were in too great a hurry, but the effect was the same. The look on his face was one of clear incredulity. Again, Rose wished she could do him bodily harm. She growled, "You heard me."

"That's ridiculous," he said flatly.

"It is not. If the police won't help us find that boy, we'll just have to do it on our own."

"And how, pray, do you intend to do that? Whoever grabbed him probably didn't take him to a mansion on the lake, you know. Do you think the two of you can wander around Chicago's worst neighborhoods without courting danger? That's the most asinine thing I've ever heard of."

If Rose had the time, she'd have grabbed him by his fancy city-suit lapels and shaken him until his brains rattled. As it was, she spoke through clenched teeth and with monumental fury. "You may or may not be aware that Little Elk and I grew up tracking game, Mr. May. You may also not be aware that tracking game and tracking people amounts to the same thing. I wouldn't be at all surprised if he and I were a whole lot better at it than any of your fancy-dancy Chicago policemen."

"Damnation, Miss Gilhooley! You don't know what you're talking about! There are street gangs in Chicago that would as soon slit your throat as look at you! And that's after they'd . . . assaulted you. All of them!"

To her storehouse of fury, Rose piled on a whole bunch of embarrassment. *Assault* assuredly meant *rape* in this case. "How dare you speak to me like that," she said in a voice shaking with indignation. "I can use a gun, a knife, and a whip better than a thousand of your Chicago ruffians. Just let any of them try to hurt me, is all I say!"

"Jesus." H.L. had his hands stuffed into his pockets. Rose got the feeling he'd like to strangle her with them and was keeping them in his pockets as a defense against committing a felonious attack. "If you hare out after this kid, you can bet your sweet life I'm going with you."

She sniffed. "Don't be absurd. You'd only slow us down and get in the way."

"I would not!"

"Would too."

"This is ridiculous."

He might have thought it ridiculous, but at least he finally shut up about it. Rose would have taken some pride in having silenced him except that she was so worried about Bear.

Bear in Winter was Little Elk's nephew, the son of his sister, and was a delightful child. He was one of Colonel Cody's favorites, and was a whiz at riding and shooting. If life had been fair to the Sioux and they'd been allowed to maintain their nomadic life on the plains and in the hills, he'd probably have made a spectacular warrior.

The free life was over for the Sioux, though. While Rose held certain opinions about savagery, which she'd garnered from her childhood on the Kansas frontier, she honestly didn't hold any grudges against any of the Sioux she knew personally. She'd learned in the cradle that life was a difficult proposition—and that's even if the culture into which you were born still thrived. She couldn't imagine what it must be like for Little Elk and his kin, who were no longer allowed to carry on as they'd done for generations, but were obliged to make do in a new and, to them, alien world. She honored Colonel Cody for giving so many of them employment, and for paying them the same wages he paid his white employees.

Some of the old Sioux skills, however, could be used in this instance, no matter what H.L. May thought. The big city was as different from the Kansas plains as night from day, but the principles of tracking were the same no matter where they were practiced. Not only that, but Rose had been taught by experts. If she had to kill a few of Chicago's ruffians while she was at it, so be it. Bear in Winter was worth it.

The three of them practically ran through the throngs of fair visitors on their way back to the Wild West. Rose was perspiring buckets in her pretty sailor suit. She was also beginning to feel distinct pangs of hunger, since she hadn't eaten anything but a sausage on a bun for lunch, and it was getting close to supper time. She reviled herself for thinking of her stomach at a time like this, but her stomach didn't care.

When they finally found the colonel, who was regaling a band of city slickers with tales of his scouting days with the army, H.L. did the talking, much to Rose's initial dismay. She discovered, however, that he could be a concise and thorough communicator when he chose to be. Probably his journalistic training.

The colonel expressed sincere dismay. "Hell, Little Elk, this is terrible. You want me to get a scouting party together and go look for the boy?"

Rose cast H.L. a superior smirk. He rolled his eyes. She wanted to kick him.

"I think we'd better report the kidnapping to the police first." H.L. sounded totally rational and cool, and Rose chalked it up to his cold heart. "After we find out if they plan to do any searching, we can better decide if there's anything the Wild West people should do."

The colonel nodded. "Good idea, son. Rosie, can you and Little Elk tell the police what happened?"

"Yes. Little Elk has a description of the man who took him."

Little Elk nodded in agreement, and the colonel said, "Very well, then. Good luck to you. Will you be back for your performance, Rosie? If you need somebody to fill in . . ."

Rose was shocked. "Oh, no, colonel! I'll be back. You don't ever have to worry about that."

He smiled beatifically at her. "You're a good little girl, Rosie. Don't know what I'd do without you."

Rose, H.L., and Little Elk rode a trolley car to the police station. Rose had never been on a trolley car before, and if the circumstances hadn't been so frightening, she might have enjoyed herself. Her insides cramped with worry about Bear in Winter, though, and she wanted to get out of the trolley and push it sometimes, it seemed so slow.

"For crying out loud, Miss Gilhooley, it's a lot faster than walking would have been," H.L. grumped at her when she expressed impatience.

"I know. I know. It's only that I'm so worried."

Little Elk, who sat on his seat in the trolley with his arms folded over his chest, and looking so much like an Indian from the wild Western frontier that the rest of the passengers actually seemed scared of him, grunted. "This thing goes fast, Wind Dancer. Calm yourself. You waste spirit with worry."

Rose glared at her oldest friend, feeling abused, misunderstood, and completely out of sorts. Was she the only one here who was worried about Bear in Winter?

It didn't help that she was still as hungry as a bear, and still had on her corset. She wasn't accustomed to wearing a corset, and she didn't feel any inclination to *get* accustomed to wearing one, either. Corsets cut off one's breath, made walking quickly difficult, and in general interfered with a woman's life. She had a grumpy suspicion that men had created them as a means of keeping women in what men recognized as their "place."

Blast all men. She hated them all with equal ferocity at the moment. "I can't help it if I'm worried about Bear, Little

Elk," she said resentfully. "He's just a little boy, and he doesn't know anything about life in a big city."

H.L. snorted. "And you do?"

She rounded on him indignantly. "I know more than Bear in Winter does. Don't forget that I've been to London and Paris—"

"And Rome. I know. But at the moment you're in Chicago, and it would probably behoove you to relax and let me take care of this problem. I know the police, and you don't. What's more, they'll be more apt to pay attention to you if you don't screech at them like you did to that poor Columbian Guard."

"I did not screech at the man." Rose crossed her own arms over her breasts and sat back with a huff. "Besides, he was a moron."

H.L. had the gall to laugh. "He might not have been the brightest candle in the box, but you gave him a touchy problem, don't forget. The most those Columbian Guards usually have to contend with is folks who've had to much beer in the German Village."

"Hmph." Rose didn't think anything about this situation was funny. "This is much more serious than that."

"Right. Which is why we're on our way to the police station right now. Don't worry, Miss Gilhooley, we'll get the boy back if it's possible to do so."

Rose had her doubts about that, if she were forced to depend on H.L. May to do it. She gave him another "Hmph," and passed the remainder of her trip staring at the city of Chicago as they traveled past it.

She was impressed, although she'd eat a bumblebee before she said so to H.L. But Chicago seemed like a nice place and pretty in spots, although Rose was more comfortable in her native wide-open spaces than in cities. Still, if one had to live in a big city, Chicago might not be a bad one in which to do it, especially if one had a good income and could buy a nice place by the lake. She liked Chicago better than New York City.

Her mother would probably love it here. Although Mrs. Gilhooley had come from a family of modest circumstances, she'd begun life in Massachusetts, in the city of Greenfield. She used to regale her children with stories about life back home, and Rose had been able to discern the longing in her voice, even though her mother had always tried to hide it.

Every time Rose thought about her poor mother, she ached inside. It made her feel better to know that the money she sent home helped ease her mother's burdens. It would *really* ease her burdens if Rose could take her away from Deadwood and find her a home somewhere in a more civilized environment.

Her mother never complained, and she loved her family more than anything else in the world, but her life had been so hard. Rose longed to make her remaining years comfortable. She had a long-standing dream of moving her entire family somewhere other than Deadwood; somewhere they could all be together, but where there were more opportunities for a decent life than there were in Deadwood.

Until she'd met the colonel, her dream had been an idle one; a mere daydream. The longer she worked with the Wild West, the less impossible it seemed. She'd never spoken aloud of her ambitions, not even to Annie, because Rose was sure people would think she was only being fanciful. Whoever heard of a woman taking care of her whole family?

Actually, *lots* of women took care of their families, but not the way Rose wanted to do it. Rose wanted more than poverty and worry, which is what the normal female-headed family experienced daily. Rose wanted peace and, if not luxury, at least comfort for her loved ones. Before they died. It was all well and good to rest in eternal peace, but Rose wanted to provide her family with a bit of peace long before then.

Fiddlesticks. She wanted everything. *Why not ask for the sun and stars while you're at it, Rose Gilhooley?*

Still and all, maybe her secret dream wasn't *too* far out of line. After all, even if she couldn't move her whole family to Chicago or somewhere else as nice as this, at least she could eventually allow them to live a better life in Kansas, and that was the main thing. With her brother's help, it should be possible, too. Good old Freddie worked hard to help their mother, just as Rose did. The two smallest girls were too young to help a whole lot, but Rose had no doubt that they'd pull their weight one of these days.

She heaved a huge sigh.

"What's the matter? Worried about Bear in Winter?"

She turned to glance at H.L., whose voice had actually sounded kind. She didn't believe it and squinted at him narrowly, trying to figure out what his game was. "Of course."

"We'll all do our best for him, Miss Gilhooley," he said, still sounding sympathetic and kindhearted.

What was going on here? Why was he being nice to her? Did he know something she didn't about the fate of kidnapped children in Chicago? Was there some kind of ring that captured loose children and did awful things to them? Obviously, *something* was amiss, if H.L. May had taken to being kind.

She didn't get the chance to ask him what terrible fate he envisioned for Bear, because the trolley pulled to a stop in front of the police station, and H.L. announced, "Here we are. Little Elk, will you help Miss Gilhooley down? I want to ask the driver something."

Rose watched him narrowly as she climbed down from the trolley. He only spent a couple of seconds with the driver, and then he climbed down, too, and joined them on the sidewalk. "I asked him if he'd seen anyone with a wooden leg and a black mustache with a little Indian boy."

"Oh." Rose hadn't even thought about asking the trolley driver if he'd seen Bear. But it was a logical question, since the trolley ran right past the Exposition, and anyone might have caught it. "And had he?"

"No."

"Oh." There was no reason for her to feel so disappointed. After all, it would have been a miracle if finding the child were to be as easy as all that.

"So," H.L. went on, "let's see what the Chicago police have to tell us."

"Right."

The three of them walked up the steps to the police station, and H.L. opened the door for Rose and Little Elk to enter before him. Rose looked around with interest. There was a counter over to one side, with a blue-uniformed man with a big walrus mustache behind it. He looked bored until he glanced up and saw H.L. Then he frowned. Rose wasn't sure, but she thought this might be an unlucky-for-Bear reaction on the policeman's part.

"What are you doing here, newshound? Didn't know we'd had any riots or police beatings lately."

The man had a thick Irish accent. For some reason, Rose wasn't surprised, perhaps because she'd heard somewhere that lots of Irishmen became policemen when they moved to the United States. Why that should be she didn't know, but she wondered if Freddie might like to take up a career in law enforcement if he moved with their mother to Chicago. She warned herself not to get sidetracked. Bear in Winter was her first priority at the moment.

"No such luck, Morty," H.L. said with a hard laugh.

Rose looked at him, surprised by this change in his tone of voice. He sounded sharp and sarcastic with this police person. Only moments earlier, he'd sounded kind and concerned. She hated people who changed their personalities this way. They were so disconcerting. One never knew how to react to them.

H.L. went on, "We're here to report a kidnapping and to get help in finding the kidnapped party."

"A kidnapping? Where'd you get a kid to nap?" The policeman barked out a laugh as if he appreciated his own wit.

"Not mine." H.L. tilted his head in Little Elk's direction. "His."

Morty, who hadn't paid any attention to Rose or Little Elk once he spotted H.L., glanced at the two of them now. His gaze came to rest on the Sioux. His eyes nearly popped from their sockets. "Jaysus, May, that there looks like a real wild Indian."

Rose bridled instantly, but H.L. put a restraining hand on her arm. When she tried to shake him off, he dug his fingers into her flesh and it was all she could do not to cry out in pain. She was so incensed, she wanted to stamp on H.L.'s foot, but finally understood that he was giving her a signal to let him handle the policeman.

She sniffed and almost told him what she thought of him, but another look at the policeman made her hold her tongue. He didn't appear, at first glance, to be a particularly cooperative individual. Maybe H.L., who evidently knew him, ought at least to handle the first part of this interview.

"This is Little Elk. He's a member of Buffalo Bill's Wild West, Morty. It's one of his kinfolk who was kidnapped, a ten-year-old boy named Bear in Winter."

"Why the devil do them Injuns give their kids such stupid names, is what I want to know." Morty cast a superior sneer at Little Elk. Rose clamped her teeth together and told herself not to shriek at the obnoxious man.

"It's nothing to you why they do anything, Morty. What matters today is that this little boy has been kidnapped."

Rose was astonished by how well H.L. May was keeping his temper, even under what seemed to her like extreme provocation. If it had been she dealing with Morty, she'd have thrown something at him by this time.

"And how do you know that, Mr. Newshound? Did you see the snatch happen?"

"No, but there were two witnesses."

"Ah, and did you bring 'em with you? Is that what these two are?" He jerked a rude nod in the direction of Rose and Little Elk. Rose decided this horrid man wasn't worth her anger. He wasn't worth anything at all.

"No. This is Miss Rose Gilhooley, who performs with the Wild West as Wind Dancer."

Rose gave the policeman a cold nod. He returned her nod with a knowing grin. He also adjusted the bow tie at his throat, as if he were trying to tidy up especially for her. *Good God,* thought Rose. *He's acting just like a thug from Deadwood.* She'd believed big-city policemen to be above such things. Which just went to show one more time how little she knew about life. What a depressing thought.

"We can, however, give you a description of the kidnapper," H.L. said loudly, presumably in an attempt to deflect Morty's attention away from Rose and back to the problem.

His fun over, Morty heaved an aggrieved sigh and drew a piece of paper toward himself. He dipped a pen in a pot of ink and held the pen over the paper. "All right, then, give me the story."

H.L. glanced over at Little Elk. The Sioux stepped forward and gave a brief description of the man who had been seen carrying Bear in Winter away.

"And you say the lad was struggling?" Morty asked, sounding as if he didn't care.

"Yes."

Rose could tell by the expression on her friend's face that Little Elk had come to the conclusion they'd be getting little or no help from this quarter. She'd heard of anarchists who threw bombs into public buildings, but she'd never felt in any way akin to them until this minute. If all the policemen in Chicago were like Morty, she'd like to throw a bomb at the lot of them.

"So," H.L. said after Morty had been scratching away with his pen for a minute or two, "do you aim to help us find the boy or not?"

Morty didn't answer for another minute or two. Rose wanted to pick up the log book at his elbow and thump him on the head with it. When he looked up from his report at last, Morty couldn't have looked less interested in their problem if he'd tried. "I'll file this report," he told them in a neutral tone.

"I see." H.L. gave Morty a long, hard look. "That means you're not going to try to find the boy, doesn't it, Morty?"

"Now see here, newshound. There are rules and regulations that govern these things. Time limits and so forth. We can't go rushing around looking for every little kid who runs away from home. It ain't worth the effort."

"I see." H.L.'s face hardened further. Rose was glad he'd never looked at her like that. "In other words, you neither care about this lost child, nor are you going to do shit to try to find him. Right, Morty?"

"Now, now, May. That's no way to talk in front of a lady." He gave Rose a leer. "If she *is* a lady, that is."

"Why, you—"

H.L. grabbed Rose before she could climb up the barrier and hit Morty with her handbag. "Don't waste your energy, Miss Gilhooley. This specimen isn't worth it. It's our misfortune that the man at the desk had to be this slug. The unfortunate truth is that Chicago's police force has far too many worthless bums just like him."

"Says you," Morty sneered.

"Say I, indeed," H.L. countered. He turned and spoke to Rose and Little Elk. "All right, we've done our duty as citizens. Since the police force won't help us, I guess we're going to have to find the boy ourselves."

"Do you mean to tell me we've wasted over an hour on a useless mission?" Rose's indignation couldn't have climbed much higher or she'd have had an attack of something.

"It's not entirely wasted," H.L. told her in a comforting tone. "For one thing, you never know. We might have found one of the few decent men on the police force on duty today.

And this way, when we do find Bear all by ourselves, I'll have an even better story to report to the good people of Chicago. They deserve to know exactly how their tax dollars are being used." He grinned. "I think I feel a call for reform in the air."

He took Rose's arm in one hand and Little Elk's in the other, and started herding them toward the door. Behind them, Rose heard a chair being shoved back and the squeak of springs as Morty rose to his feet.

"Say, now!" the policeman shouted after them. "Here! Come back here, May! You can't go printing things like that in the *Globe!*"

H.L. turned his head to cast one last glance at the irate policeman. When Rose did likewise, she saw fury and fear battling on his ugly red face.

"Watch me." H.L. opened the door and almost threw Rose outside.

"Mr. May!" she shouted at him. "I wanted to give that horrid man a piece of my mind!"

"I know you did, Miss Gilhooley," he said calmly. "That's why I shoved you outdoors. Besides, my exit line was better. We'd just be wasting our time if we stayed there while you ripped up at him."

Rose was so mad, she could only splutter incoherently. H.L. May laughed as he propelled her along the busy Chicago street.

ELEVEN

The funniest thing about the series of articles H.L. was writing for the *Globe,* he mused as he escorted the spluttering Rose Gilhooley and the stoical Little Elk down 50th Street, was that he couldn't remember ever having so much fun in his life. Yeah, yeah, he knew a kid's life was in danger—real danger. And he knew that he'd just irritated a member of Chicago's police force, which might result in consequences of one sort or another. And he knew the Columbian Exposition would end one of these days, and then where would he be?

But all that stuff didn't matter. H.L. May was having the time of his life, and it was all because of the company he'd started keeping: Rose Ellen Gilhooley from Deadwood, Kansas, and Little Elk, the Sioux Indian from God knew where.

"You're a scoundrel, H.L. May!" Rose shouted at him, oblivious to the stares of passers-by on the street. She'd realize folks were staring one of these minutes, and then she'd be embarrassed. H.L. was beginning to know her like a book.

"Probably," he said, in hopes that the word would rile her further and keep her spitting at him for another little while.

Little Elk, as always, walked along in silence, not even paying attention to Rose's diatribe. At one point, H.L. thought he caught a wink from his dark-skinned companion, but he wasn't sure, and he thought it unlikely. Did Indians wink at people? H.L. had never heard of such a thing.

"What do you mean, 'probably'?" Rose tried to stop walking, plant her fists on her hips, and shout at him from a stable position, but H.L. kept her moving.

"I guess I'm probably a scoundrel is all," he said complacently. "You obviously think I am, and I'd never doubt your opinion on such a matter, Miss Gilhooley."

"You're impossible!"

"That, too."

"That man back there ought to be fired! He ought to be called before his superiors and given a dressing down! He ought to be horsewhipped!"

Again, H.L. said, "Probably."

"But, what do you do instead of making him do his duty? You tell him you're going to write about this incident in your newspaper, and then leave!" She became incoherent for a second or two, only making sputtering noises and snorts, before she said, "I can't stand it."

"Take it easy, Miss Gilhooley. If you're through scolding me, we have to discuss how we're going to go about finding the boy."

She stopped walking this time, in spite of H.L.'s efforts to keep her moving. "What? What did you say? You mean you're going to help us find him?"

"Well, of course I am! What did you think I was going to do? Let whoever took him keep him?"

Her pretty mouth opened and closed a couple of times. H.L. watched it with longing. He really, really wanted to kiss this woman. To taste her. He wagered with himself that she'd taste sweet, rather than spicy, because she was more sweet than not, although he didn't bet too much. He gave himself slightly better than fifty-fifty odds, hedging a bit.

When Rose found her wits again, not very many words arrived with them. H.L. grinned to himself, although he deemed it prudent not to grin at Rose just yet. Because Little

Elk was looking at him impassively, and because the Indian *might* have winked at him, H.L. gave him a wink to even things up. Little Elk nodded once, which H.L. took as a signal that things were going about as he'd expected them to. H.L. was surprised when the Sioux opened his mouth to drop a tidbit into the conversation.

"I'm hungry."

Sensible man, this Sioux. H.L. said, "Me, too. Let's grab something to eat while we plot strategies."

"Plot strategies?" Rose blinked at both of them.

"Sure," H.L. said. "Here's a place. I eat here a lot, and if we take a booth in the back, we won't be overheard."

"But—but—"

Evidently, Rose hadn't recovered yet, because she didn't continue with that thought, if it was one. H.L. steered her through the doors of the restaurant and greeted the waiter by name. "Give us the best table in the house, Waldo, as long as it's a booth in the back."

"Sure, sure, H.L. I've got one just right for you."

"You're a good fellow, Waldo, even if you are a wop."

"Better'n a mick," countered Waldo with a laugh. He led them to their booth and H.L. politely gestured for Rose to enter first.

"Why don't I order for us and save time?" H.L. asked his companions.

Little Elk grunted his agreement. Rose looked startled, opened her mouth, closed it, and said nothing. H.L. took this as compliance, and told Waldo, "Bring us three plates of Joe's special spaghetti and meatballs. And lemonade for the lady. I'll have a beer." He glanced at Little Elk, recalling the stories he'd read about how alcohol was devastating Indian tribes, and wishing he'd remembered them sooner. "Little Elk?"

"Lemonade," Little Elk said in a clear voice.

H.L. breathed easier. He had no idea whether or not the stories were true, but he didn't especially want to find out when they had real work to do in order to save a child from whatever kind of hell his captors intended for him.

"Be back in a minute," Waldo said as he sauntered off.

Rose sniffed the air tentatively. If she was like H.L. and most of the rest of humanity, the aroma in Joe's Italian Ristorante would appeal to her. Joe fixed good food, and lots of it. A Sicilian by birth, Joe had come to Chicago from New York City with his family a couple of years after they'd arrived and been processed through the immigration station at the Battery. As far as H.L. was concerned, if he ever had enough money to hire a chef, the man was going to be an Italian. He loved Italian food. He sighed deeply and smiled at Rose. "Smells good in here, doesn't it?"

She nodded. The wind seemed to have gone out of her sails. H.L. hoped so, because he didn't relish another half-hour or so of being raked over the coals.

"What's a wop?"

The question startled H.L., who'd expected her to begin going over business as soon as she recovered from being startled. "Beg pardon?"

"What's a wop?" she repeated. "And what's a mick."

"Ah. A wop is an Italian. A mick is an Irishman."

"You're Irish?"

He held his hand over the table and rocked it in an equivocating gesture. "Sort of. I guess my ancestors were from the Emerald Isle. I'm from Missouri, myself."

"Missouri? Really?" Her blue eyes opened so wide, H.L. had the feeling he might just drown in them if he wasn't careful.

"Right. Why does that surprise you?"

"I—don't know. I guess I just thought of you as being from Chicago, if you know what I mean."

"I think so. I belong here. Ergo, you thought I was *of* here. Right?"

She looked at him for several seconds as if she had no

Introducing Ballad,
A LINE OF HISTORICAL ROMANCES

As a lover of historical romance, you'll adore Ballad Romances. Written by today's most popular romance authors, every book in the Ballad line is not only an individual story, but part of a two to six book series as well. You can look forward to 4 new titles each month – each taking place at a different time and place in history.

But don't take our word for how wonderful these stories are! Accept our introductory shipment of 4 Ballad Romance novels – a $23.96 value – ABSOLUTELY FREE – and see for yourself!

Once you've experienced your first 4 Ballad Romances, we're sure you'll want to continue receiving these wonderful historical romance novels each month – without ever having to leave your home – using our convenient and inexpensive home subscription service. Here's what you get for joining:

- *4 BRAND NEW Ballad Romances delivered to your door each month*
- *30% off the cover price with your home subscription.*
- *A FREE monthly newsletter filled with author interviews, book previews, special offers, and more!*
- *No risk or obligation…you're free to cancel whenever you wish… no questions asked.*

To start your membership, simply complete and return the card provided. You'll receive your Introductory Shipment of 4 FREE Ballad Romances. Then, each month, as long as your account is in good standing, you will receive the 4 newest Ballad Romances. Each shipment will be yours to examine for 10 days. If you decide to keep the books, you'll pay the preferred home subscriber's price – a savings of 30% off the cover price! (plus shipping & handling) If you want us to stop sending books, just say the word…it's that simple.

Passion-
Adventure-
Excitement-
Romance-
Ballad!

A $23.96 value – **FREE** No obligation to buy anything – ever.
4 FREE BOOKS are waiting for you! Just mail in the certificate below!

If the certificate is
missing below, write to:

**Ballad Romances,
c/o Zebra Home
Subscription Service Inc.**

**P.O. Box 5214,
Clifton, New Jersey
07015-5214**

**OR call TOLL FREE
1-800-770-1963**

BOOK CERTIFICATE

Yes! Please send me 4 Ballad Romances ABSOLUTELY FREE! After my
introductory shipment, I will receive 4 new Ballad Romances each month to
preview FREE for 10 days (as long as my account is in good standing). If I decide
to keep the books, I will pay the money-saving preferred publisher's price plus
shipping and handling. That's 30% off the cover price. I may return the shipment
within 10 days and owe nothing, and I may cancel my subscription at any time. The
4 FREE books will be mine to keep in any case.

Name_____

Address_____ Apt._____

City_____ State_____ Zip_____

Telephone (____)_____

Signature_____

(If under 18, parent or guardian must sign)

All orders subject to approval by Zebra Home Subscription Service.
Terms and prices subject to change. Offer valid only in the U.S.

DN022A

Passion...

Adventure...

Excitement...

Romance...

BALLAD ROMANCES
Zebra Home Subscription Service, Inc.
P.O. Box 5214
Clifton NJ 07015-5214

PLACE
STAMP
HERE

idea on God's green earth what he was talking about. H.L. was slightly puzzled at her reaction.

Eventually, she muttered, "I guess so."

"Antipasto, my friends!"

H.L.'s concentration had been on Rose to the exclusion of everything else, so Waldo's enthusiastic announcement surprised him. It also pleased him. He loved the tasty, meaty, olive-y salad. "Thank you, Waldo. I didn't even think of ordering antipasto."

Waldo bowed as he set the platter before them and began serving the antipasto into individual dishes. "Your companions look as though they need a hearty meal, H.L. Besides"—here he shot a wink and another bow at Rose, who stiffened—"it's not often we get so famous a guest at Joe's."

H.L. beamed at him. "Ah, so you recognize Miss Gilhooley?"

"Yes, indeed." Waldo even managed to look smitten, and H.L. gave him points for dramatic skill. "I saw you Saturday night, Miss Gilhooley, and I must say I was never more impressed. You looked like an angel riding that white horse around the arena."

H.L. noticed that Rose was not so used to people praising her that she couldn't blush. She blushed now, her cheeks turning as rosy as the tomatoes in the salad Waldo set before her with a flourish. He guessed she'd forgiven him the wink.

"Thank you. You're very kind."

"Kind? You're an angel. A princess on horseback. A vision. A—"

"Right. And more," H.L. interrupted, laughing. "You may not realize it, Waldo, but you have another famous person dining at Joe's this afternoon." He indicated his other companion. "Allow me to introduce you to Little Elk, the great Sioux warrior."

Both Little Elk and Rose stared at him, but H.L. didn't care. If they didn't know good publicity when it presented itself, he did. The expression on Waldo's face proved it, in fact.

"By golly," Waldo said in a hushed voice. "By golly. May I shake your hand, Mr. Elk?"

Little Elk, probably used to the strange and unusual ways of the white man by this time, looked vaguely resigned as he held out a rough brown hand for Waldo to shake.

"It's an honor, Mr. Elk," Waldo said, sounding reverent. "It's a true honor. Even though most people don't realize it, I read recently that it's been proven that the Indian is one of the lost tribes of Israel. It's a real honor to meet you."

H.L. feared for a moment that Waldo might actually fall on his knees and do some sort of obeisance before Little Elk, but he didn't. After another moment or two of sharing outrageous complements between Rose and Little Elk, Waldo took himself off.

"Don't mind Waldo," H.L. advised. "He's Italian."

"He seems very nice," Rose said uncertainly. "What does his being Italian have to do with anything? There were Italian soldiers at the fort near Deadwood. They seemed just like everyone else to me."

"Ah, but we each bring our culture with us into this life, Miss Gilhooley. And Waldo's Italian."

"Oh."

When he glanced at her, she was frowning and fiddling with her fork. He wondered what he'd said to bring on that frown, but didn't pursue it. He wanted to introduce his new friends to Joe's fabulous food. "Dig in," he prompted. "This is an Italian salad, and I think it's great."

He didn't have to ask twice. Apparently, Rose was as hungry as he and Little Elk were. She cut a delicate bite of lettuce and tomato, stabbed a bite of salami, and put the combination into her mouth. H.L. watched avidly as she chewed. Her eyes narrowed, then went wide, and she appeared somewhat puzzled.

"Well?" he asked when he couldn't stand the suspense any longer. "What do you think?"

She put her fork on her plate and looked at him. "I've never tasted anything like it. It's . . . different. Tasty. Um, we don't generally mix meat into our salads back home in Deadwood."

He chuckled as he tackled his own salad. "Don't reckon you do. Most folks don't, although I suppose you could look at it sort of like a cold stew." Turning to Little Elk, he asked, "What do you think?"

Little Elk seemed to be pushing his tomatoes and lettuce aside so that he could get at the salami and cheese on the plate. "Good," he said.

A man of few words, H.L. thought with amusement. Not like H.L. May, who made his living with the little suckers. After taking another big bite of his own antipasto, he said, "I like the dressing. It's tangy."

"Tangy," Rose repeated after swallowing another bite from her own plate. "Yes. That's a good word for it."

He didn't know why she appeared so unsure of herself. Hell, all she had to do at the moment was eat, and he knew she was hungry, because he'd heard her stomach growl. "You don't have to eat the whole thing if you don't want it," he said, feeling as though he'd sold out a friend to the enemy—how anybody could not like Joe's food was incomprehensible to him. "Waldo will be bringing our spaghetti pretty soon."

Rose swallowed another small bite of lettuce and tomato and cleared her throat. "Um, when we were in Rome, I think we ate spaghetti, but I'm not sure. The food was different there. But good," she added in a rush, as though she didn't want him to think she was complaining. "I, ah, have enjoyed eating different foods in different places."

"Yeah? That's good, because Chicago's got 'em all. We have Spaniards and Poles and Italians and Greeks and Irish and Bohemians and Bulgarians and Germans and just about every country in the world represented somewhere in Chicago."

"My goodness."

As H.L. had predicted, Waldo arrived bearing plates heaped with spaghetti and meatballs in a tomato sauce that smelled enticingly of garlic and other exotic spices. They were exotic to Rose, at any rate, who as a child had become used to eating beans and meat boiled together—when her mother could get meat. They'd often eaten eggs from the chickens out back, cooked with onions, and served with a side dish of some sort of greens.

After Rose had started shooting game, the family's diet improved considerably. Still, except for her mother's garden, in which she grew onions, cabbages, kale, beets, carrots, and a few other crops that could withstand the harsh Kansas weather, Rose's diet had been rather circumscribed until she'd joined the Wild West.

Even these days, she approached new foods with a certain degree of caution. Not that she didn't enjoy new experiences, but she worried about her country stomach. She wasn't precisely sure how much it could take of new and unusual foods.

After watching how H.L. tackled the long strings of spaghetti by twirling them with his fork balanced on his spoon, Rose attempted to do the same. All but one spaghetti strand slipped from her fork's tines, but she figured that was all to the good. It would be easier to swallow a little bit of something she hated than a huge fork-full. As soon as the savory mixture touched her tongue, she decided she needed more spaghetti practice.

"Oh, my! This is wonderful!"

"Good," Little Elk added. He didn't bother with H.L.'s fancy maneuvering with fork and spoon, but rather cut his spaghetti into manageable bites and spooned them into his mouth, foregoing his fork altogether. Rose deemed such an expedient solution to a messy problem quite clever on his part.

"Glad you like it."

H.L. could probably have been forgiven his smug expression, had Rose been in the forgiving mood. She was still irked with him, however, and didn't appreciate it. Nevertheless, she felt as though she were starving to death, and the food was delicious, and so she ate as quickly as she could, given the overall slipperiness of the fodder provided.

"After we eat, we need to plot strategy," H.L. said between mouthfuls.

"Indeed," said Rose, likewise engaged.

Little Elk grunted. One thing you could say for the Sioux, thought Rose indulgently, was that they didn't get sidetracked. If the problem was finding lost boys, they concentrated exclusively on that. If the matter at hand was supper, they concentrated on that. She had to admit that life was probably much simpler and more easily handled if one tackled one problem at a time. At the moment, she decided she'd be happy to concentrate on supper, except that Bear in Winter's young face kept obtruding itself into her mind's eye.

They finished their meal before too long, however, so Rose could turn her entire attention on the Bear problem. She smiled at Waldo as he picked up her plate, but the smile faded when she saw his black frown. She cast a quick glance at H.L., but his face didn't offer her any clues as to why the waiter should be displeased.

"You didn't like your supper?" Waldo asked Rose peremptorily.

"What?" She goggled for only a moment. "Oh, no! I mean, yes! I loved it. It was delicious. I've never eaten anything so tasty." Waldo eyed her narrowly, then looked down at her plate. Rose guessed she had left a lot of her spaghetti uneaten, but she'd stuffed herself until she feared she'd pop if she took one more tiny bite.

"You didn't eat much." Waldo sounded accusatory.

"Give the girl a break, Waldo," H.L. said, laughing. "She's as big as a minute. Such a small package can't hold a whole lot."

Rose bridled. If she weren't trying to soothe the waiter's temper, she'd have said something scathing to H.L. May, who was probably the rudest, most impossible, rash, and impertinent man she'd ever met in her life. Instead, she forced a smile and said, "That's it, all right. I ate as much as I could. I wish I could hold more, but I just can't."

Waldo said, "Hmmm," as if he didn't believe either of them, but he didn't look quite as upset as he had a moment earlier. Without questioning Rose further, he took the plates away.

As soon as he was out of earshot, Rose turned to H.L. "How dare you speak of me as if I were a . . . a . . . a . . ." Fiddlesticks. She didn't know a word for it.

"Commodity?" H.L. supplied, grinning at her.

"Yes." Actually, she didn't know. What was a commodity? Blast! She was going to buy herself a dictionary and read the blamed thing from A to Z as soon as they found Bear.

"I only did it to soothe Waldo's sensibilities, Miss Gilhooley. He takes it hard when people don't finish their meals."

"Good heavens, that plate held enough food to serve six people," she grumbled, feeling out of sorts—but no longer hungry.

"I eat what you don't next time," Little Elk offered.

Rose glanced at him, feeling guilty. She ought to have remembered how much Little Elk and the rest of her Sioux friends loved food. She figured it was because their generations-old way of life had been so severely compromised by white settlers in recent years that they ate whatever they could find whenever they could find it, and as much of it as possible. "I'm sorry, Little Elk. I'll remember next time."

He nodded and smiled, and she knew he didn't fault her for forgetting her manners this time.

"All right, folks, let's plan some kind of strategy in finding the lost boy."

"He's not lost," Rose reminded H.L. with feeling. "He was kidnapped."

"Right."

She resented it when he rolled his eyes, as if he found her insistence on exact wording unnecessary and annoying.

"All right. We can't dash off in all directions, because we won't get anywhere, so I have a suggestion."

Rose frowned at him. "I don't believe you have any tracking skills at all, Mr. May. How could you? You live in the city. I believe Little Elk and I would be better equipped to find the boy." He looked peeved. Rose didn't care. Bear in Winter was worth fighting for, darn it.

"Listen, Miss Gilhooley. I know you consider yourself akin to some kind of great white hunter, but before you barge off and get yourself into trouble, don't you think we ought to figure out where the lad might be?"

She sniffed, but had to admit he was right. "How do you propose to do that?"

"I have lots of contacts on the streets of Chicago, Miss Gilhooley. Many of them aren't the sorts of people you ought to be involved with. However, I'll bet I can find out where a kidnapped boy might be taken. We're fortunate in that the fellow who took him is a distinctive one. There can't be too many wooden-legged, black mustachioed men nabbing children around Chicago."

"I hope not," Rose said glumly.

"Me, too. So, since it's almost time for your performance, I recommend you and Little Elk go back to the Wild West. I'll get in touch with my informants during your show, and meet you afterwards. Tomorrow's Sunday, so you don't need to worry about getting back at any particular time."

Rose wasn't sure about this. "You mean, you think we ought to look for him at night?"

"That's probably the best time. Oddly enough, it's when most criminal activity takes place."

Rose ignored his smirk. "Bear in Winter was snatched in broad daylight," she pointed out.

"Right, but wherever they took him, I expect they'll be transporting him to wherever they want him after dark. Darkness is the criminal's friend."

"I see." Her flesh crawled, actually. But Little Elk would be there to protect her, she reminded herself, and felt better at once.

"Also, you won't like this," H.L. continued, "but I think you'd better not come with us, Little Elk."

"What?" Rose regretted the shrillness of her voice, but she'd been too startled by this pronouncement to modify her tone.

"No," said Little Elk, sounding much less hysterical than Rose, but exceptionally firm.

H.L. shook his head. "I know you want to come along, Little Elk, but you'd attract too much attention. If you and Miss Gilhooley discuss the matter before we set out, if she's as good at tracking as she says she is—"

"I am," Rose cried, stung.

"I'm sure." H.L. sounded as if he were attempting to placate a squawking child, and Rose wanted to thump him. "Anyway, if—I mean since she's good at tracking, if I can get any firm leads, she and I can follow up on them without attracting the amount of attention an Indian might. Don't you see?"

Little Elk's frown was about as black a one as Rose had ever seen on his generally impassive face. "No," he repeated stubbornly.

Scowling furiously, Rose considered H.L.'s statement. She absolutely *hated* to admit he might be right about anything, but she feared in this case he just might be. "Wait a minute, Little Elk. He might have a point." Because she didn't want H.L. to think she approved of him, no matter how right he might be every once in awhile, she shot him a scowl. He grinned back. This time she did thump him, with the toe of her foot against his shin.

"Ow! Damn it, why'd you do that?"

Rose was pleased when his smirk vanished. She batted her eyes at him. "Oh, I'm so sorry, Mr. May. I'm sure I didn't mean to kick you."

He leaned over to rub his shin. "I'll just bet."

She ignored him and spoke to Little Elk. "But in this case, I'm afraid he may have noticed something important that we didn't think about. Especially if, as he suspects, we're going to have to go into some rough neighborhoods where people might decide it would be fun to taunt an Indian."

She knew Little Elk was familiar with people like that, since there were scads of them around Deadwood. The only places where people didn't seem to take delight in being cruel to Little Elk and his kin were in lands far, far away from any lingering memories of the Little Big Horn and other of the so-called Indian troubles.

As much as she deplored the slaughter of General Custer and the Seventh, she imagined she'd fight anybody who tried to take her home away from her, too. She could, therefore, sort of understand the Sioux point of view on the matter. Besides, Rose knew Sitting Bull, who sometimes traveled with Buffalo Bill, and she liked him as much as she liked Little Elk.

The "Indian troubles" were too complicated for her, so she left them to others to figure out. All she knew was that she didn't want her friend to get hurt by any Chicago bullies.

"I don't like it," Little Elk said stubbornly.

She sighed. "I know, and I don't blame you. But it might be best for Bear. If whoever took him sees you, he'll probably know immediately that you've come to take him back, and that would give him an advantage. He won't think anything at all about seeing Mr. May and me wandering about."

"He will, too, dammit," H.L. interrupted. He sounded crabby. "You're going to have to wear something that doesn't make you look like a sweet little girl from the sticks, Miss Gilhooley, if you aim to pass unnoticed in some of the neighborhoods we're probably going to be searching."

Rose stared at him. "I beg your pardon?"

"If my suspicions are correct, somebody's grabbed the boy for a specific purpose. Otherwise, he'd have taken a kid who was easier to snag. I mean, who'd go to the World's Fair, with people all around, not to mention the Columbian Guards patrolling—"

"Ha!" Rose interjected, having formed a rather unfavorable opinion of the one representative of the Columbian Guard she'd met thus far.

"Right, I know you don't think they're worth their uniforms, but they do create a presence, and people intent on kidnapping children don't generally like to do it where they can be overseen by the authorities."

"That didn't stop Bear's kidnapper."

"Exactly. That's why I think there's more to this than a simple kidnapping."

"Simple!" Rose was offended and didn't bother to hide the fact.

H.L. patted the air in a soothing gesture. "I know, I know. Kidnapping's a rotten pastime. But you see, there are various business enterprises that buy children."

"*Buy* children! Good gracious, are you serious?" She was both scandalized and horrified. Not only that, but she was unable to comprehend the type of villainy that must be behind such enterprises, if they existed. She doubted it. Squinting hard at H.L., she said, "I don't believe you."

He shrugged, as if he'd expected nothing else of her. "Fine, don't believe me. Nevertheless, I'm still going to question my resources while you perform." He broke off suddenly and gazed at her fixedly. "Say, Miss Gilhooley, are you in any shape to perform tonight? Are you too worried to concentrate? If you fall off that horse when it's going a hundred miles an hour, you'd probably kill yourself."

Rose's exasperation and indignation spiraled. "Thank you *so* much for your concern, Mr. May, but I shall be fine. I am a professional, in case you'd forgotten."

"Oops. Didn't mean to offend you." As usual, he sounded not the least bit contrite. Rose thought about kicking him again but decided against it. He'd only chalk it up to emotionalism, and she didn't want to give him any ammunition.

"I go," said Little Elk, cutting through their fight with ease and determination.

Both H.L. and Rose turned to gaze at the Sioux, who sat like a boulder, his arms crossed over his chest, looking implacable and immovable. Rose sighed and decided to give up sparring with H.L. May. Bear in Winter was in danger, and as much as Rose hated to give Mr. May credit for anything, she feared he might be right about having better luck if Little Elk stayed at the encampment while she and May went hunting.

It took another forty-five minutes to convince the stubborn Little Elk of the wisdom of H.L.'s proposal, and another half hour before Rose conceded that she'd best array herself in trousers for the evening's excursion. As little as she wanted to look like a hick from the plains, H.L.'s vivid descriptions of what might happen to her if the scoundrels in Chicago's worst slums realized she was a woman finally convinced her.

They parted at the Wild West arena about an hour before the show was scheduled to start, and not on the best of terms. H.L. May promised to pick Rose up after the show, and swore he'd be loaded with information. Rose hoped he'd choke on it—after they got Bear in Winter safely back into the arms of his family.

TWELVE

The show was over. The crowd, after swarming Annie and Rose and the Indians and the soldiers and the colonel, had finally left the arena. Rose had stabled Fairy as usual, giving her the treat she always got after a successful performance, and Rose and Annie had trundled off to Rose's tent.

Rose was nervous about the night's impending hunt for Bear in Winter, but she wasn't going to back down. The way she looked at it, the entire Sioux ensemble traveling with the Wild West was depending on her, and she'd sooner shoot herself than let them down.

Before the performance, she'd assembled an outfit to wear during her tracking mission. She'd had a little trouble buttoning the trousers up, not having had much practice in such an endeavor. Now, however, as she stuffed the plaid flannel shirt into the waist of the trousers, she was beginning to feel rather free. "These really are comfortable, Annie. I expect they wouldn't be if they were tighter, but they're plenty loose." She performed a kick with her right leg and then with her left leg. "You can really get around in them."

Annie frowned heavily as she looked Rose up and down. She addressed Rose's comment in a roundabout manner. "I don't like this, Rose. I'm worried about you running around after dark with that man."

Rose was, too, although she wouldn't admit it to Annie. "It's for a good cause, Annie. The police don't want to do anything about getting Bear back, and Mr. May does, and I really don't want to go out there and try to track him by myself."

Aghast, Annie cried, "For heaven's sake, Rose! I wouldn't let you do such a thing. But I do think you ought to take Little Elk with you."

Peering into the mirror and trying to make the best of a costume that, while comfortable, was at best outrageous if not indecent, Rose tugged at the big Stetson hat under which she'd crammed her thick, wavy hair. "No, I hate to say it, but I think Mr. May's right about Little Elk. He'd attract too much attention."

Both women silently observed Rose in the mirror. Rose didn't have to guess at the thoughts in Annie's head: If Rose thought Little Elk might attract attention, what did Rose think *she* was going to attract? Flies? Rose admired Annie's restraint in not asking the question.

Because she was so uneasy about the night's endeavor, she answered Annie's unspoken question anyway. "I doubt that anyone will look at me twice. In the dark, I'll look like Mr. May's kid brother or something."

Annie sniffed. "Or something, is right."

"I think I look very much like a little boy," Rose said, feeling defensive.

Her bosom didn't want to squash flat, blast it. Rose had tied a bandage around it, but she still looked too bulky on top. Squinting at her reflection, she turned to get a side view and sighed heavily. "I'll wear that vest and jacket. That should take care of any . . . bulges." This was so embarrassing.

"I want you to take my Colt, Rose. I know you have your Smith and Wesson and your derringer and a knife, and I know you're good with them all, but I want to be sure you have a weapon *I* can trust."

"I'm going to be better armed than the United States Army," Rose mumbled, feeling silly.

"Better to be safe than sorry," Annie reminded her. "And

I don't trust that man to know what to do with weapons. I've heard the myth is that the pen is mightier than the sword, but I doubt that he'd get very far in fending off villains with an ink pen, however sharp it might be."

Rose chuckled. "You're right about that." She sat on her bed and drew on some heavy socks. "I hope to goodness we don't have to facedown any villains."

"Face it, Rose, it's not generally the cream of society that goes around kidnapping little boys." Annie sounded exasperated.

Rose didn't blame her. "I know, I know. We'll find him. I hope Mr. May was able to dig up some clues from his friends about where to start this evening. It will take him less time than it would me, since I don't know anybody in Chicago." Except H.L. May, who was rapidly becoming a very large presence in her life. Rose wouldn't admit that, either.

"His friends." Annie huffed as she picked up the vest Rose aimed to wear and held it out for her to slip into. "If his friends are the sorts who know where to find kidnappers, I question his value as a proper companion for you, my dear."

Getting up from the bed to take advantage of Annie's help, Rose muttered, "He says the people he was going to question help him with stories, Annie. I don't think they're his friends, exactly." She stuck her hands through the armholes of the vest and turned around to face Annie as she buttoned it up. "I expect a good reporter needs to know all sorts of people in all walks of life. They're probably a gold mine of information when he's doing research on criminal activities."

Rose didn't understand why she felt compelled to defend H.L. May against Annie's suspicions. He aggravated Rose nearly to death whenever she saw him, yet she hated it when Annie disparaged his morals and character. Rose didn't like to think of H.L. May as a vile seducer of young ladies— Rose, for example—as Annie obviously did.

"I'm sure." Annie huffed.

"It's true, Annie," Rose said, indignant on H.L. May's behalf. "He's a reporter. If he wants to be a good one, he needs to be able to talk to all types of people."

"Whatever you say, dear. Just watch yourself. I don't trust that man."

"I know you don't." Rose felt defeated, and she hadn't even started out on the night's most important job yet.

A muffled knocking sound came from outside the tent flap, and both women turned to look at the flap before exchanging glances with each other. Annie heaved a huge sigh. Rose hurried over to lift the flap. Her heart did a flying leap when she beheld H.L. May, garbed in dark clothing and carrying his ever-present notebook. She assumed it had been the notebook upon which he'd thumped in order to create the knock she and Annie had heard.

"Mr. May," she said, unaccountably flustered to see him. There was no reason for her to be agitated, since she'd known for hours that he was coming to get her tonight. "Please come in. I only have to get my jacket and put on my boots."

"Sure thing." H.L. had to stoop as he ducked under the flap and entered her tent. He spotted Annie and grinned at her. "Good evening, Mrs. Butler."

"How do you do?" Annie inquired stiffly.

H.L.'s eyes opened wide, and Rose could tell he understood precisely what Annie thought of him. Apparently, Annie's opinion amused him, because his grin broadened. "I'm quite well, thanks. You?"

"Fine, thank you."

"Good." Still smiling, H.L. allowed his gaze to stray over the insides of Rose's tent. He seemed interested in her possessions, which increased Rose's level of discomfort. He walked to her bed and lifted a picture from the night table. "Is this a picture of your folks, Miss Gilhooley?"

"Yes." She carried that picture with her everywhere she

went. It had gone to New York City, London, Paris, Rome, and all points beyond and between for six years now.

"Handsome couple. It's clear where you get your good looks."

What? Rose didn't screech the question, but she felt like it. Rather, she concentrated on picking up her boots and moving to a chair, where she sat to put them on.

H.L. placed the picture back on the night table and continued to peruse the insides of the tent. He walked to the trunk, where Rose had laid out commendations and awards she'd been given by various individuals, including heads of state, kings, princes, Indian chiefs, and even an African tribal chieftain. "This is quite an impressive array."

"You ought to see Annie's collection, if you think those are impressive." She shoved her feet into her boots, shrugged into her jacket, stood up, and stamped to get her feet to slide down properly into her boots. "I'm ready."

He turned and surveyed her. "You look swell." He laughed.

"Mr. May."

That was Annie, and her voice held a sharp edge. Both H.L. and Rose glanced at her. She was standing straight and had her hands folded at her waist. This, Rose recognized, was Annie's stern look, and it presaged a lecture. Rose hoped it wouldn't be a long, uncomfortable one.

"Yes, ma'am?" H.L. finally removed his hat, which he ought to have done as soon as he'd entered the tent. Rose wondered if this lapse in manners betokened a lack of respect for rules on his part, or a lack of respect for Rose Gilhooley. She had her suspicions.

"I don't know that I approve of this harebrained scheme to find Bear in Winter."

H.L. opened his mouth and took a breath, but Annie cut him off curtly before he could speak.

"Yes, I understand that the Chicago police aren't willing to bestir themselves on Bear's behalf. And I know Rose is probably the best white tracker in the area at the moment. I am still concerned, and I expect you to take care of her. I presume you can be trusted?"

She gave him a flinty stare. H.L.'s grin faded. He looked both surprised and a little hurt. Rose wondered if he was pretending the hurt part.

"Yes, ma'am," he said. "I aim to do everything in my power to see that Miss Gilhooley remains safe tonight, believe me."

"Hmmm."

Rose decided that, though it was nice that Annie was concerned, she was really old enough to take care of herself. "I'll be fine," she told Annie. "I've got enough arms on and about my person to fend off a hundred H.L. Mays, should they try to do anything." She was aiming to be amusing, but H.L. didn't look as if he found her comment funny.

"Say," he cried irritably. "I'm not the bad guy here. I'm out to find that kid. I'm the hero of this piece, remember?"

"Hmmm," Annie said again. "I guess we'll have to wait and see about that."

"Jeez," H.L. muttered, "you're pretty hard on a guy who's never done anything to you, if you don't mind my saying so, Mrs. Butler."

"I am concerned about my friend," Annie said flatly. "And I don't trust you."

"Annie!" Rose felt her cheeks bloom with embarrassment. "I'm sure Mr. May has never done anything to earn your mistrust."

"Not yet. We'll see," she said. "Here's the Colt. I want you to be sure to keep it at your back, as I taught you."

"Right." Opting to drop the untrustworthiness subject as too volatile to prolong, Rose was glad to take the gun. She checked it over to make sure it was loaded properly, even though she'd seen Annie load it. It was a habit, and a good one, and Rose knew Annie wouldn't object. She stuffed it carefully into the waistband of her men's trousers, at her back so that it couldn't be seen, and fiddled with it until she'd assured herself that it was both comfortable and reachable.

"Gracious, Miss Gilhooley, do you really think you'll need that?"

"Yes," said Rose.

"Yes," said Annie.

H.L. was startled by the firm duet of female voices. "Well, all right, but I sure hope you won't."

"So do I," said Rose.

"And I," said Annie.

"And I also have my derringer up my sleeve, my Smith and Wesson—that one's in my jacket pocket—and my Bowie knife."

"Lord on High. You believe in being prepared, don't you?"

"Yes," Rose told him. "I do." She gave her hat a pat and said again, "I'm ready."

"All righty. Let's be off." As Rose left the tent, H.L. turned back one last time to speak to Annie. "Try not to worry, Mrs. Butler. I'll take care of her. I promise I won't let anything happen to her."

Annie gave him a doubtful nod. "I sincerely hope so."

H.L. was honestly offended by the lack of trust demonstrated by Annie Oakley. "What does that woman think I plan to do to you, anyway?" he grumbled. "Hell, we're out to perform a rescue here."

"Annie and I both grew up in difficult circumstances, Mr. May. Annie is my best friend, and she wants me to be safe."

Rose lifted her chin in a gesture of defiance H.L. had become accustomed to long since. It tickled him every time she did it. Feeling more cheerful, he said, "Well, all right, but I think she was pretty mean to me." He eyed her from his superior height. "You're looking mighty spiffy tonight,

Miss Gilhooley." He laughed. "Nobody will ever know you're the famous Wind Dancer of Buffalo Bill's Wild West."

"Good. I don't want them to." She frowned up at him. "So, did you learn anything?"

No joking around allowed, he guessed. Vaguely disappointed, because he'd really like to get to know her better, H.L. sighed and said, "Yes. I talked to Milk-eye Pete, who hangs around at the dock. When I gave him the description of the nabber, he recognized him. He says he's part of a band of folks who occasionally take children and sell them to various people for different enterprises."

"Then you weren't joking? People honestly and truly sell children? Good Lord! Who'd do such a terrible thing? I mean, I know somebody took Bear, but—but—surely, they can't do such things on a regular basis. Can they?"

She appeared honestly horrified. H.L. found the situation moderately horrifying, too, although it wasn't news to him as it was to Rose. People could be more bestial than the beasts themselves sometimes. "Yes, they can, and no, I wasn't joking. Unfortunately, it's the truth. I guess children are a hot commodity in some quarters."

"Good gracious. It's hard to believe such things actually happen regularly."

"I agree. Milk-eye Pete doesn't like it much, either. He's not exactly an admirable character, but he doesn't like what he calls baby snatchers."

She stopped looking horrified and frowned as if some other thought had struck her. "Um, did you say Milk-eye Pete?"

"Yeah. He's got a bum eye."

"Ew." She made a face. "That's not a very nice thing to call him."

"I guess it's not. Folks on the edges of society tend to call people by descriptive terms."

"It's still not very nice."

H.L. experienced the strangest urge to pick her up and take her home with him. She was so damned adorable, he could hardly stand it. She had such spirit and gumption, and she was so innocent and so wise, all at the same time, that he just . . . well, he didn't know, but he really liked being with her.

Since he couldn't act on his urge or become a kidnapper himself, he stuck his hands into his pockets and said, "No, it's not."

They walked without talking for a few minutes. H.L. had hired a cab and a driver to take them to the dock this evening, since it was impractical to walk through some of the neighborhoods he expected to be frequenting, especially at night. After a minute or two, he pointed up the street. "That's our cab there. I decided to hire a hack so we wouldn't have to walk everywhere."

"Oh." Rose sounded doubtful.

H.L. wondered if she suspected him of motives that weren't pure. Shaking his head, he guessed he shouldn't be surprised if she did. If she and Annie Oakley were the best of friends, as she'd said they were—and he believed her—then Rose probably considered him the lowest of the low. H.L. resented that.

He'd worked hard to cultivate his devil-may-care newspaperman persona, but he wasn't a bad man, and he didn't like being taken for one. Hell, he was a good guy. If he cursed sometimes, and took a drink with the boys occasionally, and hung out with ruffians from time to time for the sake of a story, that didn't mean he wasn't an honorable fellow underneath it all. He'd never force a woman to surrender to his lusts, for instance.

The notion of Rose surrendering to his lusts on her own and without being forced was such an appealing one, he discovered he was getting hard. With a stern internal lecture, he commanded himself to keep his mind on the business at hand.

And what he wouldn't like to do with his hands on Rose's body. Oh, my, he could envision the process even as they walked together. He'd undress her slowly, slowly, making maximum use of his fingers and hands, until she was squirming beneath him and begging him to have his way with her.

"Damn," he growled, furious that his mind had wandered down such a frustrating road. As if little Rose Gilhooley would ever let him touch her.

"What's the matter, Mr. May?"

He glanced at her, scowling, and she seemed taken aback by his bitter expression. Since his own unruly feelings weren't her fault, he made a monumental effort, hauled his mind out of the gutter, and even managed to smile, sort of. "Not a thing, Miss Gilhooley. Just thinking about—things."

"Ah, yes. Bear in Winter." She cast him a worried frown. "If we can get to the general neighborhood where he's being held, I'm sure I'll be able to track him down."

They reached the hack, and H.L. gave the driver a two-fingered salute. The driver nodded back, chucked the cigarette he'd been smoking into the gutter, and said, "Thought you'd forgotten you'd hired me, Mr. May."

H.L. grinned up at him. "No such luck, Chauncy. And you're still getting a bonus for driving us around the dock, too."

"I don't like it down there. Bonus or not, if anybody tries to knife me, I'm outta there."

"Knife you?" Rose stopped in the process of entering the cab and stared up at the driver. Unfortunately, she stopped with her nicely rounded bottom in H.L.'s face. H.L. sighed deeply and decided the fates were against him tonight. "Good heavens, is it really that rough?"

"I'm afraid so," H.L. said. Because he couldn't seem to help himself, he put both hands on Rose's bottom and shoved. "In you go, little brother."

"Mr. May!"

The cabbie squinted down at H.L., who shrugged and clambered into the cab after Rose. He hissed, "Hush up. We don't want anybody, not even the cab driver, to know you're not a boy."

Rose angrily tugged at her vest and jacket. "That's no reason to put your hands on my person!"

Since she'd whispered her reprimand, H.L. didn't bother to shush her again. He muttered, "Sorry," but wasn't. The more he saw of Rose, the more he wanted to see of her. In more ways than one, darn it. He gazed at her chest and wondered how she'd managed to flatten that magnificent bosom of hers. It was a crime, that, and H.L.'s resentment against the man or men who'd snatched Bear in Winter edged up another notch.

The cab jolted into motion and Rose said no more, although she was still fuming; H.L. could clearly distinguish the signs. Because he didn't feel like wasting time arguing with her, he said, "Our first stop is to go to a certain tavern on the dock. It's a low place and full of scummy characters, so stick close to me and don't get into an argument with anybody. If you open your mouth, sure as the devil, someone will realize you're not a boy."

"I can sound like a boy," she said defensively. To prove it, she lowered her voice and added, "See? I sound just like my brother Freddie."

Actually, she did sound like a boy, although H.L. didn't have a clue as to what her brother Freddie sounded like. Nevertheless, he didn't trust her not to allow her moral outrage at the reprehensible treatment of Bear to get the better of her.

"I don't care who you sound like—keep your mouth shut." He adopted a severe expression and leaned toward her. "This is not a farce, Miss Gilhooley. The people we're going to be among tonight probably commit worse crimes than kidnapping when they're paid for it. There's every sort of villain on the dock, from prostitutes to dipsomaniacs to murderers, and I don't want any more trouble than necessary. If you aren't willing to play by my rules in this, I'll take you straight back to the Wild West and go alone."

"You can't do that!" Rose cried, forgetting to whisper. "You're no tracker!"

"No, but I'm a man, and I'm a lot bigger than you are. I don't care how good you are in the wilds of Kansas, I'm more familiar with Chicago's criminal underbelly than you are." He wagged a finger at her, as he'd seen her wag her finger at the policeman. "Admit it, Miss Gilhooley. It's the truth."

She glared at him ferociously for a few moments, then sat back and crossed her arms over her chest—her flat chest. "Oh, very well. But don't expect me not to fight if I have to."

"Never," H.L. said, after not heaving a regretful sigh over her flattened bosom, and giving himself a point of honor for it. "I've come to expect you to fight even when you don't have to."

Her glare got hotter. "And exactly what do you mean by that?"

"Nothing," he said. "Forget it." He turned to look out the window. Since night had fallen and the fog was thick, he didn't see a thing but fuzzy balls of light from the gas lamps. They didn't illuminate anything but haze, and they looked rather like enormous, nebulous fireflies in the dismal darkness.

"Fiddlesticks."

The rest of their trek to the dock was accomplished in silence. When they arrived at their destination, H.L. paid the hackie off, and told Rose they'd find another cab after they'd rescued Bear in Winter. He only hoped they could.

Fog shrouded the peeling buildings and trash-strewn boardwalks. The stench emanating from the lake around the dock blended with the tang of creosote-coated ropes, half-rotten wooden hogsheads, dried fish, cheap tobacco, stale alcohol, and back-alley garbage. Rose tried to hold her breath, but couldn't do it for very long without getting light-headed.

"It smells awful around here," she whispered to H.L., who walked beside her. She sensed that he was on the alert for malefactors.

"Yeah. It'll get worse when we get to the Sailor's Rest. These dockside taverns are disgusting."

Hard to imagine, although Rose braced herself for worse odors ahead. "Am I walking all right?" H.L. had told her not to walk like a woman, and she, taking her cue from him, had commenced swaggering in imitation of his own king-of-the-world manner.

"You're doing fine."

Something in his voice made her glance up, and she saw his white teeth gleaming in a Cheshire-cat grin. Her heart did a brief flippity-flop in her chest before she glanced away again. "Good."

"Remember not to talk unless you absolutely have to."

"Right."

Now that they'd left the cab at the dock area, Rose felt not the slightest inclination to chatter. This place scared her. It was awful. It was even worse than the saloon district of Deadwood, because it was out of the realm of her experience. She felt sort of like she had when she'd visited splendid houses and universities. Only when she'd visited splendid houses and universities in the course of her employment with the Wild West, she hadn't feared someone would leap out at her from beside a stack of barrels or a jumble of fishing nets and try to shoot her, as she did now. The weight of the weapons concealed on her person comforted her. She fingered the Smith and Wesson in her jacket pocket to ease her jitters. She was comfortable with weapons; it was people who frightened her.

"Here it is."

Rose sucked in a breath of foul-tasting air and steeled her nerves. She told herself to get a grip on her apprehension, or she'd be of no use to H.L. May and, ultimately, to Bear in Winter. That thought calmed her slightly. When H.L. opened the door and walked inside, however, it took her a second to understand he hadn't held the door for her because she was supposed to be his brother, not a lady. Bother. She scurried to catch up with him, then caught herself walking like a lady and halted to gather her wits about her.

Taking her courage in both hands, she swaggered into the saloon behind H.L. Instantly, a pall of smoke, denser and even more foul-smelling than the fog outdoors, enveloped her, and she nearly succumbed to a fit of coughing. Her eyes teared up, and she had to blink furiously to keep from crying.

"Sort of thick in here, isn't it?" H.L. said with an understanding twinkle in his eye, not to mention a mastery of understatement that Rose couldn't properly appreciate at the moment.

"Yes," she rasped when she could do so without exploding in hacks and coughs.

"Come on over here. I see a table in a corner."

"Why do we have to sit in here?" Rose wanted to bat the smoke away from her face, but didn't dare for fear the gesture would be remarked upon by the rough company.

And the company was certainly rough. Rose had seen lots of villainous men in her day, but none like these. The rowdies in Deadwood were definitely cut in the Western style. Not these Chicago toughs. She'd never seen the likes of the men in this place. Many of them fitted her notions of sailors perfectly, with empty sleeves pinned to their shoulders, presumably empty eye sockets covered with black patches, and scars to beat the band.

H.L. didn't hold a chair out for her, naturally, since she was supposed to be his brother. He also had her sit against the wall so that his own back was exposed to the rest of the room. Rose appreciated this consideration as she pulled the chair out and sat in it. She scooted closer to the table for security's sake. Not that there seemed to be much of that quality available in this room.

The floor had been sprinkled with sawdust. Glancing at it, Rose stopped herself from wrinkling her nose, but just barely. It didn't look to her as if anyone had swept the floor or spread clean sawdust in at least a century. She didn't even want to guess at what some of the detritus littering it was.

Yanking her attention from the floor and surreptitiously eyeing the unprepossessing flock of seamen seated in the tavern, she muttered, "Why are so many of these men missing limbs and eyes and so forth? Good heavens! That man over there is missing most of his ear!"

"Shhh. Try to speak more softly, please."

Rose would have heaved a sigh, except that to do so she'd have had to take on a cargo of smoke, and she feared she'd suffocate if she did. "Very well," she muttered, peeved. As if anybody could overhear anything she said over the din in this place.

"The sailor's life is a rugged one. Losing an eye is common. I understand that when the wind blows, often the yardarms will swing around and whack men in the eye. Fishermen also have to contend with hooks, nets, spikes, and the like. Whalers with their harpoons are always getting stabbed in the arm and leg and everywhere in between."

"Ugh."

"Not to mention the problems they have with sharks and storms at sea and pirates and the rest of the perils of the deep."

Rose peered at him closely. "Are you teasing me?"

"No!" He appeared honestly piqued. "I'm telling you what I've learned from interviews with sailors. It's a rough life. It's probably every bit as rough as life out on the frontier."

"I don't doubt it, if what you're telling me is true." Rose was finding it less difficult to speak softly since her throat was being scraped raw by the foul air in the tavern.

A buxom barmaid sashayed up to their table. She eyed H.L. with a smirk that Rose could only deem seductive. She felt small and unfeminine and wanted to drive the barmaid away with one of the harpoons H.L. had just told her about. She said nothing.

"What can I bring you, sweetheart?" the barmaid asked H.L. in a voice as smoky as the room.

Rose didn't scowl at her and was proud of herself.

"Beer for the both of us, darling," H.L. said with a wink.

Rose didn't kick him, either, and was doubly proud of herself. The rat. Did he honestly find females like this overstuffed beer-flinger attractive? If he did, Rose wanted nothing more to do with him, and that was that.

Good heavens, whatever was she thinking? What did it matter to *her* what kind of women H.L. May found attractive? She rubbed her eyes and wished she could remove her hat, because the air in the tavern was close as well as smoky, and the sweat was beginning to make her scalp itch.

"This little guy here don't look old enough for beer," the barmaid told H.L. with a wink of her own. "Want I should bring him a sarsparilla?"

His grin back at the woman was every bit as seductive as hers to him had been. Rose could hardly stand to watch, but didn't dare look away. "He's old enough," H.L. said. "So am I."

"I don't doubt that." The barmaid laughed and moved off, swinging her hips as if they were attached to one of those pendulum things Rose had seen in a London museum.

Concluding that she would only show herself in an unfortunate light if she were to comment on what she perceived as the overall sluttishness of the serving wench, Rose held her tongue with difficulty. She wanted to rail at H.L. May about his poor taste in women, even though she knew absolutely nothing about his taste in women, really. After all, perhaps he'd only been putting on a show for the barmaid.

While this conjecture might have been the truth, it didn't affect Rose's overall black mood. She glowered into the smoky room and wished the earth would open up and swallow H.L. May and the slutty barmaid. And if it swallowed the rest of the people in this wretched place along with them, Rose would be just as happy.

"Don't look so cranky. I might just think you're jealous."

Rose lifted her head so fast when she heard H.L.'s outrageous comment, she nearly broke her neck. *"What?"*

H.L. squeezed his eyes shut as the room went silent. Rose realized she'd shrieked, and was embarrassed. Understanding that she'd just made a horrible mistake, and that if she were discovered to be a woman in disguise, the consequences might be dire, she blustered in a voice she hoped like the devil sounded masculine. "I don't take that kind of talk from anybody. Not even my brother!" She glared daggers at H.L. and was pleased that her voice had come out ragged and hoarse. Small wonder, given the air in this joint.

H.L. muttered, "Sorry, little brother. I was only teasing."

"Hmph."

The barmaid slapped two mugs of beer on the table between them. Perceiving another opportunity to fool her audience, Rose lifted her mug, still glaring blackly at H.L., and took a gulp. She very nearly spat it back out again. Fortunately, she managed to swallow the awful brew, and the folks who'd turned to stare at her after her outcry lost interest and went back to their own business.

Oh, but the stuff tasted vile. It was all she could do not to throw up after that one swallow. She tried to hide the reflexive gagging that overtook her by wiping her mouth with the back of her hand.

Even the thick smoke couldn't hide the sparkle in H.L.'s eyes as he watched her. "Good recovery," he said. "But I don't think you'd better try that again. You look like you're about to be sick all over the table."

"I am," Rose choked out. "How can you drink this stuff?"

"Drink it? I don't drink it. It's for show. I'd advise you not to drink any more of it, either. They only serve the lousiest liquor in this place. Here. Suck on this." He reached into his vest pocket and withdrew a paper-wrapped peppermint. He palmed it and reached across the table toward Rose.

After shooting a quick glance around the room and finding nobody watching, Rose took the peppermint, unwrapped it, and slammed it into her mouth. She could scarcely do so fast enough to suit her. "Thank you."

"You're welcome. Just pretend to drink from now on, all right?"

Unable to speak, she nodded and surreptitiously wiped her eyes, which were watering from her effort not to up-chuck the unholy beer she'd swallowed.

They sat in the tavern for forty-five minutes, pretending to drink beer and carrying on a desultory conversation. Rose, miserably uncomfortable, felt as though she were choking to death and about to melt into a puddle of sweat. Worse, she was beginning to think this had been a futile effort and would come to naught, and then she'd have to live with the knowledge that she'd wasted an entire evening, nearly killing herself in the process and not even rescuing Bear at the end of it, which might have made the discomfort worth it.

She was feeling grotesquely unhappy and was about to call it a night and force H.L. to leave with her, when all of a sudden he seemed to stiffen slightly. He relaxed almost at once, then spoke out of the corner of his mouth.

"Don't turn to look, but I think our quarry just came into the room through the front door."

Being casual about it even though her heart had almost

jumped out of her chest at H.L.'s words, Rose glanced in the direction he'd indicated. She stifled a cry of amazement.

There he was! He was huge, too: a sunburned, barrel-chested ape of a man with a black mustache, grizzled dark hair, a beer belly, and a wooden leg. He swaggered up to the bar and knocked on it with a fist the size and color of a roasted turkey. She heard him bellow "Rye!" at the bartender.

"He's with the man Milk-eye Pete told me to watch for, too," H.L. said under his breath. Rose heard the quiver of excitement in his voice.

"I see," she said. "What should we do now?"

"Wait," he told her. "Wait until they leave. Then we'll have to follow them." He gave her a wink. "Are your tracking skills well honed?"

"They certainly are."

She meant it, too. She wasn't going to allow those two evil-looking scoundrels to get away with snatching one of *her* friends.

THIRTEEN

H.L. hoped Rose could stay awake long enough to follow the kidnappers if they ever left the tavern. She looked as if she was about to fall face-first onto the dirty table, overcome either by fumes or sleepiness.

He hardly blamed her. She probably wasn't used to staying up until all hours of the morning, like he was. Plus, he imagined there wasn't much oxygen in the tavern, since it was filled with as much smoke as it could hold. This was definitely an unsavory place, and he thought Rose was a real trooper to have stood it so well for so long.

"You doing all right?" he asked, leaning over the table and whispering.

The room had thinned of company in the couple of hours they'd been there, waiting for Black Mustache to leave the place. Unfortunately, old Blackie seemed determined to play cards and drink for the rest of his life.

"I think I'm going to die of suffocation if we don't get out of here soon," she muttered. "But I guess I'll last a while longer."

"Good." He reached over and gave her hand, which was resting on the table next to her now-flat beer—which probably didn't hurt it any—a pat. "You're a real sport, Rose Gilhooley."

"Thanks." She didn't sound overwhelmingly grateful for his praise.

H.L. chuckled. He really liked Rose Ellen Gilhooley. She

was a trump. Better than a trump, really, when he put together what he'd learned about her as they'd sat here pretending to drink.

He'd used his time to good purpose, persuading Rose to consent to be interviewed in order to pass the time. After taking out his notebook and jotting a few things in it, he'd surveyed the room and decided nobody was paying any untoward attention to his scribbling, from which he surmised that literacy wasn't an entirely unknown state in this vicinity. He kept tabs on people's reactions to his activity for almost an hour, but finally gave it up when he realized nobody cared what anybody else did in this place, as long as it didn't involve them. After that, he'd openly taken notes as he and Rose talked.

H.L. had been surprised at some of the things Rose had told him about herself, and not surprised about others. His overall impression was of a gallant, big-hearted, big-spirited girl who'd had to shoulder responsibilities far greater than most young people of either gender were expected to do, at far too early an age. He admired her. A lot.

She'd been embarrassed when he'd asked her about her education, or lack thereof. He'd tried hard to let her know he didn't think less of her for not being well educated. "Hell, that's not your fault," he'd told her at one point when he'd become impatient with her self-abuse. "You had better things to do with your time."

He'd seen the appreciation in her expression, although she hadn't voiced it. He'd also gotten the impression she didn't really believe him.

"Annie has helped me with my reading, writing, and ciphering," she'd said, lifting that little chin in her characteristic gesture of pride and defiance.

H.L. had experienced a mad desire to grab her out of her chair and kiss her silly. Unfortunately, that desire was becoming his constant companion these days. There was something about Rose Gilhooley that appealed to just about every aspect of his being, and he was getting worried about it.

She'd retrieved a big checked handkerchief from a pocket an hour or so earlier, and had started wiping her eyes at intervals. The smoke was hard on her. H.L. wished he could remove her from this foul den of thieves and cutthroats, but she'd never consent to go until they'd fulfilled their mission.

She wiped her eyes again now and muttered, "Do you think that horrid man will *ever* leave?"

"I'm sure he will."

She allowed her gaze to drift around the room. With a disgusted sneer, she said, "Maybe he'll just pass out like everybody else is doing."

H.L. guessed he couldn't refute her observation. "I hope not. If he does, there may be a way to intervene, although it would be risky."

She eyed him as if she didn't believe him. "How?"

He shrugged. "We can get rid of his companion and drag him off. Maybe say we're taking him to his quarters or something."

"That could be really dangerous. If anybody else in here knows the man and where he lives, they'd know we were lying."

"Yeah, yeah, well, let's not borrow trouble. With luck, he'll leave pretty soon, and we can follow him."

"If I can still see by that time."

H.L. chuckled. "You'll do fine."

"A lot you know about it."

Oops. She was getting crabby. H.L. hoped like thunder their quarry would oblige them and leave the tavern in the next little while, before she became unmanageable. He'd have liked to walk up to the fellow and dump him out of his chair, but knew he couldn't do anything so drastic—not and live to tell the tale, at any rate.

He was gazing blankly at the wall behind Rose, trying to think of more questions to ask her about her life with the

Wild West, when she suddenly uttered a muffled cry. "Look!"

When H.L. started to turn around, she grabbed his shirt-sleeve. "No! Don't look." Her voice was a harsh rasp he could barely hear. "But he's getting up."

"Maybe he's just going to the bar again." God, he hoped not. What he hoped was that the villain was finally about to depart this god-awful place. H.L. was beginning to feel as if he were suffocating, too.

"No! No! He's not going to the bar. He got his coat from the back of his chair. I think he's actually going to leave!"

She sounded so excited, H.L. hoped the bastard wouldn't disappoint her. "I'll be discreet. I'm going to turn around and pretend to look at the bar."

"Be careful," she hissed.

He was careful. And he had to admit that his own mood jumped up a few pegs when he saw that Rose had deduced correctly. The son of a bitch was going to leave the tavern! Thank God. H.L. didn't know how long he himself could have withstood the deadly atmosphere of the place, and he was used to doing stuff like this. Poor Rose must be near to dying.

The disreputable-looking peglegged person snarled something to the man who'd come in with him. H.L. couldn't catch the words, but the voice fitted the man. It was rough and gravelly and sounded as if it had been dragged over a rocky beach several times before being presented to its present owner.

The man's companion snarled something back. He sounded as if he'd swapped voices with some old tar's pet parrot.

Pegleg evidently didn't like what the other man had said, because he leaned close and snarled something else. Parrot-voice jumped to his feet and assumed a belligerent pose. He looked sort of silly, since he probably weighed a hundred pounds less than Pegleg and was a foot shorter, but he didn't back down. That signified extreme bravery or extreme stupidity to H.L., and he had a feeling he knew which one he'd pick if anyone asked.

But Pegleg didn't pop him one, or even knock him back into his chair. He only flapped a huge hand in the air in a gesture of disgust, spun around on his peg, and stomped toward the tavern's doors. Parrot-voice sank back into his chair, grumbling.

Rose and H.L. exchanged a glance. H.L. patted the air with his hand to signify they should stay put for another couple of seconds. "So as not to arouse suspicion."

He saw Rose glance around the room and twitch her mouth in a moue signifying disagreement with his order. He glanced, too, and decided she was right. Nobody would know if they left the place, mainly because they were either too drunk or too occupied in playing cards to care.

Scraping his chair backward, H.L. decided to take no chances. In case anybody was listening or watching, he said, "Come on, little brother. It's past your bedtime." He guffawed and sneered, to let everyone know he was joshing.

"Sez you," Rose mouthed as she, too, got up from her chair. She sounded like a hoodlum from the back slums, and H.L. almost smiled.

H.L. shrugged into the jacket he'd slung over the back of the chair. Rose hadn't dared to take her own jacket off, for fear, H.L. presumed, that somebody would notice her shape. Lordy, she must honestly and truly be smothering, he thought with sympathy. It was more than close in the room. It was hot and disgusting, and he wished he could offer Rose a warm bath and a bed. Preferably with him in it.

God almighty, where had that come from? Irked with his carnal side, which seemed to jump out and attack him at the least favorable times, H.L. shoved it aside unmercifully. He had to keep his wits about him now more than ever. That one-legged man was no one to trifle with.

"I hope we didn't wait too long," Rose said as soon as the

tavern doors closed behind them. H.L. heard her suck in a breath of almost-fresh air. "Oh, my, I don't think I'd have lasted much longer in there."

"Keep your voice down," H.L. reminded her, although it was hardly necessary. Her voice had suffered greatly from the contaminated air of the tavern, and she could scarcely scrape out a whisper at the moment. Nevertheless, he figured her lungs would unclog eventually, and he didn't want her hollering or anything.

"Right," she said. "Be quiet now, because I have to concentrate."

H.L. watched her with interest. She had to lean way over, since the night was dark and the fog was still as thick as barley water. Gaslights fuzzed weakly through the haze, but didn't penetrate far enough to illuminate the walkway.

"Bother. It's so dark out here." Rose inched along, searching the ground. H.L. couldn't even guess what she was looking for, but she apparently found whatever it was a moment later.

"Aha!" It would have been a cry of triumph, if she'd been able to cry.

"What?"

"His tracks." She pointed. "Clear as a bell. All right, follow me."

She sure didn't waste any time. By the time the *me* part of her sentence hit the air, Rose had vanished from H.L.'s sight. He rushed to catch up with her, suddenly panic-stricken by her disappearance. He caught up with her at once. "Damn it, don't leave me like that!"

Shooting him a nettled look over her shoulder, she snapped, "Keep up, then. There's no time to waste, and I have no idea how difficult it is to track people in the city."

In spite of her caution, she seemed to have no difficulty whatever in following Pegleg. Down one dark alley after another she led H.L., until they ended up at a hovel attached to a warehouse on the dock.

"I know this place," H.L. whispered to Rose when she stood up from her stoop and pressed a hand to her back as if it ached, which it probably did.

"You do?" She looked around. There wasn't much to see. Row upon row of warehouses lined this section of the dock area. Businesses stored excess goods here and the owners of fishing fleets kept supplies here. During the day, the place teemed with activity. At night, it was dismal and dreary and dangerous.

"He went in there." Rose pointed at the hovel. No lights were visible. Either the windows were covered or no lanterns had been lit when the man entered the building.

"You sure? How can you tell?"

"The tracks lead right straight here. And see? You can tell the door's been opened within the last few minutes."

"You can?" H.L. couldn't.

"Well, *I* can," she amended.

He didn't argue.

"Oh! And look here!" She pointed at something else that was invisible to H.L.'s eyes. "Bear's in there!"

"How can you tell?"

"He's left his mark."

Oh. Well, damn. There was more to this tracking business than H.L. had hitherto imagined. Rose had started smiling, which he took as a good sign.

She brushed her hands together. "So, what do we do now?"

Reaching into his pocket, H.L. reassured himself that the Colt revolver that he knew how to use in a vague sort of way still resided there. He'd practiced, although he wasn't a great shot. "I'm going to try the latch and see if it's open. If it isn't, I guess I'll have to kick the door in."

"We'd best make sure that's possible before you try it."

Their voices were so low, H.L. could scarcely hear them himself. "How do you propose doing that?"

"Let me do it." She didn't explain, but he watched with

fascination as she silently perused the door latch, lifted it, and then inspected the door itself as well as its hinges, all in absolute silence. When she was through, she nodded. "It'll give way if you aim at the center panel and kick it hard enough. Do you have the strength to do that?"

Irked, H.L. said, "Of course I do."

"Don't get upset. I just wanted to make sure. We don't want to make any noisy mistakes and alert that horrid man, do we? After all, Bear is probably tied up, and we can't afford to waste any time."

"I suppose not," he grumbled. He knew she'd used the royal *we* so as not to ruffle his feathers. Damn it, you'd think he was the woman here and not her, the way she talked to him. He realized he was miffed because she was the more competent tracker of the two of them. She was probably the better shot, as well.

Well, hell, a man couldn't be all things to all people. H.L. May was a damned good reporter, and that's what mattered to him. He still felt sort of small and insignificant, but he vowed not to allow the feeling to interfere with his mission.

"Let me get ready before you kick in the door," Rose whispered.

H.L. goggled as she pulled a revolver from her jacket, shrugged, and reached around to the back of her trousers to retrieve another one. She looked like a dime novelist's conception of Billy the Kid, standing there in her trousers and Stetson, aiming two guns at the dilapidated door of the hovel. He decided, *What the hell,* and drew his own gun out of his pocket. Who was he to buck tradition?

"Ready?" he asked. His heart started scrambling to catch up with his breath. He'd never performed a rescue before; it was tough breaking new ground, especially when there probably wouldn't be any room for error.

Rose nodded. She looked more grim than H.L. had ever seen her, even when she'd been angry and hollering at him for some reason. He backed up, braced himself, sucked in a bushel or so of air, nodded once, quickly plotted his trajectory, and said, "Here goes nothing."

With his gun held out before him in both hands, he made a dash at the door, raised his foot and flexed it so that the sole of his shoe would make contact with the wood, and with all his weight behind him, smashed into it. A deafening crash ripped through the air as his foot ripped through the rotten wood. The accompanying bellow of rage and alarm from Pegleg made for a truly horrific din.

H.L. hadn't counted on getting his foot stuck in the splintered wood. Swearing a blue streak, he extricated himself, aware as he did so that little Rose Gilhooley had already rushed past him into the room.

"Stop right there, you!"

When he got himself upright again, which didn't take more than five or six seconds, H.L. was aghast at the spectacle of Rose aiming two revolvers at the enormous gut of the one-legged man. Unfortunately, Pegleg in his turn had what looked like a cannon directed straight at Rose.

"Get out of here, little lady, and take that skunk with you." Pegleg sneered at Rose and jerked his head at H.L.

H.L., scared to death on Rose's behalf, decided this wasn't the time to dally. Lifting his revolver, he aimed straight at the villain's ugly face and pulled the trigger.

An explosion so loud it made his ears ring filled the room, along with a whole lot of black smoke.

"Shit! You scurvy cur, you shot me!" Pegleg roared.

Something hit H.L. in the stomach, sending him over backwards. H.L. realized a second later that it had been Rose. His brain scarcely registered her weight on his body before another explosion, louder even than the one from his own gun, boomed through the air.

"Get Bear, Mr. May! I'll take care of this man!"

Huh? His head swimming, H.L. scrambled to his feet in time to see Pegleg swat Rose away as if she'd been a fly. Rage consumed H.L. in that instant—a rage so large and fierce, it later scared him because he hadn't realized he was capable of such mindless fury.

With a roar that matched Pegleg's in volume and ferocity, H.L. plowed into the huge man's belly, head first. With a grunt, Pegleg staggered backward, fetching up against the wall behind him. Drawing on a youth spent defending himself from taunts about his name, H.L. didn't give the scoundrel time to recover, but attacked him with lefts and rights, uppercuts and jabs, whaling away at Pegleg's face and body with a strength he hadn't known he possessed.

"Mr. May!" Rose screeched at his back, but H.L. didn't care. He was going to kill the man who'd hurt Rose or know the reason why.

Through teeth clenched so tightly that his jaw ached, H.L. managed to pant out, "Get the kid."

Without looking to see if she was obeying him, he continued his assault on the kidnapper. Time and time again, his fists bludgeoned Pegleg's chest and belly. The sickening crunch of bone smashing against bone filled the air as he took time out from the cursed fiend's body and concentrated on his face for awhile.

H.L. had no notion of time. When, with a whimper that would have done justice to a babe in arms, Pegleg crumpled to the floor, H.L. wasn't through with him. Leaning over, he administered about a hundred or two parting blows.

Through the murderous fog of his rage, other sounds penetrated slowly, one by one. It wasn't until Rose's frantic "Stop it! Oh, stop it, please!" filtered into his head, that H.L. realized he'd given up on his fists, since he had to lean over too far for convenience, and had begun kicking the bastard. Hard.

"Stop it! Mr. May! You're killing him!"

"Good!" His breath had started coming in shallow gasps before H.L. finally understood that the danger had passed.

"Oh, my land, is he dead?"

Dazed, H.L. blinked down at his fallen foe. Shoot. *Was* he

dead? At the moment, H.L. felt only triumph at the notion. By God, there was *one* kidnapper who'd never ply his wicked trade again. He managed to gasp, "I dunno."

Rose squatted next to Pegleg and put two fingers to the pulse point on his neck. "He's still alive," she said doubtfully.

Hot anger sloshed through H.L. again, consuming his rational thought process in an instant. He reached down, grabbed Pegleg by the dirty bandanna tied around his neck, and started to heave him to his feet. "Oh, yeah? Well, then, I guess I'm not done yet, am I?"

He got in one good punch before Rose threw herself across the arm holding Pegleg up, causing his grip to loosen. "Stop it!" she screamed. "We've got to get Bear out of here before somebody comes!"

Feeling as if he were waking up from a very bad nightmare, H.L. stared at her. He shook his head hard. He discovered he couldn't breathe and slammed a hand over his heart. For a second, he feared he was dying of a heart seizure. Then it occurred to him that he was only winded.

He said, "What?"

Rose reached up and patted him on the cheek. Enunciating slowly and clearly, she said, "We need to leave now, Mr. May. We need to get Bear out of here before somebody else comes and realizes he's been rescued."

"Bear? There's a bear in here?" H.L. glanced around uncertainly.

"Yes. Come along, now. Bear's not been hurt, but he's been tied up since this morning, and his circulation is bad and he's a little unsteady on his feet."

"Oh." H.L. shook his head again. He realized his hands were hurting really badly and lifted them to take a look. "Good God."

"Mercy sakes, you're a mess, Mr. May. Come along. We need to soak those hands in antiseptic water."

"You fight good," a strange, young-sounding voice said

at H.L.'s back. Turning, he staggered slightly. Rose kept him from falling flat on his face by looping an arm around his waist. Her arm felt good there. For the first time, he noticed Bear in Winter, who was standing up, rubbing his wrists as if he were trying to renew the circulation therein. At last he remembered what he'd been fighting for. "Oh. I guess you're Bear," he muttered inanely.

The small boy grinned up at him. "Yes. You fight good, mister."

By God, he did fight well, didn't he? A sudden burst of pride filled H.L.'s chest. By God, he'd rescued a child from a kidnapper! "Thanks." He hoped he sounded modest. He didn't feel modest. He felt swell.

"Let's get out of here now," Rose said firmly. "This is a terrible neighborhood. We'll have to find a cab somewhere, I guess."

"Right." With one last hard shake of his head, H.L. decided he'd have to wait to gloat over his victory. Rose was correct; they had to get the hell out of the lakeside dock district, and the sooner the better. H.L. had no idea how Pegleg made contact with the buyers of the children he kidnapped, and he didn't particularly want to find out with Rose and Bear in Winter along.

God, this was going to be a good story!

He was disappointed when Rose unlooped her arm from his waist. Glancing down, he saw her pretty, piquant face peering up at him. She looked worried. He gave her the cockiest grin in his repertoire. "Hell, Miss Gilhooley, you don't have to let me go. I might fall down without your support."

She turned so pink, he could see the color bloom even in the dark. "Don't be ridiculous."

With that, she took Bear's arm and led him out of the ruined hovel. They had to step over Pegleg, since his body was so large it covered most of the floor. H.L. heard the man groan as they went through the smashed door and thought about turning back to kick him a few more times, but Rose, apparently sensing his thoughts, grabbed him by the tail of his jacket and wouldn't let him.

Rose knew it was probably wrong of her, but she couldn't help it. She was so impressed by the skill H.L. May had demonstrated in dispatching that awful villain, she wanted to kiss him.

Not that wanting to kiss him was a new sensation, she reminded herself. Annie would be upset to know of Rose's secret daydreams about this outrageous, unruly newspaper reporter.

"There's a cab," H.L. said, startling her and making her heart leap in her chest. Bother. She was really on edge.

Small wonder, after their recent encounter with that dreadful man back there. "Good. We need to get Bear back to the Wild West as soon as we can."

"I'm hungry," Bear announced suddenly. "That man, he don't feed me nothing."

Rose glanced at the boy and frowned. "Well . . . I think we really ought to get you back to your family, Bear."

The boy shrugged, resigned. Rose's heart pinched. She knew very well how much the reservation Sioux were made to suffer these days. They were supposed to be supplied with adequate amounts of food on the reservation, and they were being taught farming techniques so that they'd eventually be able to support themselves.

But the Sioux weren't farmers by nature, and the Bureau of Indian Affairs was probably the most corrupt organization in the entire government. The Sioux were forever being given bad meat and wormy grain to eat—and that was when their shipments weren't subverted entirely and they received nothing at all.

Glancing from Bear to H.L., she said doubtfully, "Do you think we could stop somewhere and get something to eat?"

H.L. pondered the question for a minute as he hailed the cab. "Why not? I could use something to eat, too. That brouhaha back there made me hungry."

The arrogant grin on his face tickled Rose. She returned it with one of her own. "Yes, I imagine you do. Beating people to a pulp must be hungry work."

He beamed down at her. "You betcha!"

"You mean we get to eat?" Bear said eagerly.

"Yes, Bear. We'll get you a meal."

"Meat?" His dark eyes sparkled.

"Meat." Rose patted his arm.

H.L. stepped aside after he opened the cab door to allow Rose and Bear to enter before him. Rose was surprised he'd remembered his manners, since he was obviously under the influence of victorious euphoria. She didn't begrudge him his moment. He'd performed heroically. She heard him speak to the cabbie before he climbed in the cab after them.

"Take us to Louie's, cabbie."

Louie's. Rose wondered if the food would be as good as that at Joe's had been. People seemed to name their eating establishments after themselves around here. As soon as H.L. flopped into the seat opposite her, making the cab rock as he did so, she asked. "What's Louie's?"

"Steak house. It's not fancy, which is why I asked the cabbie to take us there." He lifted his hands and looked ruefully at his knuckles. "I'm not looking too elegant at the moment, and neither are you."

Rose gasped since she, too, was seeing those battered and bloody knuckles fully for the first time. "Oh, my goodness! Mr. May, we need to get you fixed up before we even think about eating. It looks like your knuckles are smashed!"

"They'll be all right." He sounded nonchalant, but Rose saw him grimace as he flexed his hands.

"Nonsense! Before we do another thing, we need to get your hands cleaned and bandaged."

"Bandaged? But—"

Rose didn't wait around to listen to him fuss at her. She'd had enough experience with men to know they'd never admit when they needed help. She leaned out of the cab and used her Smith and Wesson to bang on the side of it to get the cabbie's attention. He jerked and swiveled to stare down at her from his perch.

"Take us to a hospital or a clinic, if you will, please, sir."

"Beg pardon?"

"We have an injured man in here." She used her most regal tone. It was one she'd copied from Annie, and it generally got people's attention. It worked with the cabbie. "And we need to get him bandaged."

"There's a hospital up on Silverdale."

"Good. Take us there."

"No! Wait. For God's sake, Miss Gilhooley!" H.L.'s face emerged from the window across from hers. "Take us to ten eighty-nine Gilcrest, cabbie."

"What's that?" Rose demanded. "I'm warning you, Mr. May, I'm going to get your hands taken care of before we eat."

"Good God," H.L. muttered. "All right. I admit I need to get washed up, but I'll be damned if I'll go to a hospital. I have bandages and carbolic at my place."

"Your place?"

"My place."

Rose saw his eyes twinkle, and she stiffened.

"Don't worry, Miss Gilhooley. I won't take advantage of you. Not with a witness."

"Mr. May!"

He only laughed.

Deciding she couldn't win, especially with Bear in Winter watching everything with fascinated eyes, she turned to the boy and patted his arm. "This won't take too long."

H.L. May sighed.

FOURTEEN

H.L. had to admit that his hands hurt like hell. He didn't think any of his knuckles were permanently damaged, although that bastard's jaw had been as hard as a rock and H.L. had pounded it about a hundred times.

"You're a bloody mess," Rose grumbled. "Keep your hands in that water!"

"Yes, ma'am." This was a mighty comedown for a hero. Damn it, he'd just won a battle with a man twice his size, he thought grumpily, and here he was, being bullied by a woman. Rose Gilhooley could make him feel about as big as nothing without half trying.

Nevertheless, he appreciated her nursing skills. She'd scarcely balked at entering his place of residence, although she had cast one or two apprehensive glances around to make sure nobody saw her walking up the stairs to a single man's flat. But what the hell, they had a chaperone. Damn it.

Bear in Winter was curious about his place. H.L. took time to be glad he was a basically tidy man, or he'd have been embarrassed to bring Rose here. But he didn't care for messes, and he kept his place neat. It helped, of course, that a cleaning woman came in once a week to dust, sweep the floors, and prepare a meal that kept him going for a day or two. The rest of the time, H.L. ate out. Chicago was a great place for eating establishments.

As his hands soaked and Rose set out the bandages, scissors, and carbolic acid, she, too, glanced around. "I've never been in one of these newfangled apartment buildings."

"They're not so newfangled," he told her. "This is a nice one, though. It's new. Built just a couple of years ago. I leased one of the very first flats they offered."

"It's convenient, too, I imagine."

"Yup. I only have a short walk to the *Globe,* and the El's just down the street."

"The El?"

"The Elevated Railroad. It's a great Chicago convenience. I tell you, Miss Gilhooley, Chicago's a wonderful town."

"Hmmm."

The most time-consuming aspect of H.L.'s medical treatment was the quarter-hour Rose insisted he soak his hands. She snapped at him when he said he didn't want to waste fifteen minutes. "This will prevent infection, Mr. May, and you'd be a fool not to take the time. Better fifteen minutes soaking in antiseptic water than a lifetime without the use of your hands."

Put that way, H.L. guessed a quarter of an hour wasn't all that long. She was darned good at bandages, too. By the time he changed shirts and they left his apartment, his hands looked like hams wrapped for the butcher to sell, but he could at least still use his fingers. That would come in handy when he wrote his article.

Rose had demanded that he sit still to have his face attended to, as well. He supposed he had been punched once or twice before he'd overpowered the big brute. God, he was proud of himself! He'd done a piece of work on that bastard, and no mistake.

"Your jaw is going to swell up like a pig's bladder, Mr. May, and you need to get carbolic on those scratches."

"A pig's bladder?"

She huffed. "We used them as balls when I was growing up."

Interesting. H.L. vaguely recalled doing something of the

sort back home in Missouri. When he wasn't fighting with other kids about his name.

They didn't get Bear back to his kin at the Wild West until almost dawn. Little Elk was still awake, sitting cross-legged beside a fire. Two women and an old man had also been waiting for Rose and H.L.'s return.

H.L. had told the cab driver to wait for him as he deposited his fellow travelers. The cabbie agreed to wait and settled in for a snooze.

As they approached the campfire, H.L. watched with satisfaction when Bear broke into a trot, in a hurry and happy to be back in the arms of his family. When he spotted the approaching trio, Little Elk rose slowly from his seat beside the fire. The two women jumped up and ran to meet Bear, and the old man's face, which looked as if it had been drying in the sun for a century or more, cracked into a broad smile, and he hobbled over to embrace Bear. When H.L. glanced at Rose, he was not surprised to see that she was surreptitiously brushing away tears.

A chorus of voices speaking Sioux swirled around H.L. and Rose as they were subsumed into the small reunion circle. After a minute or two, Little Elk turned to speak to them. "You found him."

H.L. thought Little Elk's statement might perhaps be both simple and profound, although he'd have to think about it to be sure. He nodded.

"We did," agreed Rose, smiling. She apparently didn't have H.L.'s penchant for analyzing other people's statements. "And Mr. May had a terrible fight with the man who kidnapped Bear."

Little Elk appeared interested. He lifted an eyebrow and asked H.L. "Did you kill him?"

H.L. shrugged. "I don't think so."

The Sioux nodded, but said, "Too bad."

Too bad he killed him, or too bad he didn't kill him? Another, more searching, survey of the Indian's face answered H.L.'s question. The law of the frontier apparently dictated that a man be killed if he kidnapped a child. H.L. guessed he could understand that, but he'd read often enough that Indians kidnapped children. Would Little Elk think it was all right if somebody killed him for snatching a child?

As he watched Rose and Little Elk converse softly about the tracking skills Rose had used in determining the place where Bear in Winter had been held captive, H.L. answered that question for himself, too. Little Elk and his Sioux brethren seemed to accept the rules of their culture as a matter of course. H.L. didn't quite understand it, having grown up among his own kind, in whose culture people expected others to forgive them but didn't necessarily believe in turnabout being fair play. It looked from where he stood that Little Elk would have expected reprisals if he'd stolen somebody's child.

Hell, he was confusing himself. Rubbing eyes that felt as though they'd been through a sandstorm, he decided he was way too tired to think about different philosophies of the world. He kept no particular hours, since his job as a reporter required him to cover stories at any hour of the night or day, but he'd put in more than a full day today.

Not only that, but he'd fought a noble fight and won it, against a powerful foe. It occurred to him that it might be nice if, say, he were a knight of old and somebody wrote a song about him and his skill as a warrior and his dashing exploit in rescuing Bear in Winter. He'd read that Indians did that, too, and he had a sudden hope that Little Elk or Bear or somebody in his tribe would sing about his brave deed in the future. Keep his legend alive, as it were.

He laughed out loud at his foolishness. Hearing him, Rose turned and gazed at him. "What's so funny?"

H.L. shook his head. "Nothing. I think I'm just dead beat." The word reminded him of his battered hands, and he added, "In a manner of speaking."

Rose smiled at him. "Yes. I'm very tired, too." She turned

back to Little Elk. "I'm awfully glad we could help, Little Elk. Please tell everyone to be careful. I don't know anything about the man who kidnapped Bear, but I wouldn't be surprised if he's the vindictive sort. He might try to take someone else or do something to retaliate."

A trifle irked, H.L. muttered, "If he can get around. He looked pretty badly maimed when we left him."

Rose patted his arm, and he got embarrassed. "Yes, yes. You did a wonderful job of overpowering him, Mr. May, and rendering him defenseless, at least for a while. I'm sure you're a hero in everyone's eyes."

He didn't appreciate the way she said that, but he didn't object, knowing that if he did so he'd be putting himself in an awkward light. But, damn it, he *had* done a wonderful job in overpowering that bastard and rendering him defenseless. "I'll see you to your tent," he muttered.

"Thank you. Yes. I'm ready for bed, all right." As if to prove it, she yawned suddenly, then put a hand over her mouth as if she thought she'd done something wrong. "I beg your pardon."

Amused, H.L. said, "It's quite all right, Miss Gilhooley."

They bade Little Elk good night. H.L. had sort of expected the Sioux women to come over and thank him, maybe give him some kind of Indian cake or something as a thank-you gift, but they didn't. Hell, he guessed he really didn't know beans about Indians.

"I really mean it, Mr. May," Rose said after they'd walked a little way in silence. "You were wonderful tonight, and Little Elk and his kin truly appreciate it."

"They didn't act like it." H.L. wished he hadn't said that as soon as the words were out. They sounded whiny, as if he expected somebody to build a statue in his honor or something. Although that would be nice, and he admitted it—to himself—he knew the real point was getting Bear back to his folks.

"The Sioux don't express themselves the way we do. I

have a feeling you'll be thanked in no uncertain terms in the days to come."

"Hmmm." That made him feel better.

He glanced down at Rose, noticed she appeared weary, and decided there was something else that would make him feel even better. "Say, Miss Gilhooley. We've known each other for quite a few days now, and we did rescue that boy together. Don't you think it's about time we started calling each other by our Christian names?"

"Oh!" She glanced up at him and looked as startled as she sounded.

H.L. frowned, wondering what the hell was so astonishing about calling each other by name. It wasn't as if he'd asked her to marry him or anything.

Where in the name of holy hell had *that* thought come from? He had no idea, and hadn't thought one up before Rose spoke again.

"Why—certainly. I guess. I mean, I'm sure that would be all right. Um, but I don't know your name, Mr. May."

"Everyone just calls me H.L.," he said, deciding to shelve the marriage issue for the moment. Cripes, he'd never, ever, not once even thought about himself and marriage, except to be glad he wasn't saddled with a wife. The mere word generally made him shudder. That he didn't shudder now, he chalked up to his being particularly tired.

"I see. Well, as you know, my name is Rose. And—well, I should think it would be fine if you call me Rose." A small frown marred the perfection of her piquant face. "I suppose I can call you H.L., if that's what you prefer, although I've never known anyone who goes by his initials before."

"If more parents named their kids awful names, I'm sure more folks would," he said.

"Oh. Yes. Well, I'm sure that must have something to do with it." She eyed him curiously. "I must say, now you have me intrigued, however. I don't suppose you'd be willing to tell me what the initials stand for, would you?"

He grinned. "I don't mind at all. The H. stands for my first name, and the L. stands for my middle name."

Rose huffed. "Thank you. That's very informative."

"Isn't it?"

They'd reached her tent, and H.L. found he was reluctant to let her go. He needed something more from her before they parted for the night, although he wasn't sure what.

Rose sighed heavily. "Thank God. I'm so tired. I think I'm going to sleep all day tomorrow. Or today." She glanced up at the sky as if she expected to see dawn creeping over the horizon.

It wasn't. H.L. pulled out his pocket watch, fumbling a bit because his bandages interfered with his movements, flicked the case open, and squinted at the dial. "It's almost four." Shoot, that was late.

"My goodness. I can't even remember the last time I stayed awake this long." She wrinkled her nose. "I'm sure Annie will want to go to church, but it had better be an evening service. I'm sure I won't be up in time for a morning one."

"Have you ever stayed up this late?" H.L. asked with a broader grin, the notion of her being worried about going to church having tickled him.

She didn't grin back. "When my father was sick, we took turns sitting up with him."

Aw, hell, he would have to go and stir up sorry memories, wouldn't he? H.L. gave himself a mental kick. In an effort to make up for it, he said, "I think we really ought to shake hands, Rose. After all, we did a good deed tonight, and we ought to congratulate each other."

Now she smiled. Thank God. "Of course. We did do a good deed, didn't we?" She held out her right hand. It was small, delicate-looking. Nobody simply looking at it would ever know it could handle a gun and a horse better than most other human hands in the world.

H.L. took it in his big, bandaged one. "Shoot, this isn't working out the way I wanted it to."

She looked confused. "It isn't?"

"No." He wanted to touch her flesh, and he couldn't feel anything through all that blasted cotton batting. "I have a better idea."

Rose resisted a little when he started reeling her in, but not enough to thwart him. His arms went around her snugly, and he peered down at her. In the darkness of the night, her eyes were large and luminous, and her expression conveyed deep doubt and a modicum of consternation. "Mr. May," she whispered.

"H.L.," he corrected her.

"H.L.," she repeated obediently.

"You're a surprising woman, Rose Gilhooley."

"I am?"

He nodded and leaned down to brush his lips against hers. She gasped slightly, but didn't wrench herself away from him. In fact, her big eyes fluttered for a split second, then closed. Ah. This was more like it. As gently as a butterfly settling on a flower petal, H.L. covered her lips with his. He brushed feathery soft kisses against her mouth for a moment, until she sighed and seemed to melt in his arms.

A powerful surge of lust, combined with a fierce sense of possessiveness, roared through H.L. He tightened his arms around her small, soft body. Damn, she felt good. She felt even better a moment later, when she began kissing him back.

Tentatively, shyly, her lips moved beneath his. His triumph in that moment was ten times what his triumph at pummeling Pegleg had been. He felt her hands, which had been bunched into tight little fists, open and splay against his back. He had too many clothes on to appreciate her touch fully, but he liked it when she caressed him hesitantly.

"You feel good, Rose. Very good," he whispered. Her damned Stetson was in his way, so he plucked it off and dropped it on the ground beside them. Her hair fell down around her shoulders, and he wanted to run his hands through it, but his bandages got in the way. "Someday," he murmured into her tousled hair. "Someday I'm going to feel your hair the way I want to."

Rose whispered, "Hmmm."

He was hard as a rock, primed and ready, and he knew he couldn't take much more of this tantalizing embrace. Fearing what he'd do if he prolonged the kiss, he reluctantly pulled back from her. Rose, not understanding his motivation for breaking the kiss, clung to him like a limpet. When he glanced down and saw her dazed, confused expression, he felt guilty. Not very guilty, but guilty nonetheless. She blinked up at him as if she didn't know what had just happened to her.

H.L. understood completely. He'd kissed lots of women in his day, but he'd never become so involved in a kiss that he'd feared for his sanity until this minute.

He had to be going nuts. There couldn't be another explanation for his sudden, overwhelming, all-consuming desire to attach Rose Gilhooley to himself. Permanently. For damned ever. Permanence regarding a woman had always seemed to H.L. May akin to a life sentence in prison or eternity in hell or something equally drastic and horrifying.

But permanence with respect to Rose Gilhooley didn't conjure up anything but bliss in his innards, which were obviously suffering some sort of dementia. He needed space and distance, and he needed them fast. Now. Instantly.

Gently, so as neither to scare nor hurt her, he pulled away and opened his mouth to say something. Anything.

Nothing came out of his mouth, so he cleared his throat. That helped his throat but didn't do anything to unscramble his brains, which hadn't yet formed a coherent sentence, much less one that was appropriate to this circumstance.

After a moment of looking as if she'd been hit by a bolt of lightning, Rose took a quick step back. She was rocky on her feet and had to grab the flap of her tent to steady herself. She lifted a hand to her lips, as if she didn't understand the sensations tingling there.

H.L. had to grit his teeth and steel himself to keep from lunging after her and drawing her into his arms again. He'd have stuck his hands in his pockets, only they wouldn't fit anymore. Thwarted, he put them behind his back. "I, ah, had better be getting along, Rose. I still have to write that article." A rock jammed his throat, and he had to clear it out again. "My, ah, editor's a bear about schedules."

"Bear? A bear?"

"I mean he's touchy about schedules."

"Ah. I thought you meant Bear. I mean—"

"I know what you mean."

She blinked a few more times, opened and closed her mouth twice, and said, "Oh. Yes. Of course. I see." She shut her eyes tight, took a deep breath, let it out, and opened her eyes again. "Yes, well, I need to get some rest."

"Right. Me, too, but I have to write my story first."

"Right. Of course."

"Well, then, I guess I'd better be off." Damn it, what was the matter with him tonight? He never had trouble leaving a woman. He almost always felt vast relief when he left one, in fact.

"Yes. Of course." Rose seemed to have difficulty turning to enter her tent.

Suddenly filled with panic at the thought of losing her, H.L. took a quick step forward before catching himself and forcing himself to get a grip on his senses. Hell, if he didn't watch his step, he'd do something that would lose him his freedom forever.

Whatever good his freedom had ever done him.

"Right," he said in an effort to clear his mind. "Right. Well, then, I'll come by tomorrow afternoon, if that's all right. I—ah—want to interview you some more, if you don't mind."

"Interview me some more?" She appeared puzzled and not altogether pleased.

"Yeah, and I'll be able to bring you a copy of the early edition. You know, the paper that will come out Monday morning. My first article about you will be in that one."

"It will?"

"Yes. I'll document Bear's rescue and how you went about finding him, using your tracking skills, in another article. Tomorrow will be an introduction." Talking about his job was easing him back into a sense of normality, thank God. Feeling slightly more chipper, he went on, "So since I still want to write a whole series, why don't I take you out to supper and interview you some more then."

"Well, all right. If you need to, I guess it's all right."

"Right. Good. Then, that's what I'll do."

"Fine, then." It seemed to H.L. that it took an effort for her to smile at him. "Thank you, then. Um, thanks for helping me get Bear back. If it hadn't been for you, I don't think I could have done it."

H.L.'s cynical side reared up at once. "Yeah? You surprise me, Rose. I thought you could do anything." He wanted to smack himself when he saw her lips press together and the stunned look evaporate completely from her face. Her eyes flashed.

"Of course, I'm sure I could have done it without your help, but not as quickly." She lifted the flap of her tent with a snap. "Good night, Mr. May. I mean, H.L." She ducked under the flap, entered her tent, and let the flap drop.

H.L. experienced a moment of total bereavement when she was lost to his sight. Muttering a soft "Damn it all to hell," he turned and slouched off, kicking at clots of dirt that he couldn't see as he went. He had the cabbie take him to the *Globe* office, where he let himself in with his key and wrote his story. This one documented Bear's rescue, and it would appear in Thursday's paper. It was a great story, damn it, and he'd been a goddamned hero in it.

So why did he feel so rotten?

H.L. decided it was probably best not to try to find an answer to that one until after he got some sleep. By that time, and with luck, his heart would have stopped whacking away at his rib cage every time he remembered kissing Rose.

Rose felt unsteady and light-headed when she entered her tent. Good heavens, H.L. May had kissed her. Worse, she'd kissed him back!

Annie would be horrified.

For that matter, Rose was horrified. She collapsed onto her bed, pressed her hands to her cheeks, and uttered a low moan.

Well, this proved a point at any rate. Annie was right. H.L. May, whose professed interest in her was only business, was a snake in the grass underneath. What's more, even knowing what she knew, having been lectured endlessly by Annie about the perfidies of men, Rose had fallen for his lures— hook, line, and sinker.

The truly appalling aspect of the situation was that Rose would love to rush outside, holler at H.L. to come back, haul him into her tent, and tell him to kiss her some more. Lifting her head and staring into the blackness surrounding her, she wondered if her character had been damaged by entering into a life that might be considered show business. She'd heard show business was bad for a person's morals.

Yet the colonel did such a good job of keeping an eye on his cast and crew, especially Rose and Annie, who were the only two white women traveling with the Wild West. He'd been especially careful of Rose, who didn't have a husband to see to her welfare, as Annie did.

So much for good intentions, thought Rose glumly. In spite of the colonel's best efforts on her behalf, Rose had managed to find someone to seduce her. She wished like thunder that being seduced by H.L. May didn't sound like such a good idea.

However would she face him in the morning—rather, this afternoon? It occurred to her that, if he arrived at the Wild West encampment in time, she could invite him to attend the evening church service with Annie and herself. That would give him a tangible, if false, impression of her moral fiber and character. But he didn't have to know that inviting him to church didn't appeal to her innermost self as much as inviting him into her tent did. That would remain her secret. She wouldn't even tell Annie.

"Bother. Rose Gilhooley, you're pathetic."

On that unhappy note, Rose fumbled for a match on her night table, which consisted of one of the trunks in which she packed her costumes, and struck it against the striker she kept next to a kerosene lamp. She lit the lamp and yawned deeply before she stood to remove her clothes and climb into her nightgown.

As she undressed, her brain kept slipping back to the kiss she'd shared with H.L. May. She wished it wouldn't, but was too exhausted to exert any control over it.

Rose had never been kissed before except by Freddie, and that didn't count, because he was her brother and his kisses had been little pecks on the cheek when she'd brought in something extra-special for supper. He'd actually pecked her cheek twice when she'd brought home two antelopes.

H.L.'s kiss had meant something entirely different. It meant he considered her a desirable woman, and it had thrilled Rose to her very core. It also frightened her an equal amount, since it meant she was vulnerable to him and his wicked ways.

Were his ways wicked? Annie would say so. Annie had much more experience of the world than Rose did. Probably Annie was right about it, but that made Rose feel bad, and she hoped she was wrong.

How did a woman tell if a man's intentions were honorable or not? Pondering this, Rose brushed out her tangled hair and plaited it into one thick braid for bed. She imagined Annie would tell her that if a man was honorable, he wouldn't kiss a lady without asking her permission first.

H.L. hadn't asked. In fact, he'd surprised her nearly into a swoon when he'd kissed her.

She frowned as she pulled down her bedclothes. Asking would take all the spontaneity and fun out of a kiss, though, wouldn't it? Rose didn't think she'd have been half so excited if H.L. had asked first.

Of course, that was probably because she'd have refused if he'd asked—and not because she didn't want him to kiss her, but because she knew that his kissing her was wrong.

Fiddlesticks. She was too tired to be thinking about any of this confusing nonsense. After a sound sleep, perhaps she'd be able to understand better what had happened this evening—morning—whatever it was—and how to proceed from now on, as concerned H.L. May.

She didn't believe herself, but she went to sleep before her conflicting sides could engage in an all-out battle.

FIFTEEN

Afternoon, hell. It was almost seven o'clock before H.L. jumped out of the cab in front of the Wild West encampment and, clutching a copy of Monday's early edition, raced to Rose's tent. He hadn't meant to come this late, but he'd stayed at the *Globe* office until nearly 8:00 A.M., writing two complete articles. By the time he'd finally fallen into his bed, he'd been dead on his feet, and he'd slept for nine hours.

He told himself he was hurrying to see Rose not because he wanted to see her, exactly, but because he wanted to interview her some more. He'd almost talked himself into believing it by the time he got to her tent and discovered she wasn't there.

"Rose!" he cried in real distress. The fact that his unhappiness was real, and that he felt as if someone had gouged a hole in his heart, made him reassess his motives. Hell, not even H.L. May, who considered himself at the top of the line when it came to ace reporting, could conscientiously allow himself to preserve the fiction that he only wanted Rose for a story.

"Damn." So much for that pleasant theory. As he stomped off, wondering where the hell she'd gotten herself off to, he berated himself as an ass.

He never should have kissed her. He wouldn't feel this intense longing to see her again if he'd kept better control over himself. But had he? No. He'd had to succumb to temptation, draw her into his arms, and kiss her. The kiss had

kindled all of his wolfish instincts, and now he wouldn't be
satisfied until he'd known her completely, in the biblical
sense.

Not that there was anything the least bit biblical about his
carnal urges regarding Rose Gilhooley. The problem was
that, when he entertained the delicious fantasy about Rose in
his bed, he didn't feel quite right about it, and that had never
happened to him before. He'd never experienced any qualms
about bedding a delectable female. Why the hell were
qualms attacking him now?

But Rose was such an innocent. She was not of this world,
in fact—or not of H.L.'s world, anyhow. She had provincial
morals and standards and wasn't sophisticated as he was.
She didn't have any big-city gloss to her. To Rose, an affair
would be a serious undertaking. She wouldn't consider a
sexual liaison with him in the light of recreation. The only
context in which Rose would condone a sexual encounter
would be within the bounds of matrimony.

H.L. shuddered at the thought of marriage. That he had to
force himself to do so because the shudder didn't come naturally, as it had always done before he'd met Rose, he chalked
up to residual weariness from a long day, a bout of energetic
fisticuffs, and insufficient sleep. He wasn't sure he believed
himself.

He'd managed to make his way to the Sioux encampment
as he pondered all of this. Spying Little Elk, he waved and
set up a holler. "Little Elk!"

He'd learned as soon as he'd awakened that evening what
Rose had meant about the Sioux thanking him in unexpected
ways for his help in rescuing Bear in Winter. When he'd
opened the door to his apartment, he'd found, tacked up with
a knife, a rawhide pouch filled with a variety of things H.L.
couldn't precisely identify.

There was a beadwork pouch inside the leather pouch,
which he assumed was for anything he wanted to use it for,
some leather moccasins also decorated with beads, some

kind of dried meat—pemmican or jerky, he'd heard that sort of thing was called—and a quillwork belt. He thought it was a belt, anyway. Whatever it was, H.L. appreciated all of it, including the knife, which had some great carvings on it and looked as if it had been fashioned of bone. He wondered if a slaughtered buffalo's bones had been the source of the haft.

Whatever the items had been made of, the gift provoked lots of images in H.L.'s mind, that's for sure. Visions of great buffalo hunts and of Indians riding across the vast plains wielding bows and arrows flickered in his head, along with pictures of Indians in feathered headbands and fringed moccasins dancing around a campfire.

He took a moment to wonder if his images bore any resemblance whatever to reality, or if he'd adopted the dime novelists' renditions of Indian traditions as fact. There was a great idea for another series of articles, if he could get any of the Sioux to talk to him. According to Rose, and he'd noticed the same thing, the Sioux weren't apt to chat with white men about their culture.

H.L. understood, although he hoped he'd be able to jostle some information out of Little Elk, even if no one else in the Sioux camp trusted him. At the moment, however, his interest in Little Elk extended only as far as to ask him if he knew where Rose was.

Little Elk frowned. "With Little Sureshot, I think."

H.L. felt confounded for a moment. "Little Sure-shot? Oh, Annie Oakley. Right. I should have thought of that myself."

The Indian nodded as if he agreed.

H.L. didn't mind. He understood that the Sioux's take on things might relegate white intelligence to a fairly low rung on the ladder. He said, "Say, Little Elk, I appreciate the gift someone left on my door today. I like it very much."

Little Elk nodded. "You save Bear in Winter."

"Right. Well, thanks." H.L. had read that Indians didn't

receive thanks in the same way whites did, and he wasn't sure how much gushing he should do.

Damn it, if he could find Rose, she could tell him. He was slightly peeved with her for running off before he'd arrived. After all, he'd *told* her he'd come by this afternoon.

"Bear said you almost kill the man who took him. That's good." Little Elk nodded again, as if to indicate H.L. had performed a good deed and was appreciated for it.

Glancing at his swollen knuckles—he'd removed the bandages, figuring fresh air might do the cuts and scratches some good—H.L. muttered, "I'm glad to have helped."

Little Elk nodded again and didn't look as if he intended to keep the conversation going, so H.L. said, "So long. I'm going to look for Rose," and took off.

He wished Little Elk hadn't mentioned that fight. H.L. had managed to forget about it in his panic over missing Rose, but as soon as Little Elk reminded him, his hands and jawbone resumed aching. His arms ached, too, not to mention his ribs. They weren't accustomed to that kind and severity of exercise. It was probably a good thing H.L. had decided to become a reporter and not a riverboat captain or something, since he didn't think he'd really enjoy that much physical exertion on a regular basis.

The balmy May day smelled of blooming flowers combined with the leftover scent of popcorn mingled with horses and a faint whiff of the stockyards. If H.L. had been in Rose's company, he'd have considered the day just about perfect. As it was, no matter how much he appreciated the elaborate gardens the fair directors had planted, and the hundreds of energetically blooming rosebushes therein, the day had a hole in. A Rose-sized hole. He'd started out in a good mood, but it was sinking with each step he took without Rose on his arm.

"Damn it," he muttered as he paused to try to remember where Annie Oakley's tent was.

He spotted Rose before he got to Annie's tent. She was

dressed to the nines in a lavender spring suit and a tiny flowered hat. His heart soared into the stratosphere, executed several front flips and a back somersault, then careened about in his body for a second or two before coming to rest in his chest. Damned heart. It was terribly unpredictable these days.

Rose hadn't seen him yet, so he set up a shout. "Rose! Rose! Here I am!"

It only occurred to him after he'd hollered that she might not have been as eager to see him as he was to see her. Although H.L. had a very good understanding of his own self-worth, the notion that she might have a different one daunted him. He was even more daunted when he saw Rose glance up, spot him, and frown.

Blast it, what was she frowning at him for? Hell, he was going to make her famous. Not that she wasn't already famous, but—aw, hell, he knew what he meant.

Because he didn't want her to know how insecure he felt, and because the feeling was as uncomfortable as it was new to him, he waved and trotted over to her. She was with Annie, and they looked as though they might be going off somewhere together. Maybe he could go with them. The notion of heading back to his lonely apartment without getting a full dose of Rose only served to depress his spirits, so he aimed to push his way in on their excursion if he could. He had faith in his brass.

Sweeping his jaunty spring straw hat from his head, he gave the two ladies a small but perfect bow. "Good afternoon, Mrs. Butler. Rose."

Annie gave him a frosty "Good evening, Mr. May."

Rose's cheeks were pink. H.L. didn't know if she was embarrassed or had only got some sun the day before. She muttered, "H.L."

Perceiving that she was edgy in his company, and in an effort to diffuse any misunderstanding on her part, he said, "Sorry I'm a little late. I spent a couple of hours at the *Globe* office after I left you this morning, and I'm afraid I slept a little longer than I'd planned."

Her stiffness eased a little, and H.L. was glad he'd made his uncharacteristic apology. He generally felt little need to apologize for anything.

"I wondered if you'd forgotten you'd asked to interview me again today," Rose said. Her voice was soft, as if she wasn't sure of him or herself.

Probably an aftermath of the kiss, H.L. told himself. The kiss loomed large in his own mind today, but since Rose hadn't nearly the experience he had when it came to kisses, she was undoubtedly feeling more than ordinarily shy. "Not a bit of it. I wouldn't be likely to forget that, would I?" He gave her one of his more dazzling smiles. This was the one he reserved for women he was trying to wear down so they'd go to bed with him.

She lowered her head and stared at the ground, as if she were inspecting something fascinating that had crawled onto her shoe. "I wouldn't know."

His immediate reaction to that was to bark something sarcastic at her because her words had irked him, but he bit back the impulse. Annie spoke next—mercifully, in H.L.'s opinion, since he didn't have any idea what to say next and he didn't have any more smiles in his repertoire.

"We're on our way to the evening service at Saint Mark's Episcopal Church, Mr. May. If you'd care to join us, I'm sure it would do you a world of good."

Annie's voice was as caustic as her words, and H.L. glanced at her keenly. What was her problem? Was she mad at him for some reason?

Oh, crap. Rose hadn't told her about that kiss, had she? A glance at Rose told him nothing since, although she'd stopped staring at her feet, she'd started fiddling with the small handbag she carried and was now staring off into space. It was clear to H.L. that she didn't want to look at him. She probably didn't want him to accompany them to church, either. To hell with them both.

Donning his cockiest demeanor, he swung around to Rose's side. "Don't mind if I do. I haven't been to church for a long time."

"I'm not surprised," Annie said with something of a snarl.

Rose allowed her shoulders to slump for only a moment. H.L. resented that slump.

Damn it, he didn't mean her any harm. Couldn't she tell that much about him, even if she was as innocent as a newborn lamb? He'd never encountered such an intriguing combination of worldly wisdom and absolute innocence. He hoped he'd captured it in his article. The good Lord knew he'd tried hard and long enough. He'd tried so hard and so long, he'd missed an entire night's sleep. That he'd managed to catch up on his sleep during the day, he chose not to remember, since he was reveling in his indignation at present.

They caught a cab and rode to church. None of them said a word the whole way. H.L. maintained his nonchalant exterior, although he wasn't feeling nonchalant inside. He was feeling abused. The feeling didn't abate as they left the cab—Annie paid before H.L. could reach into his pocket for money—and climbed the steps to the church.

St. Mark's was a pretty place, designed along Renaissance lines, with a tall bell tower. Inside, the Victorians had had a field day. There were carvings everywhere, and the stained-glass windows made an explosion of color on the pews as the sun shone through them. H.L. watched Rose as she took it all in. He'd have liked to talk to her about it, since he found a certain interest—not to say joy, which was an awfully strong word and made him nervous—in listening to her discover new things.

Although he was almost certain Rose didn't want him to, H.L. maneuvered so as to sit between the two ladies during the church service. It became clear to him as the ritual progressed that Rose wasn't familiar with the Episcopalian way of doing things.

He ventured a question while the three of them walked to the cab that would return them to the Wild West encampment. "So, Rose, did you grow up in the Episcopal Church?"

Her quick frown surprised him. "You know very well that I grew up in Deadwood—oh." Her flush was as quick as her frown had been. "I understand what you mean. No, I went to the church closest to our farm. It wasn't Episcopal."

"What denomination was it?"

"What difference does that make?" Annie snapped. "At least she went to church."

H.L. turned to Annie. He didn't understand her hostility. Even if Rose had told her about the kiss, he ought to have been forgiven by this time. After all, it wasn't everyone for whom H.L. May would attend church. "It only matters to readers, Mrs. Butler. They're eager to know all there is to know about Miss Gilhooley." It occurred to him that she might also be miffed that he and Rose were on first-name terms, although he didn't know why she should be. It wasn't any of her business.

"When I was a small child, the church didn't even have a designated denomination, as far as I know," Rose said in a rush, as if she were attempting to stave off violence between her companions.

H.L. gave up trying to wriggle his way into his companions' good graces as they approached the hack. He couldn't buck Annie's hostility and Rose's shyness in the confines of the cab. He hadn't regained his full strength yet and wasn't up to a verbal battle. Yesterday's physical one had him aching from jawbone to toenails.

They returned to the Wild West without more than two words being spoken by anyone. Once they got there and it became clear to H.L. that Rose planned to hang out with

Annie for the rest of the night, he decided his luck was out for the day.

In a foul mood by this time, he said, "Here," as he thrust the early edition at Rose. "You can read what I wrote about you. It'll appear in tomorrow's paper." Handing her another, smaller rolled-up package of papers, he said, "This will be coming out in Thursday's paper. It tells about how we rescued Bear in Winter, too."

Startled, Rose took the newspapers. "Thank you. I mean, it's nice of you to—to bring them to me."

"Yeah," said H.L. "Sure." As he turned and slunk away, he felt very low.

Rose watched him go, clutching the newspapers close to her bosom and feeling both guilty and ashamed. She was ashamed that she'd kissed him last night, and ashamed that she hadn't been nicer to him today. She felt guilty about both of those things, as well. She was also slightly annoyed with Annie, who had no reason to dislike Mr. May as much as she seemed to. She also felt guilty about that, since Annie had been her kindest friend and a surrogate family to Rose since she joined the Wild West.

"Fiddlesticks," she muttered at last. "I give up."

Annie sniffed. "I hope you're not letting that man take advantage of you, Rose."

With a sigh, Rose turned and started walking with her friend toward the Butler tent. "I'm not." What Annie didn't know wouldn't hurt her. Even more to the point, it wouldn't hurt Rose, and at the moment that was more important to her than anything else.

"I'm so tired," she mumbled as they walked slowly along. "I've never been through such a night."

"I'm sure." As if she regretted her hard edge, Annie added, "You performed a heroic act yesterday, Rose. I'm glad Mr. May wrote about it. The colonel will be beside himself with joy."

Since Annie smiled at her after she said those nice things,

Rose smiled back. She felt minutely better that her friend didn't seem inclined to give her a lecture or question her about Mr. May's possible advantage-taking.

More brightly, Annie said, "Let's take the papers to my tent, and you can read them to me. That way, I can enjoy the articles, too, and help look up words if you need me to."

"Thank you, Annie." Rose felt true gratitude, because she really did want to read what H.L. had written about her. She hoped to goodness he'd be kind about her lack of education and so forth, since she wasn't eager for the citizens of Chicago, or anywhere else for that matter, to know what an uneducated dunce she was.

Since whaleboning and Sunday-go-to-church clothes were all but suffocating her, she persuaded Annie to stop by her tent before continuing to the Butler abode. There she removed her corset, stockings, and Sunday shoes, changed into a simple skirt and shirtwaist and donned her old, soft, worn-down moccasins. She felt much more comfortable and, therefore, much more cheerful afterward.

"Oh, look, Annie!" Rose had just opened the Monday paper. The article about her was featured on the first page of the second section. "There's the picture of me that nice man, Mr. Asher, took that day when he came by to meet us. There's one of you, too." She showed Annie the photographs.

The one of Annie showed her aiming at a target that looked as if it was about a thousand yards away, thanks to the angle. She appeared very serious about what she was doing.

Rose's photograph, on the other hand, was much more exuberant. Mr. Asher had captured her in full costume, a glorious smile on her face, standing on Fairy's back with her arms flung in the air, and with one of Chicago's famous winds blowing her feathered headdress out behind her. The feathers were blurred because they'd been in motion, but that only added to the feel of the picture, which was one of exhilaration and action. At least, Rose told herself, that's the feeling she got when she looked at it, and she was vastly pleased.

She was also pleased because when she first saw the picture, her first reaction had been to notice how pretty the girl on the horse was. She only realized a second later that the pretty girl was her, Rose Gilhooley, and that's the way she really looked. It was a delicious discovery, and one Rose hugged close to her heart, although she knew it was vain of her to do so.

"That's a lovely picture of you." Even Annie appeared gratified. "Mr. Asher's a good photographer."

"I'll say."

"He really captured you, Rose. You're such a pretty girl."

"Thanks, Annie." Now Rose was embarrassed, although she didn't say anything else, fearing she was being foolish. It had been Annie herself who'd once told her that the best thing to do when one paid you a compliment was to say, "Thank you," and let it go.

Calmer now that she'd viewed the two photographs, Rose felt slightly less uneasy than she had been earlier when she started reading H.L.'s article, the one intended for the Thursday paper. She was interested to know how he'd captured the rescue in words. She cleared her throat and began slowly. She continued slowly, as well, since she hadn't mastered the art of reading aloud very well yet.

" 'Miss Rose Ellen Gilhooley was born in the rough-and-tumble community of Deadwood, Kansas,' " the article began. Rose looked up at Annie, who was seated nearby, embroidering a cloak for her white poodle, George. "So far, so good."

Annie chuckled.

Rose's complaisant mood didn't last long. Before long, she was reading even more slowly and with dawning apprehension. Maybe horror was a better word. " 'The charming

Miss Gilhooley, an uneducated and unlettered young woman'—Oh, Annie! How could he *write* that? I don't care if it's true; it's humiliating!"

Annie had laid aside her embroidery several sentences ago. Her face was set into a stern frown. "I don't know, Rose, but I fear I was right about Mr. May. He's not a nice man, and you'd be better off not speaking to him again."

Wiping tears that, in spite of her attempt to control them, had leaked from her eyes, Rose said shakily, "You're right. What a fool I was to believe him." Because she'd already begun reading the article, and because she was driven by the need to see what other shocks lay in wait for her within H.L.'s words, Rose continued reading. " 'Unable to read more than simple, basic words'—Oh, Annie, that's not even true!" Rose wiped away more tears. "Not anymore, anyhow. I'm learning. He didn't even give me credit for *learning!*"

"The man's a monster," Annie stated flatly.

Rose found she didn't want to disagree with Annie's harsh assessment of H.L. May's character. She no longer entertained the slightest inclination to defend him. She hated him. She wanted to take up one of Annie's guns and shoot him dead.

" 'Although the ravishing'—What does *ravishing* mean, Annie?" She wasn't sure she wanted to know.

"He finds you attractive," said Annie through seriously clenched teeth.

Well, that was something, anyway. Rose sniffed. " 'Although the ravishing Miss Gilhooley is unlettered and unso'—Fiddlesticks. I hate it when he uses big words. What does u-n-s-o-p-h-i-s-t-i-c-a-t-e-d spell?"

"Unsophisticated."

"Oh." Rose heaved a huge sigh and decided she guessed she was unsophisticated all right, although she despised H.L. for revealing this flaw to the whole world. Without further comment, she continued. " 'Although the unsophisticated Miss Gilhooley knows little or nothing about life in a big city, she proved herself to be an ace at tracking down lost children.' "

Crumpling the newspaper as she lowered it to her lap, she gazed at the far side of Annie's tent for a moment, contemplating the words she'd just read. "Did that sound sarcastic to you, or am I imagining it?" she asked at last.

Annie had picked up her embroidery again, although the sour expression on her face hadn't gone away. "I don't believe you're imagining a thing, dear. I think he's making fun of you."

Rose's heart crunched painfully. "That's what I was afraid of." She lifted the paper and went on, grimly determined to finish the article and learn the worst.

It took a long time, since she had to spell out many of the bigger words H.L. had used in the article. *He,* obviously, hadn't missed out on an education. Blast him. *He* could fling words around as if they were nothing at all. *He* could annihilate Rose Gilhooley in the newspaper with ease and facility. *He* probably thought Rose was too stupid to read the article in the first place.

Or . . . Maybe that wasn't true. Maybe he'd given her the newspaper to prove to her exactly what he thought of her, which was pretty much nothing except on a superficial level. She amused him. That much was clear. He thought she was pretty. That was clear, too. But he despised her as beneath him. That was painfully obvious.

Rose wanted to shoot him. Then she wanted to shoot herself. Then she wanted to jump up and down on him, wearing the one pair of heavy boots she owned. Then she wanted to throw him into Lake Michigan and laugh as he drowned.

She wanted to die.

"Rose, look at me."

Rose lifted her head and looked at Annie. She couldn't remember the last time she'd been this miserable, unless it was when her father had died. Or maybe when she'd departed Deadwood to join the Wild West, leaving her mother and brother and sisters behind. This felt worse even than that.

"You will *not* allow that man to make you unhappy," Annie commanded.

"Oh?" She couldn't make herself ask Annie how to accomplish that feat. Anyhow, it was beyond her since H.L. May had made her unhappy already.

"No. You will not. You will not speak to him again, and you won't fall for any more of his 'I-want-to-interview-you' tactics. The man has no morals and is a fiend."

"He is? A fiend, I mean."

Annie gestured at the newspaper. "Would he have called you an unschooled bumpkin if he wasn't a fiend?"

Rose winced when she recalled that part of the article. "No, I guess he wouldn't have."

"He is an insensitive boor, and if you take my advice, you'll refuse to see him again."

Rose's heart felt as if it were being gripped in an eagle's talons. It hurt *so* badly. Here she'd begun to believe H.L. May wanted to be her friend. If she were brutally honest with herself, she'd own up to something else. She'd begun to harbor a faint wish that he wanted more than friendship from her.

Annie went on, interrupting Rose's train of thought. "I hope to heaven that man hasn't taken any liberties with you, Rose. If he has, he's worse than a scoundrel."

"Liberties?" Rose almost cried out in torment when she recalled that kiss. Had that been a liberty? It had felt like heaven. Rose heaved a huge sigh. Yup. It had been a liberty. And she was a simple-minded fool. "No," she lied. "He hasn't taken liberties."

"Hmph. I wouldn't put it past him." Annie again laid her embroidery aside. She got up and joined Rose, who was sitting on the bed, and put her arms around her. "Oh, Rose, I'm so sorry. I know how much this article hurt you. It made me angry, too, although perhaps we're making more of it than is really there."

Rose had subsided into Annie's arms and allowed herself to cry. Annie would understand. Sniffling, she said, "How? It was mean, what he said."

"Perhaps he was only trying to be honest," Annie said, sounding as if she didn't believe it. "Perhaps he didn't mean to belittle you."

"Hunh!" Rose didn't buy that one. After spending so much time with H.L. May, if he hadn't come to understand how sensitive she was about her lack of education, he was a really lousy reporter, and Rose didn't believe *that* for a second.

When H.L. moseyed around to the Wild West encampment late on Monday morning, he was surprised not to find Rose exercising one of her pretty white horses in the arena. Glancing around, he saw no one at all, not even Little Elk searching for coins.

"Huh." He guessed he'd just have to go look for her, then.

She wasn't in her tent. When she didn't answer his call, he lifted the flap and peered inside. No Rose. Since she liked to hang around with Annie Oakley, he made his way to the Butlers' tent, the flap of which was down. Unusual, that. The Butlers usually kept the flap up during the day, to catch the Chicago breezes. He stood outside and hallooed.

He was startled when, a second later, Annie popped outside, dropping the tent flap behind her. She looked as if she was as mad as a wet hen, and he jogged backward a step.

"What are *you* doing here?" she asked without preamble.

Taken aback, H.L. stumbled over his response. "I-I'm looking for Rose. Miss Gilhooley. You know. Rose. Wind Dancer. To interview."

Reaching up, Annie wagged a finger in his face. H.L. blinked in time to the movement of her finger. "Rose doesn't want to see you again, Mr. May. That article you wrote about her was not only mean and degrading, it was awful. I don't know how you can live with yourself, writing things like that about people."

Dumbfounded, H.L. could only stare down at Annie, who knew an advantage when she saw one and continued to berate him.

"If you didn't discover, in all the hours you spent with Rose, that she's sensitive about her limited education, you're a pure idiot, Mr. May, and I don't believe that. I think you're too smart for your own good. You did what you did on purpose. You humiliated her in print, and that's unforgivable. You ought to be horsewhipped."

"Shot," came from inside the tent. H.L. recognized Rose's voice.

"Rose!" he cried. He was feeling sort of numb, not having anticipated this reaction from the woman he'd written about in such glowing terms.

"You can't speak to her," Annie said abruptly. "And you assuredly can't see her. You said the most dreadful things about her in that article. You made her feel *awful,* and you just get out of here now!" She whirled around and ducked back into her tent.

H.L. might have tried to enter the tent after her, except he saw, by the indentations on the canvas, that she was tying down the flap. He also didn't care to have one of Annie Oakley's famous guns aimed at him, mainly because she was too good with her weapons and he didn't want to annoy her more than she was already annoyed. His mouth hanging open, he stared at the tent flap for a few minutes, trying to think.

Damn. He'd humiliated her? Rose? He shook his head hard, attempting valiantly to figure this out. How could an article that fairly glowed with admiration for her humiliate her? How could she object to his having exalted her brilliance, both as a performer and as a person? She was angry because he'd pointed out her lack of a formal education? But he'd explained all that! Plus, he'd admired her continuing attempts to make up for her ignorance, and had written so clearly and enthusiastically in his article. How could that humiliate anyone?

He stood outside the Butlers' tent for almost ten minutes, trying to understand Rose's reaction to the pieces he'd written about her, but he couldn't. He'd meant those articles to be paeans of praise for a woman he admired above all other women in the world. How could she take them so completely the wrong way?

By the time he finally gave up and left the Wild West, he hadn't come up with an answer. The only thing he knew for certain was that he couldn't let things rest like this. He needed to talk to Rose, to make her see reason—to make her see *him*.

He had a vague and unsettling feeling in his gut that if he couldn't persuade her to see him again, he'd waste away and die.

SIXTEEN

Rose managed to clear her mind of thoughts about H.L. May so she could perform that night. She knew better than to clutter her brain with extraneous matter when she was doing potentially lethal acrobatic tricks on horseback.

The crowd roared when she rode into the arena. Although that was not unusual, this evening the yells of approval sounded even louder than normal. This surprised her, since she hadn't anticipated it. In the pit of unhappiness into which she'd sunk, she'd expected nobody to show up at all after reading that article about her. Or, if anyone showed up, she figured they'd jeer at her.

But they didn't. They applauded and cheered and clapped and whistled as if they were all madly in love with her. They even gave her a standing ovation before she'd done more than ride out of the tunnel and circle the arena. Odd, that. Rose didn't understand.

She went through her routine, keeping her mind on her business, although spontaneous eruptions of applause continued to surprise her throughout her act. When she'd taken her last dancing bow on Fairy, the crowd went wild. She looked around at the audience, and couldn't understand why they were so much more enthusiastic tonight than usual.

The colonel rode out to salute the crowd, and gave her a hug from his horse as he sometimes did. Rose feared for her ears, the clamor got so loud. The people sure loved the colonel.

"They sure love you, Rosie."

Rose jerked her head around and stared at the colonel. Did he think the audience was going crazy for *her?* She glanced back at them, decided she ought to give them another wave, did so, and almost had to clap her hands over her ears when another deafening roar split the air.

"You gotta give 'em another dance around the ring, Rosie," the colonel said, grinning from ear to ear. "They love you. That reporter fella did us all proud with that article he wrote about you."

He did? Dazed with shock, Rose didn't respond with words, but did as the colonel had suggested. Waving and smiling at her admirers even though her head was in a whirl, she circled the ring again, nudging Fairy into a high-stepping trot. After they'd made the circuit, she directed Fairy into the center of the ring, had her take one last elegant bow, and decided enough was enough. The show would get seriously behind schedule if she kept taking extra bows.

The uproarious thunder of the audience's appreciation followed her out of the ring. In a fog, she took the moccasins Annie handed up to her.

"They love you, Rose," Annie told her with a radiant smile. "They absolutely *love* you."

"Thanks, Annie," Rose mumbled, beginning to feel a trifle uncomfortable about all the noise.

She slipped her moccasins on, slid from Fairy's back, and guided the horse through the masses of cavalry and Indians waiting to head out into the arena to enact Custer's Last Stand. As she returned her friends' waves and congratulations by rote, her brain started churning.

Was the colonel right? Did that horde of people out there love her because of what H.L. May had written about her? Rose trusted the colonel implicitly, but she wasn't sure about this one, mainly because it made no sense to her.

After she'd finished reading those articles, she'd felt as if H.L. had knifed her in the back. She'd felt as if he'd stripped her naked and paraded her around Chicago, revealing to the masses every single one of her faults and deficiencies. Annie had understood exactly how she'd felt, because she'd shared her view of the articles.

Could the two of them possibly be wrong? Did the people of Chicago like her even better now, knowing she'd overcome certain obstacles? Rose gave her head a shake, making her feathers jiggle and tickle her calves, and she realized she'd forgotten to take off her headdress. She did so as she walked to the stables, still attempting to make sense of everything that had transpired in the past day or so.

She was so involved in puzzling the matter out that she didn't at first see H.L. May, who was waiting for her inside the stable. When she saw him, she stopped in her tracks, confusing Fairy, who whickered with irritation. Fairy's favorite part of the day was the few minutes after her performance, when she got pampered.

Rose blurted out, "H.L."

He pushed himself away from the wall he'd been holding up and walked over to her, ignoring the horse. "I need to talk to you, Rose."

Even as her heart soared with joy at seeing him again, she knew she didn't want to talk to him. Not about those wretched articles. She felt foolish, as if she'd made a big deal out of nothing.

Yet it hadn't been nothing to her. Those articles had hurt her so badly, she'd been totally crushed after she'd finished reading them. She was ashamed of her lack of education, and of his calling her an unschooled bumpkin. Annie had called him a fiend for that one. Just thinking about it made the heat creep up the back of her neck. The thought of the whole world learning her deepest secrets made Rose want to crawl into a hole and hide.

Knowing she was in no condition to make sense of anything, she withdrew into herself. Renewing her forward progress, much to Fairy's relief, she muttered, "About what?"

"You know about what." He fell into step beside her.

Rose felt hemmed in, as she had that first night, with H.L. on one side and the horse on the other. Uncomfortable, she sped up. H.L. kept up with her, blast him. When they got to where Rose's equipment was laid out, H.L. subsided, thank God. He went over to lean against another wall.

"I didn't mean to hurt your feelings, Rose. You *must* know that."

"Must I?" She glanced at him out of the corner of her eye as she reached for Fairy's brush.

"You have to." He sounded almost desperate. "Those articles praised you to the skies, for God's sake!"

Rose sniffed. "I didn't get that from them."

"Obviously." Now he sounded cranky. "You're too damned sensitive. Do you know that? Somebody praises you for rising above your circumstances, and all you do is get mad because they mentioned the circumstances. Did you pay any attention at all to the rest of the articles?"

"Yes," she snapped. She was beginning to feel as if he were shoving her into a corner, and she didn't enjoy the feeling. "Yes, I read the whole thing, thank you, in spite of my *unschooled* background. Of course, it took me a long time, since I had to sound out a lot of the words." She sniffed imperiously.

"Ah, Jesus." H.L. flung his arms in the air in a gesture of supreme frustration.

Rose resented that. Anybody would think it was *she* who was at fault here. She pointed the currycomb at him. "You may think it's fine and dandy to reveal a person's darkest secrets to the world, H.L. May, but some of us prefer to enjoy a little privacy. It's not enjoyable for me to have the whole world know how stupid I am."

"You're not stupid, damn it!"

He hollered so loudly, Fairy objected, dancing nervously and nudging Rose. Rose winced at the noise and comforted her horse. "There's no need to yell at me, H.L.," she grumbled. She did appreciate his emphatic renunciation of her alleged stupidity, although she'd never say so. Rather, she sniffed again.

"A lack of education doesn't mean you're stupid, damn it," H.L. went on. "Lots of people don't have the opportunity to go to school. You've done more than most people, even people *with* an education. Don't you see that?"

She glared at him, feeling silly about her reaction to his articles, but resenting them anyhow. "It's all well and good for you to say such things, H.L. May, but look at it from my point of view for a moment. How would *you* like it if the whole world learned the one thing about you that you were most ashamed of?" Embarrassed by this statement and the admission of her shame, she turned back to her horse and clucked gently to her. She started brushing her, hoping H.L. wouldn't notice how shaky she was.

"Damnation, Rose Gilhooley, you're a public figure! What's more, the public eats up the kind of stuff I wrote in those articles!"

Rose huffed, mainly because she didn't know what to say.

"You may not like it, but the fact is people want to know about their idols, and you're an idol for a whole lot of people. Especially kids."

A wrenching pain swooped through Rose as his words sank in. She dropped the currycomb and stared at H.L. "Oh, my God," she whispered. "Now every child in Chicago is going to know I have no education."

H.L. stalked up to her and took her by the arms. "Damn it, Rose, that's not what they're going to focus on!" He shook her lightly. "They're going to read today's article, and their parents are going to say to their children, 'See? This young lady came from pitiful circumstances, and look at what she's made of herself.' They're going to say, 'Don't you dare complain to me about your life. Look at Wind Dancer. See what she's done with herself. She's a big star with Buffalo Bill's Wild West, and she was so much poorer than we are; she had to shoot game for her family to eat when she was just a child. She never had a chance to go to school, yet she made something of herself.' Don't you understand, Rose?"

The only thing Rose understood at the moment was that she didn't want anybody to know what a hick she was, and that it felt wildly good to be this close to H.L. again. She resisted the urge to fling her arms about him, but it was an effort.

"Damn it, didn't you *hear* those people out there?" He shook her again, still lightly or Rose would probably have socked him. "Well? Did you?"

She admitted it. "Yes."

"You see? Those people read all about you and what you call your deficiencies, and they love you more now than they did before! And it's because they admire you and what you've made of yourself! Don't you see that?"

"Well . . ." Now she felt totally foolish. It occurred to her that she simply couldn't win with H.L. May, and the notion was darned depressing.

"Admit it, Rose. It's true. You and your friend Annie Oakley might not want to admit it, but it's the truth. You're a phenomenal example of the human spirit triumphing over circumstances. You're a real-life, honest-to-God rags-to-riches story. You're a tiny, beautiful, wonderful miracle of life."

She wanted to whack the side of her head to clear it of fluff. Had he really said all those nice things about her? Did he *mean* them? She'd really like to know but didn't feel comfortable asking. Anyhow, he was going on, so she couldn't.

"Those people admire you. *I* admire you! Hell, the whole world would admire you if they knew you. Damn it, you're special."

She swallowed, then asked in a tiny voice, "I am?"

He goggled at her. "How can you even doubt it?"

Since she didn't know, she shrugged.

"Aw, hell, Rose."

H.L. gazed down at her for several seconds, as if searching for something to say. Rose recognized the exact second he decided words weren't enough, but she didn't have time to prepare herself because she was in his arms an instant later, and he was kissing her as if there would be no tomorrow.

Rose felt his hunger and recognized it, because it matched her own. Unable to resist a moment longer, she threw her arms around his neck and clung to him.

"Ah, Rose, Rose, Rose," H.L. mumbled into her curls. "Damn, I want you."

He did? A thrill shot through her at his words. She wanted him, too, although she wasn't sure for what. She had a vague notion it had to do with one of the more basic secrets of life, however. He resumed kissing her, feathering light touches over her cheeks and throat and turning Rose to jelly in his arms.

"I can't stand knowing you're angry with me, Rose," he said after another few moments. "I was afraid you'd never speak to me again, and I couldn't have stood that."

She didn't think she could have stood it, either. Unable to form words, she only held him more tightly and ran her lips over his jawline. Recalling the punishment that jaw had taken a mere two days prior, she lifted her hand and delicately brushed her fingers against the livid bruises. "Does this still hurt?"

He didn't answer immediately. It seemed to take a moment or two for him to process her question. Pulling back slightly, he blinked down at her. "What? Oh. No, it doesn't hurt much."

"I'm glad."

He crushed her against him again. She felt his hard body against her own, and it was perfectly glorious. Something hard and long pressed against her thigh. It took her a moment to realize it was the evidence of his desire for her. She was shocked for only a second before passion subsumed her fear and replaced it with delight.

Yes! This is what she wanted from H.L. May! She wanted his passion. His desire. His—oh, Lord.

Suddenly, Rose stilled in his arms, because she understood what she wanted from him, and it frightened her—mainly because she didn't think she could get it.

Lord help her, she wanted his love.

"Rose," he whispered in her ear, "I want you so badly, I can hardly stand it."

The emotions that surged through Rose nearly rendered her speechless. Understanding was followed almost immediately by a sense of defeat. H.L. May, a man who lived through words, could never love Rose Gilhooley. He might admire her for overcoming her origins, but he'd never be happy with a woman who couldn't handle language the way he could.

Shortly on the heels of defeat came resignation and something she couldn't immediately put a name to. A second later she decided it was acceptance. If she could never secure his lasting love, perhaps she could experience a brief season of his affection and passion.

Swallowing both her dreams and her scruples, Rose whispered, "I want you, too, H.L."

His renewed kisses made her understand how much he appreciated her admission. Rose decided not to fight the heady sensations rioting in her body, but to relinquish herself to them. If she couldn't have his love, she could experience his desire and her own, and she'd make do with that. She guessed she'd have to.

As for H.L., he was lost. He wasn't sure he believed he'd really heard Rose say she wanted him, but if he hadn't he didn't want to know it, so he kept kissing her. He explored her small, sturdy body as he did so, allowing his hands to wander at will. She was perfect, as far as he could tell through touch.

Her breasts were wonderful, as he'd expected them to be. Thank the good Lord, she didn't wear a corset during her act, but only a chemise and underdrawers. He managed to get the top of her costume open with a minimum of struggle. It was crafted of lightweight calico, he presumed so as not to interfere with movement during her act, and it fastened with buttons, which he worked with ease.

"H.L. !" she cried softly when his hand covered her breast.

Worried that she'd object, he whispered, "You're so beautiful, Rose. Please . . ." He wasn't sure what he was pleading for, but it had something to do with her not making him stop.

She said no more, but sighed deeply as her nipples pebbled under his tender assault. He stroked them lightly, longing to taste them but not wanting to rush anything.

It wasn't until Fairy got fed up with being ignored during this, her favorite time of the day, and gave Rose's back a firm push with her nose, that H.L. realized what he'd been about to do. He staggered when Rose fell against him. He barely managed to straighten up with her in his arms in time to prevent them both from tumbling onto the stable floor.

He glanced around the stable, confused, before reality conked him over the head with a *thunk*.

Good God! He'd been about to ravish Rose Gilhooley, star of Buffalo Bill's Wild West and woman extraordinaire, in a horse barn! He could hardly believe such a thing of himself. Aghast, he muttered, "Good God." Then he shook his head, trying to get the jumble therein to organize itself.

"Oh, my," said Rose in a rattled whisper.

Gazing down at her, H.L. noticed that her eyes appeared about as unfocused as his own brain. This would never do. He ought to be horsewhipped, as Annie Oakley had recommended.

With tremendous effort, he forced out a word. "Rose." That was as far as he got before fuzz overtook him once more.

Rose said, "H.L.," and she, too, subsided.

He cleared his throat.

Fairy nudged Rose again, propelling her against H.L., whose arms tightened automatically around her. The temptation to continue where he'd left off was so great, he almost succumbed to it, but he knew Rose deserved better. So did he, actually. He didn't particularly fancy getting straw stuck in indelicate places.

With that thought foremost in his mind, he finally came up with a coherent suggestion. "Finish with the horse, and let's get out of here."

Rose stared up at him for a moment as if she didn't comprehend the meaning behind his words. He swallowed, praying hard that when the meaning penetrated the fog inside her, she wouldn't slap his face and rush off in the opposite direction.

She didn't. After only another few seconds of looking befuddled, Rose gave a sharp nod, wheeled around, and resumed brushing the horse. She snapped out orders to H.L. as she worked, as if she, too, wanted to finish up and get out of there to more felicitous surroundings.

"Hand me the currycomb, please."

H.L. handed her the currycomb.

"Fill that bucket with water." She jerked her head at a bucket hanging from a hook on the wall. H.L. obeyed, then stood, holding the dripping bucket, awaiting further instructions.

"Dump it in that trough there."

H.L. did so with alacrity.

"Fill that other bucket with oats from that sack over there."

H.L. filled the other bucket with oats.

"Dump it in the bin in that stall."

He did it.

"Now give Fairy a pat, H.L. She likes to know she's appreciated."

Although it had never occurred to him that horses had feelings, he was willing to do pretty much anything in order to get Rose in his arms again. Therefore, he walked up to Fairy, stroked her velvety neck and nose, and stepped back again. He was glad he'd obeyed Rose's peremptory commands when she shot him a glowing smile and led the horse to her stall.

His heart was thundering like a bass drum when Rose dropped the latch on Fairy's stall and turned to face him. They gazed at each other for what seemed like hours, but could only have been seconds. H.L. felt a sudden pang of trepidation, for fear Rose had decided, in the few minutes it had taken her to deal with the horse, that she didn't want to go through with his plans for the rest of her evening.

She opened her arms and whispered, "I'm ready," and his relief was so great, he felt lightheaded for a moment.

That didn't last long. Elation filled him a moment later, and with one giant step, he'd reached Rose and swept her up into his arms. "Shall we go to your tent, Rose?"

She nodded and buried her face in his shoulder. She made a compact and tidy little bundle, and one that felt swell in his arms as he carried her through the encampment. It was thin of people at the moment, since most of the cast were in the arena shooting at each other.

Without missing a step, he ducked under her tent flap, and fetched up a second later. It was pitch-black inside her tent. He muttered, "Bah."

Sensing his concern, Rose whispered, "There are matches and a lantern on my night table."

"Where's your night table?"

There was a smile in her voice when she said, "Set me down. I find my way in the dark all the time in this tent."

"I don't want to put you down," he objected.

"Better that than falling and breaking both our necks."

She kissed him, and he decided she was right and he could probably stand letting her go for a couple of minutes.

He set her gently on the floor of the tent, and he heard her move toward the bed, which he recalled as being more of a cot, really, but would do. He'd see to it.

A startled cry from Rose jolted him out of the pleasant contemplation of the consummation of his lust. He called out, "What is it?"

"I—I—*Oh!*"

Her cry of fright curdled H.L.'s blood. With a roar, he lunged in the direction of the sound, his arms outstretched so as to feel where he was going.

"Put me *down!*" Rose shouted.

The panic in her voice made H.L. curse. "Damn it, Rose, what's wrong?"

"That man!" she cried. "That man! He's—oomph!"

H.L. bumped into something huge and human, and bounced off. Fury consumed him. If it was that one-legged bastard, he was going to kill him for certain this—

Pain and light exploded in his head. He grunted once, then darkness engulfed him. He felt himself fall, as if from a great height, and then there was nothing.

Rose had never experienced such rage. She didn't have any idea who'd kidnapped her, but she knew good and well she'd been kidnapped, because why else would she be in this filthy burlap sack, being bounced all over the place? She struggled like a mad cat, to no avail. If she weren't so crunched up in so small a space, she might be able to reach a gun or a . . . but no. She didn't wear weapons during her act. She had nothing on her person with which to fight off whoever it was who'd taken her.

She could use her voice, though, and she did. At the top of her lungs, she shrieked, "Help! Help me! Somebody, please help me!"

"Shut up," a growly voice sounded from outside the burlap. "Shut up, or I'll shut you up."

Rose was too scared and angry to care about threats at the moment. She struggled wildly in the sack—although wildly in her present confines wasn't very. She continued to screech, though, since that was something the burlap couldn't confine.

"Help! Murder! Police!"

"Damn it, shut up!" the growly voice said again.

It sounded moderately frustrated, and Rose experienced a sense of triumph that was probably unwarranted, considering the circumstances.

"No!" she shrieked. "Let me go!"

"Damn it, if you don't shut up, I'll shut you up."

"Try it!" she bellowed. She hoped he would. If he so much as reached into the sack, she'd bite his hand off.

She hadn't counted on how painful it would be when he set the sack down, hard, on the ground. "Oomph!" Ow. She anticipated brutal bruises from this night's escapade, whatever else happened to her. And here she'd been primed for something wonderful with H.L.

The sack fell open suddenly, as if whoever had been carrying it and dumped it down had untied the rope or whatever he'd used to close it up. It took Rose only seconds to gain her feet, and she thanked God and the colonel for her years of practicing agility and nimble moves. *"You!"* she screeched when she saw the person who'd been carrying her.

"Damn your eyes, be quiet!" Pegleg snarled.

He looked quite the worse for wear, and Rose was glad to see all of his swellings and bruisings. She didn't have time to contemplate the mess H.L. had made of him, because he lifted what looked like a small beanbag, as if he aimed to hit her with it.

"Don't hurt her," another voice snarled behind her. "Al ain't going to pay for damaged goods."

Oh, this was simply splendid, Rose thought resentfully. There were two of them. That probably accounted for the sudden cessation of H.L.'s protests back there in her tent.

This beast's friend had attacked him from behind. A fresh surge of ire swept over her at the thought of one of these brutes bashing H.L. with one of those beanbags.

Rose hadn't spent years on the Kansas plains and associating with the reservation Sioux for nothing. Before Pegleg or his companion could do a thing to her, she'd caught Pegleg a kick in the groin that doubled him over with a very satisfying roar of pain. Whirling around and using a high kicking maneuver Little Elk had taught her, she bashed the man behind her on the chin with her foot. Since she wore only moccasins, it hurt like crazy. If she'd been wearing her heavy boots, she might have done something worthwhile, like breaking the creature's jaw.

"Damn you!" Pegleg's partner bellowed. Pegleg was rolling on the ground, clutching his privates and groaning. Rose darted over to him, grabbed the beanbag thing out of his loosened clasp, and bashed him over the head with it before he knew what was going on. His groans ceased. Perceiving a knife in a scabbard at his waist, Rose snatched it out and held it the way Little Elk had taught her, turning to face Pegleg's pal as she did so.

He was under the weather, too. "You bitch! You broke my jaw!"

"Good." Rose was panting hard, but the blood was pumping hard in her veins and she was ready for anything now. "I'm going to kill you next, if you don't get out of my way." She waved the knife in front of the man's face, and he shrank back, cursing her and holding his jaw with both hands. Rose saw blood dripping from his mouth and experienced a thrill of victory in battle that she imagined few women ever felt.

"Stay away from me, damn you!" she bellowed, although he hadn't done anything but cower at the sight of the gigantic knife in her hand. "I know how to use this, so don't you dare try anything else!"

It looked to her as if he believed her. After casting a frightened glance at Pegleg, who was still out cold on the ground, and giving Rose one last dirty look, he stumbled off in the opposite direction. Rose didn't dare take her gaze away from him until he was out of her sight. Even then, she didn't trust him not to come back and do something awful, but she needed to take her bearings and find out where she was.

She was at the perimeter of the Wild West encampment, at the very farthest point from the Indian encampment. Rose's breast swelled with contempt. "So, you and your friend didn't dare carry me through Indian territory, eh?"

Because she was so furious, she stalked over to Pegleg and glared down at him for a second. He hadn't awakened yet, and because she was operating under stress, adrenalin, and residual fear, she hauled her foot back and kicked him in his huge stomach, again hurting her foot.

"Blast." Scanning the darkness around her with a feverish intensity for fear the other man would return, she limped off. Now that she had time to think, she started worrying about H.L. She realized that what she'd believed to be a beanbag was actually a heavy leather sack filled with sand. She'd read that city criminals often hurt their victims with such things, and that they were called sandbags. She'd also read that such injuries could be serious.

Although her foot was still smarting from having been used as a weapon, she hurried, trotting when she could, and walking fast when her foot protested. After what seemed like forever, although she knew it couldn't have been more than a few minutes, she reached her tent.

She lifted the flap and darted inside. "H.L.! H.L., are you all right?"

He didn't answer her cry, and Rose's heart stumbled. With shaking hands, she found a match, lit the lantern on her night table, and turned to see how badly he had been hurt. She looked again. Then she pressed a hand to her head in disbelief.

He wasn't there.

SEVENTEEN

H.L. staggered through the encampment in a blind panic. His head felt as if somebody had been dancing on it in copper-toed boots, and he thought his vision was blurred, although he wasn't sure since it was dark and he couldn't see anything anyway.

Rose. He had to find Rose. Somebody had taken Rose. He needed Rose.

Damn it, they'd been just about to make beautiful love together. It was bad enough she'd been taken, but to have been taken at that precise moment smacked of some kind of devious, devilish plot. Unless his brains were scrambled from that god-awful blow he'd taken and it was no plot at all, but only bad luck.

He discovered he'd made his way to the Butlers' tent, but nobody was there. Not even their dog. Well, of course the dog wouldn't be there, since Annie used him in her act. He muttered soft "damns" and "hells" as he stumbled on past the Butlers' tent. His feet weren't working right, and he bumped into things as he went.

"Rose!" His shout made his head throb, and he groaned. He shouted again, because Rose was more important than pain. "Rose!"

"H.L.!"

He tried to stop in his tracks, but his feet didn't cooperate, and he staggered sideways before fetching up against another tent. Steadying himself on a tent post, he hoped the damned thing wouldn't collapse. "Rose!" He wasn't sure he'd actually heard her voice, since his ears were ringing, but he allowed himself to hope.

"H.L.!"

God in heaven, if that wasn't her voice, he was going to die. "Rose?"

"H.L.?"

"Rose?"

"H.L.! It's *you!*"

Rose appeared from between two tents like an apparition. H.L. didn't dare let go of the tent pole so he could grab her. Fortunately, it didn't matter, because she grabbed him.

"Oh, H.L.! I was so worried about you! When I got to my tent and you weren't there, I—oh, I thought all sorts of things!"

"Yeah?" He knew he needed to say something more, but he couldn't figure out what.

"Oh, I was so worried! Did that horrid man hit you with that sandbag thing of his?"

H.L. pried one arm from around Rose's waist so that he could feel the lump on his head. It hurt. A lot. "Is that what it was?"

Rose had begun crying, which startled H.L. He didn't expect tears from this quarter. Rose was so tough.

"Yes," she sobbed. "It was one of those stuffed leather things that beastly criminals use. See?" She reached into her costume's skirt pocket and withdrew the sandbag, holding it up even as she kept her face buried in H.L.'s shirt front.

"By God, it *is* a sandbag, isn't it? A genuine, honest-to-God, nasty little sandbag." Even though his vision was blurry and he feared for his stability, H.L. took the sandbag, lifted it to the level of his eyes, since his head hurt when he lowered it, and pondered the evil implement of his present injury. "By God, you don't see very many of these."

Rose sniffled. "That's because the only people who use

them are wicked scoundrels. It was that horrid one-legged man who took me."

H.L. would have goggled if he'd been in any condition to do any goggling. "Pegleg? I'll be damned."

To his dismay, Rose pulled away from him, an action that set him swaying. He tried to hold onto her, but she evidently had another agenda in mind.

"We have to get your wound tended, H.L.," she said, wiping her eyes with the back of her hand. "And we need to report this attack to the police. Maybe they'll pay attention to us this time, since it's not a little Indian boy they took, but me, and I'm a member of Buffalo Bill's Wild West." The sniff she gave this time was one of pure outrage. "That ought to make them worry. Think of the bad publicity they'll get."

H.L. sighed deeply. He'd had such lovely plans for this evening. Now those plans were up the flue, along with his balance, which he hoped he'd regain one of these days. He wasn't sure his head would ever recover. "Right." He knew she was right, even though he had no desire to speak to the Chicago police anytime soon.

"Can you walk?" Rose asked.

He appreciated her concern. He also appreciated the question, since he wasn't sure of the answer. He'd managed to stagger this far, but that was when he'd been propelled by fear for Rose's safety. Now that he knew she was still alive and kicking, he wasn't altogether sure whether he could walk or not.

His state of health did produce one happy prospect, however. "Put your arms around me, Rose. I think I'll be able to walk with support."

She followed his suggestion instantly, and H.L. decided he'd survive. It might take his headache a while to go away, but feeling Rose pressed against him was a sure-fire way to make the rest of him feel better.

They got to her tent after a few minutes of painful progress. She'd left the lantern burning, so when they ducked under the tent flap—causing H.L.'s aching head terrific torment as they did so, since the blood in his veins pounded like a dozen sandbags were beating on it—they could at least see where they were going. Rose guided H.L. to her bed, where he flopped down ungracefully and buried his head in his hands. "God, my head hurts."

Rose realized her front was still unbuttoned, blushed slightly, and quickly redid the buttons. When he glanced up after coddling his head for a few seconds, H.L. was sorry to see her bosom disappear under the calico, although he was too debilitated to say so.

"I'm sure it does. I'm so sorry that dreadful man hit you."

Now that Rose was safe and he was in the relative comfort of her tent, H.L.'s brain slogged back to work again, slowly and haltingly. Slitting his eyes against the blinding light of the kerosene lantern, he focused on Rose. "How'd you get away? I thought for sure they'd kidnapped you for some reason or other, and that I'd have to scour Chicago for you."

Rose gave an unladylike snort that almost made H.L. grin, but he wasn't quite up to it. "They did kidnap me, the fiends."

"How'd you get away?" he repeated when she didn't continue. She'd turned her back on him and was puttering around the place like a trained nurse. Her efficiency and industry gladdened him. He adored competent people. He adored Rose.

Oops. He must have been hurt more seriously than he'd thought. He'd never admitted adoring a woman in his life.

Before he could dwell on it, Rose spoke. "I kept yelling for help, and he put me down to try to shut me up."

"He put you down? You mean he'd been carrying you?" Rage engulfed H.L., making his blood race and his head throb. "He was *carrying* you?" Visions of Rose, unbuttoned, her breasts pressed against that gigantic scoundrel's chest, filled his already overtaxed head. He made a lunge to get up off the cot. "Where is he? I'm going to kill him for sure this time."

The old saw about the spirit being willing and the flesh being weak occurred to him a moment later when a rush of sparkling light and pain filled his head. He lost his balance, careened across the floor of Rose's tent, and came a cropper against one of her trunks. He fell heavily, sending shoots of exquisite torture through his head and the shin he'd barked.

"H.L. !" Rose cried. "What do you think you're doing? Get back to that bed this instant!"

He felt ridiculous when pitiful whimpers and groans fell from his lips. He'd meant to explain, not whimper. "I—I can't."

Rose rushed over to kneel beside him, and again put her arms around him, so he guessed he'd live. She helped him to his feet and led him back to the bed.

"I'm as weak as a kitten," he muttered, feeling unmanly and inadequate.

"Of course you are, silly. Your brains have been knocked all around."

She didn't sound as if she considered him less of a man for having been wounded in the line of duty, and he felt slightly better.

"Now don't move again, H.L. I'm trying to make a poultice for your poor head."

"A poultice?" H.L. grimaced. He'd been through a lot in his life, but he'd never been forced to use a poultice. A poultice sounded so . . . so . . . not masculine.

"Yes. A poultice." She apparently detected a certain unwillingness to endure poulticing in his voice, because she turned around to shoot him a good, hot glare. "This is good medicine, H.L. May, and you're going to keep it pressed to your head for at least a half hour. Little Elk's mother taught me how to make it, and if you balk about using it, you'll be worse than an idiot."

"An Indian poultice?" For some reason, knowing that she was going to doctor him using Indian medicaments made H.L. feel less like a simpering weakling. In fact, his reporterly instincts made a stab at awakening, although they, too, were unsteady on their feet. "What's in it?"

Rose kept puttering on the other side of the tent. H.L. missed her and wished she'd finish up over there and get back to the bed. If they couldn't make love, maybe they could at least hug for a while. "Lots of things. There's witch hazel and yarrow and aloe and several other plants and herbs that grow in Kansas. It's really quite soothing. I'm going to fix you an old Sioux remedy for headache to drink, too, and I don't want any guff from you." She frowned.

Since he hadn't said anything to account for her frown, it worried him. "Why are you frowning?"

"I beg your pardon?" She turned and gazed at him blankly for a second. Then, as if she realized what he'd asked, she said, "Oh. Well, that horrid man bruised me when he put down the burlap sack he'd stuffed me in."

"He *what?*" H.L. wished he hadn't yelled when pain stabbed through his head. Pressing a hand over the growing lump, he eyed Rose. He knew he was going to have to kill Pegleg. There were no two ways about this. Pegleg was going to pay with his life for having bruised Rose. Forcing the words out through gritted teeth, he said, "Where did he bruise you?" He squinted hard at her. "Did you say he carried you in a burlap sack?" Perhaps he'd misunderstood her.

"Yes. It was very uncomfortable, too, let me tell you. But I kept hollering, and he got mad and dumped the bag down on the ground. It hurt."

"Where did he hurt you?" After he killed Pegleg, he'd kiss Rose's bruise and make it well. Maybe he'd kiss it before he went out to kill Pegleg, since he wasn't in any condition to kill anything yet. And if it didn't make *her* better when he kissed it, it would certainly make *him* feel better, and that was a good thing.

"My—" She stopped speaking abruptly. H.L. thought he detected a faint flush invade her cheeks. She cleared her throat. "My, ah, leg. The upper part of, ah, my leg."

"Ah. I understand. That bastard bruised your butt." H.L. was going to kill him. That was all. There needn't be any muss or fuss about it. He'd shoot him, and it would be an execution of a vicious criminal, pure and simple, and nobody, not even the president of the anti-capital-punishment brigade or the Purity League, could find fault with him. Pegleg had bruised Rose's buttocks; therefore, Pegleg must die. It was simple, really. H.L. hoped his head stopped throbbing soon so he could carry out his plan. The prospect of kissing Rose's injury increased the pleasurable aspects of retribution a lot.

"You needn't be so blunt," Rose muttered.

"Nuts. That man is vicious and a danger to society."

"I won't argue with you about that." She finished doing something that required the jamming of ingredients into a cloth bag and dipping the bag into a bowl of water. Then she tied a string around the open end of the bag. "There. It's all ready for you." Turning and eyeing him critically, she said, "You really do look terrible, H.L. Loosen your tie and take off your shirt and jacket, please; then lie down. After I adjust this poultice, I'm going to go find someone to take a message to the police. Then I want to see if you have any other injuries."

He actually managed a grin. "Yeah? Take off my shirt? Your friend Annie won't be shocked?"

Rose huffed. "Don't be ridiculous. You're injured, and you need medical attention. Now take off your shirt and jacket and lie down."

She sounded ferocious, and he did as she ordered. He was pleased to see the avid expression on Rose's face as she watched him bare his torso. He had a rather fine torso if he did say so himself. Lowering himself carefully and painfully, he lay flat on her bed. His head underwent excruciating agonies as he nestled it against her pillow, but the sweet-smelling pillowcase eased his nerves. "This pillow smells like you, Rose."

"It does?" She appeared flustered for a moment. "Well, that's not surprising, I suppose."

"It smells wonderful. Like you. You smell like vanilla and wildflowers. Did you know that?" His eyes had squeezed shut from pain, but he opened them now and gazed up to see her looming over him. Looming in a good way. If he felt less pitiful, he could come up with a better word for what she was doing. For now, looming would have to do.

He realized he was already composing an article about this incident in his sore head, and came to the conclusion that Rose was good for him. She provided endless copy for his fertile imagination. Besides, she smelled great. So did her pillow.

"Here," she said softly, leaning close. "Press this to the sore spot."

H.L. had just begun to enjoy having her face practically touching his when the poultice struck. "Aaaagh! That stings."

"The skin's broken." Rose straightened away from him, and H.L. felt doubly awful. "But it's not a bad scratch, and soon it will stop stinging. Mostly, it's the swelling that's going to hurt. I'm afraid that spot will be tender for some time, but this poultice will help if you give it time."

His eyes squeezed shut in agony. "God, I feel awful."

"I'm sure you do." She sounded as if she were at least a little bit worried about him, and he thought that was nice. He heard sounds from across the tent that he presumed were made by a spoon being stirred in a glass. He wasn't looking forward to drinking whatever noxious concoction she was brewing.

Her footsteps came closer and stopped beside the bed. "Here."

H.L. pried his eyes open and frowned at the glass she held out to him. "What's that?"

"Don't sound so reluctant. This is the best cure I've ever taken for headache, and you need it."

"You sound like a prison guard," H.L. grumbled.

"Just drink it."

He drank it. "God, that stuff tastes horrible!" He wasn't altogether sure he wasn't going to return it to Rose against his will, and he had to hold his breath for a minute before he was sure it would stay down.

"Horrible or not, it will help you. Here. Chew this."

He squinted at her and took the dried twig she held out to him. "What is it?"

"Mint. Chew it. It will help the remedy stay down."

Thank God for small favors. H.L. popped the twig into his mouth and chewed. He was glad to discover Rose was right. He thought he might just live through her ministrations. He sank back against her pillow, pressing the poultice to his throbbing skull and wishing it were a couple of weeks from now and he didn't hurt anymore.

"You just stay there, now, and keep that poultice on your sore spot. I'll be back in a minute."

H.L.'s eyes popped open in horror. She was going to abandon him! Before he could voice a protest, she'd left him all alone in the tent with nothing but his pain and his poultice to keep him company. He felt really rotten.

Before his sense of being marooned in a desolate place could flourish, however, Rose was back, looking pleased with herself. H.L. frowned at her. "Where'd you go?"

She appeared surprised by his brisk tone. "Just over to the Sioux village. I sent a couple of the children to find a Columbian Guardsman and the colonel. I'm sure the Guard will get a message to the police, especially if Colonel Cody steps in and orders him to do so."

"Ah. Did you write a note to the police?"

She looked uncomfortable. "Yes."

All right. H.L. guessed she wasn't going to tell him what her note said. He also guessed he didn't care a whole lot. He asked with hope, "Are you going to fix a poultice for yourself?" He thought he'd recover quicker if he could see Rose's sweet bottom, even if it sported a bruise and a poultice. "I promise I won't do anything untoward." Bitterly, he added, "I couldn't if I wanted to, damn it."

She frowned, narrowing her eyes in thought as she contemplated his suggestion. "I suppose I might as well. That poultice really does wonders for bruises and swellings. I'm afraid I might not be able to perform for a day or two, because the spot is really quite sore. I don't think I ought to try to work my act unless I'm in top shape."

H.L.'s heart cried out in terror at the thought of Rose trying to perform some of those tricks of hers with a bum leg. "Good God, no!"

She blinked at him. "I beg your pardon?"

He tried to sit up, but she dashed over and held him down, shrieking, "Stop it!"

"No! You can't perform, Rose. Not until you're all better. Good God, Rose, you'll kill yourself!"

She patted his shoulder. "Calm down, H.L. I'll speak to the colonel as soon as possible."

He subsided but was still worried. It also occurred to him that while Rose was doctoring his head, Pegleg was probably busy escaping. He let out a groan as he settled back onto her bed. He wished she'd join him there, but he knew there were more important things to think about at the moment. Damn it, he wanted to make love to Rose. He didn't want to have to heal first.

Hell. First things first. He looked up at Rose as he obediently pressed the poultice to his sore spot again. After the first appalling seconds, during which the moistened herbs inside the calico bag felt as if they were eating the skin off his head, the spot actually began to feel sort of better. Cool.

It felt cool. "So, you managed to escape from the burlap sack. Did you run away from him, or what?"

"What?" Rose had gone back to the table upon which she'd prepared H.L.'s poultice. It looked to him as if she were getting another one ready for her own use. He hoped she'd apply it where he could see her do it. "Oh, you mean the men who kidnapped me?"

"Men? There was more than one of them?" H.L. frowned. "Oh, of course, there was more than one of them. There had to be, or I wouldn't have been beaned from behind, would I?"

"Exactly."

"So. They didn't just let you go, did they?"

Her sudden wicked grin tickled him. "Not on purpose, they didn't."

As she told him how she'd escaped, H.L. felt a swelling in the area of his heart. He'd never experienced its like, and he didn't know whether to be pleased or aghast, because he feared it meant something he'd never even contemplated happening to him.

Yet could it be happening? Could H.L. May, who'd always considered himself above such things, actually—he swallowed as the thought smote him—be falling in—he could hardly bear even to think the word—*love* with Rose Gilhooley?

"So," Rose said as she tied up another calico bag into which she'd stuffed moistened herbs. "That's how I escaped from the man you call Pegleg. As far as I know, he's still out cold, but I have no idea what happened to his friend. Wherever he is, I expect his jaw is pretty badly swollen."

She looked about as proud of herself as H.L. expected she could look, and he gave up the struggle. He was too weak to fight any longer. Damn it, he loved her. He allowed his eyes to drift shut, still pressing the poultice to his lump, and waited for the dread to strike him. He couldn't imagine falling in love and not dreading the consequences of such a damn-fool happenstance.

"I'm going to turn down the lamp," Rose told him.

H.L. opened his eyes to slits and glanced over at her. "All right, I guess, but don't you think we ought to wait for the police?"

She sniffed, reminding H.L. of a grand lady objecting to something one of her servants had done. He grinned in spite of the state of his emotions.

"They'll get here eventually, I'm sure, especially when the colonel gets involved. As for waiting for them . . . Well, what have the police ever done for us?" Rose asked coldly. "If they want to talk to us, they can do so after we take care of our bruises and bumps. If they even care."

H.L. grinned as he allowed his eyes to close again. "Oh, they'll care. After Cody gets on their case and they read my article about *this* night's work, they'll care, all right."

"Fine," Rose said. "Let them care, then. My . . . leg is beginning to stiffen up, and I need to get this poultice on the bruise."

H.L. felt sort of dreamy. "I don't suppose you'll come here and lie beside me, will you? I won't be able to do anything to you, unfortunately."

"Unfortunately?"

She sounded shocked, and H.L. considered this reaction to his comment disingenuous, considering they'd been about to consummate their passion until those two bastards showed up and kidnapped her. *Tried* to kidnap her. He chuckled. "Fudge, Rose. If I try anything, you can just bop me like you did those two crooks, and push me off the bed." Straining his eyes open one last time, he added, "Besides, where else can you do it? There's only one place in here to lie down."

Rose stood in the middle of her tent and glanced around. She was looking, unless H.L. missed his guess, for some other, less disreputable, place to apply her poultice. She gave it up after a few moments. "You're right. Very well. Move over."

He moved over. Rose winced as she lowered herself to the bed. "Close your eyes," she said.

H.L. sighed, but he closed his eyes. "It won't matter, you know. I'm going to see you in the altogether one of these days."

"H.L.!" Again, she sounded shocked.

This time, he found her reaction funny. "You don't really think I'm going to let you get away, do you, Rose? If you do, you're daft."

"Be quiet, H.L." Her voice sounded strained. "You need to rest now."

"All right."

"Are your eyes closed?"

He sighed. "Yes, Rose. My eyes are closed."

She wriggled the bottom half of her costume down her pretty legs and kicked it off. H.L. knew she had pretty legs, because he watched, having lied about his eyes being closed. He felt a smile spread through his entire body as she curled up next to him. She made sure her back was to him, but he didn't mind. He decided that from the way she lay on her poultice, it was her right thigh that had been bruised.

"There," she muttered after a few minutes. "I think that will do it. Try to sleep, H.L." She sounded very stern, as if she wanted him to think she was a toughie.

Hell, she *was* a toughie, when it came to crooks and criminals. With H.L. May, if she tried acting tough, he'd see it didn't last long. H.L. was an expert. He snaked an arm around her waist and pulled her up close to his chest.

Rose gasped. "What are you doing?"

"Holding you so you can't get away."

"For heaven's—really, H.L., you shouldn't be doing that."

"Hush, Rose. You've been through enough tonight. I won't hurt you. Hell, I can't even move, much less consummate a ravishment, damn it."

"H.L.!"

"Hush," he said again, laughing softly. "Go to sleep, Rose. We both need to rest up from our battles. Besides, we probably won't have much time to rest before the world interferes and starts asking us all sorts of questions."

She tried to sit up again, but H.L. found the strength in his body somewhere to prevent her. "Stop it!"

"But the colonel can't see us like this!"

"The colonel won't give a rap. He'll be happy you're tending to our wounds, Rose. Besides, we're not doing anything wrong."

"I don't know," she muttered.

He felt her internal struggle because it had stiffened her body. He also felt when her struggles ceased. Happiness suffused him when she relaxed.

"If anyone comes in here and sees us like this, I'll be embarrassed to death," she muttered after a minute.

"Don't worry. We'll hear them coming in time for you to get up."

"I hope so." She didn't sound satisfied.

H.L. was almost asleep. "Hell, tell 'em we're getting married, and they'll go away again."

Her body went tense for a second. H.L. wondered if he'd lost his mind. He was too worn down to care much, and when Rose relaxed after a second, he did, too, and unconsciousness claimed him a moment later.

Rose frowned into the dim light of her tent, wishing she could go to sleep with the ease H.L. May demonstrated. But she was too on-edge to succumb to the healing powers of sleep. H.L. could say whatever he wanted to, but it would be mortifying to be discovered in such a compromising situation. And, since she'd sent messages to Colonel Cody, the Columbian Guard, and the police, she expected their privacy to be interrupted any second now.

Fiddlesticks. She had to get up. She didn't want to. What she wanted to do was bask in the comforting pleasure of lying here with H.L.'s arm around her.

Suppressing a groan as her bruised bottom slid across the cot, Rose glanced back to see if she'd disturbed H.L. Her heart pinged painfully. He looked ghastly. And it was all because he'd tried to rescue her from the hands of villains.

As she brushed a lock of dark-brown hair away from his poor battered head, she felt a swell of tenderness toward him. She also wanted to take a sandbag to the other side of his head. "*Tell them we're getting married,*" her hind leg.

She huffed softly as she pushed herself to her feet. H.L. May, the decadent, cynical newspaperman, might think such a statement funny, but Rose Ellen Gilhooley didn't. To Rose, marriage was a serious topic, and his flippant remark made her heart hurt.

Which was nothing compared to the spears of pain the bruise on her bottom was sending down her right leg. "Oomph." Again glancing at H.L., Rose was glad to see her unexpected groan of pain hadn't disturbed him. She limped over to the hatrack she used as a clothes hanger, lifted her robe down, and slipped it on. She supposed it was improper to receive guests, or even policemen, in a robe, but Rose didn't care. Her insides were still in a turmoil over H.L.'s casually spoken "*Tell them we're getting married.*"

As she tied the belt to the pretty yellow brocade satin robe she'd bought in London, Rose glared at H.L. He looked so innocent lying there, pressing that poultice to his lump even as he slept.

Rose knew better. He was an insidious, lecherous creature who had almost succeeded in having his way with her this evening. If it hadn't been for Pegleg and his crony, Rose would no longer be a virgin right now.

The muffled sound of worried voices reached her, and Rose sighed heavily. She figured it was another lamentable indication of moral laxity on her part that she regretted having been spared defilement by H.L. May. Because the whole thing was too depressing to think about, she ducked through the opening of her tent to greet the newcomers and ask them to keep their voices down so as not to disturb H.L.

EIGHTEEN

"Don't you even think about your act for at least a week, young lady. You've got to get yourself well." The colonel spoke severely, but Rose saw the concern on his face, and she sniffled, touched by his goodness.

"Thank you, sir." She felt foolish when she had to wipe a tear from her cheek.

Annie put an arm around her. "Oh, Rose, I can't believe those awful men tried to kidnap you."

The women glared at the awful men, both of whom appeared to have lost their self-confidence. Any hint of the swaggering bravado Rose had detected upon her first encounter with them had been knocked out of them. The two men stared morosely at their own booted or pegged lower appendages and didn't utter a sound.

Rose's tent was awfully crowded. Generally speaking, the only person it ever contained was Rose herself and, sometimes when Annie visited, Rose and Annie. At the moment, Rose, Annie, H.L., Colonel Cody, Little Elk, a Columbian Guard representative, two burly policemen, Pegleg, and Pegleg's friend filled it. Her usually orderly and emptyish tent now reminded Rose of a tin of sardines. She huffed softly, wishing the police would take the villains away.

The two men had their wrists manacled behind their backs, and they looked dejected. Not to mention thrashed. Rose eyed their bumps and scrapes with satisfaction. While she knew she'd administered one or two of those injuries, and H.L. had delivered several others, she suspected representatives of the Chicago police force, goaded at last into doing their duty, had taken their resentment out on the two men, as well. Rose considered such tactics only fair.

The two criminals had been dragged to the Wild West in order to facilitate their identification by Rose, H.L., and Little Elk. Rose had been delighted to comply, since she didn't feel like visiting the police station. H.L., after he'd more or less come to his senses, also identified the two men. Rose would have resented it when he'd spat on the floor of her tent after he'd fingered the villains if she hadn't felt much like doing the same thing herself. Anyhow, he'd apologized, so she guessed she couldn't hold his lack of good manners against him.

A burly policeman licked the point of his pencil and painstakingly wrote a few words in the notebook he held. "Right. And you say the big feller's the one what took the Injun kid the other day?" He jerked a thumb in Pegleg's direction.

"Yes." Rose lifted her chin. "You might have caught him then and spared Mr. May and me these injuries if you'd bothered to take our report seriously," she reminded him.

The policeman grunted, frowned, and wrote some more.

"The lady's right," H.L. said. He'd regained a good deal of his bounce and fighting vigor, even though he claimed his head still ached. "We had to get the kid back ourselves; Miss Gilhooley and me. You can read all about it in Thursday's edition's of the *Globe*." When the policeman shot a scowl in H.L.'s direction, the reporter grinned.

Rose admired his gumption, even if she didn't understand it. Her whole aim in life was getting people to like her; she couldn't comprehend H.L.'s indifference to public opinion. She chalked it up to his being a reporter.

The colonel, who stood beside Rose and Annie, who were sharing seats on one of Rose's trunks, laid a hand on Rose's yellow brocade-clad shoulder. "I should say so," he boomed, his big voice filling the tent as full of sound as it was of bodies. "I can't believe you folks didn't rush right out and try to get that little boy back."

Annie said, "Hmph."

Rose said, "Indeed."

The policeman hunched his shoulders slightly, as if he were warding off blows. Feeling indignant, Rose offered a "Hmph" of her own. If he'd done his job in the first place, he wouldn't have to be doing that, would he?

"Right, well, the kid's back now, and Miss Gilhooley's all right, I reckon."

"No thanks to you," Rose reminded him haughtily.

The policeman cleared his throat and forged onward. "I think that's about all the information I need from you right now, Miss Gilhooley." He lifted his head as if he didn't want to and looked at H.L., who sat on the edge of Rose's bed, still holding the poultice to his head. He was grinning the way Rose imagined the Cheshire Cat in *Alice In Wonderland* might have done.

"Listen, boys, Miss Gilhooley and I really need to rest. If you want more details about what happened tonight, you can read all about them in the *Globe*. The article will be in the paper in a couple of days."

The policeman sighed heavily. He didn't respond to H.L.'s flip comment, but turned and scowled at the two criminals. "And you two say you were hired by Arapaho Al?"

Pegleg looked mutinous for approximately three seconds. His mutiny ended when the second policeman gave him a vicious whack on the back of the skull with his nightstick and growled, "Speak up, you."

"Cut it out," Pegleg grunted. Before the second policeman, who lifted his billy club in a threatening gesture, could administer another whack, he hastened to add, "Yes. Yes. Arapaho Al."

The first policeman asked Cody, "You know anything about this Arapaho Al, colonel?"

Cody shook his white head. "Can't say as I do, although I've heard there's a fellow calls himself Arapaho Al who's touring Europe at the moment. He operates a cheap imitation of the Wild West. Reckon he staffs his show with folks he kidnaps." His grim visage told everyone what he thought about *that*.

The police, the Columbian Guard, and the prisoners left first. Rose didn't think her tent would ever be her own again. It seemed to her that folks intended to remain and discuss the excitement, if that's what you could call it, for the rest of her life. Eventually, however, with many words of condolence, encouragement, and support, they left Rose and H.L. alone in the tent. Rose practically had to shove Annie out into the night, since she seemed determined to stay as long as H.L. did. She did it for propriety's sake, Rose knew.

The colonel finally took Annie by the arm. With a chuckle, he said, "Let's go, missie. These two want to be alone."

Rose felt her neck get hot. Annie muttered, "Well, really!" But she went.

"I'll talk to you tomorrow, Annie," Rose called after her. "I've got to get some rest now." She heaved a sigh of relief when Annie gave up trying to chaperone Rose and H.L. and marched off with the colonel. As for Cody himself, he started whistling a popular love tune and didn't release Annie's arm. Rose appreciated him a lot.

Behind her, H.L. murmured, "Thank God for privacy."

Rose turned around, frowning and feeling shy now that he and she were alone in the tent once more. She hugged her robe tightly to her body. "Yes." She sighed.

"You don't have to stand all the way over there, Rose." H.L. patted the cot at his side. "I don't bite—very often."

Rose wrinkled her nose. "Do you think you can get home, H.L.? Or do you think you'd better sleep here. I don't suppose anyone would think anything of it, considering you're such a mess and all."

"Thanks heaps, Rose." He laughed.

Rose didn't. "You know very well what I mean, H.L. It's improper for you to stay here, but I'll allow you to do so since you've suffered such a bad blow to your head. Anyhow, I'd probably better keep an eye on you to make sure you aren't going to suffer from a delayed reaction to that sand-bag."

"Absolutely. I need you to keep an eye on me."

She knew he was making fun of her, and she didn't appreciate it. "I'll have you know that it sometimes takes hours for the full extent of a head injury to be manifested. Mr. Lovelady's uncle got kicked by a horse, thought he was fine, and dropped dead two days later from a blood clot. At least, the doctor thought it was a blood clot. So it's not funny."

"Good God." H.L.'s insouciant grin faded.

Rose took some satisfaction from having rattled him.

"In that case," H.L. went on, "you can't keep an eye on me as well from across the tent as you can from over here."

Her sense of satisfaction died a quick death. Nevertheless, when she cast a glance around her tent and discerned no suitable place for her to rest except on the cot next to H.L., she gave up resisting. "Very well. But you'd better not do anything I don't approve of." She tried to sound stern and determined, but he only grinned harder.

With a funny feeling in her heart, and wondering what this night would mean to her in the long run, Rose tied her tent flaps down—she didn't fancy having any more visitors barging in during what little remained of the night—and walked over to her bed. H.L. obligingly scooted over to make room for her, lying on his side and watching her with an expression that hit her like a single sunbeam through a heavy mist.

"You might as well take that robe off, Rose. It would be a shame to get it all wrinkled."

She didn't believe the innocent look on his face for a second. "Does your head still ache?" she asked hopefully.

COMING UP ROSES 273

"Sure does."

She didn't believe that, either.

Since she had no other option except sleeping on the floor or in Annie's tent, which would be deserting her patient, Rose removed her robe and sat on the edge of the bed. She glanced at H.L. over her shoulder. He smiled sweetly at her.

"Feel free to take off your shirtwaist, too, Rose. I promise I won't tell anyone."

"I'm sure." She gave him her hottest scowl. It didn't faze him in the least, as she might have predicted.

"No, really," he said, sounding not unlike a Sunday School teacher explaining one of the parables of Jesus to a five-year-old. "I'm sure you'll be much more comfortable if you take off your clothes and wear your nightgown to bed."

Rose was sure of it, too. The notion of H.L. seeing her in her nightie, however, made odd, pulsing sensations start up in her lower belly. While she hadn't experienced them before, she feared they boded ill for her status as a proper maiden lady.

H.L. patted the bed. "Come on, Rose. I won't be bad. Promise."

She eyed him, keeping her back to him. "Promise?"

"Promise."

"Well . . ." She probably shouldn't trust a single word he said. Yet she was tired and sore and *really* wanted to get to sleep. After thinking about it for another couple of minutes, and doing battle with herself on the issue of modesty versus common sense, Rose finally gave up. Blast H.L. May, anyhow. And blast herself, too, for being so absurdly attracted to him. She got up abruptly. "Close your eyes."

H.L. looked worried. "What are you going to do?"

"Get into my nightgown."

He relaxed. "Good. That's good, Rose. I'm sure you'll sleep much better if you're in comfortable clothes."

She squinted at him. "Right." She knew she was taking a huge step, although she didn't know where it would lead her.

She repeated, "Close your eyes." She heard his sigh from across the tent.

"All right, Rose. My eyes are closed."

Rose doubted it. But she removed the rest of her clothes as quickly as she could, donned her voluminous flannel nightgown, and returned to the bed. His eyes didn't look closed to her, but she guessed it would only be embarrassing if she questioned him.

As if to reassure her, H.L. repeated, "I won't be bad, Rose. Honest."

"Good."

"I'm never bad."

She got a sinking feeling that she was missing his point.

It was long past midnight. Probably dawn wasn't far off when H.L.'s eyes drifted open and he blinked into the dim shadows of Rose's tent. She hadn't extinguished the kerosene lamp before she retired, but she'd turned it down, so there was very little light.

The sense of blissful comfort pervading his body was as foreign to H.L. as the meals he'd eaten in the Street in Cairo. It took him a minute to realize that the delicious sensation emanated from the woman sleeping next to him.

Rose. H.L. still had an arm around her. As he looked back over the events leading up to his awakening beside her, he wondered why he didn't feel worse. He'd been knocked for a loop by that damned sandbag. By rights, he should be in agony. There was a faint, faraway ache in his head, but it felt more like the memory of pain than pain itself.

He grinned, remembering the poultice Rose had made for him, and the foul-tasting potion she'd made him drink. Those Indians really knew their stuff. If they could only make that drink taste less like sewer water, they could probably make lots of money marketing it.

Carefully, so as not to awaken Rose, he began testing his

limbs one at a time. His arms seemed to work all right. His legs were operative. The big test was his head. Gingerly he lifted it from Rose's pillow. Pain didn't come back with a thump and attack him, so he dared to sit up.

Hmmm. So far, so good. Bracing his hands on the mattress, he turned and peered through the gloom at Rose. She looked as lovely and peaceful as an angel, with drifts of dark hair framing her pale, pretty face. Her dark lashes were thick and gave her the faintly mysterious look of some kind of Egyptian princess. As if he knew anything about Egyptian princesses. Still, he liked the imagery.

He lifted a hand to his lump and wondered if his senses had been knocked askew by Pegleg's sandbag. H.L. couldn't recall ever having such fanciful whimsies about a woman in his life.

On the other hand, Rose was special. She wasn't like any other woman he'd ever met. She was something brand-new to him: tough as nails, innocent as the new dawn, and as charming as a kitten.

H.L. reminded himself that he didn't like cats, but it was no use. Rose was special, and he wanted her. A lot. He, who'd believed himself impervious to love. He, who used to laugh at his fellows who went around mooning over women. He, whom the mere thought of marriage used to make cringe.

Actually, the thought of marriage still made him cringe. The thought of bedding Rose, however, was sounding better and better with each passing second. He loved the wench.

There you go. H.L. guessed he'd found his comeuppance in Rose Ellen Gilhooley: Wind Dancer, Bareback Rider Extraordinaire. Who'd have thought it? Not he, certainly.

A problem remained, however. While H.L. May knew beyond a doubt that Rose Ellen Gilhooley was the only woman in the world for him, he had yet to convince her. He'd almost succeeded before the Pegleg incident, but Rose had had plenty of time to cool off by this time. He shook his head—

carefully, in case the ache was still back there waiting to pounce—ruing circumstances and loathing Pegleg.

As he sat there, drinking in the sight of Rose in all her innocent loveliness, a thought occurred to H.L. He shook his head again, harder this time, to test its ability to withstand activity. No problem.

If he sort of sneaked up on her while she slept, she'd probably succumb pretty easily. After all, if she was unconscious, she wouldn't know what he was doing until it was too late and she was so excited she wouldn't be able to refuse him.

At once guilt stabbed him. Hell, H.L. hated guilt. It was such an inconvenient emotion. Guilt hadn't troubled him when they'd headed to Rose's tent hours earlier with the express intention of consummating their passion; why should it trouble him now?

He knew the answer to that one: It was because earlier he'd been blinded by lust and hadn't given a thought to the consequences. He was in his right mind now, and was trying to think of ways in which Rose might be coerced into giving up her maidenhood to him.

It sounded bad when he put it like that. Frowning, he tried to come up with other ways to put it, and couldn't.

"Aw, hell."

Although he hadn't spoken loudly, Rose stirred. Some incomprehensible murmur left her lovely lips, and she turned over onto her back. H.L. gazed down at her, and his heart felt all light and floaty. After a second or two, she moved again, turning onto her left side and grabbing the pillow H.L. had just vacated. She tugged it against her as if she were hugging another person, and H.L. felt a pang. He wished it were he she was holding like that.

Which brought him back to his moral dilemma. What to do; what to do?

When Rose stirred yet again and sighed deeply into the

pillow, a surge of desire shot through him that was so strong it almost wiped the slate of his conscience clean. Almost.

H.L. decided to hell with it. Almost was good enough for him. Taking care not to jostle the bed, he stood up and slipped out of his clothes. His arousal was already heavy and so powerful it almost hurt.

Then, very gently—he didn't want Rose to wake up too soon—he slid back onto the mattress until he lay on his side, facing her. Demonstrating more patience than he'd given himself credit for, considering the state of his arousal, he pried her fingers from around the pillow and thrust the pillow behind him.

Her nightgown buttoned down the front, which was convenient. H.L. took great care not to bother Rose as he unfastened the buttons. His breath snagged when, button by button, her body was revealed to his greedy eyes.

She was tiny and perfect and delicious, just as he'd expected her to be. Her breasts were a precious handful. And mouthful. As he drew the nightgown away from her body, H.L. leaned over and tasted one of them. Wonderful. She was wonderful.

Rose released a soft mewing sound and stretched in her sleep. Ah. Good. H.L.'s plan might be underhanded and dirty, but he was feeling more desperate than usual at the moment. The thought of making love to Rose was exquisite. The thought of making love to Rose and then having her hate him was unthinkable. So he didn't think about it.

Rather, he spread his palm over the warm skin of her stomach. He didn't understand how so much raw physical power could be encased in this delicate body. Her skin was as soft as a baby's. As H.L. had never felt a baby's skin, he wasn't absolutely sure about that, but he expected he was right. Her skin was soft. Very soft.

His hands caressed her tenderly, and his excitement climbed when he saw that she wasn't impervious to his touch, even though she still slept. She moaned softly and gently arched her hips. H.L. had to close his eyes for a second and tell himself to keep calm.

Leaning close to her, he brushed her lips with his, gently and tenderly, barely touching her. He saw her eyelids flutter for a moment, and then her eyes opened and she looked up at him, blinking.

"H.L." Her voice was a breathy whisper.

"You're beautiful, Rose."

She took in the sight of his naked chest and gasped. "What are you doing?"

To H.L.'s dismay, she sounded frightened. He guessed it was time to confess. "I'm making love to you, Rose."

Her mouth opened and closed, and she swallowed. "Um, you're what?"

"I'm making love to you."

Even though she was still fuddled with sleep, she gaped at him. H.L. sighed, recognizing the clear signs of shock.

Desperately he confessed, "I love you, Rose." He needed for her to believe him. This was too important to him to chance disbelief. Hell, he didn't expect such a thing ever to happen to H.L. May again in this lifetime, and he needed her to understand. "I didn't think I'd ever fall in love, but I have. With you."

Still, she didn't speak. H.L. kissed her again, harder this time, allowing his tongue to trail over her lips, craving her love in return. He couldn't imagine her allowing him to make love to her if she didn't love him. Rose Gilhooley was no floozy. She was no liberated feminist who believed in free love and indiscriminate bedding of any man who caught her fancy. She was, in her own way, an old-fashioned girl. She was also ahead of her time. She was, in short, perfect for H.L. May.

"I want you to love me back," he said at last, uneasy in the face of her continued silence.

He saw her swallow, but she didn't speak.

Finally he lost his patience. Sitting up and glaring down

at her, he said, "Damn it, Rose, speak to me. You must love me. You wouldn't let me sleep with you if you didn't."

"H.L. I—I—I don't know what to say."

Well, hell. *That* wasn't what he wanted to hear. Frustrated, he snapped, "Say you love me, damn it."

Her smile came to him out of the dark and lit up his whole soul. With a pounce, she threw her arms around him. "I love you! I love you, H.L. May. You're the most exasperating fellow on the face of the earth, and I love you."

"Thank God. Thank God." He cradled her in his arms, and his heart felt full to overflowing. Since H.L. May would sooner have people call him Horatio Lambert than admit to entertaining weepy emotions, he captured her lips with his again and ravished her mouth.

If she wasn't stunned and breathless after *that* kiss, she was made of stone, and H.L. already knew she wasn't. Lowering her to the bed again, he continued his survey of her body with his hands and his lips and tongue. Rose was soon writhing underneath him.

"Good," he whispered when she whimpered softly. "I want you to love this, Rose, because we're going to be doing it a lot."

She crammed a fist to her mouth, as if to stifle a scream. "Oh, my!"

He didn't want to scare her, but H.L. had a yen to let her know what she did to him, so he guided her other hand to his erect sex. She let out a soft cry, and he saw her big blue eyes open wide. "That's the effect you have on me, Rose. Pretty powerful, isn't it?"

"I should say so. I've never—that is, I—oh, dear."

"You've never seen a man like this before?"

She shook her head, and her curly hair caught the lantern light. H.L. was delighted to perceive golden and red highlights gleaming up at him. "I love your hair," he whispered. Then he buried his face in it and had the joy of feeling Rose's arms enfold him.

After an exquisite moment, Rose whispered, "I've seen dogs and horses before, but never a man."

H.L. couldn't help it: He laughed. Rose smacked him lightly on his shoulder blade. "It's not funny, H.L."

"Is too." Burrowing his hands under the hollow of her back, he rolled over onto his own back, taking her with him so that she was lying on top of him, her exquisite body pressing against his. He'd never felt anything so good in his life. He cupped her face in his big hands and drew it down to his. She kissed him as if her life depended on it. He knew his did.

He rolled over again until she was beneath him. As much as he was enjoying this, he feared he was going to disgrace himself if they didn't get down to business soon. He hadn't been this excited since his first time. It seemed funny to him that the most potent aphrodisiac he'd yet discovered was love, since he used to be so cynical about love.

Not any longer. With a shaking hand, he reached to cover the dark-brown curls between Rose's thighs with his hand. He heard her suck in a deep breath, but she didn't protest. By the time he found the seat of her pleasure with his thumb, his whole body was trembling. He felt as if an earthquake were happening inside him.

"Oh, my!" she exclaimed softly when he began gently manipulating his fingers against her. She lifted her hips in rhythm to his tender caresses. "Oh, H.L."

"That's the way, Rose." His voice was low and scratchy with passion. "That's the way, sweetheart. It's supposed to be good, Rose. I want it to be good for you. Does it feel good, Rose?"

"Yes. Oh, yes." She caught her breath again, her body stiffened, and then, with a cry, she shuddered beneath him.

H.L. watched, enraptured. He'd never seen anything so beautiful in his life as Rose achieving pleasure at his hand. Before she could come back down to this earthly plane, he knelt over her. "I hope this won't hurt, Rose."

Without giving her a chance to react to his hope, H.L. guided himself to her wet passage and thrust home. With his eyes squeezed tightly shut, he spared a moment to bless Rose's chosen career, because she evidently felt no pain. At least, she didn't cry out or mention it.

She felt so good. He didn't dare to move for fear he'd spill his seed before he wanted to, so he remained poised there, action suspended until he was able to trust himself again. Fearing what he might see, but needing to know how she was reacting to his intimate invasion, he cricked his eyes open and peered down at her. She looked stunned. He wasn't sure that was a good thing and guessed he'd better ask.

"Did I hurt you, Rose?" His voice, he noticed, didn't sound like it belonged to him.

She shook her head. "N-no. It feels . . . funny."

Great. Here he wanted to give her the greatest experience of her life, and he was making her feel funny. He cleared his throat. "Um, is that bad?"

Again she shook her head. "No. It feels . . . good."

Ah. That's what he'd been hoping for. With a sigh, H.L. decided he'd probably survive. "Good. I'm glad."

Very carefully, taking exquisite care so as not to frighten Rose, he began to move inside her. He watched her closely, trying to gauge her reaction.

She appeared confused for only a moment before she started tentatively meeting his thrusts with lifts of her hips. H.L. blessed her and decided he could stop being so careful and resume enjoying himself.

It didn't take him long. He'd been wanting this for so long, and he and Rose had been through so much together in the short time they'd known each other, and both H.L. and his body needed this affirmation of his love. After only a few deep thrusts, his release came, shudderingly and magnificently, and with a hoarse cry that seemed ripped from deep inside him.

Rose held on for dear life, although he didn't know it until his last shuddering spasm had been spent and he barely stopped himself from collapsing on her and crushing her. With great care, he let himself down at her side. He was still buried inside her; he wanted to stay there forever.

A deep, deep silence prevailed in the tent. To H.L., it was as if they'd been transported to another world, one in which there was nothing but Rose and himself, floating in blissful fulfillment.

Being a cynical and world-weary reporter, he knew he was out of his mind even to think such a thing for a second. Therefore, with a gut-wrenching sigh, he opened his eyes.

Nope. No other world. Rose's tent. He glanced at Rose. Her eyes were closed, and she looked as if she weren't quite sure what had happened to her. Or him, for that matter.

"Rose?" He spoke her name softly, hoping she was still willing to speak to him. Truth to tell, he hoped she still loved him. He loved her; no mistake. If he were another sort of man, he'd pick her up and carry her right off to a justice of the peace and demand he unite them in holy matrimony. Such a notion was alien to H.L. May's nature, however, and it no sooner entered his head than he thrust it aside again.

He was glad when her eyelids fluttered open. She turned her head and looked at him. "H.L.?"

"Are you all right, Rose?"

She didn't answer immediately, but seemed to be taking stock before answering. After a minute, she said, "Um, I think so."

"Good." He realized he was more than all right. He was absolutely splendid. He couldn't recall the last time he'd felt this well, actually, which was odd, since he'd recently sustained a powerful injury. His grin sneaked up on him. "I think you cured me, Rose."

She blinked. "I beg your pardon?"

Aw, hell, he felt so good, he couldn't stand it. With a whoop that made Rose cringe, he grabbed her around the waist, rolled over so that she was lying on top of him, and said, "I feel wonderful! You're the best thing that's ever happened to me, Rose Gilhooley. You cured me right up. My head doesn't hurt at all anymore."

"No?" She didn't smile back at him.

"No." He hugged her hard and for so long that she gasped for breath. He released her, but still grinned at her. "Sorry. But I feel really swell, Rose."

"Um, I'm glad."

"You ought to be, since it's all your fault."

Although she didn't seem to want to grin at him, she found no trouble frowning. "What's my fault?"

He cranked his own grin up a notch. "The fact that I feel so good is your fault. You cured me. You fixed my head, and made love with me, and I feel good. Great. Wonderful!"

At long last, she offered him a shy smile. "It felt good to me, too, H.L."

That was what he'd been waiting for. He hugged her again, hard. She gasped again. "Don't squish me!" she begged.

He rolled over so that they were lying on their sides, facing each other. "Sorry, sweetheart. Didn't mean to squish you. You're really something, Rose. Really, really something."

"So are you, H.L." She looked embarrassed.

H.L. didn't want her to be embarrassed. He wanted her to be madly in love with him. So, knowing that women needed to hear certain things, he kissed her and whispered, "I love you, Rose."

He wasn't sure, but he thought she blushed. "I love you, too, H.L."

Good. That was out of the way. The fact that it was the truth in this instance, and that H.L. had never said such a thing to another woman, made him feel good. He hadn't ever really considered himself and love in the same sentence until Rose. It made him feel akin to his fellow men that he, H.L. May, could actually fall in love. It was sort of nice, really.

"Um," Rose said, sounding tentative and as if she wasn't sure she should be speaking, "may I ask you something?"

"Certainly!" H.L. felt expansive. At the moment, he not only loved Rose, but he loved the whole world. He felt like singing. Maybe even dancing. It occurred to him that it would be nice to dance with Rose. He'd have to see about taking her to some of Chicago's night spots. He'd bet she was a good dancer. "Ask me anything you want, Rose." He loved life. He loved everything.

"Um, does this mean you want to marry me?"

H.L.'s expansive mood collapsed like a bombed building. In a heartbeat, his ecstasy plummeted into a whirlpool of sheer terror.

NINETEEN

"Don't you say another word, H.L. May. I don't want to hear you or your phony excuses." Rose was buttoning up her nightgown, although her fingers fumbled with the buttons. She was so mad she would have spit, except that she was trying so hard not to cry, her spit wouldn't come.

"Rose. Rose, don't!" H.L. was buttoning his own clothes. He looked truly awful, with his face all over bruises, and an expression of anguish in his eyes.

She didn't care. "Just get out of here, H.L. I don't ever want to see you again."

"Rose! That's not true, and you know it! You love me. You said so."

"I don't care what I said." Rose picked up one of his shoes and hurled it at him. He caught it as it struck him in the stomach, and she had the satisfaction of hearing him utter an "Umph!" and seeing him shake out the fingers of his right hand. Good. She hoped she'd broken a few of them.

"And I love you, too! Just because I hadn't considered marriage before you brought it up is no reason to—"

"Hush up!" Rose threw his other shoe at him. She was sorry he caught it before it hit. "Just hush up! I don't want to hear another word from you. Get out of here!"

"But, Rose!"

"No!" She couldn't remember ever being so enraged. Or so hurt.

"Listen, Rose . . ."

"Get out of here, H.L. May." Her voice held a truly grati-
fying degree of menace. Rose looked around her tent, trying
to remember where she'd put her Colt revolver. As angry as
she was, she wouldn't shoot the bounder, but she might be
able to put the fear of God into him.

"Rose—"

"Get *out.*"

As he finished dressing, Rose began searching through
trunks and boxes. If she could find that gun, maybe she
could at least whack him with it. A good, solid revolver
would produce a much more satisfying thwack than a shoe.

"Listen, Rose, we need to talk."

Giving up her search for the Colt, she straightened and
stared at him, trying to discern the evil she hadn't noticed
before. She didn't notice it now, either, blast it. He still
looked like the man she loved. He shouldn't. He ought, if life
were fair, to look like the devil. "You're a cad, H.L. May.
You're a coldhearted, black-hearted scoundrel. You're—"

"I'm not, either!" he cried, obviously offended.

"Ha!" If he was offended, Rose was outraged. Not to
mention completely, totally, absolutely crushed.

Annie had been right about H.L. all along. Rose should
have listened to her. Well . . . She *had* listened to her. The
problem had been that Rose hadn't wanted to believe Annie
was right about H.L. Rose had wanted to believe that H.L.
wasn't a beast like all the other men in the world. She'd
wanted to believe that H.L. May was special.

She was a fool. A naive, ignorant, stupid fool. She'd will-
fully disregarded Annie's wiser counsel, and look what had
happened. She'd allowed H.L. May to take advantage of her.
And she'd had the unmitigated idiocy to think he wanted to
marry her. As if a man like him would ever want to marry
an uneducated bumpkin like Rose Ellen Gilhooley.

Ha! He probably considered Rose no more than an interesting sidelight to a nefarious career as a woman-chaser. An
excursion into the untried frontiers of country life.

He'd managed to get both shoes on and tied and was looking around for his hat. Rose saw it first. She marched over to it and swept it up. She thrust it at him as if she were thrusting a lance. "Here. Get out."

"Rose, this isn't fair."

"What isn't fair?" she demanded, incredulous. "It isn't fair that I want you gone? It isn't fair that I asked you about marriage?"

"Damn it—"

"Stop swearing this instant, H.L. May." Rose sucked in about a gallon of air and made her eyes go squinty. "You're right. Silly me, to think you might be an honorable man."

"Now that's not true, Rose—"

"Oh, be quiet. I can't believe I let you into my bed." Or her heart. She wouldn't give him the satisfaction of hearing her say again how much she'd been fooled. She felt like *such* a dimwit. How could she have allowed herself to fall in love with a man so obviously above her in every way. Except morals. He had no morals at all.

"Rose . . ." He might have sounded pathetic if Rose weren't filtering everything through the haze of her own present misery. "Won't you please give me a chance?"

A chance at what? No matter. If Rose didn't get quit of him soon, she'd break down and cry in front of him, and she couldn't do that and maintain even a shred of her dignity. Not that she had very much dignity left. "No."

He stood there, hat in hand, looking awful and broken and miserable, for another ten seconds. Rose put her fists on her hips, glared, and tapped her foot in a show of impatience that was only half feigned. She really did want him to go away, so she could have hysterics in peace.

H.L. opened his mouth, closed it, turned, and untied the flap of her tent. He muttered, "I'm leaving now, but I'll be back."

His threat alarmed Rose, who hastened to say, "If you come back, I still won't speak to you."

He shot a glance over his shoulder, sighed, and left. Rose raced to the door and tied the flap back in place. She didn't want anyone entering into her presence before she'd composed herself. She already felt completely humiliated. She'd die before she allowed any of her friends to see her thus. Especially Annie.

She felt so stupid. And so, *so* bad.

"Oh, Lord, what have I done?" Her voice was a thready whisper and ragged with tears when she threw herself down onto the bed in which she'd only lately experienced such pleasure.

As she cried, she thumped her pillow—the pillow H.L. had said smelled like her. He'd said it as if he considered it special because her fragrance lingered there, too.

"What a fool I am!"

Rose wished she could talk to her mother. Of all the people in the world, Mrs. Gilhooley understood human frailty. Mrs. Gilhooley, who'd been through so much in her own life, understood how a girl could allow a longing to be loved to bring her to this pass. Rose's mother never made her feel stupid.

Not like H.L. May. H.L. May didn't have to do anything at all but exist in the same world she did, and Rose felt stupid. Now that he *had* done something—more than something—Rose felt lower than low, and as dumb as dirt.

She wanted Annie. Annie would sympathize with her, too. Even though Annie had advised Rose from the first not to get involved with H.L., she'd understand. Annie's life had been much like Rose's, only Annie, unlike Rose, had chosen wisely in the man department. Rose had been stupid.

In short, she wanted to die.

What the hell had happened back there? H.L. shuffled along, his hands jammed into his pockets, his brain aching. He felt lost and alone. His soul hurt. He almost wished his head still hurt, too, since it didn't seem right that so much psychic pain shouldn't be accompanied by physical pain.

But except for some bumps and bruises and a pretty big lump on his head, Rose's Indian medicaments seemed to have cured him.

Rose. "Aw, hell." The words didn't half match the anguish in his heart. Pulling his right hand out of his pocket, he splayed it over his chest, wondering why love should feel so bad.

How could he have been so stupid as not to have realized that a girl like Rose would assume the man who deflowered her would then marry her? Of *course* that's what she'd assume! He'd been so blinded by love and lust, the notion of marriage hadn't occurred to him—at least it hadn't occurred to him seriously enough that he'd concocted an answer to the question she'd surely ask him.

"Idiot. Fool. Ass." He wished there were more disparaging words in the English language, because those weren't quite vile enough to describe him.

But jeez, it's not as if he didn't love her. The fact that he hadn't considered marriage, and the fact that the thought of marriage sent cold shivers up his spine, didn't mean he didn't love her.

As he walked, H.L. considered the married state now. His automatic reaction to the word *marriage* was one of panic, although he didn't know why, exactly, it should be. His folks had been happy enough, he supposed. Still were, for that matter.

Sam, his cohort at the *Globe,* seemed content with his Daisy, and Sam was always talking about his kids. Sam seemed to think his children were something special, although as far as H.L. could tell, they were ordinary enough.

It went without saying that any children he and Rose might have had would be special. They couldn't help but be, given their parents. He and Rose were both outstanding people, after all. They would naturally produce superior off-spring.

Why the devil was he thinking about children, when the very thought of marriage made his blood run cold? He couldn't think of an answer.

Squinting at the sky, H.L. tried to determine the time of day. It must be going on toward five in the morning. The sky was turning gray, and the stars were fading. H.L. wasn't accustomed to seeing in the dawn. He knew quite a few reporters who were. That's because they reveled in their bachelor status and celebrated it by carousing all night. The newsroom was full of hung-over gents most mornings. They all joked about their lives of sin and excess.

Frowning at the sky, H.L. wondered if that was what he wanted out of life. Did he really want to drink and smoke and stay up all night and tell tales about the women he'd bedded, the stories he'd covered, and the articles he'd written? That was what he used to want. It used to sound romantic to him. At the moment, it didn't sound like any sort of aspiration at all. In fact, it sounded pathetic, although that might be only because he was bone tired.

Bone tired or not, he had work to do, so instead of heading to his flat, he flagged down a cab and told the cabbie to take him to the *Globe* building. He needed to write up the events of last night. Given his present state of mind, he didn't intend to spare the minions of the law who should have prevented Rose's kidnapping, but to state clearly and as acerbically as possible all of their shortcomings and stupidities. He hoped the Chicago police department would choke on them.

He paid off the cabbie and entered the building, hoping nobody else would be there. His luck was out, as he might have expected it would be, given the way it was running this morning.

"Jesus H. Christ, H.L., you look like hell and then some."

Glancing up, H.L. saw George Wiggins, a young pup of

a reporter who also relished his status as newshound and devil-may-care rakehell. "Yeah. I ran in to a sandbag last night."

"Shoot, really?" George, who had been sagging in his chair, sat up straight. "How'd it happen?"

H.L. didn't want to chat. Forcing a grin, he told George, "You'll be able to read all about it in the early edition. I've got to write it down now, or it won't get printed."

"I heard Haley's drooling over your fair pieces, H.L. Good going."

"Thanks." Any other day in the year, H.L. would be secretly preening over Wiggins's words. H.L. knew the young cub reporter envied him and did his best to emulate his style. Right now, H.L. would have gladly consigned Wiggins's envy and imitation to the devil, if only he could be back in Rose's tent. In Rose's arms.

How could he have bungled so miserably in what, by rights, should have been the blissful beginning to a heavenly affair?

The word gave H.L. pause. As he sat at his desk and pulled out some sheets of paper, he pondered the word *affair.* Is that what he wanted with Rose? An affair? A brief liaison that would end when the Wild West pulled up stakes and went touring elsewhere? Back to Europe, maybe? Or to New York City, where Rose might meet any number of reporters? Hell, she might even meet reporters who worked at the *New York Times.* Wouldn't that be a kicker, if Rose took up with somebody from the *Times?*

Hell, men who might be interested in Rose didn't necessarily have to be reporters. There were hundreds of millionaires back East who'd be thrilled to court and even marry the bareback-riding sensation of Buffalo Bill's Wild West. Ancient rich men were forever making asses of themselves over chorus girls and actresses. Why not bareback riders?

H.L.'s heart, which had been throbbing much as his head

had done last night, gave a sharp spasm. He slapped a hand over it.

"What's the matter, H.L.?" Wiggins asked with a laugh. "Too much excitement? You older fellows have to watch it, you know."

H.L. squinted malignantly at the younger reporter. "That so?"

His expression evidently took George Wiggins aback because he started slightly and stopped grinning. "No offense, H.L." He held up a hand in a placating gesture. Then he grinned again. "Big night?"

H.L. subdued the sudden urge to pick up his Underwood Invisible Writing Machine and heave it at George Wiggins. He growled, "Yeah," and jabbed a sheet of foolscap into the machine. Even though he hadn't even begun to think about what he planned to write, he started typing because he wanted to forestall any more ill-timed comments from his fellow reporter.

Damn George Wiggins to hell. How dare he talk about Rose as a "big night" in that crafty, winking, sly way?

Not, of course, that George knew H.L. had spent the night with Rose. Nobody knew that yet.

Suddenly, H.L.'s fingers stilled on the typewriter's keys. Crap, would anybody in the Wild West find out Rose and he had made love last night? Would Rose have to face snide comments and knowing looks this morning?

And, if she did, how the devil could he protect her from that sort of thing if she wouldn't allow him near her? He experienced a sudden painful, aching need to be with her; to shield her from the slings and arrows of outrageous people. He wanted to slam his head against his desk ten or twenty times as some sort of punishment for his sins.

How could it be a sin to love a woman? Indignation swelled in his bosom. He caught Wiggins staring at him out of the corner of his eye and forced himself to type some more. He didn't know what he was typing. Nothing, probably, but he needed to keep his fingers moving so Wiggins wouldn't suspect him of going through an episode of emotional turmoil. H.L.'s reputation would be ruined if anyone suspected him of having been bitten by the love bug.

And what good, his inner voice asked him, was a reputation, anyhow? If H.L. lost Rose forever, would his reputation be a comfort to him in a lonely old age, as Rose might be if he gave her a chance? Would his reputation love him, as Rose did? Would his reputation soothe his wounds, physical and emotional, as Rose did? Could he and his reputation produce brilliant children?

Children? Why was he thinking about children again? H.L. May didn't want children, not even the brilliant variety he and Rose would surely produce. He didn't need that kind of responsibility, for the love of God. He had a great life. A perfect life, even. Children.

He waited for a shudder to seize him, but didn't think much about it when it didn't come. But children? Good God. While H.L. might, in moments of weakness, consider marriage, he couldn't even imagine rearing children.

As his fingers pecked away at the typewriter keys, his mind wandered, and he imagined them now. Although the mere notion of children was appalling to him, he had to admit that, if he had any with Rose, they'd be really smart, good-looking kids. Hell, they couldn't help but be. Both he and Rose were smart, good-looking people.

He considered this last insight and decided that, in truth, Rose was gorgeous. Funny he hadn't noticed her true beauty at first; he'd only seen her as a fantastic subject for a series of career-making articles. But he contemplated her beauty now. In fact, H.L. couldn't recall ever seeing a woman who more perfectly matched his ideal of womanhood.

He only realized he'd sighed when Wiggins's head snapped up and the young man stared at him. H.L. quickly turned his sigh into a yawn and hoped Wiggins wouldn't catch on.

So . . . If Rose matched his ideal of womanhood and H.L. couldn't bear to think about what his life would be like when she and the Wild West packed up and left Chicago, why did the idea of marriage to her bother him so much? Naturally, the notion of marriage to anyone else in the world was anathema to him, but marriage to Rose? Hmmm . . .

He thought about it as his fingers tapped out sentences on his Underwood. He thought about it after he'd filled the first sheet of paper and as he rolled in another one. He thought about it as he figuratively tore the Chicago Police Department's attitude toward kidnapped Indian children to shreds. He thought about it as he recounted his and Rose's rescue of Bear in Winter, which became the prelude to Rose's own kidnapping. And he thought about it as he finished up with a flourished account of Rose's attempted kidnapping and her resourcefulness in rescuing herself after he, her erstwhile protector, had been sandbagged into unconsciousness.

"Thus it is," his article ended, "that Rose Ellen Gilhooley, otherwise known as Wind Dancer: Bareback Rider Extraordinaire, proves herself to be not merely beautiful, intelligent, and talented, but the possessor of a heart as big as the Kansas plains from which she hails."

H.L.'s fingers stilled on the typewriter's keys as he reread the final sentence of his article. He frowned.

"What's the matter, H.L.? At a loss for words?"

H.L. glanced up to find Wiggins grinning at him as if he'd just uttered a brilliant witticism. H.L. grunted and went back to glaring at his article.

Perhaps those shouldn't be his last words on the subject of Rose. Perhaps, if H.L. truly didn't want to lose Rose forever, he ought to tack on another paragraph. He hit the return bar, spaced in far enough for a new paragraph, and typed the letter *A*.

All the teachers of literature and journalism who'd ever tried to teach him the basics of his craft had pounded it into the heads of their students that one should never start a sentence, much less a paragraph, with the word *And*. However, H.L. had ever been one to twist the rules to suit himself.

Besides, language was a dynamic applied art. Language changed constantly. Therefore, he tossed his teachers' strictures aside and didn't give them another thought as he started the last paragraph of his article with *And*.

"And," he typed quickly, before he could lose his nerve, "if she will have him, Miss Rose Gilhooley will make this reporter the happiest man in the world and agree to marry him. This, before God and the citizens of the great city of Chicago, Illinois, is my formal proposal of marriage to the woman I love."

It would have to be, since Rose wouldn't speak to him. With a sigh, H.L. realized that, one way or the other, he'd just sealed his own fate. If Rose agreed to marry him, his days of carefree bachelorhood would be over. He might eventually even be responsible for rearing a dozen or so children of his and Rose's production. He waited for the shudder engendered by the notion of having children to hit him, but again it didn't come. He considered that a good omen and went on to the alternative to her acceptance of his proposal.

If Rose refused to marry him, his bachelor days would go on forever. H.L. knew in his soul that, while his days might be free of responsibilities in that case, they'd no longer be carefree.

All things considered, he preferred the first alternative.

In spite of the pain her bruised bottom caused her, Rose was kind of glad she couldn't perform for a few days. She didn't believe H.L. May would honor her demand that he never speak to her again any more than she believed Colonel Cody would eschew strong drink for tea.

The one was as likely as the other, and Rose figured she could dodge H.L. better if she were not adhering to her regular performing schedule. If she were trapped by duty into her usual hours, he'd catch her for sure one of these days. This way, she could keep her eyes open and make sure she spotted him before he spotted her, and in that way avoid any confrontations with him. She was absolutely certain she wouldn't be able to withstand any of his sweet words.

The bounder. The cad. The horrid, awful . . . man she loved.

"Oh, Annie, how could I have been so stupid?" she asked, the anguish vivid in her voice. She sat on a poultice, made according to Little Elk's mother's recipe, in Annie's tent. She'd confessed all to her best friend, who'd taken up the cudgel of righteousness on her behalf.

"He's a man," Annie said, drawing the doggie brush through George's curly hair. "Most men are curs." She paused to give her poodle a hug. "I'm sorry, George."

Rose heaved a huge sigh. "I didn't want to believe you were right about him, although you were all along. I don't know how I could have allowed myself to weaken so thoroughly."

Annie tutted. "Don't be so hard on yourself, Rose. It's difficult to resist a man when you long so much to believe him."

"Yes. You're right about that." As Rose knew to her everlasting sorrow.

"It will be all right, dear," Annie said soothingly. "You're not the first woman, and you assuredly won't be the last, to be fooled by a sweet-talking charmer."

Another sigh constituted Rose's reply to her friend. She felt really stupid; even more stupid than usual, mainly because H.L. hadn't really sweet-talked her. He hadn't had to. He'd just been himself, and she'd fallen for him like an avalanche. It was a lowering reflection and one she feared didn't speak well for her overall moral character.

Both women swiveled to face the flap of Annie's tent when raised voices reached them from outdoors.

"Damn it, Little Elk, I thought we were friends."

Rose and Annie exchanged a glance, and Rose's heart gave a quick, painful spasm. That was H.L.'s voice, and it sounded both aggrieved and angry.

"I need to talk to her," H.L.'s voice added in pleading accents.

"Wind Dancer my friend," Little Elk said. He, on the other hand, sounded both stoical and impenetrable. "She says she don't want to see you, so I won't let you see her."

"Bless him," Rose whispered, grateful beyond anything that Little Elk was her friend. He'd agreed to stand guard, eating popcorn and hamburgers and drinking carbonated soda, all provided by Rose and Annie, and to ward off H.L. May should he attempt to see Rose.

Before she decided to hide out in Annie's tent, Rose had contemplated H.L.'s probable plan of attack. She figured he'd go to her tent first and then, finding it empty, try to find her. She expected he'd try the Butlers' tent next, since that was logical. Therefore, she'd posted Little Elk outside Annie's tent during the day. During the evening performances, Rose made sure she was as invisible as possible by hanging out with the cowboys on the sidelines. They were all a good deal taller than she and hid her well.

"But I'm her friend, too, damn it."

Little Elk grunted. Rose heard a rustle of paper, and featured him reaching into his popcorn bag to get a handful of the crunchy morsels.

"Damn it, Little Elk, this isn't fair!"

Rose had never heard H.L. whine before. She hadn't known he had a whine in him until this minute. She muttered, "Maybe I should—"

Annie whirled on her. "No! You just stay put, Rose Gilhooley. You know very well you won't stand a chance if you go out there and try to reason with him."

Rose heaved another large sigh. "You're right." She was no match for H.L. May should they engage in a war of words. He knew too blasted many of them, and he also knew how to use them. Since she'd met him, Rose's own vocabulary had grown, but she'd never be able to use words with the facility with which he used them.

Her heart ached to see him. Her body ached to touch him. She was *so* stupid! She hated herself for harboring these longings even after he'd proved himself to be a worthless seducer of innocent females.

Not that he'd had to work very hard to seduce her, Rose acknowledged bitterly. She'd fallen into his clutches like a ripe peach from a spring branch.

"Little Elk, *please.* I only want to see her for a minute or two. I promise."

Rose imagined Little Elk shrugging, because H.L. then shouted, "This isn't fair, damn it!"

Little Elk probably thought it was amusing that a white man should be talking to a Sioux about fairness. Under other circumstances, Rose might have been amused, too. Not today. Today, she wanted to cry.

But she wouldn't. Rose Ellen Gilhooley vowed to herself that she would shed no more tears over H.L. May. She'd read that article in the *Globe,* including the last paragraph, in which he'd penned a proposal of marriage to her. She didn't believe a word of it. He'd probably only written that absurd last paragraph as a means of placating her and getting her back to his bed until he tired of her. That was the scenario Annie had proposed, anyway, and Rose had no reason to doubt Annie, whose predictions had proved catastrophically accurate so far.

Therefore, Rose sat still on her poultice, her heart throbbing out a dismal rhythm, and wished she were dead. Or at least sicker than she was, so she could sleep or something. Being awake and hurting was no darned fun.

"Little Elk . . ."

"No."

Rose imagined her friend, sitting like an immovable red

rock on the stump beside Annie's tent flap. He looked harmless enough, but Rose knew he'd do whatever it took to keep H.L. away from her. After all, he and Rose had been friends for years. Although Little Elk claimed to like H.L. all right, Rose knew where his loyalty lay, and it was with her.

She couldn't quite suppress a sniffle or a tear, but she blew her nose on her hankie and brushed the tear away angrily and decided she'd be very happy when ten years or so had passed and she no longer ached for H.L. May.

Hearing the telltale sniffle, Annie put down the doggie brush and moved to Rose. She gave her an encouraging hug. "It will be all right, dear. The man's a devil, and that's the worst kind to get over, but you'll do it. One of these days, you'll look back on this and thank God you escaped so lightly." As if to turn Rose's mind onto a cheerier path, she added with a bounce to her voice, "Did you get the cablegram off to your mother, Rose?"

Thank God for friends, Rose thought with a lift to her heart. *And thank Annie for bringing up my family.* "Yes. I'm hoping she and Lizzy and Charlotte will be able to come to Chicago in a couple of weeks." Seeing her family for the first time in several years would bolster her morale; Rose was sure of it. "They'll love seeing the fair."

"I'm sure of it," Annie said, with a patently encouraging throb to her voice.

"And I'll love seeing them again. Lizzy and Charlotte are almost grown up now. In her last letter, Charlotte told me she was stepping out with the youngest Palmer boy." Rose sighed, happy for her siblings.

Thanks to her, they were enjoying a much less rigorous life than the elder Gilhooley siblings, Rose and Freddie, had. Rose didn't begrudge her family a single penny, either. "My goodness, Annie, the last time I saw Harold Palmer, he was only thirteen years old."

"Children grow up fast," Annie said, picking up the doggie brush again. George cast a glare at the brush, but he was a beautifully trained animal and didn't try to avoid his mistress's grooming efforts.

Thinking about children, Rose allowed her mind to wander. If she and H.L. married and produced children, would they grow up fast, too? She'd love to have children one day, although she couldn't imagine ever wanting to have them with any man other than H.L. May.

Oh, for the love of heaven, Rose Gilhooley, stop mooning over that man!

Her command to herself did no good. She heard H.L. give up arguing at last. He said, "Oh, for God's sake," and stomped away from Little Elk. Rose's heart gave another painful spasm, and she feared she'd never, ever get over loving him.

TWENTY

Damn it all, she'd even posted guards to keep him away! H.L.'s indignation knew no bounds as he stormed away from Annie Oakley's tent.

Imagine Little Elk, of all people, preventing him entry into Rose's presence. Little Elk! For God's sake, H.L. was the one who'd given him his first bag of popcorn! H.L. was the one who'd paid his way onto the Ferris wheel. H.L. had assisted Little Elk and Rose in the rescue of Bear in Winter when the Chicago Police Department couldn't be bothered!

Little Elk was Rose's friend. Little Elk had taught Rose how to do all those tricks on a horse.

What had H.L. ever done for her? As he steamed away from Rose in the warm spring day, H.L. told himself he'd done a *lot* for her, damn it. He'd made her a household name in Chicago. Granted, Chicago wasn't exactly New York City, but it was about as close as you could get to New York City without actually *being* there.

He crammed his hands into his pockets as he walked and wallowed in his resentment. He'd praised her to the skies in his articles. He'd treated her only to the best. He'd helped her learn more about the world. He'd shown her Chicago and the Columbian Exposition. He'd fed her exotic foods. He'd treated her to her first hamburger. He'd taken her to see Little Egypt. He'd helped her with her damned horse. He'd— he'd—

He'd deflowered her.

But, damn it all, he loved her! Just because he'd had a momentary lapse in judgment after they'd made love and panicked when she'd mentioned marriage didn't mean anything. Just because he'd shied away from that one little word didn't mean he didn't want to keep seeing her.

Pausing in his headlong dash to leave the World's Fair for the day, H.L. realized he'd just committed another error in word choice. Damn his prejudices, anyhow. Absolute honesty compelled him to admit that he wanted more than merely to keep seeing her. He wanted to see her for the rest of his life. He wanted to be sure he had her by his side forever and ever. Even if that meant marriage.

Marriage. He braced himself for the sensations of panic and entrapment that usually accompanied the word to overwhelm him. They remained absent, so he tested the word again, even speaking it aloud.

"Marriage," he muttered into the air, scented with the fragrances of the Columbian Exposition. "Marriage to Rose Gilhooley."

When he added the *to Rose Gilhooley* part, the word didn't seem to create such blind fear in his brain. Interesting. "Rose Gilhooley May," he murmured, testing both the name and his reaction to it. Still no sense of impending doom swooped down to extinguish his nerves. "Mrs. H.L. May."

He noticed people staring at him as he stood in the middle of the Midway Plaisance talking to himself. He didn't give a hang about them, and scowled back, adding a black grimace for good measure. A little boy who'd been gazing with interest at him uttered a soft cry and hurried after his papa.

"Damned snoopy busybodies."

Nevertheless, he decided any conversations he wished to hold with himself would be better carried out away from the public's prying eyes, so he shuffled over to a beautifully sculpted marble bench and sat. He contemplated buying a bag of popcorn to help him think, but the notion of food made his stomach rebel. He'd heard that the inability to contemplate food was a classic symptom of lovesickness, but he'd never expected to be a victim of such an absurd illness himself.

The more he contemplated losing Rose, however, the more he realized that he'd already become one. He, H.L. May, was pining away for the love of a woman.

"God, what a comedown." He buried his face in his hands, dislodging his sporty, reporterly summer straw hat. When he saw his headgear from between his fingers, residing on the Midway between his feet, he had to suppress an urge to leap up and stomp it to death. Hell, it wasn't his hat's fault he was in this pickle. He was a mess because he'd allowed himself to fall in love with Rose Ellen Gilhooley. What a predicament. He heaved a stockyard-and-popcorn-scented sigh.

Then again, he supposed he couldn't be held to be a total fool for having fallen in love with Rose. After all, Rose wasn't just any woman. She was special.

Still and all . . . Marriage? H.L. scooped up his hat and set it on the bench beside him. He had to worry his hair a bit more before he put his hat back on.

Marriage would completely scuttle his image. He'd worked so hard to perfect it, too. All the young cub reporters at the *Globe* tried to emulate his style, his insouciance, his damn-it-all, go-to-hell attitude. If he got married, his image would be blown to smithereens.

Lifting his head and propping his chin in his cupped hands, H.L. thought about that. What good was a reputation if it could so easily be shattered? Surely, he'd been more adept at image creation than that. Hadn't he? The good Lord knew he'd worked hard enough at it.

"Hmmm." Cocking his head and staring without seeing at the crowd of fair-goers walking past him, H.L. contemplated the nature of self-image and the importance thereof. Crumbs, if he'd done as good a job at creating himself as he thought he had, perhaps marriage wouldn't blow it all to hell.

The word *marriage* had always brought to his mind images of men shackled and cuffed, tied to their wives and children out of duty alone. It hadn't occurred to him until Rose Gilhooley galloped into his life that perhaps those men, who had seemed akin to unwilling prisoners to him, had actually *chosen* their bonds.

"Don't be an ass, H.L.," he grumbled. Of course, they'd chosen their bonds. Only they hadn't seemed like bonds at first. The true imprisonment of marriage crept up on a fellow; it swooped down on him as he contemplated other things, and had him by the throat before he knew what had happened to him.

"Look, Papa. That poor man's talking to himself."

H.L. peered up and bared his teeth at the sweet little girl who had uttered the comment. The girl squealed and darted off. The little girl's papa cast a fulminating glance at H.L. and went off to tackle his daughter. H.L. said, "Hunh!"

A second later he sat up and swiveled his head to see where the father and daughter had gone off. He saw the man pick up his little girl, hug her close, and give her a smiling explanation of H.L.'s bad behavior. The little girl, after looking frightened for a second or two, let go of a startled laugh and hugged her father, as if he'd said the one thing that could transform her worry into something jolly and happy. As he stared, H.L. came to the reluctant conclusion that the girl's father didn't have the haggard, beleaguered appearance of a man who'd been trapped into a hateful life sentence. He looked mighty pleased with himself, as a matter of fact.

Turning and narrowing his gaze, H.L. pondered this phenomenon. After he'd done that for a minute or two, he mentally substituted himself for the father in the recently enacted scenario. Naturally, his and Rose's daughter would be much prettier than that admittedly pretty little girl, and she'd be much too intelligent to be frightened by somebody making a face at her, but still . . .

H.L. experienced the strange sensation of his heart getting

soft and gooey as he considered comforting a child of his loins. A darling little girl, perhaps. Or a sturdy lad. A lad with a decent name. H.L. would never burden a child with a name as awful as his own.

His image slapped him in his mind's eye again, and he frowned. Hell. No matter how pleasant certain aspects of the married state might appear in contemplation, there was still his image as a care-for-nobody to consider.

All of his colleagues would laugh at him if he told them he was getting married. H.L. considered the comments he'd surely receive.

"So," he imagined Wiggins saying with a sly wink, "somebody trapped you at last, eh?"

"H.L. May as a married man?" he imagined his editor saying with a loud guffaw. "You should have kept your drawers buttoned, H.L."

H.L. winced. Damn them. They didn't know Rose, or they wouldn't say such things. Rose was special. Any man would be lucky if she agreed to marry him.

He sat up straighter on the bench as the truth of his last thought sank in.

By God. Any man *would* be lucky—indeed, he'd be honored and privileged—if Rose Ellen Gilhooley agreed to marry him.

For the first time, H.L. wondered if he was approaching this marriage concept from the wrong direction. Maybe he ought to think of it in terms of his meeting with Rose as a serendipitous occurrence—an occurrence not given any other man in the world but only to him. How fortuitous had that been?

Hell, he might have lived his whole life without their paths having crossed. The thought of never having met Rose made his chest ache. He pressed a palm against the sore spot and thought some more.

By the time he'd thought himself to a near-collapse, H.L.

had decided what he had to do. He only hoped Rose would cooperate.

H.L. had stopped haunting the Wild West. He hadn't been by her tent or Annie's for three days. Rose knew it for a fact, because she'd abandoned Annie's tent for her own two days ago.

The knowledge that H.L.'s interest in her hadn't lasted a full month caused a heaviness to pervade Rose's whole being. She aimed to perform tonight and, though her bruise had healed, she wasn't sure she could summon the lightness of spirit it took to do all those tricks she had to do. She'd been practicing. All yesterday afternoon and all this morning, she and Fairy had practiced. So far, she hadn't fallen off the horse and cracked her skull, but the day was young yet.

"Stop it, Rose Gilhooley," she muttered as she slipped into her costume. As miserable as she felt about having been made a fool of by H.L. May, she still didn't really want to take a tumble from Fairy's back and kill herself. Not only might it be painful, but it would certainly be humiliating, and Rose had suffered too much humiliation lately to court any more of it.

Therefore, she had to concentrate. She'd been concentrating a lot these past few days. So eager had she been not to think about H.L. that she'd studied the lessons Annie had given her with special concentration.

Even Rose had to admit that she was a good reader by this time. She could read everything and, if she didn't know all the words in the English language, she knew how to use the dictionary, and did. She was every bit as smart as H.L. May, she told herself with a sniff of longed-for superiority, even though she wasn't as well-educated.

Bitterly she wondered where her self-respect had been hiding out when she'd first met the newspaperman. Self-respect might have done her some good then. It seemed merely superfluous now. A cynical chuckle escaped her as she considered how the word *superfluous* had simply popped into her brain as if it were as familiar to her as the word *horse.*

It wasn't, of course. Rose had learned that big word just as she'd learned how to read and write: the hard way. She'd worked diligently to achieve her present mastery of the English language, and, whereas she used to feel stupid, she now was proud of herself. It had been difficult, but she'd done it. Unlike H.L. May, whose education had been handed to him on a silver platter, Rose Gilhooley had been required to seek it out. And she had, blast him.

Stupid man. Going around flaunting his superior education and so forth. An education didn't mean a single thing except that one had been fortunate enough in one's circumstances to be able to attend school. Rose had been doing *useful* things with her talents when Mr. H.L. May had been sitting in school, learning how to use words.

Rose commanded herself to stop brooding about H.L. May. Her mother and sisters would be arriving on the noon train tomorrow, and the colonel had promised Rose that they'd be honored guests at the Wild West for as long as they remained in Chicago. What Rose prayed for was that her mother would agree to stay in Chicago from now on.

Although she hadn't spoken a word to anyone else, not even Annie or the colonel, Rose was considering retirement from the Wild West. She was tired of traveling constantly, of never having a home to call her own. In spite of H.L. May and bittersweet memories of lost love, Rose liked Chicago. It was not only a civilized place, but it was an exciting one. Rose didn't think she'd get bored very soon with all the amenities and interests Chicago had to keep one entertained.

Besides all that, she'd been offered a job. A good job. A job that would provide her with an ample salary, quite enough to support herself and her mother. She imagined her sisters would return to Deadwood because they'd made lives for themselves there. Anyhow, Charlotte was set to marry the youngest Palmer boy, so she was sure to head back to Kansas. Lizzy could attend a finishing school here and learn a profession if she didn't want to marry.

H.L. May wasn't the only one in the world who could exist without marriage. It was women who had to do all the hard work when they married, anyway. Men reaped all the benefits of the married state and had none of the responsibilities to go along with it. Well, except for money, but if one prepared oneself properly, one didn't *need* a man for that.

Rose lifted her chin, proud that she didn't need a man in order to survive in this troublesome world. She'd make sure Lizzy wouldn't need one, too. A woman could survive on her own. A woman could have a good life—a *fine* life—as a spinster. A better life, actually, because she wouldn't have to put up with a man.

A sob escaped her unbidden, and Rose stamped her foot. She'd be so glad when she stopped mooning over H.L. May and her abandoned hopes. What good were hopes? They'd only brought Rose grief, and she was sick of them.

Rose knew, because she'd grown up the hard way, that nothing in this life lasted. Therefore, even though she was going through a rough patch right now, she knew it wouldn't last. Sooner or later, her heart would heal. Broken hearts didn't kill one. As Annie and her mother had both said more than once, any experience that doesn't kill you makes you stronger.

By the time Rose was through mourning the loss of H.L. May, she'd be strong as an ox.

Not only that, but she was going to have a good job. That alone was enough to dim the edges of her grief every time she thought about it. Mrs. Lucius MacDonald Hereford, a wealthy Chicago widow and patron of the arts, had offered Rose a position as curator of a museum of popular culture, which the lady was establishing all on her own, using money she'd inherited from her late husband, a railroad magnate. Or, as Mrs. Hereford herself had put it, "a railroad robber."

Rose had liked Mrs. Hereford the moment she met her, because the woman was down to earth and enthusiastic and didn't put on airs, as so many wealthy women did. She and Rose had hit it right off, in fact. Rose had even found herself confessing a little bit about her current heartache, although she'd kept the salacious details to herself.

"You're better off, Rose," Mrs. Hereford had told her in her downright, no-nonsense manner. "Most men are asses at best and criminals at worst. Just look at my late unlamented husband if you doubt it."

Rose had laughed, although she'd also entertained the unspoken thought that at least the late Mr. Hereford had left his wife a good deal of money. Anything, from heartache to dinner, was easier to live with if one had a lot of money. Rose wasn't so naive that she'd failed to learn *that* lesson in her twenty-two years.

With a heartfelt sigh and another little lecture to buck up, she slipped her moccasins on and headed out to the stable to fetch Fairy. Tonight would be the first time she'd performed since her injury. She wondered if H.L. would be in the audience, then mentally slapped herself for it. She thought glumly that hers was going to be a long recovery.

Her performance went flawlessly, however. Rose was pleased, for she hadn't had so much time off from trick riding since she'd joined the Wild West. She didn't see H.L. in the audience, even though she scanned the first few rows as she took her bow. Her heart hurt as she rode out of the arena to thunderous applause. No matter how often she reminded herself that she was better off without a faithless newspaper reporter in her life, she still felt horrid.

She continued to feel horrid until the following day, when she met her mother and her sisters at the Chicago train station. Their reunion was joyous. Rose was happy to see that her mother didn't look nearly as haggard as she had the last time she had seen her. It was perfectly astonishing how a sufficient amount of cold, hard cash, even in so rustic a place as Deadwood, Kansas, could improve the quality of a person's life.

Lizzy and Charlotte were all grown up now. Both of her sisters were taller than Rose, and it amused Rose that when they saw each other for the first time in years, both of them treated her with a degree of awed respect. Or maybe it wasn't amusing. Rose was now a star in a wild west show, but when she'd lived with them, she'd fed them. It seemed to her that if people had their priorities straight, her sisters should have been in awe of her then instead of now.

Fame was a funny thing, she decided. After lots of hugs and kisses, and after Rose had seen them to a fancy hotel that had both sisters and her mother goggle-eyed with wonder, she took them on a brief tour of the Columbian Exposition, including popcorn, hamburgers, carbonated soda, and the Ferris wheel.

She couldn't stay with them all night, however. "I have to get ready for my show. I want to introduce you to the colonel afterwards."

"I remember the man," Mrs. Gilhooley said. This time, she seemed worshipful. Rose didn't begrudge her that. Rose fairly worshiped the colonel herself.

The show went well. Rose pulled out all the stops in order to give her family a brilliant performance. As she took her last bow to the cheers and applause of her audience, she waved to them. Then she could have smacked herself when she scanned the crowd for H.L. May.

Fudge.

It took H.L. forever to talk Annie Oakley around to his point of view. He'd almost given up when she began to weaken. Taking heart, he continued his pleas with renewed vigor, finally wearing her down, as she put it, to a nub.

H.L. was sorry he'd harassed her so badly, but his life hung in the balance, and he guessed his life was worth a little harassment. He wasn't sure Annie agreed, but she said she'd help him, so he didn't much care.

Next he tackled Rose's mother and sisters. They weren't nearly so hard to convince as Annie had been. Mrs. Gilhooley, in fact, was moved to tears by H.L.'s plight. Never one to eschew the use of emotional blackmail when it served his purposes, H.L. played up his heartache to the hilt. Rose's sisters were inclined to be romantic, so they were eager to assist him.

Mrs. Hereford, whom H.L. had met before, thought he was a sly dog and told him so, but she, too, agreed to help.

Little Elk had proven the most difficult of all, primarily because he considered that his loyalty lay with Rose. It took H.L. hours to convince him that by helping H.L., Little Elk would be proving his loyalty to Rose. By the time the Sioux finally consented to help him, H.L. was exhausted. He wasn't through, however.

He tackled Buffalo Bill Cody last of all, sensing that the colonel's assistance would be invaluable. Although H.L. had always found Cody affable and friendly, he approached the great man with trepidation. If Buffalo Bill let him down, H.L. despaired of ever achieving his mission.

Oddly enough, Cody proved the least recalcitrant of the bunch. He laughed heartily, clapped H.L. on the back, and said he thought it was a splendid idea and he'd be more than happy to help H.L. perpetrate his scheme. He even helped H.L. plot out the most strategic plan so as to prevent injury to Rose, should she be so shocked she lost her concentration.

Therefore, H.L. carefully coached his collaborators to spring the trap during Rose's very last race around the arena, when she was holding tight to Fairy's mane—or whatever she clung to during that headlong dash.

If this didn't work, he guessed he'd just have to go out to the pier, jump off, and drown himself.

* * *

Rose was pleased that her family so enjoyed Buffalo Bill's Wild West that they wanted to see it again. She was puzzled, however, when she saw them rising from their grandstand seats right before she turned a somersault and landed on Fairy's back. Perhaps one of the girls felt ill. Rose hoped not. If she was, she hoped it was nothing more than indigestion caused by devouring so many of the treats available at the Exposition.

She knew better than to think about her sisters during her act, though. If she lost her train of thought, she was done for. Therefore, she cleared her mind of extraneous worries and carried on.

It was while she was standing on her hands on Fairy's back and trotting around the arena that she first suspected something was going on. Upside down though she was, she realized that several people had walked into the arena and were now standing on the sidelines holding signs. Even on her head, Rose could discern her name on one of them.

What was going on here?

Lowering herself to Fairy's back, she nudged the little mare into her last, thrilling gallop around the arena. As was her custom, Rose leaned way over so that she created as little wind resistance as possible, and with her feathers streaming out behind her, she took off like the wind.

She blinked when she saw a huge sign painted on white board in bright red letters that had been sprinkled with glitter: ROSE GILHOOLEY.

Whatever did this mean?

A second later, she read another sign. I LOVE YOU.

Good heavens.

I'M SORRY popped up next in her line of sight.

FOR BEING SUCH AN ASS.

H.L. This had to be H.L.'s doing. No one else she knew would use such inelegant language in a public arena.

MARRY ME, ROSE.

Good God. Rose felt light-headed for only a second. She steadied herself before she could tumble off her horse.

PLEASE SAY YES.

Rose was totally rattled by the time she drew Fairy up in the center of the ring. Because she didn't know what else to do, she made her usual bows. The crowd, she noticed, was practically hysterical with joy and laughter. Small wonder, she thought sourly. They probably didn't get to witness such outlandish marriage proposals on a regular basis.

Neither did Rose, and she didn't know what to make of it. It was no use trying to pretend everything was proceeding normally, because the crowd had started chanting.

"Marry him! Marry him!"

Fiddlesticks. Rose wasn't used to improvisation. She didn't know how to react. When a thunderous cheer went up, she breathed more easily, knowing that meant the appearance of the colonel. Her relief when she turned on her horse's bare back to witness his arrival turned into pure shock when she beheld, not Colonel Cody, but H.L. May trotting out into the arena. His form on horseback, she couldn't help but notice, was abysmal.

He was also holding up a last sign: PLEASE MARRY ME, ROSE. I LOVE YOU. H.L.

The crowd roared with delight.

"That was a dirty, underhanded trick, H.L. May."

Rose lay naked on the bed in H.L.'s apartment. He lay panting beside her, so happy, he was surprised his body didn't float up off the bed and bounce against the ceiling. "Maybe, but it worked, didn't it?"

She smacked him lightly on his washboard belly. "I thought you didn't believe in marriage."

"I thought so, too," he admitted. "I was wrong."

"And to involve my family . . . Well, I just don't know about you, H.L."

"You're going to have years to find out all about me, Rose. I love you too much to risk losing you again."

"Good."

"And think about children, Rose!" H.L. couldn't recall exactly when he'd become enthusiastic about having children, but now he could hardly wait. "I can see them now. They'll be so smart and beautiful. We're going to have the best, brightest, most wonderful children in the whole world."

Rose turned over, threw her arms around his naked body, and planted a kiss on his lips. He responded with enthusiasm, and it wasn't very long before the embrace turned passionate.

"I love you more than life itself, Rose," H.L. whispered as he prepared to plunge his hard shaft into her welcoming passage. "I was such an ass."

"Yes," she agreed happily. "You certainly were."

H.L. hadn't known lovemaking could be so joyful. He was very happy to have found it out.

The marriage of Miss Rose Ellen Gilhooley to Mr. H.L. May was one of the highlights of the year for the citizens of the great city of Chicago. Colonel William F. "Buffalo Bill" Cody gave the bride away, and her weeping siblings were her attendants. Mrs. Gilhooley watched from the bleachers, dabbing her eyes with an embroidered handkerchief.

Rose's brother, Freddie, and his wife, Suzanne, had been rushed from Deadwood, Kansas, to Chicago in record time so that they could attend the nuptials. H.L.'s parents rode the train in from Missouri.

Rose had never been happier in her life.

Neither had H.L.

And the crowd went wild.

If you liked COMING UP ROSES, be sure to look for JUST NORTH OF BLISS, the second book in Alice's new series, *Meet Me at the Fair,* available everywhere books are sold in May 2002.

Belle Monroe has already scandalized her family down to its proud Georgia roots by choosing to work as a nanny up North rather than languish in genteel poverty. Her mother would swoon if she knew that her precious daughter was considering letting a handsome stranger at the World's Columbian Exposition in Chicago take her portrait and plaster it all across America to publicize the fair. Though she's terrified of posing for Winslow Asher, the persistent photographer's tender advances soon make Belle wonder if this brash northerner and a proper southern girl like her could actually be meant for each other. If Win has his way, she'll stop wondering . . . and find out.

COMING IN MARCH 2002 FROM
ZEBRA BALLAD ROMANCES

__LIGHT A SINGLE CANDLE: The MacInnes Legacy
    by Julie Moffett   0-8217-7270-8 $5.99US/$7.99CAN
Bridget Goodwell is determined that nothing will prevent her coming wedding. But three weeks before the ceremony, her first love drops anchor in Salem's harbor, threatening everything she has planned. Bridget is horrified to discover that her love for him will lead her to an ancient curse—unless the passion between them breaks a powerful spell. . . .

__LUCK OF THE DRAW: The Gamblers
    by Pat Pritchard   0-8217-7254-6 $5.99US/$7.99CAN
Cal Preston wins a half interest in an eastern Colorado ranch from a reckless youth. Cal finds his way to the property, where he is met by widowed owner Lily McCord. Without his help, she will lose the ranch—and he can't stand by and watch that happen. Now Cal is prepared to do whatever it takes to keep Lily in his life, even if it means risking everything to win her heart. . . .

__THE SEDUCTION: Men of Honor
    by Kathryn Fox   0-8217-7243-0 $5.99US/$7.99CAN
Journalist Samantha Wilder was certain that at least one of the North West Mounted Police had to be on the take. But even cynical Sam was shocked when clues led to well-respected Inspector Duncan McLeod. Still, the truth had to be told, and she would be the one to tell it. Until Duncan's passionate kisses had her falling in love with the subject of her investigation.

__TWICE BLESSED: Haven
    by Jo Ann Ferguson   0-8217-7309-7 $5.99US/$7.99CAN
Emma Delancy ran from her past to Haven, Ohio, seven years before. Then handsome newcomer Noah Sawyer accused an orphan boy of stealing, and Emma found herself fostering the youngster. Destiny seemed to throw them together at every turn. Emma knows her secret will only make matters worse—unless the love they have found can shelter the family they long to make . . . together.

Use this coupon to order by mail.
ALL BOOKS AVAILABLE MARCH 01, 2002.

Name_____

Address_____

City_____ State _____ Zip _____

Please send me the books that I have checked above.

I am enclosing $_____

Plus postage and handling* $_____

Sales tax (in NY and TN) $_____

Total amount enclosed $_____

*Add $2.50 for the first book and $.50 for each additional book.

Send check or money order (no cash or CODs) to: **Kensington Publishing Corp., Dept. C.O., 850 Third Avenue, New York, NY 10022.**

Prices and numbers subject to change without notice. Valid only in the U.S.

All orders subject to availability. **NO ADVANCE ORDERS.**

Visit our website at **www.kensingtonbooks.com.**

DO YOU HAVE THE HOHL COLLECTION?

Celebrate Romance With
Meryl Sawyer

Romantic Suspense from

Lisa Jackson